BIG PAPA

WOLVES OF IRON VALOR MC BOOK 4

DEX HAVEN

UNDER A TEXAS SKY PRESS

For inquiries or permissions, please contact:

mailto: dex@dexhavenauthor.com

Website: DexHavenAuthor.com

Mean Man

I'm so blessed that you saw past my scars to find the beauty.

CONTENTS

A Note to Readers

In the worlds I build, it's always the women who win.

Not because the monsters are soft or because the odds are ever in anyone's favor. Sometimes, the darkness comes for them. But there's a point—a turning, a clever twist in the shadows where the women realize how much they love the darkness. Where the love comes laced with danger, pain, or a hunger bigger than the two of them put together. You may read about women who made the wrong choice and never regretted it. You could read about the men—who take what they want, and in taking, turn the woman into someone new. You may see yourself in these pages, even if you don't tell anyone.

There are people who will say you shouldn't like this. That you should be ashamed of what you want. That wanting to be ruined, or devoured, or loved so hard it bruises is a sickness. You and I know better. Shame is for people who take life too seriously. For the rest of us, the dark is where we finally get to take off the mask and breathe.

In these pages sometimes, the women do the saving. Sometimes, they burn the world down and build something better from the bones.

Keep reading, darling. Keep wanting. There's no darkness that can hold you for long.

If you are a person who is triggered, please trust your instincts before reading. Big Papa includes scenes of graphic intimacy, themes of power exchange, and violence (not sexual). A list of trigger warnings may be found on my website: www.dexhavenauthor.com

CHAPTER 1

Aspen

I wasn't supposed to cry. Mama always said tears were for the weak, and if there was anything a Waters woman wasn't, it was weak. Still, I let the tears stream down my cheeks anyway, hot and stinging, as I sat on the edge of her narrow bed and held her papery hand in mine. She'd wasted away over the past three weeks, her once-strong arms gone to twigs, her golden skin gone the color of spent beeswax. Now, she looked less like the wild, laughing woman who'd raised me, and more like a shadow pressed thin beneath the handmade quilt I'd outgrown in the eighth grade.

She could barely catch her breath, but she tried anyway. "Baby, come closer. I want... I need to talk to you."

I leaned in, ignoring the pain in my knees against the wooden floorboards. Our little cottage wasn't anything spectacular, but my mom had made it a home. And I'd known it could have been so much more, but she wasn't about expensive personal possessions. It was cozy and filled with the scents of dried lavender and old recipe books and more love than the walls could contain. Moonlight from the lone window slanted across her bed, setting the dust motes to drifting. I could see my own reflection in the glass: complexion white as snow, black-haired, my eyes that impossible green. Mama always joked I looked like a Halloween cat. I wish we had time for jokes now. But we didn't now that she was dying, and the coven was waiting like vultures to pick over her carcass.

She coughed; a wet, rattling sound that left a red fleck at the corner of her lips. I pressed the damp handkerchief to her mouth, then dabbed it away. I didn't recoil. I was used to blood.

"You're so beautiful, Aspen," she whispered, and I believed her, even though most days I had to remind myself.

"You should rest," I murmured, stroking her hair back from her forehead. It was still soft, still the color of molasses, but the roots were snowing in with gray. "Wyrdmother Elaina said she'd come by at noon tomorrow to check on you. Hopefully she can heal you."

Mama's lips twisted in a bitter smile. "That old bitch would sooner slit my throat than heal me. Don't be fooled, Aspen."

The word bitch hung in the room, thick and forbidden. Mama wasn't shy with her opinions, not even now. But it scared me, the way she talked about the coven lately—like they were enemies, not family. Like they were wolves waiting at the door.

"I'm not a child," I said, and I wasn't. Twenty-five felt a hundred years old these days.

She squeezed my hand; her knuckles bird-brittle under my fingers. "No, you're not. That's why you need to listen. It's not safe here, not anymore."

My chest constricted. "Then we'll leave, Mama. We can go to Atlanta or Savannah. Nobody'll think to look for us there."

She smiled again, softer this time, and brought my hand to her mouth to kiss it. I felt her breath, warm and sour and fading.

"Listen to me," she said, and her voice was so clear it cut the air. "I've kept things from you. I thought I had time to tell you; to teach you. But I no longer have the luxury of time because of this curse. And that's exactly what this is. The thing that is killing me it's not sickness; it's a punishment. Because I voted against the Wyrdmother those weeks ago..

When the Council had to vote regarding King Bridger Hardin and Queen Savannah Calloway's mate bond being a true fated mate bond, I advised the Wyrdmother that the bond was genuine, not some trick. She didn't want to hear it. And when I stood up for what's right, the coven turned. There was a reason other than truth that caused the Wyrdmother to vote against them, Aspen. It was something other than justice. I realized then, nothing was sacred. Nothing was safe."

She coughed again, and I felt a small, hot panic rising in my gut.

"You're part of that world," I argued. "You always said—"

She cut me off with a look. "I knew that not everyone was honorable, honey. But in matters of great importance, I had to believe that honor counted. When I saw that the Wyrdmother was willing to lie to sever a loving couple's true fated mating bond, that was when I knew she was a leader I could no longer support. She could read my thoughts. She knew she'd lost me, and she could not let that stand. Before I could get our house in order, she'd somehow worked a curse that I could not break. I know this is overwhelming, darling, but there is more."

She asked for a drink, and I held the glass to her lips before she continued.

"When I realized I would not recover, that's when I sold the herb shop. I knew I had to make provisions for you. Because there is one other thing you must know. I know I always told you I didn't know who your father was. I'm so sorry my darling, but that wasn't true. I was trying to protect you. I still will not tell you who he is, but I will tell you he is not human and he is not a witch. It is enough for you to know that he is 'other' and you are in danger because of who he is."

"What *am* I?" The words crawled out of my throat. "I'm not even a proper witch. I can't cast, Mama. The other girls call me Dud. I thought... maybe magical ability skipped a generation, or..."

She shook her head. "Magic doesn't skip generations, baby. It gets diluted sometimes. Mixed with other blood. But there's nothing wrong with *your* magic, sweet girl." She tried to sit up, and I eased her forward, propping her with a pillow.

I wrung my hands. "What am I supposed to do?"

She closed her eyes, and I thought for a moment she'd gone, but then she squeezed my hand, just enough to feel. "Lift the loose floorboard beside my bed. You'll find my grimoire there and a large brown envelope. In the envelope are the deed and keys to a small bakery in the town of Dairyville, Texas. There is also a phone and credit card. Pack your belongings right now and prepare to leave as soon as you're done. Open that bakery and find a new life and happiness for yourself. If you have any problems or run into trouble in Dairyville, seek out the Iron Valor Pack Alpha Bronc. He is honorable and will help you."

I let the words sink in. The Iron Valor Pack? The one wolf pack everyone knows? The devils in leather, no one dares to cross? I'd sooner have stuck my hand in a blender than go to them. But Mama's eyes, even dying, left no room for argument.

"Promise me," she whispered.

I nodded, tears falling again. "I promise, Mama. I'll go."

She smiled, so faint I might've missed it, then relaxed back into her pillow, her hand still clutching mine. "Good girl," she said, softer than a prayer. "Now go. I think this curse was set to last a specific number of days and if I'm right, I'll be dead by morning. You don't have to see me die, daughter. I know how much you love me."

The moon had shifted now, throwing the long shadow of the cottage roof across the bed. I watched her chest rise and fall, each breath a battle. Around us, the little home she'd built for us—our sanctuary—felt suddenly like a coffin.

I felt as though my soul had slipped its moorings. "You have given me the best possible life, Mama. Even with its hardships, you taught me how to laugh and love. And every hour we spent baking was an hour you poured your wisdom into my heart. And every minute I spent working with you at the herb store was experience I'll take with me to my bakery, which I cannot believe you bought for me." I said through my tears.

She took a shallow breath. "I have been proud of you every day of your life. Go and find your destiny. I love you my darling."

"I love you, Mama." I told her as I went to my room to pack.

I grabbed the battered duffel from beneath the bed, and stuffed it with the basics: underwear, jeans, a couple of hoodies, a couple of my favorite dresses, the old quilt for good measure. In the bathroom, I scooped up Mama's brush, her favorite lotion, the little tin of beeswax lip balm we'd made together last spring. I hesitated over the photos pinned to my wall—me as a baby, the two of us at the county fair, Mama caught mid-laugh at my thirteenth birthday. I tore down the smallest one, tucked it in my back pocket, and left the rest.

Then I knelt by the bed, pried up the loose floorboard beneath the rocking chair, and reached into the darkness. My fingers closed on rough, oiled leather—the grimoire. It was heavier than I remembered. I pulled it out, turned it over in my hands. The cover was stamped with our sigil: a circle of willow branches, three dots at the center. I'd never been able to open it; the magic was locked tight, waiting for a true witch.

Maybe now it would answer to me.

Underneath the grimoire was the large brown envelope. *Aspen*, it said in Mama's script. My throat knotted up, but I shoved it into my bag, too.

From the pantry, I gathered a couple jars of honey, a loaf of sourdough, and the last two apples. I wanted to linger, to take in every line and corner of our life together, but I needed to leave before the world outside started waking up. I thought I heard the crunch of footsteps on the gravel path, and the shrill voices echoing across the commons.

I laced up my boots, slung the duffel over my shoulder, and tiptoed back to Mama's side. I pressed a kiss to her forehead, just above the place where the skin was warmest, and lingered for three heartbeats.

I made my way to the back door and then turned one last time to see her sleeping form. "May the earth remember your kindness," I said, voice barely above a whisper. "May the wind sing your memory, and the waters carry you safe."

It was the old way, the words she'd taught me when I was little and didn't understand what death meant. Now, saying them, I felt a slice of comfort, so small I almost missed it.

"Love you, Mama," I said, voice thick and rough. "Don't forget me."

There was a rap at the front door—three hard knocks. I froze.

A second, then a third. More urgent now.

I crept to the back of the house, unlatched the screen door, and slipped into the darkness. The air was sharp with frost, and the grass crunched beneath my boots. I ducked behind the woodpile and circled wide through the little kitchen garden. When I looked back, I saw shadows moving through the cottage window. The front door crashed open, and a voice—a man's—shouted my name.

I ran then, straight into the trees, the bag thumping against my back, the grimoire like a stone in my chest. I didn't dare look back.

If Mama had taught me anything, it was that running wasn't weakness. Sometimes, it was the only way to survive.

I made it to the edge of the forest the moon lighting my way. There was a battered Subaru waiting on the dirt road, exactly where Mama and I always left it after foraging trips. I'd patched it up so many times I knew its engine better than my own heartbeat. The backseat was loaded down with laundry, textbooks, and at least three jars of pickles that'd rolled loose from last summer's canning. I threw my duffel onto the passenger seat, slammed the door, and cranked the ignition. The engine purred to life—stubborn as a stray dog.

"Come on, now. Don't you give up on me," I muttered, patting the dash. It felt silly to talk to a car, but it was better than talking to the woods behind me. I didn't want to imagine what or who was waiting in those shadows.

I bounced down the rutted road toward the highway, breath shallow and jittery. My hands shook on the steering wheel, but my mind was clear. Clearer than it had been in days. Maybe knowing what I was running from made it easier.

The further I got from Verdant Hollow, the less real it seemed. Maybe the coven was already searching for me, calling in their familiars, setting hexes on the crossroads. Or maybe they'd just be glad I was gone—a blemish erased from the bloodline. My skin prickled with every passing mile.

The first gas station was a graveyard of fluorescent lights and stale coffee. I filled the tank, hands shaking, eyes scanning every stranger for a sign they'd recognize me. But no one did. I looked like any other runaway—short, thick, too pale, hair wild and tangled. I bought a bag of jerky and two bottles of water, paid cash, and got back on the road.

I drove straight through the night, past fields gone gold with winter rye, past strip malls and empty drive-ins and motels whose vacancy signs never seemed to turn off. Sometimes, I'd check the rearview, expecting to see a shadow or a pair of headlights holding steady behind me. But it was just me, and the endless blacktop.

Somewhere near the Alabama line, I pulled off onto a dirt road and killed the engine. The air was thick with pine and river mud. I spread the grimoire on the hood of the car and ran my fingers over the cover, wondering if it would open for me now.

It didn't. The clasp held tight. But I felt a hum just under my skin, like it was waking up, or maybe just waiting. I unscrewed a jar of salt from Mama's bag and poured a circle around the car, then mashed up some rosemary with the butt of my water bottle and smeared it on the door handles. I couldn't cast, but I knew how to hide. If the coven sent anything after me, I'd make myself as invisible as a snake in grass.

The map Mama left was hand drawn, with little stars marking safe towns, potential enemies, and, circled three times in blue, Dairyville. That was my target. That, and the bakery she'd left in my name. The idea of running a bakery made me laugh and cry at the same time. My mama knew the one thing I was good at. Baking any and everything. I'd pulled the phone out of the envelope. A shiny new iPhone. Even though Mama had drawn a pretty map, I'd plugged the address of the bakery into the GPS figuring that between Mama's map and Google, I'd find the place without too much of a problem.

"Just keep movin', Aspen. Don't look back," I said, the accent thicker now, like it needed to anchor me. "That's what she'd want."

I drove on, using the back roads, stopping only when I was too tired to keep my eyes open. I slept in the car, hoodie pulled over my face, every sound in the darkness a possible threat. Sometimes I dreamed of Mama, her arms warm and alive, braiding my hair and humming to herself as she always did. Waking up hurt, but I kept going.

Near the state line, the roads grew wide and lonely. Truck stops gave way to nothing but open prairie and the scent of distant rain. I ate cold jerky, drank water, and counted the days since Mama died: one, two, three. Grief felt different in the car—less sharp, more like a bruise that flared whenever I stopped to think.

The sky was purple when I hit the Texas border, clouds lit from beneath by the promise of sunrise. I pulled over, just to see it, and let the engine idle while the world went from night to blue.

For a second, I thought about turning around. Going back to what little I had left. But there was nothing for me in Verdant Hollow, nothing at all.

So I pressed on, into the new day, with the bakery and the Iron Valor Pack waiting somewhere ahead.

I hoped Mama was right—that I'd find something beautiful at the end of this road.

If it wasn't beautiful when I got there, I'd do my best to make it so.

Chapter 2

Aspen

It was dawn when I rolled into Dairyville. I'd made it through the long dark highway by mainlining black coffee and heartbreak, counting down the mile markers like the beads of a rosary. The sky above the High Plains was a pale, lidless blue, empty of clouds and mercy. I expected Texas to hit me with wildness and gunfire, but Dairyville had the kind of calm you only found in places that had forgotten the world outside.

The town square was best described as charming. It consisted of a couple of streets with pretty little storefronts painted in various colors. There were street lamps and park benches that dotted the square that begged you to sit down and take a load off. The buildings were all stitched together by their old awnings and different lettering and logos on their windows: JONES HARDWARE, SHEAR ECSTASY SALON, and, squeezed between them like an afterthought, BUTTER-CREAM & BLESSINGS BAKERY.

I let the Subaru idle at the curb, my hands clenched on the wheel, waiting for the place to wake up. It was still early, too early for much life, but the streetlamps glowed against the dark like they refused to give up the night. At the heart of the square stood a perfect little gazebo, white as a wedding cake with Victorian trim. There was even a plaque on one of the gazebo pillars, though I couldn't read it from the car.

I spotted a sign taped to the bakery window advertising the "Iron Valor Christmas Toy Run." The date was December 25, and it was currently the end of January, but nobody'd bothered to take it down. I guess not having an owner, the bakery got lost in the aftermath.

I cut the engine, and for a minute the silence rang in my ears. My brain, wrung out from the last three days, tried to fill the emptiness with Mama's voice. "You make your own luck, Aspen. Don't wait for the world to hand it to you." I wondered if she'd say the same, seeing me now, strung out on exhaustion and clutching the steering wheel like it could save me.

I slid out of the car, concrete solid under my boots. The air was cold but dry, the kind of cold that slid right through your jacket and turned your nose red.

The building itself wasn't terribly wide. I'd guess 25 feet or so. The front window was smudged, the displayed cake stands were cracked, and it held a faded sign that said, "Happy 4th of July." The paint on the outside was a dull, washed-out mustard, with streaks of darker yellow running down in sad little tears. I tried to imagine what it looked like when the color was fresh. Maybe like sunshine, if sunshine had a nervous breakdown.

I checked the sidewalk. There was no one. Not a single soul, not even a stray dog. I ran a hand through my hair, which was tangled and greasy and absolutely not ready to meet the public. My coat felt tight over the hoodie I was wearing, and I was past due for a shower. It was just as well there was no one for me to meet at this hour.

I walked up to the bakery door, which had a bell but no lock. The key Mama left worked on the deadbolt, but the handle turned easily, as if the place had been waiting for me all along. I held my breath and went inside.

The real shock wasn't how bad the place looked, but how bad it felt. Buttercream & Blessings had seen better days—maybe better decades—but now it looked like someone had just up and quit halfway through closing. The air inside was thick with the sweet rot of old sugar and the metallic ghost of burned coffee. I walked the bakery's length with my arms tucked tight to my ribs, trying not to touch anything I couldn't wash off.

Flour moved in lazy drifts across the tile. It caked every knob and switch, turned the black-and-white checkered floor into a blurry, ashy painting. There was sugar dried to glass on the stovetop, and in the back kitchen a film of yellowed butter crusted the prep table. I flicked the light switch by the door and nearly wept with relief when the fluorescents flickered to life. I half-expected the lights to catch fire, the way everything else looked ready to combust.

First order of business: see if anything actually worked.

The walk-in cooler, which took up most of the back wall, rattled when I yanked the handle. I stepped inside and felt the temperature drop a grand total of zero degrees. Dead. All the metal racks were empty except for one shriveled orange and a single, bloated tub of what I guessed was margarine. I prodded it with the toe of my boot; it shivered like jelly, refusing to move.

Next up, the sinks. I turned the faucet on full blast and heard nothing but the gurgle of a thousand dead pipes. No water, not even a cough. The steel basin was filled with a brown scum I didn't want to inspect further.

The oven. My last hope. I flipped the preheat switch and waited, counting the seconds the way Mama had taught me. Ten, twenty, thirty. No click, no glow, nothing but the familiar scent of defeat. I sat down on a flour sack, stuck my head between my knees, and tried not to scream.

Instead, I laughed. It came out broken and high, and sounded exactly like Mama on her worst days. The woman could cuss out a car that wouldn't start with the creative force of a preacher at a tent revival. But right now, I didn't even have the energy for profanity.

I dragged myself into the dining area, slumped into one of the mismatched chairs, and stared at the dark street outside. Morning sunlight cut sharp lines across the bakery's filmy windows. I wondered what the people in this town would see, looking in: a pale, chubby girl in a hand-me-down coat, face blotched from crying, elbows sunk into a dirty bakery table.

I tried to cry, but the tears wouldn't come. I was past crying, past anger, somewhere in the numb void where you either quit or doubled down.

The chair wobbled under me as I fished my phone from my coat pocket. The battery was almost dead, but I still had just enough juice to open the text Mama sent while the phone was still in the box. The last words she ever sent to me.

Check your bank account, honey. You'll need it. I believe in you.

She'd sent it two days before she died, while I was out buying groceries she'd never eat. I clicked into the banking app, expecting to see the usual: double digits, maybe three if I was lucky.

Instead, the number nearly blinded me. $25,313.16.

For a second, I thought it was a glitch. Or maybe Mama had stolen someone's identity to give me a head start in life. But there it was, staring back, real as sunlight. This must be what was left of the proceeds from selling her herb store after purchasing this bakery. The little herb store she ran in Verdant Hollow was actually quite successful. I loved the days we spent there and the customers we served. I thought I'd inherit it someday. I guess I did, just not how I'd expected to.

My hands shook. I set the phone down, afraid I'd drop it. The tears came, and I let them. There wasn't anything pretty about the crying this time—no delicate sniffles, no pretty weeping. I just let it out, ugly and animal, until my throat felt raw and my cheeks burned. The whole bakery echoed with the sound, but no one heard except me and the ghosts.

When I finally got hold of myself, I wiped my face on the hem of my shirt and forced a laugh. "Okay, Mama," I said to the empty chairs. "I get the point."

If she'd gone through all this trouble, the least I could do was get the place up and running. I had money, or at least more than I'd ever seen in my life. I could call the plumbers, fix the cooler, order flour and sugar and eggs by the ton. I could buy every self-help book in the world and line the windows with them, if I wanted.

But first, I needed water. And a working oven. And maybe a new chair that didn't threaten to collapse under my ass.

I made a list on the back of an old invoice; the pen shaking in my fingers:

- Call utilities (water/gas/electric)
- Find plumber
- Fix oven
- Clean EVERYTHING
- Inventory supplies
- Sleep (ha)
- Open for business

I stared at the list for a long time, waiting for the panic to come back. But it didn't. The fear had burned itself out, replaced with a hollow, reckless hope.

I pressed my palms flat to the table, felt the stickiness of spilled syrup, and swore an oath right then and there:

No matter what, I would make this bakery work. For Mama. For me. For the dumb little town that was now home.

The apartment above the bakery was tiny, but it had a couple of windows to let in some natural light, and the heat worked when I twisted the dial on the thermostat. That alone made it better than sleeping in my car. The bedroom had a full-size bed complete with an old, lumpy mattress, but it wasn't the floor. The kitchen was a galley with a tiny sink, a fridge that moaned like it was trying to simply live another day, and a stove so ancient the brand name had worn away. I opened a few cabinets and found exactly what I expected: mismatched cups, plates, a coffee pot with a cracked handle. Mama had to buy the place sight unseen, and I know she trusted the universe to give me just enough. This was certainly exactly *just* enough.

I spent twenty minutes making mental notes. There were sheets on the bed, a towel hung over the bathroom door, and a bar of soap that smelled like hotel shampoo. No food in the fridge except for a single bottle of mustard and two cans of Diet Coke. I made a list: groceries, new pillows, towels, toiletries, and so many other things. But that was a start.

First priority, though: a new mattress. If I were going to survive this, I needed sleep that didn't come with springs poking at my kidneys. I checked Google Maps—turns out, Dairyville had exactly one furniture store, on the square, just two doors down from my own building. I called; the woman on the other end sounded so chipper I wanted to hang up. Yes, they delivered. Yes, today. I ordered a queen-size mattress and frame, nothing fancy, and paid with some of that newfound money.

Next, I dialed the water company, putting them on speaker so I could start unloading cleaning supplies downstairs. The hold music was a nightmare loop of eighties country, and I had to repeat my name four times before the woman believed I was real. When I told her the address, there was a long pause.

"You said Buttercream & Blessings Bakery?" she asked, her voice suddenly wary.

"That's right."

"Place has been empty a while," she said, as if I didn't already know. "Last owner packed up in the middle of the night; rumor is she owed half the county money."

I tried to sound cheerful. "Well, I paid the bill. Or, my mother did. I'm starting fresh. Can you send someone out to turn the water on?"

She promised a technician within the hour. For the gas, I needed a plumber to sign off, and for the oven I'd need to wait until everything was up and running. I thanked her, told her to have a lovely day, and hung up.

Without water, I decided to start removing trash and sweeping.

I started at the top and worked my way down, as Mama always said. Dust before you sweep, sweep before you mop, then wipe every surface twice. I found the cleaning supplies in a plastic bucket under the sink—mostly vinegar and bleach, plus a terrifying pink sponge that looked older than me. I threw the sponge away and raided the hardware store for fresh supplies.

The man behind the counter was about sixty, with a face like beef jerky and hands that could crush walnuts. He watched me the whole time I shopped, his eyes following me down every aisle. I bought gloves, rags, a broom, and a gallon of lemon-scented cleaner. At the checkout, he rang everything up in silence.

"Y'all are new to Dairyville, aren't you?" he said finally.

I nodded, offering a half-smile. "Moved in this morning. I'm opening the bakery back up."

He grunted, not quite friendly, not quite unfriendly. "People here like things the way they are. Don't much care for change."

"I'm not here to change anything," I said carefully. "Just bake some pastries, maybe a few cakes. Hopefully, I'll make a few friends."

He slid the bags across the counter. "You let me know if you need a contractor. My son does odd jobs—painting, repairs, whatever." His gaze softened, just a hair. "Good luck."

I stopped at the door. "Matter of fact, I could use a painter. I'd love to have the front painted a pretty, sunny yellow. If he's available and not too expensive." He gave me a quote, and it seemed reasonable. And suddenly, I'd hired the man's son and apparently had a new friend to boot.

When I got back to the store, I heard water running in the kitchen sink. I'd clearly left the faucet open, and someone had turned the water on while I was at the hardware store. So, I rolled up my sleeves and got to work. I scrubbed the windows until my knuckles ached, cleared the cobwebs from the corners, and polished the glass case next to the front counter until I could see my own puffy-eyed reflection. Every sweep of the rag peeled away a layer of grime, a decade of lost hope. It wasn't pretty yet, but it was starting to look alive.

The lemon cleaner made the whole place smell like a Florida orchard, sharp and clean. I set up the tables in the front room, arranging the mismatched chairs so they wouldn't look so lonely. There were only six tables, enough to seat maybe twenty people if they squeezed. I dusted each one, scoured the salt and pepper shakers, and the sugar caddies to get them ready to be filled with the first grocery delivery that would soon arrive.

Around noon, a battered pickup rolled up in front of the bakery. The driver was a guy in paint-spattered jeans and a camo hat, carrying a five-gallon bucket and a ladder. He knocked once, hard.

"You Aspen?"

"That's me."

"Dad said you needed the outside painted." He didn't wait for me to answer, just started unloading. The paint cans were sunshine yellow, the kind of color you couldn't look at straight on without smiling. He covered the front door with plastic, taped off the windows, and set to work like he'd been born with a brush in his hand.

I watched from the inside, every stroke a little brighter than the last. The old mustard color was gone within the hour, replaced by the bold, almost absurd optimism of fresh paint. I couldn't help but think of Mama, and how she used to paint our rooms every spring, chasing away the gloom of winter with wild shades of turquoise and coral.

The plumber showed up next, a woman in coveralls and a bandana. She took one look at the mess in the kitchen and shook her head.

"You got your work cut out for you, girl," she said, hands on hips.

"I know," I replied. "But I have a secret weapon."

She raised an eyebrow. "Yeah?"

I smiled for real this time. "Stubbornness."

She laughed and got to work under the sink.

It was so odd that, speaking to strangers around here turned out to be much easier than speaking to the coven members back home.

By the time the sun set, things looked much better. I still had a ways to go, but as I sat down in a chair by the front window, with a real cup of coffee in my hands, for the first time, I felt like maybe I could do this.

I glanced up at the sign, now freshly painted and clean.

Buttercream & Blessings Bakery.

I whispered it to myself, letting the words settle on my tongue. I thought about changing the name, but I kind of loved it as it was. Why fix something that wasn't broken?

My mattress was delivered, and I'd made a Walmart run, grabbing new sheets, towels, and toiletries. A trip to the laundrette to wash everything, a shower, and a quick meal at a place called Pearl's (which I think was full of wolves), and I was in bed just after midnight, dead to the world.

I'd tackle more cleaning tomorrow and hopefully get to baking soon.

Cleaning ended up taking me another couple of days. But it was so much easier than getting the appliances working for the official start of baking. On that day, I was up before sunrise, hair twisted in a bun. I'd picked up some new clothes on one of my shopping trips for supplies. No more shapeless dresses for me. I had on some cute yoga pants and a long top that hit right below my rounded ass. I felt cute and ready to make some magic; as much as I could. The kitchen was mine now—every polished handle, every clean bowl, every square inch of the ancient butcher block.

I decided to keep the existing oven. The expense of an industrial bakery oven would have set me back several thousand dollars, and this oven wasn't actually all that old. It just looked like hell from the abuse it had taken from the previous owner. It took a couple of days, but I scrubbed it until it looked so bright and hopeful.

I was willing to do anything to make the old thing work. I'd even sing to it, the way Mama used to when she wanted a loaf to rise just so. I'd made a batch of cinnamon roll dough and left it to proof while I checked the oven to see if it would preheat.

The plumber had signed off; the gas was flowing, and the thermostat blinked in neon orange. But when I pressed the preheat button, nothing happened. The click of the igniter was just air; the burners stayed cold, unblinking. I tried again, slower this time, reciting the steps from memory like a prayer.

Still nothing.

I stared at the empty racks inside, willing them to heat up, and for a minute I wanted to smash the oven windows. Then I remembered how Mama had talked to the kitchen when things went sideways. Not just muttering, but full-out bargaining. I felt stupid, but desperation is stronger than pride.

I set my hands on the oven's cold steel, closed my eyes, and tried to remember the kinds of things she said. I set my intention and spoke, "Come on, baby," I murmured, slow and low. "You're stronger than this. You're made for helping to create delicious things with your heat. Don't let me down. It's your time to shine."

Nothing at first, just the hum of the cooler and the tick of the wall clock. Then, in the space where my palms met the metal, a warmth buzzed through my skin. It tingled up my arms, a charge that made my hair stand on end. The oven shuddered once, then sparked to life with a roar that was half mechanical, half alive.

I jumped back, nearly tripped over my own feet, and stared at the oven like it was a living thing. The burners glowed. Heat poured out, thick and sweet, and a single tear rolled down my cheek; not from sadness, but relief.

"Mama?" I said, half-laughing. "Did you see that?"

The kitchen didn't answer, but I felt something settle in the room, a softness, like someone had wrapped me in honey.

I went back to the dough, rolled it out, then added the cinnamon mixture and cut it into neat strips. I rolled the spirals and loaded them onto trays. The oven was perfect—hot, steady, faithful. I tried the same trick on the coffeemaker, and when it coughed to life, I felt the same pulse in my fingertips. The industrial mixer, too. The more I spoke to them, the more they responded. Every whir and beep and hum felt like a conversation, a secret language I'd never known I spoke.

I started to wonder if all those years in Verdant Hollow, I'd been more than just a dud. Maybe the coven had bound my magic, kept it tamped down until I was alone and too far gone to matter. Maybe Mama had known, and that's why she bought me this place; to give me a chance to grow.

By early afternoon, the bakery was full of the smell of cinnamon, sugar, and fresh bread. I stacked pastries in the window, lined cookies on cooling racks, and filled the air with the sharp, dark scent of strong coffee. I played Mama's old playlists on my phone, singing along to country ballads and golden oldies, dancing from counter to counter like no one was watching.

I worked until my feet hurt and my arms ached, but it was a good kind of pain—a building pain, not a breaking one. For every tray of muffins I pulled from the oven, I whispered a thank you. For every loaf that rose just right, I patted the countertop and said, "Good job, sweetheart." I wiped the sweat from my brow, looked at the full display case, and felt a surge of pride so fierce I nearly burst.

When the sun set, I turned off the lights, locked the doors, and stood outside to look at the bakery. The yellow paint glowed under the street-lamps, every window bright and inviting. For a second, I imagined Mama standing next to me, arms crossed, a smirk on her face.

"You did it, baby," I said, just for her. "We did it."

I'd built something beautiful from nothing, and no one could take that from me.

As I sipped my coffee, I made a wish: that the people of Dairyville would come. That they'd smell the bread, see the light, and maybe, just maybe, give me a chance.

I'd been here for several days now, and lots of people had stopped to look in the window. Today I'd finally put some teaser items in the window. Guess I'd find out tomorrow if they'd take the bait.

CHAPTER 3

Big Papa

The best part about being the Iron Valor's chaplain was never the Sunday services, and it sure as hell wasn't handholding the half-drunk prospects through their first come-to-Jesus talk. It was these moments, right before "church" officially started, when all the club officers crowded into the conference room, each man carrying his own brand of quiet.

We met every Monday, rain or shine, in a room that was too clean to belong to a biker compound and too battered to ever pass for professional. The table had gouges and burn marks, and every chair was a different height—Wrecker had sawed an inch off Gunner's legs as a joke two months back, and nobody had bothered to fix it.

Of course, this was the new bunker conference room that had been built after the old compound had been blown to hell by the Greenbriar pack. Wrecker's mate was in the building at the time. She told him she'd died. Saw her dead mother and everything. But, thing is, there's this angel named Archon who showed up, as he does from time to time, and seems he touched Parker. Cuz she's as alive as I am. And now, that girl is angel touched and little miracles seem to follow her. Hell, maybe she'd be a better chaplain. Then again, I recently passed away as well, and that same angel brought me back from the other side. I got no miracles to my name at this time, but the day's still young.

This morning, the whole place smelled like burnt coffee, and the ghost of last night's pulled pork. Sunlight cut stripes through the shades, landing square on Bronc's knuckles where he sat at the head, frowning into his third cup of black.

Juliet, our Luna, had arrived early and put out donuts. She lingered by the window, arms folded, profile sharp as a scythe. Her mate had finally claimed her in a way that didn't let her out of his sight, but she still liked to haunt the perimeter, like a wolf circling the herd. That woman had been to the pits of hell and came out the other side stronger than steel; a Luna we proudly would die for.

Next to me sat Gunner, slouched back so far his boots nearly propped against the table. He nursed his coffee with two hands, eyes half-lidded and chin speckled with stubble, cowboy hat low on his head. The big Texan's voice was slow and syrupy, but the brain behind it was sharper than most gave him credit for.

Wrecker, our newly named VP, paced at the back, restless as ever. He ran a thumb along the edge of his patch, occasionally pausing to glare at his phone. There was a rumor he slept with it under his pillow, and I'd yet to see him go five minutes without checking it.

Doc had arrived late, as always, sliding into his seat with a nod and a tired smile. The man looked like he belonged at a university, not a biker club, but he fit here better than most. He'd been up all night with a broken arm and a birth; he had the exhaustion to prove it. He adjusted his black-framed glasses when he sat.

Bronc waited until the last chair creaked before he spoke.

"Let's get this started," he said, voice dry as gravel. "Anyone wanna open with a prayer?"

A few snickers circled the table. I raised my hand. "Lord, grant us the patience to deal with each other, the wisdom to out-think our enemies, and the appetite to get through whatever the hell Gunner brought for breakfast."

Gunner grinned, eyes flicking to the donut box. "Amen."

The laughter died quick. Bronc set his cup down and steepled his fingers, the blue in his eyes gone hard and cold. "Rafe's called a Council. It'll happen in a few days. He's not letting any grass grow under this one. It's priority one."

Juliet let out a low sigh, her gaze shifting to the floor. She hated the politics of the packs, but it was her burden now, same as Bronc's, especially when it came to our territory king, Rafe Mayfield.

"What's his angle?" Wrecker asked, arms crossed. "He hasn't called one in ages."

"To get to the bottom of the Greenbriar attempted massacre," Doc said, tapping a finger against the table. "He wants to see if he can make Maltraz and Otero squirm. And to make sure nobody tries to come back on us for wiping out Greenbriar."

Gunner shifted forward. "We handled Greenbriar by the old rules. They poisoned our water—killed seven of our own, including a damn child. They came at us. We mopped the floor. I assume nobody is questioning our response."

Bronc met Gunner's stare. "He's gonna make damn sure nobody gets the chance. He's using our situation as leverage."

Wrecker grunted. "King Rafe doesn't breathe unless he can profit from it. So who's he aiming at?"

"Look, we know there is no love lost between Rafe and the demons," Bronc answered. "It's about the same with that vampire prick. Rafe wants to lay the water attack at their feet and force a formal alliance among shifters. There's no taking out those factions, but maybe that can be weakened or something. Shit, I don't know why Rafe does what Rafe does. But he's our king, and we gotta believe he'll stand up for us. Plus, Menace may be the Midwest king, but he's our king too. If it's possible to make them pay for the attack, they had a hand in, I'm all for it."

There was a beat of silence. My wolf, usually calm, bristled with the memory of the attack on our compound: the first death had been quick, the rest less so. We buried the child ourselves. When it came to payback, Iron Valor hadn't left a single Greenbriar standing.

"He's not wrong about the demons," I said, remembering how they'd attacked me in that field. They'd literally killed me and possessed my body. "I'd like them to pay for what they did to me." I said with a shiver, then continued. "And they're getting bolder. Maltraz is trying to carve a route across New Mexico, and the vamps run supplies for him."

Juliet's lips twisted. "Supplies. You mean human cargo."

I nodded. "And witches. They're abducting the solitary ones anywhere they can nab 'em. The ones with real power."

Doc slid his hands into his hoodie, knuckles white. "How do we get ahead of it?"

Bronc flicked his gaze at me. "You and Wrecker and Parker take point on the research. Every move Maltraz or Otero's made in the last twelve months, I want it on my desk after the ceremony. Gunner, you're in charge of security at the compound. Have Tyler help with double patrols, all hours. Juliet, you coordinate with Pearl—if there's a threat to the young or the elders, I want them safe before anyone else knows there's danger."

He ran through the rest of the assignments, his voice never raising, but every word hammered into our skulls. If he told us to jump, we'd ask how high on the way up.

Wrecker set his mug down. "This all means we need to pull off the mating ceremony without a hitch. If there's trouble, it'll happen while the pack's focused on the party."

Juliet smirked. "Typical. We can't even have a mating night without plotting murder."

Bronc's face softened, just a hair. "Three weeks. It's happening. Whether Rafe's Council goes to shit or not."

Pearl breezed in through the side door, carrying a tray of fresh biscuits and a carafe that steamed like a volcano. She wore pearls around her neck and a look that could shush a hurricane.

"Y'all look like you're about to start a funeral instead of a wedding," she said, setting the tray down. "Eat. I need the bridegroom and his Luna alive, not plotting world domination on empty stomachs."

"Thank you, Ma," Bronc said, meaning it.

Pearl poured coffee for everyone, topping off my cup, black the way I liked it. She eyed the rest of us. "So, have you picked a cake yet, or are you planning on serving Little Debbies to 200 hungry wolves?"

Juliet raised an eyebrow. "You think I'm eating cake with this morning sickness? Not a chance."

Pearl winked. "You could at least taste it. There's a new bakery on the square, open just this morning. Owner's adorable. But she's definitely not human. And she's not wolf, either."

Gunner perked up. "She single?"

Pearl shot him a glare. "That's not what you should be asking, young man. But yes. Single. Runs the place solo, and rumor is she bakes a cinnamon roll so good it's practically illegal."

Gunner grinned. "I'll volunteer to be taster."

"No, you won't," Juliet said. "You're on security. Big Papa, you go."

It took me a second to realize she had told *me* to go. I blinked. "Why me?"

"Because you're the only one with a palate. And you're the only person I trust not to sleep with the baker before we've even hired her," Juliet said, deadpan.

Even Bronc cracked a smile. "She's right. You're the best we've got."

I tried to protest, but Pearl just patted my arm. "It's settled. Go around noon, be nice to her, and don't scare her off. She's new to Dairyville and looks like she's been through hell. You, of all people, should understand that, son."

The room dissolved into laughter and groans. I finished my coffee and watched the others file out, each to their assignments, their burdens stitched into the backs of their jackets. Bronc lingered a moment, giving me that measured, piercing look.

He nodded once, then left, boots thudding down the hall. I could hear Juliet scolding Wrecker in the hallway for not bringing Parker, Gunner's laughter booming, and Pearl's voice trailing after her son like a prayer.

I stared at my empty cup, then out the window, where the wind was already picking up dust from the canyon and sending it across the empty plains. There was a wedding to plan, and a Council to survive, and a whole world of uncertainty that could be waiting to tear us apart.

And apparently, I had a cake to order.

I pushed to my feet, grabbed my jacket, and headed for the door. It was a long walk across the compound to my bike, and I needed the air to clear my head. The wind tasted like dry grass and pine; the sky already sharpening to blue.

The last thing Pearl had said played in my head: Be nice to her. I was nice to everyone. It's who I was. Don't know why I felt like I wanted to be *not* nice to this girl.

I'd try. But if she put raisins in the cinnamon rolls, we'd definitely have problems.

I decided to reserve judgement just like I wanted people to do with me.

The sun was just starting to bake the streets when I made it into Dairyville proper. My bike rumbled under me, stubborn and loud and comforting.

The main square was buzzing: the hardware store's lights flickering, drug store clerk propping the door with her hip, a couple of ranch hands sipping coffee from to-go cups on the courthouse steps.

The bakery was impossible to miss. The yellow paint didn't just stand out; it shouted. Looked like somebody had poured a can of daylight over the old facade. On either side, the buildings were more subdued—hardware store to the left, hair salon to the right, both painted a tasteful gray and navy. The bakery blazed in the middle like a beacon of warmth.

I parked at the curb, killed the engine, and took a breath. There was a sweetness in the air that hit me even outside, something rich and golden, like the memory of Sunday mornings our housekeeper baking delicious treats my mom was too busy to be bothered with. My stomach gave a hopeful twitch. So did my wolf the moment I stepped through the door.

The bell above the entrance announced me with a happy little jingle. The sound was so at odds with the world I came from that it almost made me shiver. I squared my shoulders like I was looking for a fight, and stepped inside, boots leaving a dust mark on the freshly mopped tile.

It was bright in here. Sunlight pooled on every surface, bouncing off lemon-painted walls and glass display cases. The counters gleamed. There were several small tables, each with mismatched chairs, and the smell—God, the smell—was a full-bodied gut punch: vanilla, caramelizing sugar, a sharp drift of citrus that made my teeth ache. I wasn't sure if it was the pastries or the beauty standing at the counter.

There she was, five feet five inches of delicious curves and softness. She stood, back straight, hands folded on the counter, waiting as I took her in. Even from here, I could see her subtle nervousness. Her skin was pale as fresh milk, hair a black river of silk falling over one shoulder. Her eyes, like two emeralds, sharp, and assessing.

I knew before she opened her mouth or even smiled that she wasn't human. It was in the stillness of her hands, in the unnatural green of her eyes, and in the way her presence pressed against my chest. My wolf bristled, then settled, as if recognizing some ancient rule.

"Mornin'," she said, with a voice soft as air. Southern, maybe Savannah or Atlanta, with a sweetness I didn't want to trust. "Can I help you?"

I tried not to let the military training take over. I kept my voice easy. "Depends. You the new owner?"

She tilted slightly. "That's what the deed says," she affirmed. I wondered if she was using magic on me right then. Her voice had a definite, natural, magical lilt. "I'm Aspen."

Aspen. It suited her. Delicate but tough, the kind of name you give something that survives bad winters.

"Big Papa," I said, offering the club nickname out of habit. "I'm with Iron Valor."

Her eyes darted to my jacket, to the patch. She didn't flinch, but something in her posture shifted. "I heard about y'all. From the hardware guy. He said your club runs most of the town."

I shrugged. "We don't run it. We just keep things quiet."

She smiled, a quick flash of white teeth. "That's what people say right before they admit they run things."

My lips twitched. I liked her for all of three seconds. Then I caught a glint of a large leather-bound book on a shelf behind the counter. A grimoire. The reminder that she was a witch. I stiffened, old habits coming back.

"You're a witch," I blurted.

She blinked hard as though she had misheard. "Excuse me?"

I nodded toward the shelf. "That's a grimoire. You can't deny it."

A flush crawled up her neck, but she held my stare. "So what if I am?"

"I just like to know what I'm eating," I said, deadpan.

The friendly atmosphere I'd been enjoying had gone frosty. She looked at her hands, then back up. "You're here for the cake tasting."

I wondered if she was clairvoyant as well. "Mind reader, also?"

She rolled her eyes at me. "Pearl called this morning. She said you'd be coming."

Of course. Pearl never left anything to chance.

She gestured to a table. Yep, the charming beauty was all business now. "Sit. Let me just hop on my broom and fly back to the kitchen to get your samples."

I just stared at her for a minute.

"It's called sarcasm. Geez." She called over her shoulder as she walked back to the kitchen, unaware that the luscious sway of her hips was almost as intriguing as her personality.

I picked the chair that put my back to the wall. Old habit, again. She disappeared into the kitchen, and for a moment I just sat there, breathing in the sugar and butter and watching sunlight creep across the floor.

She came back with a wooden tray, four slices of cake on clean white plates, each with a tiny fork stuck in the side.

"Carrot, chocolate, strawberry, and lemon."

I glanced at the slices. The carrot was topped with a smear of cream cheese icing so white it glowed. The chocolate was almost black, dusted with something golden. The lemon wasn't fancy but was iced with some kind of fluffy icing and had a creamy curd-type filling.

I tried the carrot first. It was good. Too sweet for my taste, but the texture was right, and the frosting had that tang people liked.

The chocolate was dense, and rich, and bitter in a way I respected. She watched my every move, her eyes anxious and curious at the same time.

The strawberry was fresh, moist and full of flavor. The icing creamy.

Then I tried the lemon. The moment I did, the world just about stopped.

The cake was light, so delicate I barely tasted it before it melted away. But the flavor—it was sun-warmed, sharp, so perfectly balanced it nearly made me angry. And that acid bite hit right in the jaw.

I set the fork down.

She waited, holding her breath.

"What did you put in this?" I asked, almost accusing.

Her brows pinched together. "Lemon. Sugar. Eggs. Butter. Little bit of buttermilk, maybe."

"No magic?"

Her face closed up. Now she just looked hurt. "I promise you mister, if I had any discernible magical abilities, I likely wouldn't even know how to bake. Now, do you like the damn cakes or not?"

I tried to read her, but all I saw was exhaustion, and wounds that ran about as deep as the scars I carried. I knew that look. I'd seen it in the mirror off and on for years.

"I'm not judging," I said, voice softer now. "Wolves and witches don't usually mix. Experience makes me a little skeptical."

She laughed a sarcastic laugh. "Really? I wasn't aware of the ancient history between wolves and witches." She looked away, then back at me. "Someone told me the Iron Valor Pack was different. That I might be safe if I were to move here alone. Maybe they were mistaken?"

Shit. She looked so small and vulnerable. "I didn't mean anything by that. Iron Valor judges people strictly on their merit." I told her.

"Maybe you could have given me that courtesy before you threw out accusations." She attempted to glare at me. Cutest thing ever.

She was right. I came in here with a chip on my shoulder ready to judge her. "Again, my apologies."

I looked down at the cake, then up at her again. "You ever bake for two hundred?"

She blinked. "Two hundred?"

"We're doing a mating ceremony in three weeks. Might be more like two-twenty if the vampires show."

Her jaw dropped, just enough to be funny. "Vampires?"

I nodded. "They're friends of ours. You'll know them when you see them. Pale, overdressed, allergic to small talk."

She grinned, but it faded quick. "Who's ceremony?"

"Our Alpha and Luna," I said. "Pretty big deal. We need something good."

She was quiet for a moment, then said, "I can do it."

I believed her.

There was a pause, long enough for the clock over the counter to tick three times. I tried to picture her in this place, alone at dawn, mixing batter and humming to herself. I wondered if it made her happy, why she was here alone.

"What's your story?" I asked.

She raised an eyebrow. "You mean, why is a witch baking cakes in the middle of wolf country?"

"Something like that."

She looked at her hands, then out the window. "My mom died. Before she did, for some reason she bought me this place. Said it'd be safer here than with my coven. She actually told me to run. So I ran."

"Sorry about your mom. Why would you need to run from your coven? Thought they are usually your family."

"Thanks." She didn't say anything for a long time, then, "My entire coven always said I wasn't much of a witch. Treated me like garbage. Never called me by my name, just 'dud.' I could never do what the others did. Never reached the point to where my magic manifested. But my mother, who was the most powerful witch in our coven next to the Wyrdmother, taught me how to bake. Don't know if she knew what the future held or what, but here I am."

The last word trembled, and I saw it for what it was: a plea not to push any further.

I cleared my throat. "We'll take the lemon. It's delicious."

She tried to hide her smile. "That's the first real compliment I've had since I can't remember."

Her reaction to the praise hit me in the balls. "Well, you should get used to it."

She hesitated, then said, "What's your actual name, Big Papa?"

I considered lying, then thought better of it. "Jonas. But everyone calls me JT, or just Rice."

She nodded. "Nice to meet you, Jonas."

I looked at her again, really looked, and the urge to run had faded. There was an edge to her. She wore the look of someone who'd been through her own hell and survived it, same as I did.

"I'll send payment through Pearl," I said, standing.

She followed me to the door. "I'll make a small sample cake by tomorrow. Prefer a style? I can do fancy, but I like it simple."

"Simple's better," I said. "And Aspen?"

"Yeah?"

"Keep the magic to yourself. Most folks in Dairyville are human, and they don't like what they can't explain."

She nodded, but there was a spark of defiant humor in her eyes. "If I ever figure out how to make my magic work, I'll be sure to keep it under my witch's hat."

I smiled, despite myself. "See you around."

As I stepped outside, the sunlight hit me like a slap. My wolf grumbled inside, annoyed at how I'd handled her, like I should've been softer or at least less of an ass. Because I truly was mostly a nice guy.

I turned back. She was in the window, hands pressed around a coffee mug, looking after me like she half expected I'd vanish.

My wolf growled, deep and low, a wordless warning. Then he said the word that I'd already had rolling around in my brain and had been trying desperately to dismiss:

"Mate."

I started my bike, the engine snarling, and took off down Main. The taste of cake was still on my tongue. The girl was still in my head. This was something I didn't need right now with everything else that was on my plate. How could I explain it? I didn't know any examples of wolf and witch mated couples. Was this even a thing? Maybe I just hadn't been laid in so damn long my dick was just confused by the first new gorgeous flesh it had seen in forever.

"NO, MATE."

"Alright. Calm the fuck down. Her flesh *is* gorgeous. You just want to sink your teeth into her."

Great. Now I'm arguing with my wolf. Life just keeps getting better and better. That little witch said she had no ability to use magic, but she sure as shit put a spell on me.

Chapter 4

Aspen

By the time dusk settled over Dairyville, my body ached in places I'd forgotten I even had. I was cleaning up the bakery, hands raw from the lemon-scented soap and arms spattered with the ghosts of dough and glaze, and thinking, *this is the kind of pain you earn*. I stood at the kitchen's edge, surveying the aftermath: mixing bowls stacked, cooling racks half-filled with tomorrow's ambition, a single, beautiful cinnamon bun left on a parchment square like a consolation prize. It was the sort of exhaustion that curled up deep in the muscles and radiated a slow, low fire through my ribs. Satisfying in a way I couldn't quite put into words.

The last customer of the day—some woman in blue jeans and a band t-shirt, hair up in a messy bun and a kid at each hip—had called me "hon," paid in cash, and left with a box of cookies and a "see you tomorrow." She was the third or fourth person to say that, which felt both like a blessing and a threat. I'd never worked so hard to fit in. I tried to make every customer feel seen and even made larger purchases extra special by tying them up in boxes with a white string that, according to the internet, was part of the "brand experience."

I set the mop in the bucket, wiped my palms on my apron, and took a long, slow breath. The bakery looked cleaner than I imagined it had in years. The air was scrubbed free of its sugar rot, replaced with something sharp and hopeful. The display case gleamed. A girl with flour in her hair and dark circles under her eyes looked back at me in the reflection. A sense of accomplishment that I'd never felt filled my being.

For the first time since I'd arrived in Dairyville, I wasn't afraid to stand still. There was a fragile hope in my chest, almost like pride, though that was a feeling I'd never known well. Maybe that was what Mama had tried to teach me—how to plant roots without getting choked out by the dirt.

I went to the front door and flipped the sign from OPEN to CLOSED; the bell tinkling its final note of the day. It was early afternoon, and people were still shopping at the antique stores and boutiques. Come dusk, the streets outside would be mostly empty, as the last of the sun dragged shadows up the sides of the buildings. This little town looked like it belonged to another time. I started to believe I could like it here.

I looked up at my own yellow awning, bright and cheerful against the blue of the Texas sky. I thought of Mama, and how she'd have been happy with her decision. I closed the door and leaned against it, glancing around the bakery. Goosebumps suddenly ran up my spine, and a gentle breeze brushed across my neck. I heard a voice, small and light. *"I knew you could do it. I always believed in you, even when you didn't believe in yourself. Now,* **you** *have to start believing. You are more, so much more, than what people have said about you. You have everything you need to be great already inside of you. Find a way to grasp it."* I stopped and looked around the dining room.

"Mama?" A tear ran down my face. I knew I'd not be able to see her, but I absolutely heard her voice; heard what she'd said. "I'll find a way, Mama. I promise I will."

As I locked up, my thoughts drifted to JT—Big Papa Rice—and the way he'd looked at me earlier. He had been the first person, the first to actually compliment my food. He'd been standoffish and kind of a jackass, but sincere. It seemed like he was battling with himself. I think his instinct told him that all witches were bad. And honestly, I couldn't blame him for thinking that. *I* feel that way about most witches.

But there was something about him. And it went beyond the fact that he's maybe the most beautiful man I'd ever seen. Yes, he carried scars on his face and neck, and probably across his body, but that does not detract from his innate attractiveness. He had a light around him that drew me in. Even when I wanted to punch him. He clearly worked to keep his dark blonde hair styled and his beard neat and trimmed. I wondered if that was because of his scars or if he'd always been meticulous. Maybe I'd find out someday.

"Oh, girl, what are you even thinking about? That guy hated you. You're never gonna find out anything personal about him." I had this conversation with myself as I went back to the kitchen and started tomorrow's prep. I needed to get his sample cake made. I lined up the baking sheets, measured out flour and sugar, and set the coffee to auto-brew at five thirty. I liked the rituals, the way they anchored me to the present. Mama always said that purpose was the best shield against grief, but tonight the old ache pressed in at the edges of my mind. I let it hang there, just out of reach.

As I worked, I couldn't help but think about how the townsfolk kept their distance. Polite, yes. Kind, even. But there was a wariness in the way they watched me—a slight tilt of the head, a narrowing of the eyes when I handed them their change. It wasn't hostility. More like curiosity, the way a person looks at a snake in the grass and tries to decide whether it's venomous. I'd grown up with that look. In Verdant Hollow, it was sharper, more direct. Here, it was soft and hidden behind layers of small talk and neighborly goodwill, but it stung just the same.

Papa's warning surfaced in my mind: 'Dairyville is almost a hundred percent human. We keep all the supernatural stuff under the radar. They can sense when you're different.' I hadn't tried to hide, but I hadn't advertised myself, either. I was just the girl from Georgia with the odd name and the knack for cinnamon rolls. That was enough, for now.

I finished cleaning the last mixing bowl, got the cakes out to cool, and wiped down the counter with a fresh rag. The kitchen was quiet but not empty; it buzzed with the memory of today's work, of laughter and music and the constant hum of the ovens. I liked the idea that I could fill a space with my own energy, make it a little less lonely. After I wrapped the cooled cake layers and got them into the cooler, I washed up the last two pans. I thanked all the appliances for their hard work today as I walked out of the kitchen.

Pearl's Bar & Grill smelled like salvation, or at least like home. It was all fried food and sweet pie and old wood that'd seen more laughter and heartbreak than any church pew. When I stepped inside, the place was humming, half the town jammed into vinyl booths and wood tables, the air so thick with gossip you could slice it and serve it with a side of ranch. I didn't know where to stand, so I just hovered by the coat rack, hoping not to get trampled by the high school football team demolishing burgers at a long table.

Pearl herself spotted me before I had a chance to sit. She sailed out from behind the bar, hands spread like she might actually hug me, and I braced myself for the impact. There was something about her—this kinetic energy wrapped in pastel sweaters and pearls—that made you feel instantly seen, maybe even known.

"Look at you, little flower," she crowed, with an easy smile on her face. "You worked yourself to the bone today, didn't you?" Her eyes swept me from head to toe and found all my rough edges. "Come, come. I've got a booth with your name on it. Right by the window. That's the best seat, trust me."

She steered me, gentle but insistent, past a row of men in Carhartt jackets and women who didn't so much as glance up from their chicken fried steaks. I slid into the corner booth, the red vinyl sticky against my legs, and tried not to notice the way a few people's eyes bounced off me like I was just another ghost passing through town.

Pearl pressed a menu into my hands but didn't bother to give me time to read it. "We've got meatloaf tonight, or you can do the catfish. Don't ask for a salad unless you want to watch me die of disappointment." She plucked the menu away, already certain she knew what I needed. "And you'll get the pie. It's pecan, just made this morning."

I tried to protest, but she patted my arm and sailed away, leaving me with a glass of sweet tea and a sudden, unspooling sense of comfort I hadn't known I missed. The table was covered in little carvings—hearts, initials, the odd dirty word—and I traced them absently, letting my mind drift.

Mama would have loved this place. She'd have found the corner with the best light, ordered a daily special, and made best friends with the entire kitchen staff by the end of the night. She'd have told me to smile more, to loosen up, to let myself be taken care of for once. It made my chest tight, remembering.

The food arrived before I could get too lost in the memory. Pearl herself set the plate down, balancing three others on her arm for the neighboring table. "Eat," she commanded, like it was the admission charge for sitting in the booth.

I picked at the meatloaf, poking at the mashed potatoes until the brown gravy made little rivers on the plate. It tasted like Sunday afternoons, heavy and rich, but my stomach was knotted up as my mind drifted back to Big Papa Rice. I took a few bites anyway, determined not to let Pearl down.

I was halfway through the pie—perfectly sweet, with a crust that flaked apart in my mouth—when someone slid into the booth across from me. She was my age, maybe younger, with hair the color of campfire smoke and eyes that sparkled like she was always one step from starting a commotion. She grinned wide and unapologetic, and propped her chin on her fists.

"You smell like rosemary and trouble," she said.

I blinked, thrown by the greeting. "Excuse me?"

She leaned in, voice lowered but playful. "That's not a bad thing. I'm just saying. You're new, and you smell like you don't quite belong yet, but you're trying really hard to pretend you do. I respect that." She offered her hand. "Maddie."

I took it, and her grip was strong, warm, a little reckless. "Aspen. I...uh...just opened the bakery on Main."

She snapped her fingers. "I knew it! I had a cookie from there at lunch. Best cookie I've eaten since I can't remember when." She paused, tilting her head. "Hear you're from Georgia. Is that right, or did Pearl get her wires crossed?"

"It's true," I said, the words heavier than I meant them. "I came here to start over. Or maybe just to start."

Maddie looked at me for a long time, like she could see the cracks under the surface. Then she smiled again, all mischief and understanding. "Well, whatever you're doing, it's working. You got half the ladies at the salon talking about you. And the men, too. Well, you got the men *lookin'* anyways."

I laughed, surprised by the sound. It was the first real laugh I'd managed since leaving Verdant Hollow. Maddie noticed and looked pleased with herself.

"So, what do *you* do?" I asked, desperate to change the subject.

She shrugged. "Work at my brother Bronc's motorcycle shop; sometimes I help my Ma here. I basically do what I want." She leaned in closer, conspiratorial. "I'm really trying to find Mr. Right, have a few pups, you know, live the life."

I know my eyes had to be as big as saucers. I'd never met anyone so honest.

"Wow. You getting close to finding him?"

"Not yet. But you never know. He could come walking through my door when I least expect it." She beamed.

I immediately thought of Big Papa, then smiled and nodded.

Before I knew it, an hour had passed. Pearl came by with a to-go box and the check. She squeezed my shoulder. "You call if you need anything. Anything at all."

I promised I would, and she nodded, satisfied.

As Maddie slid out of the booth, she caught my gaze and grinned. "I'm coming by tomorrow morning for a cinnamon roll. Don't you dare sell out before I get there."

"Deal," I said, feeling lighter than I had in months.

We said our goodbyes at the door, Maddie disappearing into the night with a wave. I lingered a moment, watching the empty street, the way the yellow paint of my bakery caught the moonlight from across the square.

As I was about to walk out, Pearl called after me, "Aspen! Hold up!"

I turned, surprised.

She hustled over, her steps quick for someone her age. She stopped just short of hugging me again, and her eyes shone with a kindness I wanted to believe in.

"I nearly forgot. I need a chocolate cake. For the diner. By the slice. You think you can swing that by tomorrow afternoon?"

I nodded, swallowing the sudden lump in my throat. "Yes, ma'am."

She smiled, satisfied. "Knew you could. And Aspen? Don't be afraid to rest. You're safe here. Understand?"

It was such a simple thing, but the words nearly undid me.

"Yes, ma'am," I whispered.

She watched me a moment longer, then turned back to the diner.

I started the walk home, the winter air biting at my cheeks and my heart aching in a way I couldn't quite explain. I was still haunted, still uncertain. But for the first time since I'd lost Mama, I felt the edge of hope, sharp and bright as the stars overhead.

I toed off my boots, peeled out of my coat, and put my takeout box in the small fridge. For a second, I just stood there, staring at my little living space. The tiny couch that I'd traded for the pitiful thing that was there when I'd first arrived sat in the center of the room. I'd added cute pillows and a soft throw. The kitchenette was on the left and the bedroom to the right. The space was perfectly functional. I'd add plants soon in the hopes it would eventually feel like home.

For now, all I wanted was to scrub the day off my skin, so I grabbed a towel and headed straight for the shower. The water came out hotter than I meant to set it, stinging my scalp and shoulders, but I let it burn. Sometimes the only way to feel clean is to scorch the nerves right off. I closed my eyes and braced my hands against the tile, letting the steam fill my lungs until the mirror was a blank fog.

Tiredness clung to me, bone-deep, the kind that seeps into your marrow and makes it impossible to think in straight lines. I lingered until the water ran cold, then wrung out my hair and stepped out and wrapped myself in the towel. I pulled on some warm pajamas and then brushed and started the arduous task of drying my waist-length hair. Thankfully, I only had to do this part once a week.

I crawled into my new queen-size bed—the tag still on the frame. I didn't care that the bed was way too big for the room. The mattress was like sleeping on a cloud, so it was worth the cramped space. Beneath the quilt, I pulled my knees tight to my chest. I lay there a while, shivering and exhausted, staring at the ceiling as Pearl's words replayed in my head on a loop:

Don't be afraid to rest. You're safe here.

The phrase echoed in the silence, bouncing off the bare walls and the lamp-lit corners, until I almost believed it. For a second, I could even hear Mama's voice layered over Pearl's, that gentle hush she used whenever I worked myself into a panic. *"It's okay, baby. Just let it go. Let the world turn without you for a night."*

I let my eyes close, but the calm didn't last. Out of nowhere, grief hit me in the gut—sharp and sudden and mean. I sat up, teeth clenched, and grabbed the battered duffel from the end of the bed. Inside wrapped in a dish towel was Mama's grimoire.

The book was heavier than it looked; the leather warped and cracked; the edges stained with years of handling and spilled coffee. The sigil on the cover—three willow branches circled tight, dots at the center—looked different in the dim light. More ominous somehow, like it was warning me not to try. I didn't listen. I held the book in my lap and let the tears come, hot and silent, sliding down my cheeks to splatter on the worn leather.

I turned it in my hands, fingers tracing the pattern over and over, looking for a weak point. The clasp was as stubborn as ever; the lock refused to give even when I pressed hard enough to leave a crescent-shaped dent in my thumb. The defeat was nothing new, but tonight it tasted even more bitter. Like the book was keeping secrets on purpose, just to spite me.

I wiped my nose on my wrist, then let out a half-laugh, half-sob. "You'd think," I said out loud, "that you'd have a chapter on starting over." The words sounded pathetic in the empty room, but it made me feel a little better, talking to the book like it could actually hear.

I slid it under my pillow, feeling the hard edge dig into my neck, and killed the light. The darkness swept in fast, smothering every thought except the hope that tomorrow might be as good as today was. Maybe even better.

I fell asleep in less than a minute, dead to the world, the grimoire pressed close like it might actually keep me safe.

I woke up with a start, heart hammering so loud I could hear it in my ears. Sunlight poured through the thin white curtains, making strange patterns on the ceiling and painting my skin in pale gold. For a second, I didn't know where I was—Georgia, maybe, or in that dream that was scraping the edges of my mind. But then the sounds of Dairyville crept in: a distant train whistle, a truck downshifting on Main, and the dull, steady tick of the wall clock over my bed.

It was morning, real and raw, and I was alone in my bakery apartment, the quilt tangled around my legs and my pajamas plastered to my back with sweat.

I shoved myself upright, trying to shake off the weight of the dream. It clung to me like cobwebs, sticky and persistent. I rubbed my eyes, then reached under my pillow for the grimoire—half expecting it to be gone, or changed, or maybe still thrumming with that light.

It was still there. But the second my fingers closed over it, I yanked my hand back in surprise. The leather was warm. Not just warm, but almost hot, like the book had been lying in a sunbeam all night. My heart hiccuped, and for a moment I just stared at the thing, waiting for it to move or speak or burst into flames.

Nothing happened. But when I finally picked it up and cradled it in my lap, I saw that the sigil on the cover wasn't the same as last night. The willow branches had twisted, reshaping themselves into a tighter knot, and the dots in the center—three, like always—had drifted a little, forming a triangle where before they'd been in a line.

I traced the new pattern with my thumb, and something cold and electric zipped up my arm. I gasped and dropped the book, but it only bounced once on the quilt before sliding to the floor. My right hand tingled all the way to the wrist.

That's when I noticed it. A mark on the back of my hand—faint, silvery, like it had been drawn with the world's tiniest paintbrush. It was the same as the new sigil on the grimoire, willow branches and all, only instead of dots it shimmered with a little pulse of light, as if it were breathing.

I stared at it, holding my breath, half convinced I was still asleep. But the rest of me said, *No, this is real, this is happening, don't you dare flinch.*

The mark glowed for maybe a minute, the light barely visible in the morning sun. Then, slowly, it faded, seeping into my skin until only the faintest outline remained. I touched it, expecting it to hurt or at least feel weird, but it was smooth as ever, warm to the touch.

I picked up the grimoire again, feeling the heat now more as a comfort than a threat. The book was still locked, the clasp still stubborn, but I didn't try to force it. For the first time, I thought maybe the thing wasn't refusing me out of spite. Maybe it was just... waiting.

I flexed my fingers, watching the skin stretch where the mark had been. I didn't know whether to be scared or grateful. But I knew one thing for certain: nothing in my life would ever be the same.

I got dressed, braided my hair back, and went to the kitchen to start the day. The whole time, I couldn't stop glancing at my hand, or at the grimoire that I'd brought downstairs and set on a table in the kitchen. Even the light seemed different—brighter, richer, like the air itself was filled with new possibility.

Maybe that's what hope was. Not a promise that everything would be okay, but a way to keep moving even when you had no idea what came next.

I rolled up my sleeves, scrubbed my hands, and went to work.

The coffeepot had just started to gurgle, letting me know it had completed its brew.

"You might want to rethink the cinnamon ratio in that crumble topping. Bit heavy-handed, if I may."

I froze, one hand halfway to the flour canister, and stared at the empty kitchen.

"Over-spicing is a very common error among witches trying to distract themselves. Happens all the time. Emotional baking is highly unpredictable."

The voice—dry, crisp, and unmistakably British—wasn't in the room. It was in my *head*.

I spun around anyway. "Hello?"

Nothing. No one. Just the quiet hiss of the kettle and the faint creak of the wooden floorboards.

"Over here, darling."

I looked behind me.

And there, sitting on the back counter with his tiny paws folded like some kind of rodent librarian, was a prairie dog. Tawny fur, beady little eyes, wearing a navy blue jacket, plaid vest, and an expression that could only be described as *judgmental.*

He blinked slowly. *"Took you long enough."*

I stumbled back, almost knocking over the canister. "What the actual hell—?"

"Language," he said primly. *"Honestly. Is this how your mother raised you?"*

"You're a talking prairie dog," I snapped.

He gave a short sigh and appeared on the counter next to me in an instant. *"Technically, I'm your familiar. Though I'll admit I've had better introductions."*

"Familiar?" I repeated, because clearly the universe had decided I hadn't had enough weird for one morning. "I don't recall my mother having a familiar."

"Yes, I'm your familiar. And your mother didn't need one—absolute powerhouse, that one—but you, my dear, clearly require some... assistance."

I stared. "You're in my *head.*"

"Yes, well. I prefer it to shouting. I find vocal cords so... primitive."

He sniffed, then sat down like he owned the place.

"You may call me Oscar B. Wilde, or just Oscar, if you like."

I blinked.

"What, were you expecting Whiskers or Buttons or some such nonsense? Absolutely not. I have standards."

I leaned against the counter, not sure if I was losing my mind or if this was just Tuesday now.

"So let me get this straight. You just... showed up?"

"Well," he said, grooming a paw, *"the book called me. Or rather, your mark did. You activated it, and here I am."*

"And what exactly are you here for?"

"Guidance. Insight. Occasional insults if you insist on poor magical form." He paused. *"Also snacks. I do like a good scone."*

I stared for a long second, then reached for a lemon scone from the tray.

He took it delicately, sniffed, and gave a satisfied nod. *"Excellent. You and I are going to get along famously."*

I just shook my head and got back to baking. What else was I supposed to do? I was a witch, and some witches had familiars. Although it was generally witches with significant power, but I wouldn't look a gift gopher in the mouth.

"Prairie dog, if you please."

"Shit, sorry. Wait! I didn't realize you could hear everything I was *thinking.*"

"Well, I can. And we'll work on making it so I can't unless you want me to. It might come in handy someday."

CHAPTER 5

Wyrdmother, Verdant Hollow Coven

The stench of wilted rosemary and burnt tallow clung to the walls like mold. I stepped over the corpse of a shattered mixing bowl and waded through the carnage of the Waters cottage, my patience unspooling with every crunch of glass under my shoe. I'd sent Olive, Maggie, and Teela ahead, but of course it took a proper witch to see that their search amounted to little more than a tea party for sociopaths.

"Check the floorboards again," I said, and Olive—the tallest of the three, her strawberry-blonde hair yanked back in a too-tight bun—hunched her shoulders and poked a broom handle at the plank seams. They all reeked of nerves. I watched, lips pressed thin, as Maggie, she of the constantly peeling cuticles and wandering eye, scoured the stone hearth with a pocket mirror, looking for charms or sigils Laurel might have left behind.

None of them would dare look at me.

It still astonished me that Laurel Waters had managed to die without leaving so much as a strand of hair for me to use. Even now, her body lay embalmed on ice, waiting for whatever sanctimonious send-off the Hollow would cobble together. And not one of these idiots had thought to collect a single personal effect.

Olive hovered in the doorway to Aspen's room, hands fluttering like anxious doves. "There's nothing here, Wyrdmother. Every drawer's empty, and the grimoire's gone. We checked the loft too. Just old linens."

I advanced, letting the heavy silence work on her. The room had been stripped to the bone. The girl's duffel, the single quilt, even the photograph by the window had been taken. I surveyed the emptiness, then eyed the place where, as rumor had it, Laurel used to stash her potions: an alcove behind the bed, veiled with a strand of dried marjoram. The marjoram was gone, its scent obliterated by panic.

"Is it so hard to believe she saw us coming?" I muttered, more to myself than to them. "The last of her line, and she didn't even try to hide."

Maggie sidled up, a pair of latex gloves snapped over her hands. "Should we try a calling spell, Wyrdmother? If the grimoire's in range, maybe we can—"

"No," I cut her off. "She'd have shielded it by now. If that girl has half the brains her mother had, it'll take more than a calling spell to flush her out." I grabbed the edge of the mattress and flipped it, sending a drift of stale feathers into the air. A spider scrambled for cover; I flicked it away.

Behind me, Teela had started sorting through the kitchen trash, desperate for approval. She found nothing but coffee grounds and broken crockery. I snorted and moved to the living room, where the fire had been left to die a quiet, ashy death. I squatted beside the hearth, fingers searching for scorch marks, hidden sigils, any hint of what Laurel had been working on in her final hours.

There was nothing but a faint blue residue on the bricks. A charm for protection, maybe. It hadn't worked.

Olive waited for me to stand before reporting, "The men you sent after Aspen—"

"Failed." I finished for her, rising. "Of course they did. She's her mother's daughter, even if the magic never fully came in." I dusted my hands, then turned a withering stare on the trio. "Which one of you watched the back road?"

Silence. Then, finally, Teela: "I did, Wyrdmother."

"Then it's your failure. Let it eat at you." I let the words land, savoring the way she flinched. "Aspen Waters slipped into the woods and is halfway to freedom, grimoire in tow. Do you know how many generations of Waters witches that book spans? The spells within are older than the Hollow itself. I just hope I don't have to explain to the High Coven that I lost it to a chubby little half-witch."

I spat the last word, and the room seemed to contract around me. And even the Coven did not know the one spell that I was certain that book held. The spell that would set me at the head of the High Coven and the Council itself. It would set me at the head of the entire supernatural world.

Maggie tried to rally. "We have her mother's blood. If you'd allow it, I can work an echoing spell—maybe use the blood to locate—"

I whirled on her. "There is no blood. You left the body on ice, didn't you? Once it's been preserved, it's useless. You'd know that if you'd spent less time whoring around with the Garrets and more time reading the codex."

Maggie blanched and shrank behind Olive.

I straightened my dress and gave myself a moment to collect my thoughts. Losing the grimoire was humiliating, but not irreversible. Aspen would be found eventually. What worried me was the feeling, sharp and cold in my gut, that Laurel had managed a final trick, one last act of defiance. The vote against me, the public declaration that Menace and Savannah's bond was "true and just," had been the first slap in the face. Now, even dead, she was laughing at me.

I curled my fist and drove it into the wall, relishing the shock it sent through my knuckles and the little plume of plaster dust. Teela let out a gasp. I ignored her.

"We're leaving," I announced. "This place is contaminated. There's nothing left but ashes." I gestured at the three of them, gathered like crows around a carcass. "Teela, clean up this mess. Maggie, call a car to the edge of the woods and tell them not to use the main road. Olive, you're with me."

We exited into the hard winter sunlight, the wind instantly cutting through the gauzy black sleeves of my dress. Olive kept her eyes on the ground as we walked.

After a stretch of silence, I decided she'd earned a crumb of explanation. "Do you know why I hated Laurel so much, Olive?"

She shook her head, braid stiff as a whip against her back.

"Laurel Waters was as powerful as I am. Maybe more so, in some ways. And she never, not once, let the Council see her true strength. She kept secrets, hid her lineage, and refused to tell a soul who fathered that pathetic little daughter. That's what makes Aspen dangerous. She's the only one of her kind, and we don't know what she's capable of."

Olive swallowed, voice nearly lost in the wind. "Do you think the grimoire will open for her, Wyrdmother?"

"Not yet," I said. "But it will. It always does eventually. And when it does, we need to be ready."

We reached the car, a black town car with windows so tinted they might as well have been painted on. Maggie and Teela were already inside, whispering in low, urgent tones. I slid into the front passenger seat and watched the woods blur past as we drove.

After a while, Olive asked, "Should we go after her? Aspen, I mean."

I smiled, all teeth. "No need. She'll come to us. The world isn't kind to girls like her, and she doesn't know the first thing about hiding. We'll put word out along the supernatural lines—let the wolves and the vamps play their games. Eventually, she'll land in our lap."

I spent the rest of the ride picking the dried wax from my fingernails, thinking about how Laurel's eyes had looked in her final hours: defiant, but also...relieved. As if dying on her own terms was victory enough.

That had been my mistake; underestimating the sentimental.

When we reached the train station, Maggie jumped out and pulled the bags from the trunk. She kept her eyes on the ground, waiting for my permission to speak.

"What is it?" I snapped.

"I have the Council agenda, Wyrdmother. They moved the meeting up to tomorrow. They say the Iron Valor pack is to be discussed."

My smile, this time, was real. "Of course it is."

As we boarded, I let myself imagine Aspen's face; afraid, cornered, clutching the grimoire as if it could save her. It would, for a time. But not forever.

As the train lurched away from Verdant Hollow, I allowed myself a small, private laugh.

"We'd all be better off if that pack were wiped from the earth," I said, to no one in particular. Olive heard, but she knew better than to reply.

The trees gave way to open country. In the reflection of the glass, I watched myself smile, a thin crescent of satisfaction.

Council chambers always looked the same, no matter the continent or species. I suppose there are only so many ways to arrange a parade of monsters and egomaniacs so that everyone can pretend it's all civil.

The Chicago High Supernatural Council room was an old bank vault, stripped of its safe deposit boxes and dressed up with too much velvet. They'd taken pains to etch the stone walls with every sigil of peace and truce the ancient orders could muster, but it just made the place feel more like a tomb. Around the circular table—a massive thing, polished so smooth you could almost forget the blood that'd been spilled across its grain over centuries—sat the worst of the worst, each perched on their little throne of power.

I strode in first, Olive and Maggie flanking me, Teela trailing behind with the luggage and a face full of open awe. The witches' seats were nearest the entrance, four cold iron chairs that always left the thighs numb and the ego bruised. Not that I cared; I'd sat through enough of these charades to know the real work never happened at the table. It happened in the shadows, in the bathrooms, in the alleys behind the host hotels.

King Rafe Mayfield of the Southwest Wolves was already here, pacing behind his chair like a panther denied its kill. In a perfectly tailored black suit, the size of him defied sense: six-four, biceps straining the seams, hands like river rocks. His onyx eyes flicked over us once, registering and discarding in the space of a blink.

Next to Mayfield sat the newly minted Midwest Wolf King himself, that arrogant prick Bridger "Menace" Hardin. The former Iron Valor pack member was decked out in a three thousand dollar suit, not a hair out of place. The mirrored aviators hid his eyes, but I'd bet my grimoire they were shooting daggers at those of us who voted against his claim on his fated mate. Those of us still breathing, anyway.

Hardin leaned over, whispering to the formidable Kazimir Kozlov, the ancient Eastern Vampire King. Kazimir's sleek black hair cascaded past his shoulders, contrasting with the red satin jacket he wore open, exposing the physique of a man centuries younger. The close ties between him and Iron Valor struck me as odd, but word was his daughter and their Luna were thick as thieves since college. I'd never known Kozlov to care at all for wolves. It defied nature.

The newest face at the table was Griffin Calloway, freshly crowned king of the Eastern Packs, courtesy of Hardin. Griffin, son of the recently executed King Declan Calloway, had ascended mere weeks ago. Apparently, killing your daughter's fated mate is enough to get the Council's attention, even if the angel brought the bastard back. Griffin looked like a deer in the headlights. I stifled a laugh. I loathed Declan. Good riddance.

Varek Otero, King of the Western Vampires, was hard to miss in his white silk suit, tailored to emphasize his otherworldly pallor. He lounged in his seat, one leg carelessly draped over the armrest, idly fiddling with his signet ring. His long silver hair framed a face that was both alluring and unsettling in its post-human perfection.

Farthest from the door sat Maltraz, the Demon King, disguised as a dark-skinned man with a clean-shaven head and mismatched eyes; one brown, one blood-red. His suit reeked of new money, and his left hand still sported untrimmed, razor-sharp black nails that clicked against the glass pitcher as he reached for water.

Slade Stewart, ruler of the Western Packs, was the last Wolf King to arrive. He'd been scarce lately, mourning his dead mate. His auburn hair had lost some of its luster, and he looked thinner. In my eyes, it only proved the weakness of taking a mate; the Achilles heel of every ruler who had one. He nodded to the room, putting on a show of having pulled himself together.

Archon Seraphael, the Angel King, kept his distance from our motley assortment of leaders. An enigma of ethereal, golden-eyed beauty, who spoke rarely, but possessed the wisdom of the Great Creator. Of course, he'd clearly fucked up royally to get himself and a thousand of his kind banished to our plane. Still, his power was unquestioned. He had the kind of power that could raise the dead, as we'd all witnessed weeks ago when he'd resurrected Menace after that fool Calloway planted a blade in his heart.

That left the witches' covens. We mostly clustered together, while Fallon O'Connell of the Astral Spire Coven tried to set herself apart. She'd been the lone coven leader to side with Bridger and Savannah. Apparently, she'd never owed Declan any favors. Lucky bitch.

The Gloamreach and Emberthorn Covens' leaders occupied their seats, an eccentric pair. I wondered if they found me as odd as I found them as I graced them with a respectful nod.

Shasta Tierney, the High Flame Caller from Emberthorn, touched my arm and leaned toward me. "Sorry to hear of the death of Laurel Waters." She whispered, suspicion in her voice.

I fought to keep a sympathetic face as I nodded in her direction and answered quietly. "Yes. Such a tragedy." My mind was running through the possibilities of how she could have known about her death.

Otero glanced at the clock on the wall and gave a perfunctory yawn. "I must remind everyone, sunrise comes early this time of year. Some of us keep more delicate hours."

Rafe stopped his pacing and glared. "I didn't drag my ass to this city to listen to you whine, Otero. But yes. Let's get to the point."

Maltraz smiled, all teeth. "By all means, the mighty King Mayfield wants the floor, as usual." He gestured with his arms wide.

The chair of the Council brought her gavel down and officially brought the session to order. "King Mayfield, I believe you have a matter to bring before the Council."

Rafe's voice dropped half an octave, the sweet Alabama in his accent curdling into something darker. "Several days ago, in a territory under my protection, the Iron Valor shifters lost seven of their pack in a blatant, cowardly attack that had obviously meant to wipe out every member. This was a biological attack in which their water system was infiltrated with a deadly toxin. Every household in the territory was infected. Over the course of a week, pack members became weaker until their organs began to fail. Six of their elderly and one very young child died as a result."

A few gasps traveled around the room.

Some members sat up.

Rafe withdrew a manila envelope and dropped it on the table. "Here are the autopsy reports. Our doctors couldn't synthesize the poison. It was too dangerous for any wolf to touch. Kazimir was good enough to have his people run the tests." He snapped his fingers, and an attendant, a human, sweat-beaded and trying not to tremble, entered, carrying a locked case. Rafe opened it, withdrew a heavy glass vial filled with black liquid, and rolled it toward Maltraz.

The demon king didn't even blink. He took the vial, unscrewed the cap, and took a deep inhalation. His eyes glazed over for a split second before returning to normal. "Curious," he said, rolling the vial in his hands. "Why bring this to me, Alpha?"

"Because," Rafe said, voice low, "I couldn't help but notice your sigil stamped on all the bottles."

Maltraz licked his lips, feigning offense. "I can assure you, the demons have no interest in hunting wolves. Not in this age of peace."

Otero let out a bored sigh, tapping his nails on the tabletop. "I fail to see how a little old-fashioned pack culling requires all this melodrama. Wolves die. So do vampires, so do humans. What's your point, Mayfield?"

Rafe's fist hit the table. "Iron Valor is the strongest pack in my territory! How 'bout I cull a few hundred vampires, Otero?"

The lead Councilwoman banged her gavel. "This is getting us nowhere. Threats and flippant remarks about people dying are not acceptable."

Rafe took a deep breath before he continued. "There was a secondary attack that occurred as well. There was an attempt to drain the Iron Valor pack's bank accounts the same week the water supply was poisoned. The person who attempted to funnel money from their accounts also had your sigil Maltraz."

Maltraz sat up, amused now. "Prove it."

Rafe bared his teeth. "Already did. The records are in that file. You can pretend to be bored, but we know damn well what you've been up to. Curious if you knew those funds you were draining weren't real."

Maltraz froze. A look of surprised anger crossed his face for a moment before it vanished.

He quickly recovered. "I can assure you it makes no difference to me, real or false, funds moved here or there, as I had no part in it. However, if some rogue demons in my organization acted without my knowledge, they will be dealt with." Maltraz's smile widened. "Of course. The demons want only peace."

It was Menace's turn to let out a sarcastic laugh. "Oh yes. Demons are well known for being peaceful creatures. You see, Maltraz, I was there when the Greenbriar pack attacked Iron Valor, thinking they had succumbed to the virus. They brought a few vampires and several demons to fight with them. Curious, don't you think?"

Voices raised around the room.

The gavel came down again. The Councilwoman gave Maltraz and Otero a chance to answer the charges.

Maltraz thoughtfully dragged his finger along the edge of the table. "I'm as shocked as anyone to hear that demons were a part of the fight. I have no beef with Iron Valor. I am the king of demonkind. Why would I care about a random wolf pack? Sadly, it sounds as though there may be rogues who hold a grudge against them for one reason or another. I vow to put my people on it. This act of cruel violence against innocent people should be answered. If I find who was involved, rest assured, King Mayfield, they will be dealt with."

Otero gave the same simpering assurances.

I almost grinned at how smoothly they lied. And the looks of utter disbelief on Mayfield and Hardin's faces were priceless. This Council was such a farce. Rarely was justice ever served. I thought of little Aspen Waters, running for her life. For the first time in years, I felt a pinprick of pity. How would she survive when even here, in the sanctum of peace, it was all just theater and power games?

The meeting wound down with the usual empty resolutions. Maltraz signed a statement of intent, Rafe added his blood to the paper (a ritual I'd always found tacky), and everyone pretended to be satisfied. The room emptied, the echoes of boot heels and designer loafers bouncing off the stone.

I stood, motioned for my girls to pack up, and slipped into the corridor. The Council's administrative maze was a warren of marble and glass, but I knew the shortcuts. I rounded a corner and nearly collided with Maltraz, who loomed a foot taller and radiated the sort of hungry, patient malice that set every hair on my arms bristling.

"Wyrdmother," he said, and the word oozed out, thick as sap.

"Maltraz." I didn't waste time on pleasantries. "A word?"

He gestured for me to lead the way. We ducked into a side chamber, a space just wide enough to be private, just small enough to feel like a threat.

He leaned against the wall, arms folded, those mismatched eyes boring into me. "You want something."

"Don't we always?" I asked. "But this time it benefits you, too." I waited for his nod, then continued. "There's a witch on the run. Waters line, name of Aspen. She's taken a grimoire, possibly two, and she has no idea what she's holding."

He smirked. "And you want me to retrieve her?"

I shook my head. "Nothing so crude. But I thought you'd want to know. She left Georgia over a week ago. Trust me when I tell you, this girl is a mystery worth unraveling. She could be a key to...something." I told him, raising an eyebrow.

Maltraz's eyes glittered, the red one flashing briefly. "And if I decide to pass?"

"Your choice," I said, turning to go. "But if you let her slip, the next time the Council meets I might be the person holding all the aces and you'll have no choice but to fold."

He watched me walk away. "You're colder than your reputation, Rowan."

I glanced back, letting the mask slip for just a second. "That's because I don't have a soul to burn, Maltraz. Remember that."

As I merged back into the crowd, Olive fell into step beside me, voice low. "What did you tell him?"

I smiled, savoring the bitter aftertaste. "Enough to kick him into gear."

The chamber was emptying; the night outside was deeper than sin. I paused at the exit, listening to the bickering of two centuries' worth of monsters, and felt—just for a second—the old, exhilarating certainty of having the upper hand.

Let them chase the bait. Let them tear each other apart.

When the dust cleared, I'd be the one left standing.

And the weapon in my hand would be enough to have them all on their knees before me.

CHAPTER 6

Big Papa

The mornings always came early at the Iron Valor compound, but today, the cold bit straight through to the bone. The sun was barely a hint behind the scrub of mesquite and winter-bare hackberry, but the lot was already full. Chrome glinted under a skin of dew; exhaust from the warm-up runs hung above the bikes like prayer smoke. It felt right. The way the world froze and burned at the same time reminded you that life was always close to the edge.

I shook the frost off my boots and walked up to the clubhouse, the sound of my steps lost in the low drone of a half-dozen men talking at once. Someone'd fixed the front steps since last week; the boards didn't creak under my weight. It was the kind of detail most people missed, but I made a habit of noticing the small things. It's what kept the brothers alive, more often than not.

Inside, the conference room was already humming. Bronc had claimed the head of the table, eyes bright and blue and scanning every man as he filtered in. His hands were steepled in front of him—his tell that this wasn't going to be a bullshit session, but a meeting where you left with a job and probably an ulcer. Arsenal and Gunner had the left and right flanks, hands busy with mugs of black coffee, plates of bacon and eggs, and the pack's daily banter. Doc, always punctual, sat with his black-framed glasses perched on his nose, reading a patient's chart while he waited. Wrecker was late as usual, but his voice echoed from the hallway, carrying some foul joke about what happened if you crossed a succubus with a dairy cow.

I sidled in, catching Juliet's scent from the open kitchen. She was there, back straight, hands on hips, giving the griddle hell. The woman ran a tight ship. She saw me and nodded once, a signal that she'd have a plate out in a minute. I nodded back and turned my attention to Bronc.

He didn't say a word until every chair was filled. Then he leaned forward and, without preamble, spoke in that low growl that always demanded respect.

"We got word from the council last night. King Rafe delivered the news himself." His gaze went around the table, pausing on each man like he was checking for cracks in the foundation. "We know Maltraz worked with Silas on the poisoning. His sigil on the bottles wasn't proof enough for the Council."

Bronc's jaw clenched. "Council isn't taking action. Say they can't prove it was actually him and not some rogue in his organization. They want us to keep the peace, bide our time, and let the proper channels work."

"Always the fucking same. Proper channels?" Arsenal spat, voice soft but loaded. "We lost seven people. Almost lost our Alpha *and* our Luna."

Gunner stared into his coffee, the anger in his eyes sharp enough to skin a man. "They won't be satisfied until Iron Valor is burned to the motherfucking ground."

I felt the old, familiar tension run the length of my spine. It was never rage with me, just a slow, building pressure, like the earth settling before an earthquake. "What about the bank hits?" I asked, careful to keep my voice level. "Anything on that?"

Bronc nodded. "Rafe sprung that on him." He shot a look at me. "Said that was worth the look on Maltraz's face. He hadn't figured out we'd put the screws to him there. He still thought those transactions were real. Guarantee he ran from that room to check on those accounts only to find out they actually stole zero dollars from us."

Wrecker wore a shit eatin' grin. "My little bird leaving a backdoor open for us saved us a shit ton of money there. Although I guess I need to keep an eye on her. He'll know she's the one who screwed him on the bank transaction side."

Bronc got serious. "We'll keep an eye on *everything*. Maltraz is gonna be pissed he failed on all sides."

Juliet walked in with a tray, cutting the tension in half just by existing. She set plates down with more force than strictly necessary and topped off everyone's mugs. "Y'all are welcome, by the way," she muttered, and I caught the flicker of pride in her eyes when Bronc reached for his plate first.

"Thanks, darlin'," he said, his voice overflowing with affection. The gratitude wasn't just for the food.

Gunner had just swallowed a bite of food. "So, what's the verdict on the bakery hottie? I may or may not have strolled by there yesterday and took a peek in the window. Holy shit! Girl's got curves for days! Does she bake as good as she looks?"

I had to grit my teeth. I wanted to take Gunner's eyes, so he'd never be able to look at Aspen again. "Hey asshole, how 'bout some respect." I growled at him.

He threw up his hands in surrender. "Whoa, sorry, man. Just making an observation."

Shit. I shouldn't have reacted like that. I cleared my throat. "She's an excellent baker." I continued like I hadn't just acted like I wanted to remove his head. "Of the choices, the lemon was definitely the best. I'm going by there today to pick up a sample cake for everyone."

Wrecker's eyes lit up. "Well now. Maybe the day's not a total loss."

"So, you gonna tell us anything else? What's her story? Is she single like we heard?"

I felt the heat rise in my cheeks, but I didn't shy away from the question. "Her name's Aspen. She's from Georgia. Lost her mom, moved out here to start fresh." I kept my voice casual, like it wasn't the most important fact in my life at the moment. "And she's different."

Arsenal raised an eyebrow. "Different how? She a shifter?"

"Nope," I said. "She's definitely a witch. From one of the old Southern covens. But she's not like any witch I've ever come across. Said her magic never came in right. Swears she doesn't have any magical abilities."

Bronc's eyes narrowed, and for a second I thought he'd shut me down right there. Instead, he asked, "She left her coven? She running from something?"

I considered my answer and nodded. "Her coven itself sounds like. I didn't exactly get off on the right foot with her, so she wasn't totally forthcoming. She just mentioned that as her mother was dying; she told her she'd bought her that bakery. Then told her to run. So she ran. But Aspen seemed afraid of her coven."

Gunner's hand hovered over his coffee mug. "So we're harboring a fugitive?"

"Didn't say that. Don't know that. Right now, she just seems like a girl trying to survive. And get this, her mother told her if she got into any trouble, to seek out the Iron Valor Pack, that she could trust us."

A silence fell—heavy, but not dangerous. The men, thinking. Arsenal finally broke it. "Well, if she can make a good carrot cake Gunner might marry her himself."

Wrecker hooted. "Might have his pups, too."

Gunner ignored them, but his smile was real.

Bronc leaned back, weighing his words. "You trust her?"

"Too soon to know," I said, and meant it. "She got damn offended when I accused her of infusing her cakes with magic to make them taste so good, though. She seemed so innocent. I don't think the girl has ever been on her own."

Bronc nodded, just once. "Well, you know the deal. We protect our own. If she brings trouble to this door—"

"All due respect, Alpha, every woman any of us has brought in around here seems to have had a bucket of trouble in tow." I told him.

"Well, hell," he breathed out on a heavy sigh. "I can't argue with that. Guess they've all been worth the trouble they've hauled in."

Nobody dared disagree with him.

The meeting rolled on, talk shifting to logistics for the ceremony, how many people to expect, who was on perimeter duty the night of the event. I took notes, and thought of any details we might be missing.

Wrecker nudged me under the table. "You gonna bring her to the party?"

I shrugged. "Maybe. If she doesn't hate me."

He busted out laughing. "Like anybody could hate you, JT."

"I was an ass to her. I don't know what happened." I ran my hand through my beard.

Doc spoke up. "Maybe you felt a connection, and it scared you. Honestly, Papa, you're used to keeping people, especially women, at arm's length. Her being a witch was a good excuse to push her away."

It was Bronc's turn to chime in. "He's right, Papa. I'm not saying you shouldn't be cautious. But you also shouldn't close yourself off either."

"Shit, when did y'all suddenly become Dr. Phil?" Everyone around the table laughed. But I knew they were right.

The meeting broke up soon after, men filing out in twos and threes, talking about bike repairs and security assignments and who'd pay up at poker night. I hung back, watching Bronc as he lingered by the window, arms folded, deep in thought.

I waited until the room was empty before approaching him. He didn't turn until I spoke.

"You worried about me, boss?"

He kept his eyes on the frost outside. "Man, I just want you to find your happiness."

"I'm keeping my eyes open," I said, keeping my voice even.

He finally turned, and I saw something in his eyes I'd never seen before: fear. Not for himself, but for me. "Just be careful, Papa. There is an unknown factor here. Listen to your heart and your instincts."

We stood there a moment, silent, then he turned back to the window. I took that as my cue and headed out, the chill air sharp and bracing after the heat of the room.

I took my truck to Dairyville since I was picking up that bigger cake. I sank into the soft leather and cranked up the radio, letting the music take me to a place where I knew who I was and things made sense.

The drive to Dairyville always cleared my head. The bakery's bright yellow awning slanted up into the sharp morning light, a flag for lost souls and sugar addicts alike. The smell hit me a block away—vanilla, yeast, and whatever Aspen's special touch was.

I found a spot to park and killed the engine. For a second, I just sat and watched the world go about its business. Towns like this didn't change much, but people noticed a six-foot-five man in a leather jacket, especially when he favored a limp and had a beard no matter how neatly trimmed. The trick was to act like you belonged. The real trick was to believe it.

Inside, the bakery was chaos in miniature. With almost every table full, the counter lined three deep, the din of conversation and laughter sparring with the country ballads that leaked from the old speaker in the corner. Aspen was at the center, hair twisted up in a knot, hands moving fast and sure as she pulled cinnamon rolls from the oven and rang up orders with a smile that looked friendly, but stressed. She wore a blue apron dusted with flour, and I could see, even from the door, the way her eyes lit up whenever she solved a problem, filled a plate, or made someone's day a little happier.

What I saw—what no one else in that room could see—was the light. Not a literal halo, but something close. A warmth, a shimmer at the edges, like sun through a honey jar. The longer I looked, the brighter it got, until the rest of the bakery faded into white noise and all I could do was stand there and stare like a fool. That light reminded me of something.

I glanced out the window toward the gazebo on the square. People milled about town. And Aspen was here, adding her own ray of sunshine to anyone lucky enough to encounter her. I decided right then that before I left with my cake, I would know more of who she was. Why exactly was she in Dairyville?

She looked up and saw me standing by the door. I certainly didn't deserve the smile she graced me with after how I'd acted yesterday. She gave a small wave and indicated she'd be with me in a few minutes.

When the last customer cleared out, she told me to follow her back to the kitchen area where she pulled two layers of cake out of the cooler.

"I am so sorry I haven't been able to fill and ice your cake yet. Happily, I've been busy non-stop today." She beamed, and I'd never seen anything more beautiful.

I reassured her that it was no problem. Truth is, it was a joy to watch her work. Everyone who left the store seemed happier for it. I still wondered if she wasn't using magic, even if she hadn't realized it.

"Do you mind watching me work on your cake?"

I was surprised she'd allow it. She seemed a little nervous; kept checking under her work table like she'd lost something.

"I'd love to watch you work. And I hate to ask, but my Alpha had a few questions about your past if you didn't mind answering. Just to know again, how you made your way to Dairyville and what your mother's connection to Iron Valor might have been."

She suddenly paused squeezing the bottle of liquid that she'd been infusing the cakes with. "Oh, yeah. I suppose he would. I am going to be feeding your entire pack. I understand that."

"There is no accusation involved, Aspen. A few weeks ago we lived through our entire pack being poisoned through our water system. We had several die. We're just being cautious. Please understand."

I was shocked when she stepped towards me and took my hands into her much smaller ones. A tear traced down her cheek.

"I'm horrified that y'all had to live through that. I am not offended. I'm a stranger to your pack. And a witch on top of that. I'm so very sorry for the loss of your pack members. I know that had to be very painful."

I wanted to wrap her in my arms. To feel her body against mine. But I let go. "Thank you for understanding."

She moved to the cooler again and pulled out a tub of something creamy that smelled like lemons and a tub of what looked like buttercream.

She smiled. "I prepared these last night. I'll work while I tell my sad little story, hmm?" She looked at me, her green eyes glistening with what I swear were unshed tears.

I simply nodded.

"I was a member of the Verdant Hollow Coven where my mother was one of the most powerful members. Her power rivaled the Wyrdmother's herself. Everything was fine until my mother advised Elaina, the Wyrdmother that she should vote in favor of King Menace's mating claim with Queen Savannah. The Wyrdmother had no intention of doing that, and she was furious that my mother took a public stand against her decision. Shortly after my mother became gravely ill. My mother was an excellent healer and potion mixer, but couldn't come up with anything that could cure whatever had made her sick. She told me she believed she had been cursed. Apparently, upon the realization, she set about getting her house in order, which meant making sure I would be financially secure in the event of her passing." She grabbed a napkin and wiped the tears from her eyes.

I reached over and squeezed her elbow. A feeling of connection ran up my arm. "I'm sorry to put you through this, Aspen."

"No, I understand," she said through sniffles. "I'm good. So, the night she passed she told me to pack immediately and go to Dairyville, Texas. That's when she informed me about the bakery. She mentioned the Iron Valor Pack and said that if I got into any trouble to seek y'all out. I grabbed her grimoire and a large envelope with the bakery deed and keys, bank account information, and other documents from her hiding place. She also told me she had lied all these years. That she knew who my father was but couldn't tell me because he was *other* and if anyone found out I'd be in great danger. More danger than I was already in. I asked her what she meant, and she just said, 'run Aspen. Get away from here as fast as you can.' And then she died. I packed what I could and ran through the woods until I got to our car then drove until I got here." She took another deep breath.

"And that's all you know?"

She laughed. "That's it. And it makes no sense. I promise you, I'm nothing. When I told you I have no magic, that was the truth. The other girls in the coven had a nickname for me. They literally called me 'The Dud.' I could do only the smallest things. I never got any real magic when all the other girls were conjuring spells, making flowers grow, controlling wind, commanding fire. I just watched from the sidelines or was being pelted by the elements they commanded as they laughed at me. So unless they just want my mother's grimoire, which I can't even open, I don't get it."

"You can't open the book?" I was surprised at this.

"Nope." She popped the "p" in the word.

"Can I see it?"

She reached to the counter behind her, again looking around, and gathered the book in her arms.

"Something weird has happened with this book, though."

She proceeded to tell me how she'd had it under her pillow and had had a dream that she cannot remember. When she woke, the sigil on the cover had changed, and the book was warm to the touch. I could feel the heat from the book. The clasp was warmer than the leather.

"Definitely warm."

"Well, it's not like I'm gonna lie about it."

I couldn't hide my grin. I liked her fire. "No, Sunshine. I don't suppose you would. Can you tell me about the dream you had when the grimoire heated up?"

"That's just it. I cannot remember it. I believe that dream may hold the answer to who my father is. Or maybe it's just another way I'm defective."

I walked around the prep table and touched her cheek.

"Aspen. You are anything but defective. You are brave and beautiful, and if I can do anything to help you, please know I am only a phone call away."

I stepped back before I made her uncomfortable. She likely didn't want me crowding her space.

She had put the finishing touches on the small tasting cake. It looked amazing. I was proud to take it back to the compound for everyone to taste.

"So you have my number in your phone, right?"

She grabbed her phone to check. When she discovered she didn't, I had her give hers to me, and I texted her so I was sure she'd have it. And now I had her number. I needed Wrecker to get a tracker onto her phone just in case.

Aspen walked me to the door with the cake boxed up, surprised to see I was in a truck.

"Little known secret: We don't always ride our bikes. Especially when transporting things like delicious cakes."

She laughed, and it sounded like heaven to my ears.

"I hope you stop by again, even though we've all but completed our cake business." She told me at the door.

"You can count on it, Sunshine." I turned back toward the bakery when she put the CLOSED sign on the door and locked it, and I swear there was a gopher or a prairie dog wearing a jacket, walking beside her as she made her way back to the kitchen.

By 7:15, the energy in my body had nowhere left to go. That's when I called Gunner.

He showed up at my door ten minutes later, still wearing the same sweat-stained T-shirt from his evening run. He looked at me, took in the tightness of my jaw, and just shook his head.

"Tell me you're not gonna keep being weird about the bakery girl," he said, still calming his breath from his run.

I let out a bark of a laugh. "Wouldn't dream of it. But if I don't burn off some of this, I'll be a liability while I'm trying to write the words for the ceremony."

"Fair." He nodded toward the woods. "Arsenal's game. I saw him by the barn. Let's run it."

The next five minutes were a blur of muscle memory—stripping down, shifting, the skin-crawl shudder that came with dropping the human shell. There's no dignity in the change, no matter what the movies say. It's ugly, primal, and loud. My body twisted, bones crackling like dry wood. I felt my fingers fuse, my teeth lengthen, the world tilt as my senses dialed up to eleven.

When I came up on four legs, Gunner and Arsenal were already waiting at the tree line. Gunner's wolf was a ruddy giant, bigger than most, with a lazy, unhurried lope that belied how fast he could really move.

Arsenal—jet black, lean, mean—was already pacing, tail high and eyes sharp.

We shot through the woods like bullets. The world was sound and motion and the thudding, electric pulse of pack-mind: every step, every turn, synced like a drummer's hands. We weaved through the low pines, tore through thickets, bounded over the dry creek bed in a flying leap that left Gunner rolling with laughter on the far side.

On the first incline, I cut right and nipped Gunner's flank—just enough to leave a mark and start a chase. He spun and barreled after me, teeth bared but tongue out in that wolfy, shit-eating grin. We ran until the air was knives in our lungs, the frost sharp enough to sting even through a fur coat. At the ridge, we paused and howled, long and low and rolling over the valley.

Arsenal was the first to start the teasing.

He loped up, nipped my ear, then flopped onto his back and kicked his paws in the air. Gunner picked up on it right away. Even in wolf form, they had perfected the art of sarcasm.

If you didn't know better, you'd think wolves weren't supposed to laugh, but we did. We cackled and yipped and tumbled down the slope, three grown men reduced to overgrown pups. The run wasn't about territory or dominance. It was about life, the reckless thrill of being alive after thinking you might not make it to next month.

We wrestled until my side hurt, and Gunner's tongue was lolling. Then we collapsed in a heap, fur tangled, noses buried in the ground. This was a part of our brotherhood. We were bound by more than friendship. It was a bone-deep sense of belonging that we each shared. We had each other's backs even if we didn't understand or agree with every decision we made. We'd fight anybody who tried to stand in our way.

CHAPTER 7

Aspen

The sky over Dairyville was the color of crème brûlée, all golden swirl with a burnt sugar edge, and the chilly wind whipped through the naked trees lining the square. There was comfort in the rhythm I'd fallen into here—the bakery's silence in the early hours broken up by conversations with Oscar before the first caffeine-deprived regular shuffled through the door. He popped in and out whenever the mood struck him.

"Do you think I should add eclairs to my menu?"

"An eclair made correctly creates a delightful burst of both flavor and texture on the palate. If you're up for the challenge, I think you should." He sounded like he was narrating a show on a cooking channel. I loved his enthusiasm.

"So your young man has come to see you quite often. He has a wolf living inside him you know. It's my bet he's chosen you as his mate." He offered this little bit of information out of the blue.

The cannoli cream I was piping into the pastry exploded out the end. "WHAT? What does that even mean, Oscar?"

"It simply means that wolves mate for life my dear. And I believe the young man is in love with you and his wolf chose you as his mate for life."

I'd seen Papa almost every day since he'd picked up the tasting cake, and I'd started to look forward to it. Whether it was his stopping in for coffee or just picking up pastries for the guys, I was happy anytime I got to be near him. I saw the ease with which he moved, like the world bent around him, and it fascinated me. He always made time to check in on me; never pushy, never too much, just... there.

What surprised me most was how much he'd cared when I told him about the way my coven used to treat me. Most people didn't know what to do with that kind of truth, but Papa didn't flinch. He just listened. And when he opened up about nearly losing his entire pack, about how close *he* came to dying, it hit me like a gut punch. I hadn't expected to *ache* for someone I barely knew. But I did.

And each time I saw him after that, something small shifted. A joke he cracked that actually made me laugh-snort. The way he looked at me like I was *real*, not some broken thing to pity, not some puzzle to solve, just *me.* Every day, I caught myself noticing something new. The rough rasp of his laugh. The warmth in his eyes when he talked about his brothers. The way he held space without needing to fill it.

I felt foolish, like some schoolgirl with a crush, but I'd never had this before. I was twenty-five and had never so much as been asked on a date. Maybe I was just starved for attention. But it didn't feel like that. Men came into the bakery every day, handsome ones, even, but none of them made my blood hum the way Big Papa did.

He had this wicked, dry sense of humor that snuck up on me. And he actually liked the smart-ass side of me, the one my mama always said would get me in trouble one day. Hell, I thought *he* was trouble when I first met him. Big, broody, grumpy as all get out. I never would've guessed he'd turn out to be the man I feel safest with.

I was jolted out of my revelry when Maddie showed up, bursting through the bakery door like a confetti cannon. She wore a pair of black leggings with stars down the side, her hair pulled into a perfect ponytail that bounced like it had its own opinions.

She didn't say hello, just barreled up to the counter and hollered, "You got cinnamon rolls yet, or am I too early?"

I laughed, wiping my hands on my apron. "You are right on time, Maddie. Hot out of the oven. You want frosting on top or on the side?"

She rolled her eyes. "On top, obviously. You gotta let it melt all the way in, otherwise what's the point?" She leaned over the counter, chin in her hand, and watched me drizzle the icing. "So. You and Big Papa, huh?"

I nearly dropped the icing bag. "What?"

She grinned, teeth showing. "I heard you made him a sample cake the other day. That's basically a Dairyville engagement."

I wanted to argue but knew it would only dig me deeper. "He's nice. And that cake was for everyone else to taste."

She arched one eyebrow so high it nearly met her hairline. "Sure. Next thing I know, you're running off to the courthouse together." She reached across and stole a bit of icing with her finger, popped it in her mouth, and made an obscene little moan. "God, that is so good. You are a wizard."

"Lordy, don't say that too loud," I muttered, cutting the roll and sliding it onto a plate. "People will be accusin' me of turning 'em into toads or worse."

Maddie picked up the roll and took a massive bite, then talked around the pastry. "You wanna go out tonight?"

I blinked. "Out...where?"

She swallowed and gave me a look. "The County Line. The bar. A pack member owns it, so it's safe. Come on! It's Saturday night. It's there or at the clubhouse, and I don't feel like hanging out with families and little kids."

I hesitated. "I've never... I mean, I don't even know what to wear to a bar. I've never drunk like that."

She waved that away. "You don't have to drink or you can try it if you want to. You just need to wear something cute, and if you want, I can get you an appointment at the salon next door so you can get a conditioning treatment on that gorgeous hair and get all waxed. Then I'll come by and help you get ready. Whaddaya say? It'll be fun, Aspen. Promise."

My stomach swooped. It was the first real invitation I'd ever gotten that didn't have strings attached. "Okay," I said, trying not to sound as terrified as I felt. "But, um, waxed?"

She waved her hands as if it were nothing. "Yeah. You've had your brows waxed?"

I nodded. "My mama waxed mine every couple of months."

She smiled. "It's like that. Only it's not just your brows." She waggled her own eyebrows. "I'll be here at six. You just bake your magic and get ready to let loose."

I almost wished she'd insult me instead. This was worse somehow. Nice made me nervous.

The rest of the morning went by in a rush: a steady stream of regulars, a couple of teenagers on a donut run, one old man who always asked for plain white bread even though we didn't make it ("No time to fix what's broken," he'd say, and I'd just nod like I understood). I liked the blur of motion, the constant focus on flour and measurements, and the comforting rhythm of the kitchen.

But around noon, something changed. A man walked in, not unusual in itself, but there was something off about him. He was tall, but not in the way Papa was—his height was stretched, too-thin, like a willow sapling that hadn't found the sun yet. He wore a heavy green jacket even though the bakery was warm, and his hair was a nondescript brown that looked like it'd shed the moment you ran a hand through it.

He didn't speak when he came in. Didn't even look at the menu or the case. Just walked up to the counter, eyes flicking over the pastries, then up to me. There was no warmth in his gaze, just a weird, assessing hunger. He pointed at a scone—cranberry orange, still warm from the oven.

I bagged it up, forcing a smile. "You want coffee to go with that?"

He nodded, never breaking eye contact, and handed over exact change in coins. Then he took the scone, walked to the corner table, and sat down. He didn't eat, just set the scone on the paper bag and folded his hands, staring at me every time I turned my back. I tried not to look, but the feeling crawled over my neck like cold sweat.

He stayed there for an hour. Then, as quietly as he'd come in, he got up and left, leaving the scone untouched on the table.

I waited until the door closed, then walked over to clean up, fighting the urge to check the street through the window. The scone was still there, but the paper bag had a smear of ink on it, a shape like a triangle or maybe a stylized A. I didn't think anything of it, just threw it out with the rest of the trash.

The rest of the afternoon was busier, but that unsettled feeling clung to me. Every time the bell over the door rang, I flinched. Every time a stranger came in, I checked for the green jacket.

It wasn't until close that I saw him again, across the square by the gazebo. He stood perfectly still, arms crossed, eyes fixed on my bakery like he was memorizing the window pattern. I ducked behind the cash register, heart racing, and when I looked again, he was gone.

I told myself it was nothing, just someone new. But I still made sure to lock every bolt on the bakery door before heading upstairs to the apartment.

When I hit my apartment, I saw Oscar sitting on the couch.

"Did you see that strange man in the green jacket who came in right before closing?"

He tilted his little head. *"I did, and that was no man. I'm not sure what he was, but he was either spelled or possessed. We'll need to figure out who he is and who sent him. And you need to be extra careful tonight with your friend."*

"I promise I will."

It wasn't until I started running the bath for a quick soak that I remembered Maddie's invitation. I had three hours to figure out how to look cute and not like a terrified shut-in.

I sat on the edge of the tub, staring at the condensation curling down the mirror, and wondered if this was what normal girls felt before a big night. Maybe the difference was, normal girls didn't have to worry about witches or curses or green-jacketed men who left triangles on paper bags. Maybe they just worried about lipstick and whether the boy they liked would notice them.

I thought about Big Papa, about the way he'd looked at me like he actually saw someone worth looking at. I wondered if he'd be at the bar tonight. I wondered if I wanted him to be.

I stood up, checked the lock on the window, and told myself, "You are not prey. You are not a victim. Not here."

I wasn't sure if I believed it. But I was willing to try.

I peeled off my work clothes and dug through my tiny closet for anything that didn't scream "hiding from the world."

In the end, I settled on a black and white plaid skirt that hit just above the knee (too short, maybe, but Maddie had said "cute"), a black v-neck sweater that I hoped showed just enough cleavage, (with my boobs there was always cleavage), and a pair of thick black tights I'd bought but never worn.

Before getting dressed to go out, I pulled on some leggings and an oversized shirt and ran to the salon next door. I'd never allowed myself to be pampered by anyone but myself, and I thought if they had the time to do it, I would take advantage.

Inside, the air hummed with the sound of blow dryers and local gossip. A wall-length mirror reflected three stylists in matching tie-dye aprons, each one mid-hustle with a client in their chair. I hovered by the front desk, already feeling a sunburn of regret for ever agreeing to Maddie's "just go get a quick wax, it'll change your life" advice.

The youngest stylist—maybe twenty, with purple ombre hair and a septum ring—gave me a once-over, then brightened. "Oh, you're the new bakery girl, right? Maddie said you might come in today!"

I nodded, not sure if I should admit I'd never had my eyebrows done by anyone but my mom. "I don't really...do this," I confessed, motioning at my long hair and generally unplucked face. "But I have a thing tonight. I guess I need a wax, maybe clean up my hair a little?"

She beamed. "No prob. I'm Brie, by the way. C'mon, I'll hook you up. You are gorgeous, by the way."

There was nothing quite like the ritual humiliation of small-town self-care. Brie took me into a private room and told me to strip off my leggings and panties and then lie on the waxing table. There was a large warm towel to cover myself with. I suddenly knew why Maddie had that conspiratorial look on her face when she told me to get waxed. Brie matter-of-factly asked me if I wanted a Brazilian, which was apparently removing every bit of hair down there. Or if I wanted a landing strip or a triangle.

I generally kept things tidy down there but certainly not shaved clean. Brie casually removed the towel. She didn't flinch when she saw my soft belly and thick thighs. I'd opted to leave a nice small triangle of hair there. She slathered an area with something that smelled like honey, placed a strip of soft cotton over it, and, with zero warning, yanked the strip off with a sound like ripping denim. Holy shit! I grit my teeth. My skin flared, then settled into a low tingle. She repeated this process until all was clean. Then she did my brows.

She didn't let me up. "Your lips are, like, naturally perfect, but lemme just get this little fuzz—" More wax, more burning, but at least it was quick. She let me up to get my panties and leggings back on. The area still tingled, but she'd slathered on some gel that cooled it all down so it was bearable. Next came the hair. Brie spritzed, massaged, and applied a minty scalp treatment that made my whole head feel like a chilled limeade.

"So, you nervous about tonight?" she asked, gently detangling my hair with her fingers.

"A little. I've never been to a bar before. I'm sure it's obvious, but unless I'm baking and sharing pastries, I'm a tad bit awkward." I tried to laugh, but it came out small.

She winked at me in the mirror. "Just follow Maddie's lead. That girl could talk a priest into buying her a shot." She blew my hair out straight, then curled the ends with a round brush so they bounced in perfect, glossy waves.

Brie finished up by adding a powdered foundation to my face. Then she grabbed an eyeliner pencil and expertly lined my eyes with a slight cat-eye look, followed by a coat of mascara. With a touch of pink lip gloss, she was done. She angled the mirror. "What do you think?"

I almost didn't recognize myself. My eyebrows were sharp as a knife, my hair shining, my lips glossy. My cheeks were red but in a cute, blushing way, not in the usual "flustered at being alive" way.

"It's perfect," I said, amazed. "Thank you."

She grinned. "You'll knock 'em dead."

I paid, left a tip that I hoped would convey my appreciation, and scurried out into the cold. The sun had fully set, leaving the square cast in deep blue shadows and the bright yellow glow of streetlamps. The awning of the bakery emitted an aura of joy, but the empty square felt less peaceful than usual. Every sound echoed a little too long; every movement, even the wind, seemed suspicious.

I unlocked the door, shouldered inside, and double-checked the dead-bolt behind me. I flipped on the back lights, then went room to room, checking every nook and pantry just in case someone had slipped in. It was ridiculous. But the feeling from earlier, that cold-eyed man and his silent scrutiny, still clung to me like static.

Only after making a full sweep did I allow myself to breathe.

Upstairs, my little apartment felt like a greenhouse in winter: tight, safe, and almost too warm after the chill outside. I hung my coat, glanced at the clock, and realized I had less than an hour before Maddie showed up. My stomach twisted.

The first thing I did was check the window in my bedroom. I distinctly remembered locking it this morning; I always did. But when I got there, the sash was cracked open three inches; the curtains fluttering in a draft so cold it stung my skin. I froze, staring at the window, then peered out at the blackness beyond.

Nothing. No movement, no footprints in the new snow on the roof below. Still, the hair on my neck stood at attention. I closed and latched the window tight, pulled the curtains, and retreated to the safety of the bathroom.

I stared at my reflection, half expecting to see someone standing behind me. But it was just me, pink-faced and wild-eyed, hair still smooth and shiny from the salon. I ran cold water over my wrists, willing my pulse to settle.

"I wish you'd taught me a protection spell, Mama," I whispered. "Or at least how not to be a damn chicken."

I wiped my hands, then made straight for my secret spot. The beadboard wall behind the head of my bed looked normal, but if you slid out the second slat, there was a hollow just big enough to stash something important. I knelt and reached in, feeling for the leather edge of the grimoire. It was still there, heavy and warm, the cover as stubborn as ever.

I breathed easier, replaced the slat, and let myself believe, for a moment, that I'd done something right.

I texted Maddie and told her I didn't need help finding an outfit. I had it under control. She texted back a kissy-face emoji. Getting dressed felt different tonight. For once, I wasn't trying to hide. I pulled on the black and white plaid skirt. The black v-neck sweater I'd ordered the other day fit my curves perfectly. I liked how it fit loose at the bottom so it slid over my ass and hit a few inches above the hem of the skirt. I threw the wide black belt on over the sweater so it cinched my waist just right. The neckline of my top dipped low enough that my cleavage had no choice but to say hello to the world, but with the tights and boots it felt more badass than desperate.

I turned, checked the back. The skirt flared out at my hips but didn't ride up, and the boots made my legs look longer than usual. I ran a hand over my hair—still soft, the scent of salon shampoo lingering like a promise.

I dug out my jewelry box, found a pair of silver hoops, and put them on. Then I dabbed a touch of pink gloss on my lips, just like Brie had, and tried not to think about who might be watching from the darkness outside.

For the first time in my life, I thought I looked more than cute. I looked pretty. Sexy, actually. My curves were on full display, my hair was glossy, and my eyes had a spark I didn't recognize.

I looked like a girl with a future, not an escapee.

Oscar was waiting on the couch when I came out of my bedroom. He was enjoying a cinnamon scone and had crumbs in his whiskers.

"Miss, you look quite lovely this evening. Would you like me to accompany you on your night out?"

"That's very sweet of you, Oscar, but I'd really like you to keep an eye on the bakery and apartment tonight, if you would."

He sat up as tall as possible.

"Of course, Miss. I will endeavor to keep things safe here in your absence. And you need to be careful while you are on the town."

When I heard Maddie's horn, I nearly jumped out of my boots. I patted Oscar's head, checked the bakery lights one more time, set the alarm, and locked the doors behind me. The night air was brutal, but I walked out to her car with my head high, every step daring anyone to try me.

At the curb, Maddie rolled down the window, eyes wide. "Girl! You look amazing. Get in here before you freeze your ass off."

I slid into the passenger seat, cheeks already numb. "You don't think it's too much?"

She gave me a look. "If anything, it's not enough. Wait until you see what the girls at the bar are wearing." She put the car in drive. "You ready?"

I tried to say yes, but it stuck. I nodded instead, my heart thudding like a bass drum.

We drove off, the bakery lights fading behind us, and I let myself feel it—a weird, giddy thrill.

Tonight, I'd try to be someone new.

Someone brave.

Someone who, when she looked in the mirror, finally liked what she saw.

⁂

We cruised west of Dairyville, past downtown and toward the county line. Maddie kept the radio up and the conversation light, but I could feel her studying me, checking my mood every few minutes.

"You ever been around a bunch of wolves before?" she asked.

I shook my head. "Not unless you count the ones I've served scones to."

She cackled. "Trust me, the scones are the least dangerous thing about them. Just remember: if a guy gets weird, tell him you know the Alpha's sister. They'll back off."

I nodded, but it sounded more like folklore than advice.

"And if you need anything, anything, you tell me," she added. "Also, dance at least once. It's required."

"I don't know how to dance," I confessed, my voice barely above a whisper.

Maddie gave a one-shoulder shrug. "Neither do most of the guys. Just move. It's fun if you let yourself." She glanced over, then grinned again. "Did you tell Papa you were coming out tonight?"

I frowned. "Why would he care?"

She laughed so hard she had to slap the steering wheel. "Oh, he'd care alright. Wait until you see his face if you run into him tonight."

I blushed so fast I could feel the heat rise up my cheeks and into my scalp.

The parking lot of the bar was packed, mostly pickups and battered SUVs, some bikes lined up in a row near the door. The sign above the building just said "County Line Bar". From inside, the sound of thumping bass and a hundred loud conversations spilled out every time the door opened.

Maddie parked, looked at me, and did her best to be gentle. "You okay?"

I nodded, then shook my head, then nodded again. "I've never even been in a bar before."

She squeezed my hand, warm and steady. "Just stick close. It's not so bad. The worst part is the bathrooms, and I know how to jimmy the door if you get locked in."

With that, she hauled me out of the car and up the walk. The bouncer at the door, a guy who looked like he'd bench-pressed a refrigerator for fun, barely glanced at our IDs before waving us inside. Maddie went first, dragging me along by the wrist.

Inside, it was a blast of color and light and noise. The air smelled like beer and perfume and those cheap pink urinal cakes. Tables crowded almost every inch of floor space, with people yelling to be heard over the jukebox. At least two dozen people were on the dance floor, swaying to a country song I half-recognized. At the bar itself, a cluster of men in leather jackets drank from giant mugs and watched wrestling on the TV overhead.

I scanned the crowd, looking for anything familiar, but it was just a blur of faces. Maddie leaned in and yelled over the noise, "Let's get a drink first! Bars are always less scary with a drink in your hand."

She wedged us through the bodies until we landed at the edge of the bar. The bartender—a guy Maddie introduced as "Gator," had a buzz cut and arms covered in tattoos of alligators, naturally. He grinned when he saw Maddie, and his whole face changed, going from "could crush a beer can in his teeth" to "puppy dog at Christmas."

"Hey, Mads! You brought the new girl!" Gator said, giving me a look that was friendly but with a clear "don't fuck with Maddie's friends" vibe.

"Gator, this is Aspen. She's never had a real drink before, so be gentle." Maddie gave him a look, then added, "And can you stash our bags behind the bar? I don't want anyone snatching 'em."

He nodded, took our purses, and slid them behind the bar. "First one's on me, bakery girl. What'll it be?"

I looked at Maddie for help.

"She'll have a Shiner Bock, and I'll take a whiskey sour," she declared.

Gator poured, slid the dark bottle to me, and I took a sip before thinking. The taste was awful—bitter, with a weird syrupy finish—but I forced myself to swallow and pretend it was fine.

Maddie saw right through me. "Not a fan?"

I made a face. "Tastes like bread and regret."

She snorted. "You'll like the next one better. Beer's just tradition."

We found a table wedged between the jukebox and the pool tables. Maddie took the seat facing the room and left me the wall. "Safer this way," she said. "If anyone starts trouble, you've got an escape route."

I took another sip of beer and tried to look casual. Maddie chatted, introducing me to two girls she knew from the salon, both wearing more eyeliner than I'd thought possible without permanent marker. They were nice, though, and we talked about movies and music and who had the best pancakes in town. I started to relax. By the time the band set up for their first set, I'd even managed to finish half my beer.

Gator brought another drink, pink, in a martini glass, and winked. "Cosmo. You'll like it."

He was right. It tasted like lime and cranberry and sugar, and I downed half of it before I realized I should probably pace myself.

Maddie watched me, amused. "Careful, Georgia girl. These sneak up on you."

I was feeling freer already. "You said I should dance," I reminded her, finishing my drink. "So let's do that."

The dance floor was packed, but the music was loud and bouncy, and nobody seemed to care if you knew what you were doing. Maddie shimmied and stomped and made me laugh until I forgot to be embarrassed. I let the music buzz through my veins, let the lights and the crowd and the wildness of it all lift me up. I even sang along, yelling the words when I didn't know them.

After a while, more drinks appeared. Sometimes I didn't even see who brought them; Maddie just grabbed a glass from a passing hand and checked it for me before I took a sip.

"Never drink something you didn't see poured," she warned. "Even here."

"Even in a bar full of wolves?" I asked, giggling.

She looked at me suddenly serious. "Especially in a bar full of wolves. Some of them don't take 'no' so well."

I nodded, but the warning was hard to hold on to in the blur of music and laughter. The drinks made everything loose, all the sharp edges dulled down.

It was on my third Cosmo that I realized I somehow missed Big Papa. I wanted him to see me like this—alive, happy, not just the bakery girl.

I leaned into Maddie, trying to whisper but probably just yelling, "I wish he were here. Papa, I mean. He's so big and beautiful. He makes me feel...safe."

Maddie grinned, wicked. "You got it bad, girl."

I pouted. "You don't even know. I love his face. I love his hands. I love his hair, even the way it goes messy when he's being all grumpy." I giggled again. "He has a good beard. Like, a really good beard."

Maddie doubled over with laughter. "Wait, say that again? The last part."

I repeated all the things I adored about Papa. I took another sip, steadied myself, and declared, "Big Papa has the best beard in Texas. In the world. I want to—" But then a hand landed on my shoulder, heavy and hot even through my sweater.

I whipped around, expecting Papa, but instead it was a man I'd never seen before. He was tall, broad, with black hair pulled into a tight braid and skin like river clay. His eyes were dark, almost black, and he grinned at me in a way that made all my good feelings shrivel.

He didn't say hello. Just leaned in and said, "Hey beautiful. Why don't you dance with me?"

I tried to pull back, but his grip tightened, just enough to warn me he wasn't asking.

Maddie was instantly between us, sharp as a switchblade. "She's with me, asshole. Move along."

The man sneered, but Maddie's voice drew attention. Two men by the bar glanced over, and Gator shot a look like he was ready to vault the counter if needed.

He let go, holding up his hands. "Didn't mean any offense. Just being friendly." But his gaze lingered, a silent promise I didn't like at all.

He disappeared into the crowd. I could feel my heart hammering, the flush of panic colder than the beer in my stomach.

Maddie steadied me. "You okay?"

I nodded, breathless. "Yeah. Thanks."

She smiled, but it didn't quite reach her eyes. "Told you. Wolves don't always play nice."

Chapter 8

Big Papa

The Iron Valor clubhouse felt different at night, especially after a day where nothing went sideways. The lot was packed; every Harley in the club just about lined up in military precision, reflecting the moonlight like wolf eyes in a brush fire. Inside, the men had gathered in their off-duty gear, leathers open and sleeves rolled up, the air thick with cigarette smoke and the better kind of laughter—the kind that said no one was dead or in the hospital and the world could, for once, be easy.

I had a cold Lone Star in hand and my feet up on the battered coffee table, half-listening to Wrecker and Gunner debate the merits of fried okra versus hushpuppies as a side to chicken-fried steak. It wasn't a night for deep thoughts, but I found myself stuck in my own head anyway, thinking about Aspen and the way she'd smiled at me through the bakery window that morning. It had haunted me all day, the way she'd seen my scars, but looked past them.

Arsenal sat beside me, cleaning a pistol that didn't need cleaning, and Bronc had disappeared to the front porch to make a call to Juliet. I envied him sometimes. Not the power, not the bullshit politics, but the simplicity of loving someone and being loved back, consequences be damned.

That's when my phone vibrated. Not a text, not a call, but a FaceTime request—Maddie's name in all-caps, with a string of little wolf emojis behind it. Wrecker saw the screen and let out a cackle. "Uh oh, Papa's about to get a show."

I rolled my eyes and accepted, holding the phone at arm's length, but the moment it connected, the screen filled with chaos. Music blared, the bar's neon signs flashing behind a blur of faces and drinks. Maddie was there, front and center, holding up her own phone with an unsteady hand.

"Say all that again!" she hollered, and the camera swung wildly until it landed on Aspen.

She looked radiant and completely toasted, cheeks flushed pink, hair wild and falling over her face in dark, glossy waves. Her eyes glittered, not with magic, but with a kind of joy I hadn't seen on her before. For a second, she looked straight at me through the screen, and my heart did a double-clutch.

"I wish JT were here!" Aspen said, her accent deepening until it was syrupy enough to pour on pancakes. "He's so big and beautiful. He makes me feel safe, and small."

Maddie grinned, all teeth and trouble. "She's been talking about you all night, Papa. But she keeps chickening out. But it's right there from the source!"

Wrecker and Gunner crowded in behind me, peering over my shoulders. Even Arsenal stopped his compulsive pistol cleaning to watch.

"Yeah, Aspen," Wrecker called out, voice booming through the speakers, "tell Papa what you really think."

Aspen couldn't hear the guys. She didn't know Maddie was sharing this.

"Come on, sweet pea, just say it. The man's right here!"

Maddie egged her on. "You have it so bad, girl."

Aspen looked off in the distance all dreamy. "You don't even know. I love his face. I love his hands. I love his hair, even the way it goes messy when he's being all grumpy." Her giggle was precious. "He has a good beard. Like, a really good beard."

Gunner made a strangled sound and ducked his head, fighting laughter, but I couldn't look away from the screen. Aspen's words hit me straight in the gut. The real kind, not the pretty kind. The kind that said she meant every syllable. It was like poetry to my ears, anyway.

Maddie whooped. "She's got it bad, Big Papa! You'd better show up and sweep her off her feet before someone else does."

Aspen just realized what Maddie was doing. "Wait, you have Papa on the phone?"

Maddie's laughter carried over the music. "I do, girl. Actually, I'm FaceTiming him. You wanna see?"

Maybe it was the alcohol, or maybe it was the years of being ignored and unappreciated, but she found her courage and leaned in closer.

"I do," she said, almost in a whisper. "I wish you could have seen me like this tonight. To see I can be more than the bakery girl. And I *do* think you're beautiful. The most beautiful man I've ever seen."

A chorus of howls erupted around the clubhouse. Even Arsenal cracked a smile.

I could have died happy in that moment, except everything changed in the next heartbeat.

The camera caught a flash of movement behind Aspen. A big man in a brown leather jacket stepped up behind her, his hands landing on her hips like he'd done it a hundred times before. He was tall, with a face like old granite and eyes the color of black coffee, and the way he touched her made every muscle in my body snap tight.

On screen, Aspen froze. The light in her eyes guttered out, replaced by something small and wary. She tried to wriggle free, but the man leaned down, his mouth too close to her ear, and whatever he said made her whole body tense.

Maddie saw it, too. She twisted around and shoved the man's arm. "Back off, asshole. She's with us tonight."

The man just smiled, but it was the smile of a wolf who already knows the lamb's got nowhere left to run. He gave Aspen a squeeze, then let go, but he didn't leave. He stood there, looming, watching the screen with dead-eyed amusement.

Wrecker's mood evaporated. Gunner stiffened, and Arsenal looked at me with a warning in his gaze.

But I was already on my feet, the phone clattering to the table as my hands balled into fists.

"County Line, NOW," I barked, voice low and lethal.

Bronc reappeared, reading the room in a split second. "What's going on?"

Gunner told him, quick and clipped: "Aspen's at the County Line. Someone's messing with her. Papa's about to lose his shit."

Bronc's eyes narrowed, but his voice stayed steady. "JT, sit the fuck down. We'll handle it. You go in there, you'll start a war."

But the beast in my chest had already shredded the leash. "If another man had his hands on your *MATE*, how calm would you be, Bronc?"

The silence that followed was total. Even the men in the hall stopped moving.

Bronc's jaw flexed. He saw the truth of it—saw that it wasn't about pride or territory, but the bare fact that Aspen was mine, and she was in danger. His voice, when it came, was soft but absolute.

"Wrecker, Arsenal, Gunner, you're with me. Let's go."

I didn't wait for the others. I was out the door and in my truck before anyone could try to stop me. The cold air slapped me awake, but nothing could dull the red haze at the edge of my vision, or the way my heart howled for blood.

They could say what they wanted about wolves being monsters. But this—this was love. And there wasn't a force on earth strong enough to keep me from her.

The bikes thundered to life behind me, a wall of noise that promised violence and retribution. I stomped on the gas pedal and aimed myself at the County Line Bar, praying I wasn't already too late.

The County Line Bar looked like every roadhouse in Texas, but tonight it felt like the only thing on earth that mattered. The parking lot was already full—Fords, Chevys, the odd Ram, and a neat row of bikes I didn't recognize—but our arrival, a snarl of six Harleys rolling in together, sucked the sound out of the place. People at the picnic tables on the porch straightened, drinks paused mid-drink. They all recognized our cuts and decided they needed a smoke break instead.

I barely noticed. My world had narrowed to a tunnel: get inside, find Aspen, break anyone who hurt her.

Wrecker and Arsenal flanked me, Gunner a step behind. Bronc led, his presence enough to part the line at the door like the Red Sea. The bouncer, a kid I didn't know, tried to step up, but Bronc looked at him once and the poor bastard all but curtsied. We entered as a unit, the noise of the bar folding down to a single note. A pack member owned this bar, so we owned this bar.

First thing I did was scan the room: dance floor to the left, pool tables to the right, a long wooden bar running the length of the back wall. I didn't see her at first, but I caught her scent—rosemary and vanilla, sweet and sharp—cutting through the sweat and cigarette haze.

But before I could move, Gator appeared from behind the bar, arms crossed, tattoos rippling with each step. He raised his chin at me, then Bronc.

"Thought you boys might show," he said, voice steady but wary. "It's handled."

I stopped, my whole body humming with the need to do something, anything. "Handled how?"

He thumbed over his shoulder. "Asshole from Morgantown pack got grabby with your girl. I tossed him, no blood, no drama. Maddie decked him pretty good too. He left with his tail between his legs."

The name clicked—Morgantown was fifty miles south. Small pack, all assholes. Known for thinking anything unattached was fair game.

I let out a slow breath, my heart still galloping. "He gone?"

Gator nodded, eyes sympathetic. "Gone. He won't be back tonight."

I nodded my thanks, but I still had to see her with my own eyes.

The pack broke rank; the other guys fanned out, casing the room with practiced ease. I followed my nose and found Aspen and Maddie at a high-top in the far corner, half hidden by the edge of the dance floor. Aspen sat hunched over a mostly empty Cosmo, cheeks wet, hair a little wild. Maddie had her arm around her, giving comfort but also keeping her upright.

When Maddie saw me, she flagged me over with a look that said help, then slid out of the chair and gave me the space. Aspen looked up, blinking slow. Her green eyes were glassy and rimmed with red, the eyeliner smeared to raccoon levels.

"Oh, hey," she slurred, trying to muster a smile. "It's Big Papa. What chu doin' here?"

I put a hand on the table to keep from shaking. "I might ask you the same thing, Sunshine. What are *you* doing here?"

She laughed, weak but real. "I was...having fun. I wanted to try being normal."

Maddie hovered behind her, eyes wide, but didn't say a word.

I tried to keep my voice gentle, but it came out as a growl. "You call *this* normal? Getting drunk until you can't stand, letting some piece of shit put his hands on you?"

Aspen shrank into herself, and the anger in me twisted, quick as a snake, into something else. Guilt, maybe. Fear. Love.

She blinked, and for a second I saw the old Aspen—the one who was free with her sarcasm. "I didn't *let* him butthead," she whispered. "He just...did it."

I glanced at Maddie, and she nodded. "She told him to back off. He didn't listen. I made sure he got the message. Gator took care of the rest."

I nodded, my chest still tight. "You don't understand. You could've been hurt."

Aspen shook her head, then stopped, hand to her forehead. "No. *You* don't understand. I wanted to be brave. I wanted to be like everyone else for once. But I'm not."

The words hit me sideways, and I realized I'd scared her more than the asshole from Morgantown had. I reached out, my hand shaking, and tucked her hair behind her ear.

"You don't have to be like anyone else," I said. "You just have to be you."

She looked at me, and the mask fell away. All the pain, all the hope, every ounce of pride—gone. Just a girl who'd been hurt too many times, and wanted someone to say she was enough.

"Can you take me home?" she asked, so soft I almost didn't hear it.

I nodded. "Yeah. I can."

Maddie helped her up, and Aspen wobbled, then sagged into my side. I wrapped an arm around her, careful but tight enough that she knew she was safe. I looked at Maddie, who smiled—a real smile, relieved.

"Thank you," I told her. "You did good."

She shrugged and handed me Aspen's purse. "That's what friends are for."

I led Aspen toward the door. The bar watched us go, silent. Wrecker and Arsenal formed a screen as we passed, and the rest of the pack fell in behind.

At the truck, I unlocked the door and guided her inside, buckling her seatbelt before I got behind the wheel. The guys waited, engines idling, ready to follow if I needed them. But this wasn't a mission for the pack. This was mine.

The drive to her place was quiet. She leaned her head against the window, watching the streetlights go by. She didn't speak until we were almost home.

"I made a fool of myself," she said, not looking at me.

"No, you didn't," I told her. "You tried something new. It just didn't work out. That's all."

She turned, face blurry with tears and booze. "I ruined everything. You probably hate me now."

I pulled the truck over, right there on the shoulder, and turned to face her. "I could never hate you, Aspen. Not in a million years."

She stared at me, searching for the lie, but there wasn't one to find.

She nodded, then closed her eyes, and I drove the rest of the way with my hand resting on her knee, her scent filling the cab, my wolf finally at peace.

When we pulled up in front of the bakery, I parked and turned off the engine. Aspen didn't move. She just sat there, eyes closed, breathing slow and deep.

I got out, walked around, and opened her door. She slid out, more graceful than I expected, and stood on her own two feet.

But she didn't make it two steps before she turned and threw her arms around me, burying her face in my chest. She shook, maybe from the cold, maybe from everything she'd held in all night.

I held her tight, the only thing in the world that made sense.

"It's okay," I whispered. "You're safe now."

She nodded against my shirt, and I felt her start to relax.

"I'm sorry," she said, muffled.

"Don't be. Not ever."

I picked her up bridal style, and carried her to the door, her keys jangling in my hand. She laughed, weak but alive.

"You know, you don't have to do this," she said.

I smiled. "I like holding you."

She looked up at me, and for the first time all night, she smiled back.

I set her down inside the apartment and closed the door behind us. She slumped onto the couch, and I knelt down to take off her boots.

"I think I drank too much," she said, voice small.

"Probably."

"Will you stay until I fall asleep?"

"I'll stay as long as you want."

There are a hundred ways to spend a night with the woman you want. This wasn't any of them. Aspen barely made it to the bathroom before she was on her knees, and I dropped beside her, holding her hair back as she puked up a night's worth of courage and heartbreak into the toilet. I stroked her spine, slow and steady, the way I'd comforted a hundred wounded wolves before her. She heaved and shook, tiny, shivering, and at one point started crying and apologizing in the same breath.

"I'm so sorry," she sobbed, knuckles white on the rim. "I didn't mean to—oh God—" She launched again, and I kept her hair in a ponytail with one hand, rubbing circles into her back with the other.

"Shhh, you're okay, Sunshine. Happens to the best of us." I grabbed a washcloth, ran it under cool water, and held it to her forehead while she spat, wiped her mouth, and started another round of tears.

"I'm a mess," she whimpered, slumping against the tub. "You probably think I'm disgusting."

"Not even close." I wiped her face, gentle as I could, and grabbed a hair tie from her counter. "You look adorable, even like this."

She closed her eyes and let me clean her up. I rinsed her mouth with water, found a fresh toothbrush under the sink, and waited as she brushed with the grim focus of a soldier field-dressing a wound.

When she finished, Aspen let herself collapse against my chest, half-buried in my arms, and the smell of her sweat and vanilla shampoo was so sharp and right I nearly lost my own composure.

"Can you get me to the bed?" she whispered. "I don't think I can walk."

I picked her up again and carried her across the hall and into her bedroom. The quilt on the mattress was a patchwork of blue and yellow, brighter than any I'd ever seen. I set her down and turned away, giving her a sliver of dignity. She fumbled with her top, but her hands were too uncoordinated to do much more than tangle in the fabric.

I hesitated, then cleared my throat. "Want me to help?"

She nodded, not meeting my eyes. "Please."

I unhooked her belt and then lifted her arms out of her sweater with the care of a man handling a live grenade. I tried to be clinical, but her skin was soft and warm under my fingers, and the line of her collarbone, the curve of her shoulder, made my mouth go dry. I pulled it the rest of the way over her head. She wore a plain black bra beneath, full coverage but somehow more intimate than anything lacy. I looked away as I slid the sweater off, but I saw her smiling, shy and fierce, in the lamplight.

I removed her boots and then had her stand as I knelt before her and unzipped her skirt. It fell away and pooled at her feet, and I tapped each leg for her to step out so I could set it aside. My hands shook as I reached up for the waistband of her tights. I wanted so much to take her panties down with them and bury my face in her sweet-smelling pussy then eat her until the sun came up. The scent of her arousal was making everything I did almost impossible.

"Sit down, Sunshine." She followed my order immediately her eyes not leaving mine. Good fucking witchling. I pulled a long t-shirt from the dresser. "Arms up." I slipped it over her head. The whole time, I kept my hands gentle, my movements deliberate, but I knew my wolf's eyes were glowing in the dark. "Good girl. Now lie back on your pillow."

I tucked her under the quilt, then sat on the edge of the bed, heart thudding in my throat.

She stared at me, wide-eyed, a single tear tracking down her cheek. "I really, really wanted to kiss you tonight," she whispered. "But I didn't want to screw it up by being...this."

I brushed the tear from her cheek with my thumb. "You can't screw this up. Not even if you tried."

She reached up, fingers tracing the edge of my jaw. "I've never felt like this before. I don't even know what to do with it."

"Let it happen," I said, my voice rough.

She smiled, then yawned, eyes drifting shut. "I've been kinda scared all day even before the bar." She was mumbling.

I was brushing her hair back from her face. "Why have you been afraid, Aspen?" My instincts were raised..

"The man in the bakery."

"Sunshine, I need you to stay awake just a few more minutes, okay? What man in the bakery scared you today?"

"Green jacket man. He looked wrong. And he just stared at me, and didn't eat his scone. Oscar says he's spelled or possessed." She said through a yawn.

"What did he do with his scone, baby? And who's Oscar? I need you to tell me, then you can go to sleep."

There was a long pause. I was afraid she'd already dozed off. "He left it with the drawing on the bag. And Oscar is my prairie dog friend."

Shit. What? One thing at a time. I sat up. "What drawing, sweetie? Do you still have it?"

"Umm, it's in the trash."

I stood up. I needed to find that bag first.

"Go on to sleep, Sunshine."

"Will you be here when I wake up?"

I leaned down and kissed her forehead. "Always."

She fell asleep in less than a minute, breath slow and sweet, lips parted in a tiny smile.

I went back to the living room and checked the window. It was locked tight, but the sash was loose. Someone with enough skill could have worked it open from the outside, if they had the ability to access it at that height. I prowled the bakery, double-checking every bolt and door, then returned to the kitchen. The trash cans were empty. She'd taken the bags to the outside dumpster. Damn it. I went out the back door to the alley. I felt something out here; one of those ominous feelings. Something was stalking my mate. I went to the dumpster and opened the lid. Empty. I hoped like hell she'd remember what the symbol looked like.

I sent a message to Wrecker and told him what was going on. He texted back. *"Let me know what you find out. Sounds like someone's got eyes on your girl. We need to find out who and why."*

My pulse spiked, but I kept it quiet. I crept back to the bedroom, checked Aspen, and found her sleeping on her side, arms curled around the pillow. I brushed her hair from her face, memorizing every line.

I texted Wrecker again: *"Send guys to keep watch tonight. Watch for freaky shit. Guy in a green jacket specifically."*

His reply was a thumbs up and a simple phrase: *"We've got your back, brother."*

I set my phone down and eased myself onto the floor beside Aspen's bed. The room was warm, and her scent filled every inch. I let myself drift, half awake, half guarding the door, ears tuned for the slightest sound.

If I were lucky, nothing would happen tonight.

But if anyone came for her, they'd have to go through me.

My wolf was ready for it. So was I.

No one—witch, wolf, or otherwise—would ever touch her again.

I watched her as the hours ticked by, every breath a promise.

She'd be safe.

She'd be mine.

From now until forever.

CHAPTER 9

Aspen

I woke with a splitting headache, dry-mouthed and stiff all over. For a second I panicked, certain I'd passed out on the bar's sticky floor. But instead of beer stench and neon, the world was soft lamplight and the lavender scent of my own pillow. Quilt bunched around my knees, flannel sheets twisted at my waist. I blinked, squinting against the morning, and found myself alone in my bed—alone except for the shadow slumped against the side of the mattress, knees drawn up, arms crossed like some kind of sentry.

Papa sat on the floor beside me, head tipped back against the bedframe, breathing slow and heavy with sleep. His beard rough, hair mashed into strange little wings above his ears, arms crossed like he could keep watch even in his dreams. The sight nearly made me forget my hangover.

Nearly.

My mouth tasted like a biscuit left out in the rain, and my tongue was so dry I could've used it to sand a tabletop. But it was nothing compared to the ache in my chest as the memories of last night started coming back in ugly, overlapping fragments: the bar, the music, the drinks I'd pounded like a woman on a mission to forget her own name. The sick, humiliating lurch of panic when that man had grabbed me. Papa's voice, hot and furious, followed by the cold reality of me puking my guts out in front of him. My face burned, even before I tried to sit up.

I risked a peek at the digital clock: not quite seven. I'd been asleep for maybe five hours. Or maybe forever. I let my head flop back onto the pillow and stared at the ceiling, mind racing the way it always did when my body was too tired to keep up. This was supposed to be a new start. I'd tried so hard to fit in, to be normal, and now here I was—helpless as a baby, with the one person I liked best in the world literally propping up the side of my bed.

Why would anyone want to take care of me? I could still see the look on his face as I'd leaned over the toilet, the way he'd held my hair back and wiped the sweat from my neck, never once looking disgusted. It should have made me feel safe. Instead, I wanted to dig a hole in the mattress and crawl in.

I closed my eyes, letting my thoughts twist around themselves like a bowl of overcooked spaghetti. All the ways I'd failed last night, all the ways I'd been a disappointment; not just to Papa, but to myself, to Mama, to anyone who ever thought I was meant for something more than being the town's pity project.

I needed to get up and use the bathroom, but I couldn't bring myself to disturb him. Besides, what if he woke up and saw me? What if he tried to talk to me about last night, about how reckless I'd been, or how he had to swoop in and rescue me like some battered puppy?

You don't deserve a man like him; I thought. He's a war hero, an Alpha's best friend, a walking mountain with a heart bigger than Texas. You're just...a defective little witch who can't even hold her liquor.

I tried to hold still, but the need to pee became impossible to ignore. I eased my leg out from under the quilt, careful as a burglar, but of course the bed frame creaked. Papa's eyes snapped open. Even groggy, his gaze was sharp as a blade.

"Good morning, Sunshine," he said. His voice was a sandpaper rumble, softer than I'd ever heard it. "You been awake long?"

I shook my head, then instantly regretted it. "No, sir," I croaked. "Just now."

He smirked, then rubbed the bridge of his nose. "You need the bathroom, don't you?"

I flushed so hard I thought my ears would pop. "Um. Yes, sir."

He stood, slow and deliberate, then held out a hand for me. "Come on. I can hear your mind racing from here."

I took his hand, expecting him to yank me to my feet, but instead he cradled my palm like it was made of blown glass. I slid off the bed and instantly wobbled. His arm caught me around the waist, steady as a fencepost. He walked me to the door, only letting go when I reached the threshold.

"Take your time," he said. "I'll make coffee."

I closed the door and leaned against it for a second, trying not to let the wave of gratitude drown me. I took care of business, washed my face, and stared at the girl in the mirror: hair in a fright, skin ghost-pale except for the flush in my cheeks, eyes puffy and rimmed in red. I splashed water on my face again, hoping to trick myself into feeling alive.

I opened the medicine cabinet, found the bottle of ibuprofen, and shook out three. I dry-swallowed them, knowing I'd need at least that many if I was going to survive this day.

By the time I cracked the door, the smell of coffee was already drifting down the hall. I shuffled toward the kitchen in my t-shirt and nothing else, only remembering halfway that the shirt only hit me mid-thigh. I almost turned around, but the smell of breakfast stopped me in my tracks.

Papa was at the stove, tossing scrambled eggs in a pan like it was the most natural thing in the world. Bacon sizzled beside it, and the coffeepot gurgled on the counter. He'd found my favorite mug—blue, with a little pink cow design—and poured me a cup without asking how I took it. He knew. He'd remembered.

I ducked my head and slid into the nearest chair. My heart was thumping so loud I could hear it in my ears. I wrapped my hands around the mug and tried not to look at him.

"Eggs'll be ready in a minute," he said. "Toast is on the way."

I just nodded, then sipped. The coffee was perfect—creamy, sweet, just the way Mama used to make it when she knew I'd needed some comfort. I felt a lump rise in my throat, and I did my best to swallow it down.

Papa set a plate in front of me: eggs, bacon, two slices of toast with jam. He took the chair opposite, watching me with those unreadable gray eyes.

"Eat something," he said. "You'll feel better."

I took a bite of toast, chewed, and almost started crying. The sweetness of the jam, the warmth of the bread—simple, solid, like being anchored back to earth.

"I'm sorry," I blurted out, unable to hold it in any longer. "About last night. About all of it."

He tilted his head, considering. "What are you sorry for exactly?"

I stared at my plate. "For making a mess of everything. For needing you to bail me out. For being—" I almost said "a disappointment," but the word stuck. "—for being a pain in the ass."

He snorted. "Sunshine, if you think puking your guts out is gonna scare me off, you don't know me at all."

I looked up, surprised.

He leaned forward, elbows on the table. "I've seen men shot, stabbed, and set on fire. I've seen the inside of more toilets than I care to count. None of that even comes close to what you did last night."

I winced. "You mean being a drunk idiot?"

He shook his head. "No. Standing up for yourself. Telling that asshole off. Trying to be brave, even when you were scared shitless."

I stared at him; the words stung more than I expected. "I didn't feel brave."

"Most people don't," he said. "But you were. I'm proud of you."

I felt tears prick at the corners of my eyes, and I wiped them away with the heel of my hand. "I don't know why you'd be proud of me."

He gave me a look equal parts exasperation and affection. "Because you fought for yourself. And because you let me help you."

That did it. The tears came, hot and quick, and for a moment I couldn't even look at him. I just stared at my eggs, letting them go cold, and tried to remember the last time anyone had said they were proud of me.

He reached across the table and put his hand over mine. "You don't have to do this alone," he said, voice low. "Not anymore."

I nodded, breath hitching.

"Finish your breakfast," he said, voice soft but firm. "You've got a long day ahead."

I ate, slow but steady, until my stomach stopped twisting. The pain in my head faded to a dull ache, and my body felt almost normal again.

Papa cleared the plates, rinsed them, and stacked them in the sink. Then he walked to the fridge, opened it, and pulled out a bottle of Gatorade.

"For you," he said, unscrewing the cap and sliding it over.

I took it, sipped, and smiled. "Thank you," I said, voice barely more than a whisper.

He smiled back, then nodded toward the hallway. "Go shower if you want. I'll be here."

I nodded, then padded off to the bathroom, desperate to scrub the last of the shame and sweat from my skin.

I turned on the shower; the bathroom steamed up. I saw that he'd left a fresh set of my clothes—underwear, bra, and a long-sleeved dress I liked—on the counter. I stared at the little stack, a fist of feeling squeezing my chest.

Nobody had ever done something like that for me. Not even Mama, who loved me more than the sun loved the sky.

I peeled off my shirt and stepped into the shower, letting the water run as hot as I could stand it. I closed my eyes and let the spray pummel me, washing away the guilt and the fear, the memory of strange hands and dark voices, the old ache of never quite being enough.

I scrubbed my hair and scrubbed every inch of my skin desperate to start fresh. When I got out, the towel was still warm. I dried off, then picked up the underwear and pressed it to my face, feeling the tears come again. Not sad tears, but something softer. Gratitude, maybe. Or hope.

I got dressed, brushed and dried my hair, and went to face the day.

This time, I didn't feel defective at all.

I felt like maybe, just maybe, I could be someone worth loving.

I found him right where I'd left him, leaning against the kitchen counter with a mug of coffee cradled between both hands, eyes fixed on the empty parking lot outside my window. He looked like a man who could out-wait the sunrise if he put his mind to it, but when he saw me, his entire face softened. Maybe it was just the hangover, but the sight made my pulse trip over itself.

He grinned. "Look at you. Hair's all shiny."

"Don't make fun," I said, even though I knew he wasn't. "That was the closest I've come to dying."

He shook his head, set his coffee down, and poured a second mug—mine, already doctored the way I liked it. He slid it across the counter. I took it, warm between my hands, and tried not to let my heart show on my face.

"Eat something else?" he asked. "I made extra toast."

I sat at the table, folded my hands around the mug, and nodded. "Yes, please."

He set a fresh plate in front of me. Toasted bread, buttered to perfection with just the right amount of strawberry jelly sat on top of it. I bit into it and closed my eyes, letting the taste anchor me.

We sat in companionable silence for a minute. I could feel him watching me, waiting for the right moment to bring up the thing I least wanted to talk about.

"You want to tell me what you were thinking last night?" He asked, voice low.

I took another bite, chewed slow. "About the bar?"

He nodded.

I set my fork down and tried to remember the moment it had all gone sideways. "I just wanted to feel... normal," I said. "Like everyone else. Not the weird girl with the haunted past. Just a person who could laugh and dance and drink a little too much and maybe get hit on, but in a fun way."

He nodded, but the lines around his eyes deepened. "You know why I was mad, right?"

I nodded. "Yeah. Because I scared you."

He let out a huff. "Not the word I'd use, but close enough." He ran his hand over his mouth, then looked me dead in the eye. "You're not just the weird girl, Aspen. You're a target."

I wanted to protest, but the memory of the man in the bar—his hands, the way he looked at me like I was something to be owned—killed the urge. I stared at my plate, appetite gone.

Papa reached across the table, curled his hand around my wrist. "I'm not saying you can't go out, or that you have to change. But I need you to promise me something."

I nodded, eyes stinging. "What?"

"Don't go alone. Not for a while." His grip was gentle, but there was steel in his voice. "Let us keep you safe, at least until we figure out what's really going on."

I nodded, trying to swallow past the lump in my throat. "Okay."

He squeezed my wrist and then let go. "Good girl."

Warmth spread through me, chasing away the shame. It was nice, I realized, to have someone care enough to scold you. Not because they wanted to control you, but because they gave a damn if you made it to tomorrow.

He leaned back, expression softening. "Now. First thing. Who is Oscar?"

I froze mid-sip. "Oscar? I mentioned Oscar?"

"Yeah, you did. Said he was your prairie dog friend."

I needed to tell him. He's not a secret after all.

"Oscar is my familiar. He showed up after the weird dream when the book heated up. He said the book called him. He's here for me. To help me."

Papa stared at me for a second. "Can I meet him?"

Just like that, Oscar was sitting on the kitchen counter. Only this time, the little sucker spoke out loud. "Oscar B. Wilde, at your service." He gave a small bow.

Papa startled and then gave him a nod. "Good to meet you."

He returned his attention to me. "Now, you tell me about the guy in the green jacket."

The shift was abrupt, but I was grateful for it. I rolled my mug between my palms and tried to summon every detail. "He came in right before close. Didn't say anything, just stared at me. He had these... I don't know, dead eyes. He bought a scone and paid in coins. Then he sat in the corner for almost an hour, watching me."

"Did he eat?"

I shook my head. "Never even touched it. When he left, he left the scone on the table, but the bag had a symbol drawn on it."

Papa straightened. "Describe the symbol."

I closed my eyes, trying to picture it. "It was a triangle, I think. Maybe a stripe through it? Or dots inside?" I opened my eyes, frustration rising. "I threw it out without even thinking. I should have paid more attention."

He nodded, not judging. "Triangle with a stripe, or dots. Anything else?"

I shook my head. "That's all I remember."

He drummed his fingers on the table. "You said he looked at you like he knew you. Not like a customer. More like...?"

"Like he was studying me," I said, the words coming out cold. "Like I was a puzzle or something. I didn't really notice it at the time, just that he was odd. I had a bunch of other people here."

He nodded, accepting it.

"You think it's a witch thing?" I asked, voice small.

Papa stared out the window, jaw tight. "More like it's a hunting thing, that's for damn sure. Could be witch, could be demon, could be something else. But the fact that he left a symbol means he wanted you to see it."

Oscar spoke up. "I agree with Big Papa. I believe he is associated with whoever is hunting you. I don't know if he is aware. His eyes seemed empty. He may be under someone else's control."

I shivered, hugging my arms around myself. "What does it mean?"

He shrugged, but there was nothing casual about it. "Not sure yet. But we'll find out."

I looked at him, searching for the part of the conversation where he'd say something reassuring, or promise it would all be okay. He didn't. He just kept his gaze on mine, steady and unbreakable.

"You're not alone," he said. "We'll figure this out together."

Something loosened inside me; a knot I hadn't even realized was there. "Thank you," I whispered.

He gave me a half-smile, the kind that creased the scar on his cheek. "You're welcome."

We finished in silence, but it was the good kind, like a peace treaty between two people who'd finally admitted they needed each other.

After the dishes were cleared, he poured another round of coffee and set his mug down with a deliberate thump. "We need to figure out that symbol."

My heart lurched. "You think that will tell us who is stalking me?"

"I think it will tell us something more than we know right now."

He looked at Oscar. "You have any ideas?"

Oscar shook his head. "Sadly, I do not. I didn't know about it until after she had thrown it away. And what she has described doesn't sound familiar to me."

He grinned, all wolf. "Well, you've got an entire pack behind you now. And I know someone who's very good at finding the answers people don't want found."

I blinked, surprised. "You do?"

He nodded. "Wrecker and his mate, Parker. She's a tech genius, best hacker in the county. If anyone can figure out what that triangle means, it's her."

My stomach flipped. "You really think she can help?"

He looked confident. "If anyone can it's her. But you'll have to tell her everything you know."

I nodded, heart pounding. "Okay."

Papa finished his coffee, then stood and stretched, all six-foot-five of him filling the little kitchen. "Get your coat," he said. "We'll head over there in ten."

I watched him move around the apartment, cleaning up. He never stopped moving, as if he were afraid the universe would catch up if he stood still too long.

But when he came over, coat in hand, he stopped in front of me and bent down so we were eye to eye.

"You did good today," he said, voice low. "I'm proud of you."

I just smiled, and let the warmth of his words carry me into whatever came next.

The drive out to pack land was oddly soothing. The road wound away from town and into a wide sweep of prairie, then dipped through a patch of winter-brown woods, the sun flickering through bare branches and some evergreens like a strobe. Papa kept his hand resting on my knee, thumb tracing slow circles while he hummed along to the radio. I could have spent the whole day in that truck, just listening to his deep, steady breathing and the rumble of the tires on the old caliche road.

But then the houses started to pop up—one after another, each one a little different but all with the same look: strong, practical, but built for family. We pulled into the drive of a pale blue ranch with a big porch and a battered mailbox in the shape of a motorcycle. There was a big Harley and a fabulous sports car parked out front, shining in the winter sun.

We got out, boots crunching on the gravel, and I had just enough time to smooth my skirt before the front door opened and a woman stepped out, propping her hands on her hips. She was shorter than me, with a compact, athletic build and the kind of presence that made her seem taller. Her hair was spiked short, brunette with streaks of pink, and one side was buzzed close to the scalp. Her eyes were a blue so blue they looked like someone had Photoshopped them. She wore black joggers and a t-shirt that said, "Nerd? I prefer the term Intellectual Badass."

She smiled wide and a little wicked. "You brought the bakery girl! Knew it."

Papa put his hand on my shoulder, like he was introducing me at a debutante ball. "Aspen, meet Parker. Parker, this is my friend Aspen."

She yanked the screen door open and ushered us inside. The house was warm and smelled like toasted bagels and cedar. The great room boasted a large sectional that sat in front of a grand fireplace that had a giant TV mounted on the wall above it. A wall of bookshelves anchored the opposite wall. There were piles of books everywhere: romance novels, code manuals, ancient histories, thrillers with bright, torn covers. I felt at home instantly.

I was about to say something when a dog bounded out of the back room—a shaggy Yorkie mix, compact, with one ear up and the other flopped over like a soggy taco shell. He skidded to a stop in front of us and gave a little yip. I crouched down, and he licked my hand, tail whipping so hard it thudded against the wall.

"That's Rocket," Parker said, fondness softening her voice. "Ugliest dog in the world, but he's family."

I knelt down and scratched Rocket behind his good ear, and he melted to the floor, tongue hanging out. "He's perfect," I said. "Aren't you boy? Yes, you are! Such a good boy!" I loved dogs and went on dog-speak autopilot whenever I was around one. I looked up to see two faces staring down at Rocket and me. Parker broke the temporary silence.

"See?" she threw her hands up. "Validation at last."

There was a clatter from the kitchen, and a man appeared, ducking under the archway with a grace that shouldn't have been possible for someone so massive. Wrecker was big, even by shifter standards—almost as tall as Papa but leaner, with shoulders like a barn door and arms covered in sleeve tattoos, black and blue and a riot of red. He had tan skin, a scruff of dark beard, and eyes the color of storm clouds. He wore a sleeveless black hoodie and faded jeans, but he carried himself like the room belonged to him.

He nodded at Papa, then fixed his gaze on me. It wasn't hostile—just that careful, weighing look that said he didn't hand out trust lightly.

"Wrecker," he said, offering a hand.

"Aspen," I managed, shaking it. His grip was warm and surprisingly gentle.

"Coffee?" Parker asked, already heading for the kitchen.

Papa shot me a wink. "She makes the best pour-over in the state."

"Sit," Wrecker said, motioning toward the couch. "We can talk in here."

I perched on the edge of the cushion, Rocket wedged between my ankles, and folded my hands in my lap. Papa sat next to me, arm draped over the back of the couch. Wrecker took the armchair, posture loose but eyes locked on me.

"So," he said, "you've got a stalker with a triangle thing. Parker and I looked at the text."

Parker came back with four mugs, each a different color, and handed them out. "Drink. It helps."

I sipped, and the coffee was dark and rich, sweet enough to make my teeth ache. It felt like a warm hug.

Parker pulled a battered tablet from the coffee table and tapped it awake. "Tell me everything," she said, eyes meeting mine. "Start from when you first saw him."

I closed my eyes, thinking. "He came in right before close. He wore a green jacket—army style, I think—his hair was brown, nothing special. He never really looked at the pastry case; he just pointed at the scones. When I asked if he wanted the scone, he just nodded at me."

"Eyes?" she asked.

"Empty. Brown. Almost black."

Parker nodded, scribbling notes with her fingertip. "Height, build?"

"A little over six feet, I think? Not muscled, more... stringy."

"Hands?" she asked. "Anything weird? Rings, gloves, scars?"

I frowned, trying to picture it. "He wore gloves. I think. Not the work kind—more like... driving gloves? Black leather."

Papa squeezed my shoulder. "You're doing great. Anything else?"

I shook my head, frustrated. "It's like I can't remember the details. Sorry. That's all."

Parker smiled, a flash of approval. "Tell me about the symbol."

I inhaled, pushing away the nerves. "It was a triangle, but I don't remember if it pointed up or down. There might have been a line through it, or dots? I don't know why I can't remember." My hands trembled, so I hid them in the sleeves of my dress.

Wrecker's eyes softened a little. "It's okay. Knowing it could mean danger makes details go fuzzy. We'll get it."

Papa reached across and took my hand in his. "Try to draw it," he said, voice soothing. "Sometimes that helps."

Parker handed me a notepad and a pen. I stared at the blank page, heart thudding, then sketched a triangle. My hand shook, so I scratched it out, drew it again, over and over until the paper was a mess of ink and smeared lines.

I started to feel stupid, heat creeping up my neck. "I'm sorry. It's not coming."

Papa leaned in close, his breath warm on my ear. "Take your time. No rush."

I swallowed, tried again. This time, I drew a triangle with a horizontal stripe halfway up. Then one with a dot in the center. I remembered the bag; the ink had bled a little, so maybe it had been a filled-in dot. Or maybe two? I circled both options.

Parker took the page, scanned it with her tablet, and started typing.

"Okay," she said, "I'll run this through every database I've got. Symbolic, occult, military, witch, even corporate. We'll get a hit."

Papa grinned at me, proud. "See? Not so hard."

I tried to smile, but my insides still buzzed with anxiety. I wanted so badly to be useful, to not waste anyone's time.

Rocket nudged my hand, tongue lolling, and I scratched his head. He sighed, content, and the little surge of joy I got from it cut through the panic.

Wrecker took a sip of coffee, then spoke. "You ever see this guy before yesterday?"

I shook my head. "No. Never."

He nodded, like that was the answer he'd expected.

Papa shot him a look. "What are you thinking?"

Wrecker shrugged. "If she'd seen him before, I'd say we had a local problem. But this feels... planted. Like someone sent him."

"Could be," Parker said. "I'll run facial recognition too, see if there's a match."

She turned to me, expression gentle. "You did good, Aspen."

I bit my lip, blinking fast. "Thanks."

Papa squeezed my hand, then stood. "Can we have a minute?" he asked, but it wasn't really a question. Wrecker nodded, and Parker waved us off.

We stepped out onto the back deck, which overlooked a little yard and a fringe of woods beyond. The air was sharp and cold, but the sun was out, and the deck boards were warm under my feet.

Papa leaned against the railing, then looked at me, really looked at me, the way he always did when he had something important to say.

"You alright?" he asked, soft.

I nodded and then shook my head. "I feel like an idiot. I can't even remember a stupid drawing."

He stepped close, so close I could feel the heat from his chest, and cupped my face in his hands.

"You are not an idiot," he said. "You're the bravest person I know."

I let out a shaky laugh. "You must not know many people."

He didn't smile. "I know exactly enough. And I know I want you. All of you."

He bent down, and I thought he was going to kiss my forehead, but instead his mouth found mine, gentle at first, then growing in heat and pressure until my knees nearly gave out. His hands were big and rough, but he touched me like I was something precious.

I opened for him, let him in, and for the first time I understood why people got drunk on kissing. His tongue swept over mine, slow and thorough, and my body woke up in ways I didn't know it could. My fingers curled into his shirt, needing something to hold on to. I tasted coffee and the deep, dark hunger I'd seen in his eyes.

He broke away, breath ragged, and pressed his forehead to mine.

"I don't care what you think about yourself," he said. "You are it for me, Aspen Waters."

I blinked, stunned. "You mean that?"

He kissed me again, softer this time, like a promise. "Every word."

I let myself believe him, just for a second, and the ache in my chest turned to something warm and bright.

"Come on," he said, tugging me back toward the house. "We've got a mystery to solve."

Inside, Wrecker watched the door, but his eyes crinkled when he saw us. "Come on, he grinned. Let's go back to the tech room." There Parker sat at her desk, typing furiously, screens filling with images of triangles and esoteric symbols. I glanced around at the screens lit up with numbers and symbols I had no hope of understanding.

I looked down and saw Rocket begging to be picked up. With the little mutt in my arms and Papa at my side, I didn't feel like an intruder or a liability. I felt like part of a team. Part of a family, even. We'd find the answer together. Whatever it was, I wouldn't have to face it alone.

CHAPTER 10

Big Papa

Aspen sat shotgun in my truck, both hands gripping a waxed paper cup Parker had filled with the last of her fancy pour-over. She was staring out at the moonlit fields as if she expected a ghost to sprint across the road and flag us down; her face was caught half in shadow, half in the faded light from the dash. The roads out here were empty at this hour, when even the deer stayed bedded down.

When we left Wrecker and Parker's place, she'd been quiet, as if her brain was processing something big. I didn't push. As a wolf who'd spent his life corralling trauma, I knew to let the ripples settle before skimming another stone. I just let the radio fill the space—old George Jones tonight, music that played like a bruise on your heart—and watched her reflection in the passenger window.

She glanced over as we hit the turnoff for my street. "Is this where you live?" she asked, voice a little excited.

I nodded, tapping the blinker even though nobody for miles would see. "Yup. Two miles down, split-rail fence, mailbox shaped like a tractor." I could tell she wanted to ask more, but her lips pressed together, holding the words in. I loved that about her; she never filled the silence just to fill it.

We rumbled down the drive and I eased up to the porch, my truck's headlights cutting a bright wound through the black. I saw her eyes widen as she took in the house—a ranch style, three bedrooms, all wide hallways and overbuilt windows. It was a place made for a man my size who hated feeling boxed in. The wraparound porch looked out over the fields, still flecked with frost even though spring was flirting at the edges of every tree line. A porch swing groaned on its chains in the wind.

Inside, the house was warm, dry, and dimly lit. I'd left one lamp on in the front room and nothing else. The floors were polished wood, smooth enough you could slide in socks all the way from the mudroom to the kitchen. The furniture was as oversized as I was—big armchairs, a sectional that'd seat ten if it had to, every piece of it battered and broken in. The walls were spare except for a few old black-and-whites: my parents on their wedding day, me and the guys from combat years, before the bomb, Mama's favorite Polaroid of me as a kid covered in pancake batter.

Aspen hovered in the doorway, her whole body drawing up tight to make herself smaller. I stepped past her and dropped the keys on a hook. "You want a tour?"

She hesitated, then smiled, a little lost. "I'd love that, actually."

I led her through, pointing out the dumb little things: "That door goes to the guest wing, but I never use it. Kitchen's this way. Those cabinets are original, but I swapped the handles out because the old ones caught on my jeans." She trailed a finger over the edge of the countertop as if she were reading the house by touch. I wondered how long it had been since she'd been truly welcome in another person's house. I led her to take a seat on the sofa.

"Sunshine, I wanted to talk to you about some things," I said. The words barely landed before Aspen's eyes sharpened, as if she was bracing for a gentle let-down. I felt the small tremor in her as she slowly sat, boots barely touching the floor, hands folded in her lap like she didn't want to leave crumbs on my upholstery.

My house was the polar opposite of the Iron Valor clubhouse—no animal heads, no neon beer signs, just navy walls, wooden shelves lined with books, and a brick fireplace I'd built with my own hands two summers ago. The couch was big, brown, and overstuffed; it'd held me through every heartbreak, injury, and playoff disaster since I'd retired from the service. This was my bunker, and tonight she was the only person on earth who could breach it.

"Bathroom's the first door on your right," I told her, voice low. "I left something in there for you to change into. If you want. You're welcome to stay in that if you're more comfortable, but you might want out of those boots."

She looked up, relief already winning out over nerves. "Thank you," she said, and the words came out soft, round, just like her. She shuffled off, boots thumping on the floor, and I let myself have a few seconds to catch my breath.

I'd made up my mind before we left Wrecker's house. There were lines I wouldn't cross, not until I knew exactly where Aspen's lines were. I'd seen too many men mistake softness for an invitation, and I swore to myself I'd never be that kind of fool.

Still, when I heard the bathroom door open, my heart did a little double-time.

She came out wearing the pink plaid flannel pants I'd set aside, rolled twice at the waist and twice again at the ankle. The t-shirt swallowed her whole, the sleeves grazing her wrists. Her hair was down, a little damp from the sink, and she looked so goddamn wholesome I wanted to drop to my knees and thank the Great Creator for her.

She hesitated in the doorway, one hand gripping her elbow. "I love these. They're so soft. And the shirt smells like you." She quickly added, "I like your house," she said, turning her head to look at me instead of the floor. "It feels like it's got a story."

I'd poured two fresh mugs of coffee, made hers creamy and sweet, plain black for me, then walked her back to the living room. "That's 'cause it does. I built it when I got out of the corps. Didn't know what the hell to do with myself, but I knew I needed something that wouldn't blow away if the wind changed. The pack helped with the roof. Wrecker did all the wiring. Even Bronc hammered nails on the weekends. My parents wanted to send in a team of contractors to put in all the bells and whistles. Mom was convinced I'd lost the use of all my limbs. She forgot I was a wolf. I'd been blown to hell, but we heal up close to perfect if you can get to all the parts fast enough. I was damn lucky."

"I'm glad you were." She smiled when she took the mug, cradling it in both hands, and sipped. Her lashes fluttered as the taste hit her. "You remembered how I like it," she said, voice just a whisper.

"Of course I did." I watched the blush rise up her throat, a hot pink that made me want to bite down and see if it spread.

She took the cup and sat down beside me on the sofa, her bare toes curling into the rug. We watched each other in the lamplight, the silence comfortable but charged.

"I meant what I said," I started. "I want to talk."

She nodded, waiting.

"Can I ask you some personal stuff?"

She took a sip of coffee, then set the mug on the table. "If you wanna know if I've ever been with anyone, the answer is no. Not even close. The girls at the coven made sure I never forgot what a nobody I was. You were my first kiss, Papa. The very first." She was looking down at her hands, that twisted in her lap.

"Closest I ever got to a date turned out to be the worst night of my life. Care to hear that sad story?"

I squeezed her hand. "I want to know every single thing about you." I told her. And I meant it.

"In my last year of school, a boy asked me to the Winter Ball. I couldn't believe it. I'd never had a boyfriend or a date or anything. I was so excited. I bought a pretty dress and everything. I was to meet him at the dance. When I got there, I saw him kissing one of the girls in my coven. I just stood there, frozen. Before I could run out, they saw me, and several of them walked up to me giggling. I asked him why he'd done such an awful thing. He just laughed and told me it was a joke. And another girl told me they'd been practicing a new spell. A hex."

She looked down at the table as a tear slid down her cheek.

"They turned my nose into a pig snout and gave me pink pointed ears. I even felt my tailbone extend into a curly tail. Thank God you couldn't see it through my dress. As I ran out of the gym to my car, I heard them yelling 'Run, piggy piggy.' I hated going home. My mother wanted to go right back up there. But I begged her not to. She was so powerful, she'd have killed them all. Then where would I have been? Thank goodness the spell wore off by morning, and she just withdrew me from school. I finished online. "

My fists curled tight. I'd seen grown men laugh at shit like that in basic, but never at a child. "Jesus, Aspen."

She smiled, but it was a brittle thing. "Mama told me it's the people who are the ugliest on the inside who try the hardest to destroy the most beautiful things." She shrugged. "I try to remember that."

I didn't say anything for a long minute. Instead, I let my anger bleed off, then reached for her face, cupping her jaw so she had to look at me. "If you had been mine back then, I'd have burned that whole fucking coven to the ground."

She laughed for real this time, the sound wet and free. "That's the scariest and sweetest thing anyone's ever said to me."

"I mean it," I told her, voice gone rough. "Nobody makes you feel less again. Not while I'm breathing." I tried to find the right words, measured and careful. "I've been with people, Aspen. Enough to know that what I want with you is more than a one-night deal. I've never felt about anyone the way I feel about you." I looked at her, searching for any sign of fear. "I need you to know what you're signing up for."

She bit her lower lip, her eyes going big and honest. "What am I signing up for exactly?"

"Me. All of me. Which is a lot," I said, and she smiled, the tension breaking like a thin layer of ice. "If we take this next step, I won't want to stop. Not tonight, not tomorrow, not ever."

She let that hang in the air, then reached for my hand. Her fingers were small and cool, and she interlaced them with mine like it was the most natural thing in the world.

"I want that too," she said, voice trembling with both nerves and hope. "But I don't know how to do this. I'm scared I'll mess it up."

I shook my head, squeezing her hand. "You won't. I promise you. If you ever feel uncomfortable, you tell me and I'll stop. No questions, no pressure. That's how it's supposed to be."

She looked at me like I'd offered her the sun and the moon. "That's not how it works where I'm from."

"Then we're making our own rules," I told her. "From scratch."

I brought her hand up, kissed the back of it, then traced her knuckles with my thumb. "You're braver than you give yourself credit for, Aspen. You walked away from everything you'd ever known. That takes more guts than most people have."

I watched the shyness fade from her face, replaced by something fierce. "Can I ask you something else?" she said.

"Anything."

"If I tell you to kiss me again, will you?"

I smiled. "No. But if you ask, I might."

She rolled her eyes, then took a steadying breath. "Will you kiss me, Jonas?"

I leaned in, slow, giving her all the time in the world to change her mind. When our lips met, it was so goddamn sweet it almost hurt. She sighed into my mouth, fingers threading through my beard, pulling me closer.

This time, I didn't hold back. I kissed her like I'd never get another chance, and maybe I wouldn't. The world was dangerous, cruel, and full of people who would tear her down for daring to shine.

But not tonight.

When I pulled back, she was breathless and smiling, her cheeks flushed and her eyes half-lidded.

"You're good at that," she said, voice barely above a whisper.

"Practice," I said. "And maybe a little fate."

We sat in the golden glow of the living room, her feet tucked inside my legs, my hand cradling hers so careful I could feel every tiny shift of her pulse. The urge to pull her closer, to wrap her up and claim her in every way a man could, fought with the need to make this slow, memorable, and right. I'd spent a lifetime wrestling monsters, but tonight the only monster in me was hunger, and I didn't want to let it win.

Aspen finally broke the hush. "Papa, can I ask something kind of stupid?"

"There's no such thing as a stupid question," I said, and meant it.

She stared down at her lap, fingers fiddling with the hem of the oversized t-shirt. "I saw those women at the bar. Maddie and the others. They're all—" She made a motion that was more curve than straight line, but the meaning was clear. "They're just so fit and...well, perfect. When I look in the mirror, I see someone who's never been perfect in her whole damn life."

The tremor in her voice made me want to shake the earth until it explained itself. Instead, I sat back, let her finish, and marshaled every ounce of gentleness I had.

"I want you to listen to me," I said, the chaplain tone slipping in without warning. "There's a thousand types of beauty in this world, Aspen.

You might not be built like a wolf runner, but every time I see you, I swear it does something to my blood." I hesitated, searching for the right words. "All my life I've been surrounded by women who could deadlift a tractor and run fifty miles before breakfast. Strong, yes. Beautiful, sure. Some of their bodies are firm and toned, but some are softer. But *you* walk into a room, all curves and sass; it's like the air gets heavier. All I can see is you."

She didn't look convinced, but she did look up. "You sure you're not just saying that to be nice?"

"Why would I lie? I simply wouldn't waste my time saying anything at all if it weren't true. Instead, I'm sitting here hard as a rock because of the way you look in those pajamas."

She went, the blush rising from her collar to the tips of her ears.

I waited, letting her process it, then added, "I've wanted you from the moment you gave me that first smartass reply over the pastry case. You have no idea how much you affect me."

She let out a laugh that was part disbelief, part relief. "That's... good to know. I guess."

I had to make sure she understood the depth of my feelings. "Aspen, there is one more thing. Before we take this step in our relationship, you need to know that this cannot be a one and done deal with me. I feel way too much for you. I don't know how things work in the witch world, but for a wolf, at some point in our lives, if we are very blessed, fate brings one person made specifically for us into our lives. I knew the moment I met you that you were my mate. My wolf shouted it to me even as I was being an ass to you. I wanted to get to know you first. That's why I've tried to spend so much time with you. I wanted to know you as a person and for you to get to know me too. The more I know you, the more I love you. If you don't feel you share these feelings, we need to wait before we take this any further. If this is only physical for you, let's wait a bit longer."

A tear ran down her face. "I never hoped to hear these beautiful words from any man, much less from the most amazing man in the world. And

I don't know what it feels like to have another part of me telling me who my mate is; all I have is my heart and my soul telling me that without you I will never know complete happiness or joy. All I know at a soul level is you are the other half of me, and I love you deeply."

She drew in a breath that sounded like a prayer. "I'm nervous, but...I want this. I want you."

I stood and pulled her up. "Good," I said, and led her down the hall.

The master bedroom was warm, the fire in the corner hearth already down to small flames but still enough to throw a little light. Bedside table lamps cast a soft light in the room. The comforter was turned down, the sheets clean and soft, and the mattress, specially made, king-plus, reinforced to hold a man my size, looked big enough to swallow her whole.

She hovered in the doorway, bare toes curling on the hardwood, and I knew the nerves were back.

"You want me to turn off the lights?" I asked, voice gentle.

"No," she said. "I want to see you."

She watched me with big, unblinking eyes as I peeled off my shirt. I'd never liked the way I looked shirtless with scars from shrapnel, from fights, from the bomb that cost me a chunk of my thigh. But I wanted to show her I wasn't perfect, either. I stood there, chest bare, tattooed, letting her take it all in.

She moved closer, ran her hand down my shoulder, tracing the line of a scar that ran like a white river down my side.

"Does it hurt?" she whispered.

"Not anymore," I said. "Old wounds. They don't matter when you've got new life in your arms."

She smiled, and the last of her shyness melted.

I reached for the drawstring on her pajama pants, tugged it loose. She held still, watching my face for any hint of mockery or disappointment. When I slid the pants down, I let my hands run slowly over her hips, reverent. Her thighs were soft, the skin so pale it almost glowed. I lifted the t-shirt over her head, her hair falling like a black silken waterfall over her shoulders in its wake, revealing a pretty pink bra beneath. Her hands flew to cover her stomach, but I caught them and pressed them to her sides.

"Let me look at you," I said, and she did.

She was all curves—generous, lush, the kind of woman men used to write poetry about before advertising and the internet ruined everything. Her breasts were full, straining the cups, and I wanted to sink my teeth into the rise of her shoulder just to see if she'd moan or giggle.

I took my time, tracing the dip of her waist, the small rise of her tummy, the powerful curve of her thighs. My wolf was howling, claws scraping at my insides, but I kept my touch feather-light.

"You're fucking gorgeous," I said, and when she looked up, there were tears in her eyes. Not sad tears, just relief, like maybe she finally believed it.

I walked her to the bed and eased her down, laying her out in the middle on the pillow like a present I was afraid to unwrap too quickly. The mattress barely dipped under her weight, but when I crawled up beside her, it cradled us both.

She shivered, and I reached for the throw at the foot of the bed, tucking it around her shoulders. "Cold?" I asked.

"No, just... overwhelmed."

I cupped her face, running my thumb along her jaw. "We can stop anytime, Aspen. Say the word, and I'll hold you all night, nothing else."

She shook her head, hair spilling over the pillow. "Don't you dare stop."

I grinned. "Your wish is my command, ma'am."

She gave a short laugh; the tension breaking. "I like the sound of that."

"Tonight, I'm all yours," I admitted.

She reached for me, shy at first, then bolder. Her fingers traced my scars, my ribs, the flat line of my stomach. When her hand dropped lower, I shuddered, barely catching myself before I let the wolf off the leash.

I slid the straps of her bra down, slow enough to give her plenty of time to object. She didn't. The cups fell away, and her breasts tumbled free, full and perfect, the nipples already peaked and blushing a sweet, impossible pink. I had her lean up so I could free the clasp.

I covered one with my palm, feeling the weight and heat of her. She arched, pressing into my hand, and when I leaned down to kiss her breast, she gasped, a high, clear sound that made my cock jump.

"Is that okay?" I asked, voice rough.

"More than," she breathed. "It's amazing."

I alternated between her breasts, kissing, sucking, rolling the tips between my fingers. She writhed beneath me, hips rolling like she didn't know what else to do with herself.

"God, you smell good," I said, nuzzling into the hollow of her neck. "I could stay here forever."

"You make me feel—" She cut off, lost the words.

"Safe?" I prompted.

She nodded.

"Desired?"

Another nod. Another moan.

"Worshipped?"

That made her laugh, breathless and real. "Now, that's a strong word."

"It's the right one," I told her, and meant it.

My mouth found her lips again, and this time the kiss was slow, almost lazy, like we had all night. My hand drifted down her side, pausing at the waistband of her panties.

I stopped, waiting for her to say it was okay. She bit her lip, then whispered, "Please."

I slid them off, letting my fingers linger on the swell of her ass, the tender inside of her thighs. When she was finally bare before me, I had to shut my eyes for a moment just to keep from losing it right there.

She trembled, but not from fear. "JT," she whispered, "I... I don't know what to do."

"You're doing so good, Sunshine," I said. "Just let me take care of you."

She nodded, then closed her eyes and let me have my way.

I settled between her legs, one hand kneading her breast, the other running slow circles over her stomach. I kissed down her body, tasting every inch of her, memorizing the texture and heat of her skin. When I reached the juncture of her thighs, she tensed.

I looked up, checking in. "Okay?"

She hesitated, then nodded. "Yeah. I just... I feel awkward."

"Let go, baby," I said. "If I do anything you don't like, you can tell me."

She shivered, then whispered, "Maybe... tell me what to do."

Every man's dream.

"Of course, sweetheart. Can you open your legs for me? Just pull your knees up and let them fall open." She opened herself up to me. Her pussy was dripping, just begging for my tongue.

Her scent hit me like a fist, and my wolf nearly lost its mind. I kissed her inner thigh, then edged closer, letting her feel my breath before my tongue. When I finally tasted her, it was like nothing I'd ever known—sweet, tart, uniquely her.

She gasped, hips lifting off the bed, and I wrapped my arms around her thighs to hold her still.

"That's it, beautiful," I murmured. "Just feel."

I licked her slow at first, then faster, matching the rhythm of her breathing.

"You are a fucking masterpiece. Okay, love, I'm going to slip my finger inside you. I want to stretch you a bit so you can get ready for my cock."

When I slipped a finger inside, her whole body arched. I could tell she was right at the edge, so I pulled back and slowed down, not wanting it to be over too soon.

She groaned, frustrated and needy, and I smiled against her skin. "Patience, Sunshine."

I looked up at her through her legs to find she'd lifted herself up on her elbows so she could see me going to town on her pussy. The look on her face was nothing less than ecstasy.

"Please," she begged.

I went harder, sucking her clit, curling my fingers inside her until she shattered, throwing her head back, crying out my name. I never much liked being called Jonas, but when she screamed it in the throes of her release, I'd never heard a sweeter word. The sound echoed off the walls, wild and free, and I drank it in like a benediction.

I'd never seen anything sexier in my whole goddamn life.

When she finally came down, she was boneless, loose; her face glowing and hair wild.

I crawled over her body and devoured her mouth. I wanted to crawl inside her. My hands tugged at her hair as my mouth ravaged hers. She wrapped her legs around my waist as her fingers ran through my hair.

I pulled back and looked at her swollen lips. I almost felt bad for how rough I was being, but I saw nothing but wild hunger in her eyes.

"I have to be inside you now."

She groaned, eyes shining. "Oh, thank fuck. I need more."

And I vowed right then and there to give her everything.

I ran my hand down her body, savoring the velvety softness of her skin. I knew that she'd have some difficulty receiving my size, so I wanted her pussy wet and slick as possible. I pressed a finger inside her again as I kissed and sucked on one of her peaked nipples. Her moans ratcheted up; the sound was a symphony. Her hips writhed against my hand.

I released her breast with a small pop and then licked my way up her neck as I added a second finger to her entrance.

"Let me... see you. All of you." She murmured between my lips.

I pulled my hand free of her pussy, licked my fingers clean, then leaned up on my knees and pulled down my boxers. My cock sprang free, bobbing up to my stomach. Her eyes went wide, then wider. "Oh."

I gripped myself. "See why?" I said, not sure if I should be proud or embarrassed.

She bit her lip, shook her head. "Wow. It will fit, right?"

I laughed, then spread her thighs with my knee, easing myself between her legs as I continued to stroke my length.

"I have no doubt my love. You were made for me."

She stared down at where our bodies touched, the contrast between my dark tan and somewhat mottled and her pale, perfect skin so stark it looked unreal. I rubbed the head of my cock up and down her pussy, gathering her wetness, hitting her clit several times until she was begging me for release.

"You ready?" I asked, voice gone hoarse.

She nodded. "Please!"

I lined myself up, then stopped, catching her gaze. "It's going to hurt a little at first. I'll go slow, I promise."

When I leaned over her, she grabbed my shoulders, nails digging in just enough to let me know she didn't want to wait.

I pushed in, slow and steady, inch by inch. She gasped, and I felt her tense, so I stilled, waiting for her to breathe through it.

"You're doing great, sweetheart. Relax as much as you can," I murmured, kissing her eyelids, her nose, her cheek. "Tell me if it's too much."

She shook her head, tears at the corners of her eyes but smiling all the same. "Keep going. Please."

I slid in until I felt the resistance of her virginity.

"Okay, baby, this will hurt just a minute, but I'll make it better so fast." I started rubbing her clit as I quickly went hard into her. She flinched just for a moment as I was seated all the way.

The heat of her, the pressure, the way she gripped me—it was like nothing I'd ever felt. I braced myself above her, barely moving, just letting her get used to the fullness. My wolf sat up at attention. *"Mate."* He'd made the declaration often since I'd met her, but oh, I felt it in my soul in this moment. I don't know how this would work, but Aspen *was* my mate; there was no denying it.

I shook myself as she caught her breath, then laughed, a startled, joyous sound. "Oh my God, I'm so full of you. You're everywhere."

"That's because I've filled you entirely." I whispered, rocking my hips in tiny, slow motions.

She moaned, the sound low and desperate, lifting her hips. "Papa, you can... you don't have to go so slow."

"Yes, I do," I said, and kissed her hard.

I started a rhythm, slow but building, every stroke matched to her breath and the way her nails bit into my back. She wrapped her legs around my waist, pulling me deeper, her body learning the rhythm as we moved together.

The fire painted us gold, flickers of light racing over her skin. I watched every ripple of pleasure cross her face, every bite of her lip, every time she tried to hide her sounds behind the back of her hand. I pinned her hands down, made her look at me.

"Don't hide," I said. "I want to see everything."

She didn't look away. Not once.

Her walls fluttered around me, and I knew she was close, so I reached between us, rubbed slow circles around her clit, and her whole body went rigid. She came again, her voice breaking on my name, and the sight of her undid me. I poured everything I was into her, holding her tight as I came, shaking and gasping like a man starved too long at last allowed to feast. Again my wolf howled inside of me, *"Mate."* I wanted to knot her; I'd felt the urge. My teeth started to elongate for my bite, but I'd willed them to stop. I had to wait. I didn't want to hurt her.

For a long minute, we just breathed together, heartbeats thumping in sync.

I pulled out and rolled us onto our sides, spooning her close, tucking her against my chest. She burrowed into me, wrapping my arm around her waist.

"Is this okay?" I asked, not wanting to break the spell.

She nodded, sleep already heavy in her voice. "I've never felt this safe. Or happy."

I kissed the back of her head, inhaled her scent, and let myself believe the universe might finally be on my side.

After a few minutes, I got up and went to the en suite and soaked a cloth in hot water. She was drifting off to sleep when I carefully spread her legs and cleaned the evidence of our lovemaking. Her contented sigh gave me a sense of wholeness I'd not felt since before I'd experienced the terror of that bomb almost ten years ago. I crawled into bed next to her and pulled her against me and slept peacefully for the first time in years.

CHAPTER 11

Aspen

When I woke, the sky outside Papa's bedroom was still lavender with the last whispers of night. The air was soft and a little chilly, and the only sounds were the faint hum of the heater and the rustle of the expensive sheet over our tangled legs. His bed was enormous, the mattress cradling me so deep I felt like a pearl inside an oyster shell. I didn't move at first, just lay there, memorizing the warmth of his bare chest under my hand as I lay cuddled to his side. I could feel his heartbeat where my forearm lay across his ribs, steady and slow.

I looked at his sleeping face slanted towards me, lips slightly parted. In the half-light, he looked even more enormous than usual. Hair a mess, lashes thick and dark against his cheekbones, his beard shaggy from sleep. His arm opposite of where I lay cuddled, broad and muscled and battered from the remnants of war, was tucked back behind his head. His right leg was bent at the knee, his foot resting against his left knee. He looked like peace personified.

Looking at him caused something else too; a heat, low and insistent, to coil at the base of my spine. Every part of me was sore and humming from the night before, but all it took was the memory of his mouth, the way he'd looked at me like I was the answer to every prayer, and my body came alive again, hungry for more.

I propped myself up on one elbow, careful not to wake him, and watched the slow rise and fall of his chest. The sheets had slipped down to his hips, and the early light made a study in shadows of every line and scar across his torso. There were so many—some white and flat, some ridged and rough, a patchwork of old wounds stitched into the map of his body. I wanted to trace every single one with my tongue.

I scooted a little closer, the mattress barely dipping beneath my weight. His cock, half-hard, peeked out from beneath the sheet, and I felt a rush of heat that made my knees go weak all over again. I'd never seen one up close before last night, not really, and even now it seemed unreal—thick, beautiful, curved toward his stomach. I reached out, slow, barely breathing, and let my fingertips hover a hairsbreadth from his skin.

I hesitated, my confidence still new and fragile, but the urge to touch him, to know him, was stronger than my nerves. I let my hand drift over his abs, pausing at every scar, every dip and hollow. I pressed a soft kiss to his belly, then another to the edge of a jagged line near his ribs. His breath hitched, just a little, but he didn't wake.

I worked my way down, kissing my way along the path of old wounds until I reached the sheet. My heart was hammering so loud I was afraid it would wake him, but I didn't stop. I slid the sheet down, exposing his hips and the dark line of hair that arrowed down from his belly button. I pressed my mouth to the top of his thigh, tasting salt and sleep and something uniquely him.

I let my hand wrap gently around his cock as far as it would go, not squeezing, just holding him. He twitched in my palm, swelling instantly to full hardness. The feel of him, so hot and alive, made my mouth go dry.

His voice came, rough and low, eyes still closed: "Sunshine. What are you up to?"

I froze, mortified, but he opened one eye and grinned at me, all sleepy wolf.

I lay across his belly with a small giggle. "I just wanted to touch it; to see how it feels."

"Well, by all means, don't let me stop you." He waved his hand toward his erection.

The heat in my face could have lit a small town. "I, uh, wasn't sure if you'd want—"

"I always want," he said, rolling his other arm under his head. His cock stood proud, thick and heavy, flushed full against the tan of his stomach. He tilted his head, eyes soft. "You don't have to be shy with me, Aspen. Not ever."

"Only thing is...I don't know what I'm doing."

"Do what feels right, sweetheart. I'll tell you if I want something different. Just watch your teeth."

That gave me courage. I shifted, tucking my legs under me, and leaned down to run my tongue along the thick ridge of his shaft. I felt him shudder, felt the muscle in his thigh jump. His hand found my hair, gentle, threading through the dark strands, not pushing but guiding.

"Like that, sweetheart," he murmured.

I kept at it, slow at first, then bolder, wrapping my lips around the head and swirling my tongue the way I remembered him doing to me. The taste was earthy, salty, and not delicious, but I loved the taste because it was his.

"That's it. Wet it all the way down and move your hands up and down where your mouth can't reach. I'm not opposed to your gently touching my balls."

I smiled against his hardness at his instructions. His deep groans made my pussy clench when my fingers made their way across his tightening balls. His head was back, and his beautiful face was lost in a look of pure bliss. I relaxed my throat as much as I could and took him deeper until the head of his cock hit my throat. My tongue moved in a sucking motion as I tried to swallow him down, letting my hands pump the base, and was rewarded by the low, helpless groan he let out.

"Fuuuck, you're a quick study," he said, voice strained.

I couldn't help but smile around him. I looked up, searching for his eyes, and found them glassy and dark, fixed on my face like I was the only thing in the universe.

He let me keep going for a long, glorious minute, but then he squeezed my shoulder and gently pulled me up.

"Come here," he said, voice gone gravel. He sat up, grabbed my hips, and hauled me onto his lap like I weighed nothing at all. I straddled him, knees on either side of his waist, and the feel of his cock hard against my slick, aching center almost made me come right then and there.

He pushed my t-shirt up and over my head, baring my breasts, and bent to take one in his mouth, sucking until I moaned. His hands were everywhere—up my back, down to cup my ass, then in my hair, tilting my head so he could kiss me, open and deep.

I ground down against him, desperate, and he lined himself up and slid inside, slow and careful, like he was savoring every inch. The stretch was intense, but there was no pain this time, just a delicious fullness that made my toes curl.

He held still, buried balls deep, and stroked my spine with his palm. "You good?"

"So good," I whispered, rocking my hips.

He thrust up, slow and controlled, letting me set the pace. I rode him, leaning back to brace my hands on his knees, and watched his eyes as I took him deeper, harder. He bit his lip, jaw clenched, but his hands were gentle on my hips, guiding, holding, never taking.

"Goddamn, you're beautiful," he said, voice thick.

I felt the orgasm building; the pressure coiling in my belly, and I chased it, moving faster, grinding down on him until the world blurred at the edges. He knew, he always knew, and reached between us, rubbing his thumb over my clit in tight, perfect circles.

I broke apart with a cry, body clenching around him, and he followed, pulling me down so hard I thought we might fuse together. He came with a grunt, arms wrapped tight around me, and for a long, endless moment, neither of us moved.

After, he held me close, rocking me gently in his lap, his breath in my hair. "That was a hell of a way to wake up, Sunshine."

I laughed, giddy and a little dazed. "Best morning ever."

He cupped my chin, kissed me again, softer now, lingering like he didn't want to let go. "You're dangerous, you know that?" he said, lips brushing my cheek.

"That's me Aspen Waters, dangerous newly curious sex machine," I giggled.

He pulled me into his chest, and we lay back together, arms and legs tangled, hearts pounding in the hush before sunrise.

There was no hurry now. No shame. No doubt.

Just the heat of his skin, the promise of the day ahead, and the bright, impossible hope that maybe I'd finally found the place where I belonged.

The next time I surfaced, the sun was a pale, smudgy smear behind the frosted glass above the shower. I could hear the pipes ticking as they came alive, and then the hiss of water hitting tile. I blinked sleep out of my eyes and realized Papa was already up, his side of the bed still warm, the sheets rucked halfway to the floor. I stretched, luxuriating in the ache between my legs and the floaty, sated feeling that made every nerve in my body tingle.

The bathroom was attached to the bedroom—a big, open space with stone floors and a bench built right into the wall. When I padded in, he was standing under the spray, head tilted back, water streaming down over his shoulders and chest. Steam curled in the air and beaded on every mirror. The sight of him naked, all muscle and strength, but completely at ease, made my knees a little wobbly.

He caught me staring in the mirror and grinned, then reached out a hand. "C'mere, Sunshine."

I hesitated, a little shy again, but the air was so warm and he looked so inviting that I stepped right in, letting the heat and the closeness wash over me. He pulled me gently into the spray, turning me until my back pressed against his chest. His hands went straight to my hair, gathering it up and wringing out the tangles with more patience than I would've believed possible.

He twisted my hair into a messy bun and secured it with a black elastic he'd produced from somewhere—I didn't even ask—and then set about soaping me down, shoulders to toes, never missing a spot. He washed himself too, but fast, like he didn't want to waste a second that could be spent on me.

When he was satisfied we were both clean, he shut off the water and reached for a towel—thick, soft, and the color of fresh cream. He wrapped it around me and lifted me out of the shower as if I weighed nothing, holding me tight to his chest.

"I could get used to this," he said, shoulders dry. "Having you here."

The words hit me square in the heart. I hugged the towel tighter, feeling small and safe and a little dazed.

He walked me over to the vanity and set me on a stool, then went to the dresser in the bedroom and came back with a fresh pair of boxers and some joggers—navy, with a drawstring—and one of his oversized gray t-shirts. He helped me into the boxers first. He rolled them a few times until he was sure they would stay put. Then the pants. He cinched the waist and rolled the cuffs up so they didn't drag, then tugged the shirt over my head.

It smelled like him: smoke and citrus and something warm and deep that I could never quite name.

I stared at myself in the mirror, barely recognizing the girl looking back. My cheeks were pink, my hair a wild knot on top of my head, the shirt swallowing me whole. I looked like I belonged here.

Papa stood behind me, arms folded around me, a little smile on his lips. He leaned down and kissed the side of my neck, then turned me gently on the stool so I faced him.

"Listen," he said, and for the first time since I'd met him, I saw real nerves in his eyes. "I know we're moving fast. I know you've got a lot going on with the bakery, and the stalker, and the pack, and... everything. But after last night, hell, after this morning, I can't stand the thought of you in that apartment alone. Not with everything that's happening."

My pulse jumped. I bit my lip, afraid to hope for what he might say next.

"I want you here, Aspen. For good. Or at least until we get this mess with the stalker sorted out." He squeezed my hands, voice low and urgent. "You can have your own room if you want, or take over the entire house, I don't care. Just—be here. With me."

I blinked, stunned. "Are you... asking me to move in with you?"

His smile crooked up, a little sheepish. "Yeah. I guess I am."

The relief that washed over me was so strong I almost started crying. I'd been so certain he'd think I was too much, that this was a one-night or one-weekend kind of thing. But here he was, asking me to stay, because I mattered to him.

"I'd like that," I said, voice trembling. "A lot."

He looked so happy it made my chest ache. "Good. Then after we eat at Pearl's this afternoon, we'll go to your place and pack up your things. You're not going back there alone."

I nodded, not trusting myself to speak. I couldn't remember ever being wanted this way. My mama loved me, but she had to. That was the rule.

He pressed a kiss to my forehead. "Finish doing what you need to do in here. I'll make breakfast."

He left me in the bathroom, but I could hear him humming as he padded down the hall. I dried off, straightened my hair as best I could, and cinched the drawstring on the joggers a little tighter. I brushed my teeth with the spare toothbrush he'd already set out for me, then padded into the kitchen on bare feet.

He'd already started the coffee, the smell filling the house. There were eggs and bacon on the stove, and he was slicing thick bread for toast. He moved with the quiet confidence of someone who'd done this a thousand times, but every so often he'd glance over and check that I was still there, still real.

I poured myself a cup of coffee, doctored it up just the way I liked, and slid onto a barstool at the kitchen counter.

He set a plate in front of me—eggs scrambled with sharp cheddar, bacon crisp and perfect, two slices of toast dripping with butter and honey. It was so good I almost moaned.

We ate in easy silence, the morning sun climbing higher outside the window, glinting off the fields and setting the whole kitchen aglow.

When we'd finished, he took my hand and pulled me in for a long, slow kiss. "You sure you're ready for this?" he asked, voice just a whisper.

"I've never been more sure of anything in my life," I said, and meant it.

He smiled, then gave me a little swat on the butt. "Go grab your stuff. We'll head out soon."

I watched him for a second, the way his back bent over the sink as he rinsed our plates, the way his arms flexed even in something as simple as pouring more coffee. I tried to memorize the sound of his voice, the shape of his hands, the bright way my heart beat when I thought about what came next.

On the way to the bakery, he told me about his family. I was surprised to learn that his parents didn't live in pack territory. They and his brother owned and ran an oil and gas company, so they lived in West Texas. JT declined to partake in the family business when he left the military, but his name is still a part of the business, so he has shares that pay him dividends. That's why he can basically work at Bronc's shop and do assignments for him whenever he needs him. I guess the oil business pays well.

"I hope your parents won't be disappointed that you chose me."

He squeezed my knee.

"There is no way they won't love you, sweetheart. How could they not adore someone who adores their son?"

"I *do* adore you, you know?" I told him. And never were truer words spoken.

"I've gotten that feeling." He winked at me.

We got to the bakery, and I started gathering up the new clothes I'd purchased since I got here weeks ago. Papa helped in packing everything. He ran next door to the hardware store and picked up a couple of duffel bags since I'd left the coven with almost nothing and needed something to put all of my things in.

Oscar appeared at the foot of my bed. "Are we moving?"

I about jumped out of my skin at his sudden appearance. "So, you're just gonna pop in and speak aloud from now on?"

"It's rude to carry on private conversations in front of other people. Your mate would likely be offended, and I don't want to anger the giant wolf."

I laughed, in spite of myself. "You're right. I need to tie a bell around your neck so I'd have some warning."

"You'll do no such thing. I have my pride you know." He was so offended.

I went to my secret place behind the loosened wall slat and pulled out my mother's grimoire. It vibrated slightly in my hand when I removed it from the wall. I almost dropped it. I made a surprised sound.

Papa came into the room. "Everything okay in here? Oh, hello, Oscar."

Oscar nodded toward him. "Sir. And yes, I've decided to just speak out loud from now on. It's rude to have quiet conversations when others are around."

Papa's face was priceless. "I think that's a nice thing, Oscar. Thank you. Now, *you*." He looked down at me on the floor. "You okay?"

I was sitting on the floor with the book on my lap.

"I'm good. The book just has a life of its own sometimes. It's trying to tell me something but still refuses to let me open it to make it easier."

Chapter 12

Big Papa

Most mornings, Iron Valor's clubhouse was a shrine to hangovers and burnt coffee, but on Mondays, it woke up mean and sharp for the mandatory all-officer meet. I rolled up just after dawn, engine ticking in the cold and sunrise fighting through a haze of wood smoke and diesel exhaust. I left Aspen at the bakery when it opened and headed back to the compound. I walked up the steps, hands jammed in the pockets of my hoodie, because the wind out on the prairie didn't give a shit about your pedigree.

Inside, the long main room was already alive with wolf scent and the clatter of boots on concrete. Bronc presided from his usual spot at the head of the battered oak table. He wore jeans, a black t-shirt that said, "MAKE IT HURT," and his leather vest with the Iron Valor patch stitched proud across the back. He looked every inch the Alpha: hair peppered with more silver than last year, blue eyes that could freeze a bar fight mid-swing, and a mug of black coffee that steamed like a hot spring. Wrecker and Arsenal flanked him, both with their own mugs, both eyeing the rest of us as we filed in. Gunner had the kitchen detail, but he'd already laid out a pile of breakfast tacos and a tray of coffee mugs.

I nodded to Bronc, squeezed in next to Wrecker, and grabbed the nearest taco. The tortillas were buttery and grilled to perfection. The eggs, sausage and cheese inside tasted just right swimming in salsa, and my wolf was already awake and wanting fuel. Maddie, the only civilian at the table, hovered at the far end with her own thermos and a notebook, ready to record every word.

Bronc smacked the table to start. "Settle in. We got a week to the mating ceremony, and a list of shit to cover before then. First up, Arsenal. Security check."

Arsenal leaned back, eyes scanning the room like he was counting possible exits. "Ceremony will be in the clearing. The perimeter will be cleared by 3:00. But we'll have Wrecker's new motion sensors on every trailhead, plus two volunteers in the woods with night scopes. If your people are on the list, their names better match their faces, or you're not coming in."

Bronc gave him a slow nod. "Good. Can't have ghosts gettin' in. Wrecker?"

Wrecker looked up, steel-gray eyes bright under the dim bulbs. "I've run every background check twice. Anyone who even smells like a threat is already flagged in my system. I'll sweep comms morning of, so no one's leaking the time or place. Security feed is clean, no signs of pack warfare coming our way, only outsiders on the invite list are the Kozlovs, Rafe, and Archon, but I'll keep an eye on chatter."

I sipped my coffee, feeling the last scraps of fatigue burn off. Arsenal never missed a trick, and Wrecker could out-think a NASA mission control team, but something in Bronc's posture said the real agenda was still circling the room, teeth bared.

"Gunner," Bronc called. "What's the plan for food and drink?"

Gunner grinned from his perch by the window. "Full open bar, kegs on ice. Maddie and Pearl are running the kitchen, menu's already set. Brisket, sausage, and more sides than you can count. Veggies for the weirdos. There'll be food for three days, so nobody goes home sober if they don't want to."

Bronc made a small smile and turned his gaze on me. "Big Papa. Update on your end?"

I cleared my throat, all eyes shifting my way. "Aspen's got the cake on lockdown. It'll be good to go morning of. We'll deliver 3:00 for assembly on site. I moved her into my place. We're running an escort whenever she has to be in town alone, but mostly she's locked down tight in the house. Her familiar appeared several days ago. A prairie dog with a British accent named Oscar. He is with her at all times—hell, the guy's probably got more vigilance than half this room. I trust him to sound the alarm if anything weird happens."

A small ripple of surprise moved through the table. Wrecker arched one eyebrow. "Moved in? That official, or just a security thing?"

"Both," I said. "Given what went down at County Line, I'm not taking any chances. She's a target."

Gunner whistled low. "Yeah, about that—Arsenal, why the hell would Morgantown send muscle up here when they got their own bars and women closer to home? We got no beef with them."

Arsenal leaned forward, voice dropping to a dangerous hush. "That's what I'm trying to figure. Morgantown's Alpha is a greedy bastard, but he's not dumb. He doesn't let his dogs off the chain without reason. I ran the plates of the guy who grabbed Aspen at the bar—nothing in the system, but I bet my left nut he's a paid runner. They wanted to see what would happen if they pushed our buttons."

"Testing boundaries," Bronc growled, a muscle jumping in his jaw. "Next time, we break a few."

"Next time, there won't be a warning," I promised. My wolf didn't like the idea of anyone laying hands on Aspen. My human side liked it even less.

Bronc's gaze flicked to Wrecker. "Status on the green jacket man?"

Wrecker cleared his throat. "I wanted to wait until we were all together before I brought this news."

I leaned back in the creaky chair, the smell of burnt coffee and gun oil thick in the air, as Wrecker slapped the grainy photo of that damn symbol onto the table. My knuckles went white around the edge of the wood. "Spit it out," I growled, though the dread pooling in my gut already knew.

"Demonic tracking sigil," Wrecker said, voice like gravel. "Old. Nasty. Burns a trail straight to whatever poor bastard it's latched onto." The scar on my jaw twitched. "Maltraz had to have sent him. Why? That's the big question."

"That Verdant Hollow Wyrdmother must have something on him." My teeth ground hard enough to spark. Maltraz was her dog now, sniffing out Aspen like she was some prize to drag back. That green-jacketed bastard at the bakery hadn't just been passing through—he'd marked her. Left a breadcrumb for hell itself to follow.

Arsenal leaned back, calculating. "It was just a matter of time. We just have to step up patrols. Maltraz isn't stupid enough to come at us himself. We're not letting anyone who doesn't belong get to any of our people."

"Oscar seems to think the real enemy won't show up until they think Aspen's vulnerable. Right now, we're a locked gate. They're probing for weak links."

Arsenal shrugged. "So we become a wall. Simple."

"Simple until it isn't," I said. "There's another variable. The grimoire."

That got everyone's attention. Wrecker shut the laptop and stared hard at me. "She still has it?"

"She's never let it out of her sight. Until now. Now, it's at my house, in a safe when she's not trying to get it open. Then the rodent is on guard even when she sleeps. But it's waking up. There's a pulse to it, like a heartbeat. Some mornings, it vibrates so hard she can't keep it on the shelf."

Maddie spoke up for the first time, eyes shining with curiosity. "Does it talk to her? Or is it more like a magic 8-ball—shakes and gives a cryptic hint?"

"She says it feels like her mom trying to warn her, but nothing concrete. No voices, just instincts. Seems like her magic has been locked up, and there's a chance the grimoire is the only thing standing between her and whatever's hunting her."

Bronc rubbed his chin. "Is there a risk it could fall into the wrong hands?"

I shook my head. "Not unless someone can break the safe, outsmart Oscar, and get past a territory full of trained killers. Then there's still the matter of who the hell her father is."

Gunner let out a slow, "Well, shit."

Wrecker looked at me, calculating. "You think her old coven knows, so they want to take her out because of it?"

"I think that coven leader is pissed that she doesn't know, but she mostly just wants to get her hands on that book. But it wouldn't surprise me if they wanted her bloodline too. But fuck us. Since that's a worst-case scenario situation, and we're Iron Valor and we deal almost specifically in worst-case situations—I'd say the odds are likely that's how the chips will fall."

Arsenal grunted, then asked the queen mother of dumbass questions. "Have you asked her who her father is?"

I looked at him like he'd grown a second head. "Are you *serious* right now, dude? I thought I'd explained that her mother didn't fucking tell her! The only thing she knows is that he wasn't a witch, and she suspects he was supernatural. He's 'other' whatever the *fuck* that means. But if even *that* information gets out, it puts a bullseye on her forehead. Is that clear enough for you?"

My patience was at an end.

Arsenal put his hands up in surrender. I love my brothers, all of them. But Arsenal was the most bullheaded and most hard assed of all of us. He sometimes acted like his shit didn't stink, and he was always the quickest to judge and be suspicious, especially of the women that had joined our pack.

Bronc's voice was gentle but absolute. "Well, just be ready cuz I got a nagging feeling that now that the demons might have helped locate her, they might be scared of that bitch Wyrdmother. We just need to be on guard for whatever she might send our way."

Arsenal leaned in, voice flat and final. "So, what do we do?"

I locked eyes with Bronc, then Arsenal, then around the whole table. "We keep her safe. We watch every road, every shadow, every oddball who comes near the territory. And if anyone tries to take her—witch, demon, or otherwise—they answer to me first."

Bronc looked at me for a long moment. His mouth twitched, just barely, into a smile. "You heard him. Aspen Waters is now Iron Valor business. Anyone comes after her, they're coming after all of us. With the mating ceremony on the horizon, I need heads on swivels. This won't be anything we can't handle. Now, let's get out there and take care of our business. Meeting adjourned."

The table emptied fast, most of the men heading out to the yard to start the day's work or to the range behind the barn. Bronc motioned me aside before I could leave. "You alright, Papa? You've got a look about you."

I considered lying, then shrugged. "I'm fine. Just don't want to see her get hurt."

"It's your mate bond I'd guess."

I gave him a worried look. "That's another thing I'm worried about. How is this supposed to work? The claim? How does our bond work, especially since she's a hybrid and not a wolf at all? I want to bite, knot, and claim her, Alpha! But since she's not a wolf and not built to take it, I'm afraid I'd rip her apart. I mean, shit. Will her body work like an omega's body since we're mated? Will it open to accommodate me? This is unfamiliar territory for me here." I raked my hands through my hair.

He clapped a hand on my shoulder, almost making me drop my coffee. "You got yourself a brand new dilemma, brother. One I don't have the slightest clue about. Get in touch with Menace. He's got a big, fancy library on his compound. He can do some research on wolf and witch mating. Since you've had the urge to bite and knot her, my inclination is that's nature telling you that's what is supposed to happen."

I thought about it. "I've just been so careful with her. I don't want to harm her."

"Get Menace to do some research and go from there," he said. He gave me another pat on the back and then let me go. "Tell Aspen we're behind her. Tell her she's got family now, whether she likes it or not."

I finished my coffee and headed into the control room Wrecker had set up that he used to monitor Teams face-to-face meetings. I dialed up Menace. After two rings, my former VP's face filled the screen.

"Big Papa! I did *not* expect to see your beautiful face on the other end of this call this morning. What's up?"

I explained my dilemma to him and asked for his help. Luckily for me, he not only has a vast library, he also has several librarians on staff who do the work for him. He promised me by day's end I'd have all the information I could want on wolf/witch mating.

"Hey brother, I cannot thank you enough for this. I want to do only what is best for my mate. I know you understand." I told him.

He looked at me with the eyes of a man who had almost lost his mate. "I know what it is to be going crazy over an issue with your mate. That's why we're gonna figure this out as quick as possible. Keep her safe, man, and we'll talk soon." With that, the screen when blank.

I was ready to get my eyes on my mate. I sent her a quick text message. *Headed your way. Be there in twenty. Hope you're having a great morning.*

Her reply was almost instant: *We've been busy, busy. Oscar's standing guard; my invisible sentry. And I made lemon scones for you.*

I shook my head, grinning at the phone. If anyone could make a potential attack feel like a sleepover, it was her.

Normal closing time for the bakery was 2:00 p.m. but when I got to town at 10:00 a.m. a chalkboard sign in the window read, "CLOSED FOR LUNCH." I circled the building, searching the street for any trace of trouble, but nothing looked out of place except for a flower pot knocked over outside the store, spilling its dirt on the walkway like it had given up on life. I looked through the window and saw that the lights were off. The door was locked. I knocked anxiously.

Aspen opened the door a crack. Her hair was pulled back in a messy knot, and she wore leggings and boots and an Amarillo State University sweatshirt that hung off one shoulder. There was a look in her eyes I'd never seen before: wary, a little wild, and underneath, furious.

"Oh good, you're here," she said as she yanked me into the store by my arm.

She pulled me inside and dead-bolted the door behind us. The bakery was neat as always—display cases wiped, chairs stacked on the tables—but it smelled less like rising dough and more like the aftermath of a kitchen fire. Aspen motioned me to the back. I followed, wolf senses on high alert, and spotted Oscar on the counter, fur standing straight up and his little claws leaving white scuffs in the laminate as he paced back and forth.

Aspen gestured at the espresso machine. "Want a coffee?" Her voice was too bright. I recognized it from the war: the sound of someone who had just survived an ambush.

"Sit down, Sunshine," I said gently. "Tell me what happened."

She hesitated, then pulled out a chair and sat, hands in her lap. I watched her take three slow breaths before she started.

"She must have waited until the shop was empty. At about nine twenty-five, someone came in." She shook her head. "Not the green jacket man. Different, but the same kind of wrong." She looked up, eyes searching mine for judgment. "It was a woman this time. She looked like a customer at first—skinny, fake blonde, nice purse—but the minute she opened her mouth I knew."

"Knew what?" I said, voice soft.

"That she hated me," Aspen whispered. "She called me the 'fat witch who thinks she can hide.' She said she recognized me from the coven. Then she asked if I was ready to pay for what I'd done."

My hand curled into a fist under the table. "Did you recognize her?"

Aspen shook her head. "No. But she knew all about me. She said things that nobody but the old coven would know. Then she reached across the counter and tried to grab me."

Oscar, who had been pacing, stopped cold. "She intended harm, sir. If I had not intervened—"

Aspen reached over and stroked the top of his head, calming him. "Oscar jumped up and, I don't know, did something. There was a light, like a flashbulb, and a wind that knocked the woman backward. She screamed and ran out."

"She say anything else?" I asked.

Aspen nodded, jaw clenched. "She said she'd be back. She said the next time, I wouldn't have my 'furry little friend' to protect me." Aspen shuddered but didn't look away. "She wanted to make me hurt. Like they did before."

I wanted to break something. "She's not coming back," I said, and meant it. I took off my jacket and draped it over her shoulders. She tensed at first, then leaned in, letting the weight settle. My wolf pressed against my skin, demanding blood, but I pushed it down.

"I'm sorry," Aspen whispered. "I should be stronger. I'm just so tired of being—"

"Stop," I said. "You don't have to be strong all the time. Not with me. You did everything right."

She blinked, then covered her face with her hands. I sat beside her, pulled her close. The bakery was silent except for Oscar's little claws click-clicking across the counter and the hum of the fridge.

After a minute, Aspen straightened. "I'm done being helpless," she said, and this time her voice rang clear. "Oscar and I are opening the grimoire tonight. I'm going to learn what it's been trying to teach me. I don't care if it burns my hands off."

Oscar puffed up, proud. "I concur, Miss. It is time."

She met my gaze, all green fire and stubborn hope. "Mama left me that book for a reason. I've just accepted things are the way they are my whole life, Papa. I've let people bully me, and I've hidden myself away and allowed them to push me inside myself. But this is my home now. I'm done hiding. I've always had a spark of magic. I think that place held it down. But no more."

I brushed the hair from her cheek and kissed her forehead. "I'll be right beside you," I promised. "Every step. No one's getting through me or Oscar. Not ever."

She nodded, her hand finding mine. "Let's go home," she said. "I want to start right away."

Oscar hopped onto my shoulder, tiny paws gripping the fabric of my shirt. "We will need supplies. Candles, sea salt, perhaps a lemon and three eggs. And a number of other supplies."

Aspen rolled her eyes. "He's been reading too many recipe books."

"Preparation is key, Miss," Oscar replied, tone regal as always.

We packed up the register, locked the doors tight, and left the bakery behind. As we walked out into the daylight, I felt a new current running between us. Aspen's spine was straighter, her gaze steadier. The fear was still there, but it was laced with something harder, something that would not be moved.

By the time we reached the truck, I realized it wasn't just me protecting her anymore.

Aspen was ready to fight back, and the world had better be ready for her.

CHAPTER 13

Wyrdmother, Verdant Hollow Coven

The only sound in the chamber was the brittle staccato of my fingernails drumming on the edge of the obsidian table. I found it soothing, this steady beat a reminder of the discipline that had seen me through four wars, seven betrayals, and the slow, sticky decay of power that threatened every Wyrdmother once the first streak of gray curled into her hair. Of course, my own hair had long since abandoned color, but I wore it in a crown of wild silver and platinum, thick as wire and twice as sharp. No one dared call me old. Not if they liked the current shape of their bones.

The chamber was the heart of Verdant Hollow, and it reflected my tastes: black marble floors laced with gold, high leaded windows in the southern tradition, velvet drapes the color of dried blood. One entire wall was devoted to the spoils of my reign—row upon row of glass vials, each labeled with names in a script only three living witches could read. Some vials contained venom, some tears, some whispers. The rest were more dangerous.

I'd had my trackers on the hunt for Aspen since the day she'd fled. I had heard she'd been found and was about to receive confirmation. The anteroom doors swung open with the hush of oiled hinges and the cautious shuffle of women who'd spent a lifetime learning to read my moods.

Olive led, tall and too thin in the face, her robes immaculate, her eyes sharp as an undertaker's scalpel. Maggie and Teela trailed behind, both clutching black leather satchels and avoiding my gaze with the subservient air of junior nuns in a room with the Pope.

Olive bowed her head just so, enough to acknowledge my status, not so much as to seem afraid. She set a small lacquered box before me and unlatched the gold clasp. The smell that drifted out was not quite floral, not quite sweet. It was the scent of blood magic, old and raw.

"She has been found, Wyrdmother."

She produced a square of receipt, folded into a neat triangle. "From Dairyville. A bakery called Buttercream & Blessings." I felt my pulse quicken.

"And?"

She didn't smile, but the corners of her mouth twitched. "Owned by one Aspen Waters."

Maggie produced another item; a clear zippered pouch holding a small tuft of gray-brown fur. She held it at arm's length, as if it might sprout fangs and bite. "This was found outside the girl's residence."

I reached for the bag, pinching the fur between two fingers. Instantly, a current ran up my arm—a tingle of residual energy, familiar and disgusting. "Wolf," I confirmed. "Male. Unbonded. The only pack in Dairyville, Texas is Iron Valor." I spat the name like a curse.

Teela's hand shook as she scribbled my words into her ledger.

"So," I said, letting the syllable hang like a sword, "the little dud has run to the mongrels. How poetic. Laurel always did have a sense for melodrama."

I let them bask in the humiliation for a moment, then snapped my fingers. We needed more information about her relationships. I had to know how she could be exploited for the easiest extraction.

I looked at my girls and let them know we had a bit more work to do.

"Get the bowl."

"Understood, Wyrdmother."

Olive took her place on my left, then silently handed me a small silk pouch, weighted at the bottom by something dense and slightly moist. "What we have of her hair, Wyrdmother," she murmured, eyes on her folded hands.

"Put it in the bowl," I said. Her fingers trembled just slightly as she worked the drawstring and dropped the hair into the oil. It hissed, then vanished.

Maggie and Teela crowded together. Maggie reeked of burned sage and cheap gin, but her instincts were good and her sense of loyalty, though mercenary, was at least predictable. Teela trailed behind, her bare feet leaving little ghostly prints on the flagstones. She was the least skilled of the three, but the most sensitive, and therefore the most useful for scrying.

They stood around the bowl with me, hands linked, heads bowed in anticipation.

"Let's see our little wayward child," I said, and dipped my own hand into the oil, just to the wrist. The surface clouded and then cleared. In the shimmering dark, Aspen Waters appeared, framed by the bright yellow and white awning around the window of a bakery. She wore her hair loose, like her mother always had, and the sight of her hands—capable, steady, dusted with flour—almost made me nostalgic.

Almost.

Teela exhaled, her voice dreamy. "She's with them now. The wolves, seems to be attached to one of them in particular. The scarred one."

Now, this piece of information changed things and gave me something I could work with.

"Describe the perimeter," I ordered.

Teela's brow furrowed. "No wards on the outermost fence. Protected by brute force. She comes and goes freely."

"Of course she does," I said. "She never learned to build a proper shield. Assemble an extraction team. I have a plan." I traced the edge of the scrying bowl with a single nail, leaving a thin red track in the oil. The best way to draw your prey was to use the proper bait.

Chapter 14

Aspen

I sat at the dining table in Papa's house, well...my house now, which I still could not believe. My hands were settled on either side of the ancient book, not quite ready to touch its cover. The grimoire still thrummed with its own little heartbeat, and the echo of this morning's attack in the bakery made me flinch at every vibration. The dining room was all polished wood and sunlight, a world apart from the wreckage inside my chest. But the scent of bacon, coffee, and sweet cream made me feel somehow safe.

"Don't be afraid of it, Miss," Oscar said, perched on a folded tea towel on the table. "It cannot harm you unless you wish it. Or unless you drop it on your foot. Which, given the size, would be most unpleasant." He flicked an imaginary speck of dust from his vest and adjusted his little wire-framed glasses, because apparently this was his serious familiar outfit.

I tried to laugh, but the sound stuck in my throat. "What if it doesn't open for me? What if I'm a big ol' failure just like all the other times?"

Oscar leveled his shiny black eyes at me. "Miss, if you can bake a perfect lemon scone while fending off the harpies of your past, you can open a family grimoire. It is far less hazardous to your self-esteem, I assure you." He flicked his tail with a flourish. "Now. Focus."

I pressed both palms to the book, letting its low thrum center me. The grimoire was heavy and old—bound in leather; the edges sealed with wax and some kind of silvery twine that reminded me of spiderwebs in moonlight. Whenever I tried to open it before, the clasp refused to budge, as if it had to be convinced of my worthiness. I'd pulled it from the safe when we'd gotten home from the bakery after the "grabby, creepy hag of rudeness" incident this morning. I thought it so thoughtful of Papa to insist on having the book stowed in the safe anytime we were out of the house. The grimoire was too large and heavy to haul around with us; that was for sure. Papa was a man who knew how to prepare for the worst.

The man himself bustled behind me in the kitchen, slicing tomatoes with the care of a bomb technician. He'd laid out everything for BLTs—bacon crisp and stacked, tomatoes salted and drained, lettuce so cold it snapped when you tore it. He was humming a country song, one I knew from childhood, and his voice was so low and even it vibrated through the chair into my bones. I found myself matching my breaths to his rhythm, like if I kept the same beat, I'd be invincible too.

He slid a mug of coffee toward me and topped it off, the dark liquid steaming, then added just enough cream to turn it the color of river mud. "You need to eat something," he said, giving my shoulder a gentle squeeze. "Can't open ancient tomes on an empty stomach."

His hand lingered a second longer than necessary. I looked up at him, saw the worry in his eyes, the same look he'd worn all morning. I wondered if he'd ever not be worried about me, if he'd ever be able to relax knowing I was safe. That a look of love mingled in that look gave my tummy a little tumble.

He set down the sandwiches—mine cut into neat triangles, his in two enormous halves—and set down a small bowl of fresh spinach and some small chopped carrots for Oscar even though as a familiar he didn't actually need to eat unless he just wanted to. Turned out, he did. He took his place at the head of the table, but didn't touch his food. Instead, he propped his elbows and watched, as if I was about to perform a magic trick that might blow up the house.

"I can leave if you want," he said softly. "If you need it to be just you and Oscar."

I shook my head. "No. I want you here." Then, because I felt like I owed him something after the morning he'd had, I added, "If you see sparks, please don't put me out with the fire extinguisher."

He smiled, that slow, crooked grin that always made my pulse skip. "Only if you turn green. I like you the way you are."

We ate in companionable silence, Oscar crunching away at his carrots and spinach deep in thought. Every few bites, I caught Papa staring at the book, like it might leap off the table and bite him. I almost told him he was being silly, but considering everything that'd happened lately, I kept my mouth shut.

Halfway through his second sandwich, his phone buzzed. He looked at the screen, frowned, then pushed away from the table. "It's Menace," he said, nodding toward the porch. "I need to take this."

I watched him retreat to the porch; the door closing behind him with a solid, comforting thunk. The windows let in strips of sun, making the dust motes sparkle. For a minute, I just listened to the quiet: the tick of the fridge, Oscar's little sighs, the far-off rumble of Papa's voice through the porch wall.

Oscar waited until he was sure Papa was out of earshot, then turned back to me, all business. "Right, Miss. We must be quick. That phone call won't last forever, and time is of the essence."

I glanced at the book, heart pounding. "What now?"

"Now, you center yourself. Recall your mother's voice. Let her be your guide." Oscar scooted closer, his claws trailing across the tea towel. "Place your hands upon the cover. Yes, both of them. Good. Now close your eyes. You, most importantly need to relax and remember this book contains the magic of your ancestors. Your family. This magic belongs to you. It's yours."

I did as I was told, swallowing hard.

Oscar's voice dropped to a whisper. "Remember her. Think of the days you baked together. Think of the first time you made her proud."

I thought back—past the anger, past the years of not fitting in, to the handful of moments when I'd belonged. Mama's hands on mine, showing me how to knead dough without breaking it. Her laugh, a wild guffaw when I turned on the mixer and sent flour everywhere, the way she brushed it off like nothing in the world mattered but me. I remembered the feel of her arms, strong and soft, holding me when I cried after the other girls mocked my magic. She never called me a dud. She just said I was different, and someday that would save me. I recalled her beauty, her long dark hair she'd braid and twist on top of her head, and her beautiful flawless skin and bright eyes.

Oscar must have sensed something in me shift. "Good, good. Hold that feeling."

I squeezed my eyes tighter, feeling the book grow hotter under my palms.

The world rippled and dissolved, and suddenly I was nowhere near the kitchen table or the comfort of Oscar's soft little voice. I was back inside the dream, the one I'd had a couple of weeks ago and woke up not being able to remember any details. It was the night the grimoire awoke. The details of the dream now came into focus.

The first thing I noticed was the cold. Not Texas cold, not that brittle morning air that made you hunch your shoulders and hurry to the truck, but something older, a wet-chill that got inside your bones and shivered up your spine. I looked down. I wasn't wearing cute leggings and a college sweatshirt—I was barefoot in a white dress, the hem already damp and dirty from dew and mud.

The land stretched away in every direction: wild grass, rolling hills, sky so wide it made your heart ache. But the thing that drew my eyes—and kept them there—was the ring of stones ahead of me, each one as tall as a man and black as sin. They were arranged in a perfect circle, the ground inside scraped flat and bare except for a spiral of salt, laid so carefully it must have been poured by hand. Every stone was carved with marks I didn't recognize, but some part of me understood them, anyway. They were the bones of my bloodline, and they hummed with a promise that felt half welcome, half terrifying.

I stepped forward, the grass icy against my skin, and the stones seemed to lean in, like curious elders sizing up the family disappointment. I half-expected to see Oscar at my feet, but I was alone, the only sound the wind and my own heartbeat.

I reached the edge of the spiral and stopped, not daring to break the salt. For a minute, nothing happened. The silence pressed in, so heavy I thought it would split me open.

Then, from the far side of the circle, a figure stepped out of the mist.

She moved slow, as if the air was thicker for her, but every step was certain. I recognized her right away—not because of her face, which was as blurred and shifting as a photograph left out in the rain, but because of the way she walked. Like the world owed her an explanation, and she'd wait forever to get it.

Mama.

Her dress was blue, the exact shade she used to wear on the days we baked together, and her hair was pinned up with the bone comb she'd inherited from her mother. She looked both younger and older than I remembered—her skin smooth, but her eyes carrying the weight of a thousand secrets.

She stopped at the spiral and waited, hands folded over her stomach. "Aspen," she said, her voice like home and heartache all at once. "You made it."

I tried to speak, but the words caught. I felt five years old again, hiding behind her legs while the world burned around us.

"You always were the stubborn one," Mama said, her mouth curling into a smile. "That's why you're here and not with them."

I stared at the spiral, not sure if I was supposed to cross it. "Am I dead?" I asked, and my own voice sounded small.

She laughed, a wild chuckle that rang off the stones. "If you were dead, you'd know. No, child, you're just dreaming. Dreaming true for the first time in your life."

The wind picked up, swirling the salt. I tasted it on my lips, sharp and old. "Why here?" I asked. "Why now?"

Mama looked at me, the smile fading. "Because it's time. They're coming, Aspen. And you need to be ready."

I swallowed, the chill in my feet climbing up my legs. "The wolves?"

She shook her head, sad. "The wolf is your salvation, your completion. I'm so proud that you found your wolf. But you know that already."

I still needed answers, so I asked, "Why did you make me leave?"

Her gaze softened. "Because if you'd stayed, you'd be dead already. Or worse." She touched her collarbone, where the grimoire pendant used to rest, and I saw a flash of firelight, a memory that wasn't mine. "I did everything I could to keep you safe, but it was never enough. You were meant for more than that little coven. Meant for more than being a dud."

The word stung, even from her. "Then what am I meant for?"

Mama's face grew distant, like she was watching something play out in the sky behind me. "Your strength is in the making, Aspen. In what you create, not what you destroy. The world needs more of that. More of you."

The stones began to pulse, faint at first, then stronger, until I could feel it in my teeth. The spiral at my feet glowed, each grain of salt a tiny sun. My heart beat faster. I thought of Papa, of Oscar, of the way I felt baking in the early hours—how sometimes, just sometimes, I felt like I was bending the world into sweetness.

I stepped closer. The salt should have burned, but it felt warm and clean, like stepping into the shallow end of a summer river.

Mama watched, proud and sad all at once.

I wanted to ask her everything—the truth about my father, the reason I could never make magic work the way the others did. But what came out was, "Why did you lie about him?"

She winced, the lines in her face deepening. "To keep you safe. If they knew what you were, they'd have torn you apart before you could walk." She looked away, then back, her eyes fierce. "You have the blood, Aspen. You have the book. And you have a heart stronger than anyone I've ever known."

The stones began to hum louder. My skin prickled with power.

Mama stepped forward, the spiral closing behind her. She reached out and took my hand, her touch warm and solid. "They will come for you," she said, voice shaking. "But you are ready. You can do what I could not."

I gripped her hand, refusing to let go. "What about the grimoire? It won't let me in. Not really."

She smiled, a secret in it. "Because it's waiting for you to be brave. To bleed for it. It's not about the words, Aspen. It's about the will." She traced the back of my hand, where the sigil had appeared. She tapped it, gentle. "Blood remembers, love. Blood forgives."

I tried to hold on to the moment, but already the world was fading at the edges, the colors running together like wet paint.

"Mama, wait—"

She pulled me close, hugged me tight, and whispered into my ear. "The book won't give you everything. There are things too dangerous to know. But it will show you all you need to learn. Trust yourself. And trust the wolf, too. He loves you more than he knows."

I opened my mouth to answer, but the world went white.

When I blinked again, I was back in the kitchen, the smell of bacon and coffee washing over me like a wave. My hands still rested on the grimoire, but now the cover was warm, almost pulsing under my touch.

Oscar stared up at me, eyes wide. "Well?" he prompted, voice trembling with excitement. "What did you see?"

I breathed out, slow and shaky, and told him everything.

He listened without interruption, tail curled around his feet, and when I finished, he nodded once, solemn as a judge. "You must open the book with blood," he said. "I suspected as much. It is the only way."

I laughed, surprised at the relief that flooded me. "You have quite a flair for the dramatic, Oscar."

He puffed up, offended. "Witchcraft is always dramatic, Miss. It's rather the point. I don't make the rules."

I looked at my hand, and a faint outline of the sigil that matched the one on the grimoire glowed faintly.

Oscar saw where I was looking. "Use the same hand, Miss. It will remember you."

I looked around the kitchen, searching for a knife, but thought better of it. Instead, I rummaged in the junk drawer for a safety pin. After moving around some batteries and a roll of tape, I found one.

Oscar hopped onto the table, watching with rapt attention. "Go on, then."

I took a deep breath, held the pin to my thumb, and pressed. The pain was sharp and bright, but quick. A bead of blood welled up, dark and perfect.

I smeared it across the clasp of the grimoire.

Nothing happened for a second. Then, with a soft click, the lock slid open.

Oscar gasped, paws covering his mouth. "By the Queen's whiskers," he whispered. "You did it."

I grinned, tears in my eyes, and flipped the book open.

Every page was different—some thick with pasted flowers or faded herbs, others dense with tiny handwriting or explosions of color, ink so old it blurred at the edges. The first entries were in a hand I didn't know—slanted, stern, and old. They spoke of harvests and hard winters, of names I'd never heard, of bargains struck at moonrise and secrets paid in coin or tears.

I turned the page. My mother's script danced across the paper; familiar, warm, a little rushed, always running out of room before the margin. The first line was dated just months before she died:

If you're reading this, it means you survived.

I blinked back sudden tears. Oscar, seeing my struggle, gently nudged the crook of my arm.

"Go on," he whispered. "She's waiting."

I paged through, mouth dry, heart drumming. There were pie recipes and curse-breaking rituals jumbled together, diagrams of plant roots and star patterns, lists of enemies and their weaknesses, lists of friends and their true names. Some pages were sealed with wax, some folded into pockets, some blacked out entirely with heavy strokes of charcoal.

Oscar scanned each one over my shoulder, muttering small approvals. "Ah, yes, that's elder thorn, rare these days... Oh, and here, the healing draft—useful if you're poisoned or merely heartbroken... Oh, look at that, she added her own notes to the Wyrdmother's Sleep!"

I kept turning pages faster and faster, growing dizzy with the sheer wealth of it. My mother had left a map for every possible disaster, and the further I got, the more I understood: she'd been scared, but she'd never been powerless.

I wanted that, too.

Oscar finally hopped onto the book itself, tapping the page with a tiny claw. "Here," he said. "This is where you must begin."

I read aloud. "Protection circle, bloodline variant. For use against those who mean you harm. Best performed at full moon, but potent if performed with true intent."

I looked up. "We can do this, right?"

Oscar's little mouth curled in a knowing smile. "Of course, Miss. With your wolf to guard you, and me at your side, there is nothing you cannot face."

I grinned, reckless and alive. "What next?"

Oscar considered, then nodded at the grimoire. "We must research the symbol. The one the man left on your bag. There is power in it, and a message for you. But first, we strengthen your shields. No more running, not for you."

I nodded. "No more running."

Outside, I could hear the distant sound of Papa wrapping up his call, boots crossing the porch. The sky beyond the window had gone full gold, the day bright and hard and real.

I looked down at the open book, then at Oscar, who adjusted his tiny glasses and regarded me with the pride of a hundred generations.

"What do we need to look for first?" I asked, my voice steady now, my hands ready.

Oscar grinned. "We begin with protecting your bakery, then we continue to learn, to grow, and then—we fight."

It felt like a switch had been flipped inside of me, and I was coming alive.

The grimoire glowed between us, warm as hearth light, waiting for me to write the next chapter.

CHAPTER 15

Big Papa

The sky over Dairyville was that late-winter blue that always looked deeper than it ought to, a color you could drown in if you didn't keep your feet on the boards. I paced the length of my porch, boots drumming hollow over the wood, every other footstep sending up a protest from my old left knee. I had my phone pinned to my ear, but the line was silent for three seconds, maybe four, before Menace's voice rolled out of it, thick as river gravel and twice as hard to budge.

"Big Papa, you still there, or did you finally let the old man put you under with that death trap coffee?"

I huffed. "Still here. Haven't touched the sludge since you warned me it was hazardous material."

A distant, wolfish chuckle. "Smart boy. You said you needed the mate-bond files. I've got answers, but you're not gonna like all of them. First: wolf-witch pairings are so rare there's maybe five or six on record, but I found a study from an old Scandinavian pack who documented it. You want the short version, or the version that'll keep you up nights?"

"Lay it on me. I need it straight."

There was a pause as he shuffled paper, or maybe just collected his own thoughts. "Alright. The fated mate bond—if it's real, and I have zero doubt yours is—it'll override any normal biological issues. Witches aren't built to handle the full physical force of a wolf's claim, but a true mate bond brings magic into play. Her blood, her lineage; it'll start to change her at the cellular level. Not all at once, but fast enough your instincts will notice."

I gripped the porch railing, feeling the bite of cold wood through my palm. "Change her how, exactly?"

"First, her magic's gonna spike. Might see symptoms: light from the bite mark, increased appetite, erratic mood, dreams about the pack. Second, the bite itself, yours, specifically, will anchor both of you. If she's willing, you'll be able to mark her without lasting harm. There'll be pain, but her magic will blunt the worst of it. Third; this is the one they never mention in the old stories. The knot? It's only possible if her body and spirit accept you. If she rejects you, even unconsciously, it'll never take."

I shivered, thinking of Aspen's skin, soft and white as a communion wafer, and the wild green in her eyes when she looked at me like I was her sun and her horizon both. "And if she accepts me?"

"You'll know. There won't be any fear or pain, only heat. You'll knot her, and it'll seal the mate bond. That's when the real fun starts. She'll pull your magic through her, and the two of you will get into a feedback loop. Like an addiction, but less messy. Separation could get physically painful for a few days. And if one of you dies—"

"Stop there." My voice was sharp as a snapped chain. "Don't need that part right now."

Another low laugh from Menace, gentler this time. "Didn't think you would, but a man's got to be thorough."

"Just do it right. Bond her; let her magic lead. It'll be messy, it'll be wild, but it'll be the strongest mate bond this state's ever seen." Menace paused, then added, "I wish I could be there to see it. Parker still owes me fifty bucks from the last time we bet on you."

The air around me shifted, charged with something electric, and for the first time in years, my wolf pressed close to the surface. Not to fight, or to kill, but to howl for the promise of a future.

"Thank you," I said, and meant it.

Menace's voice softened, a rare thing. "You're good for her, Jonas. And she's good for you. You deserve this."

The call ended with a final, deliberate click. I pocketed my phone and let the wind scour my face until my eyes watered and my blood cooled. I stood there for a while, letting the porch creak under my weight, the memories of war and pain and all the old disappointments sifting through my mind like sand. Then I turned and headed inside, ready to claim what was mine.

Tonight, I would take Aspen Waters. Not with violence, but with every ounce of devotion and longing I'd kept hidden. I'd bind her to me, let her magic thread itself through every scar, every healed broken bone, every breath I had left to draw.

Let the world watch.

I stepped over the threshold of my house and stopped dead in my tracks, because the living room looked nothing like the one I'd left. It was as if a hundred fireflies had taken up residence in the air, sparkling and shifting with every breath. In the center of it all sat Aspen and Oscar, hunched together at the dining table like the world's strangest study group. The grimoire lay open before them, its pages bathed in a gentle blue-gold glow, so alive with magic I could feel it rippling through my teeth and nails.

Aspen didn't notice me right away. Her whole body leaned toward the book, her eyes wide with wonder, fingers tracing the lines of a sigil as if reading Braille on a lover's back. The light caught her face and painted it in all the colors of sunrise: gold at the brow, pink at the cheeks, a fierce green glint to her eyes that made her look otherworldly. Oscar sat ramrod straight at her elbow, forepaws folded with the solemnity of a royal advisor.

He peered at the book, then at Aspen, then at me, and nodded once like I'd passed some secret test.

I just watched her, let the warmth of the moment settle over my bones. For all the chaos that had brought us together, there was nothing but peaceful "rightness" in that room—like the universe had finally stopped fighting itself, just for one evening, so a girl and a prairie dog and a broken old wolf could breathe the same air without fear.

She caught my stare and beamed at me, her whole face opening like the first full sun after winter. "Hey, Papa. You're back."

"I'm always coming back to you, Sunshine," I said, and the words came out easier than breathing. "What've you got there?"

She giggled, just a little. "We found my mom's spell for protecting the bakery. Oscar says it's the best one in the whole book. He also says we need to do it first thing tomorrow."

Oscar bowed in my direction, voice crisp as starched linen. "It is my professional opinion that you copulate and complete your mating bond at the earliest available opportunity, sir. Your mutual longing is so potent I am shocked there isn't structural damage to the house."

I laughed, feeling every old ache slide away. "Noted, Oscar. You're a hell of a wingman."

"Thank you. I am, as ever, at your service." He glanced at Aspen, then back at me, and for a second, I could have sworn he winked. Then he blinked out of existence, leaving a little puff of stardust on the tabletop and a scent like fresh lemons in the air.

Aspen closed the grimoire, the magic fading to a dull shimmer along the leather. She turned to face me, her knees knocking the table as she stood. I held out my hand, and she took it with both of hers, her grip cool but her touch electric.

For a long second, neither of us spoke. I felt my pulse pick up, the wolf in me howling for what he knew was coming.

"You sure about this?" I asked, voice so low it barely cleared my own throat.

She nodded, eyes bright and wet. "I want to be yours in every way."

I drew her in, held her close, her hair tangling in my beard as she pressed her cheek to my chest. I could feel the heartbeat through her shirt, and it matched mine, beat for beat.

I picked her up, one arm under her legs, the other behind her back, and carried her down the hall. She buried her face in my neck and laughed, breathless. "You're really going to do it. The big claim."

"Only if you want it," I whispered.

She kissed my jaw, the tip of my chin, the corner of my mouth. "I want it," she said. "I want you, Papa. I want everything."

When we reached the bedroom, I set her down and closed the door behind us. The house was silent. The world was silent. There was only the two of us, and all the heat and want and hope that had ever been bottled up, finally let loose in the same room.

She turned to face me, hands at her sides, body trembling just a little.

I took a step forward, then another, until there was nothing between us but the question of how long we'd make it before we lost ourselves. I wanted to take my time, but the wolf in me was already clawing for the surface. Aspen saw it in my eyes and smiled, sharp as any predator.

She belonged to me, and I belonged to her, and if the world wanted to pry us apart, it would have to tear the earth in two.

"Tell me everything," she whispered. "Tell me what happens next."

I sat her down on the edge of my bed, the weight of her body making a small impression on the king-sized mattress. Her feet dangled off the side, bare toes not reaching the thick rug. She looked up at me with a blend of mischief and awe, eyes big as a prairie sky. I stood over her, hands clenched at my sides, trying to keep myself from devouring her right then.

There was so much I wanted to say. Too much. But I'd promised honesty, and I was gonna deliver, even if my tongue got stuck in my teeth.

"Before we start, I need you to know what's coming," I said, voice gravel. "Menace called. He found everything there is to know about wolf-witch bonds. About us."

She drew her knees up, hugging them like a little kid. "Is it bad? Am I gonna turn into a frog or sprout a tail or something?"

I shook my head, smiling. "No, but you're about to get a crash course in what it's like to be loved by a wolf. The full package."

She blinked, then grinned. "Lay it on me, Papa."

I paced a little, hands behind my back. "When wolves mate, truly mate, it's more than sex. We give a claiming bite to our partners, usually at the base of the neck and shoulder. It's instinct, but it's also how the bond is sealed. For a witch, it might be more intense, because your blood is magic. The bite won't hurt, not really, but it'll mark you forever. And after that—" I trailed off, felt my cheeks heat.

She arched a brow. "After that?"

"When we make love, my wolf will want to knot you," I said, voice just above a whisper. "You know what that means?"

She blushed, but her gaze didn't waver. "I'm not a total innocent, Papa. I've read the books. I even saw some videos once."

"Okay, so you get it. My knot's...well, it's big. Your magic will help your body adjust, but it still might be uncomfortable. I'll try to stay in control, but when we're joined, my wolf's gonna take over. I need you to trust me. If it's too much, you say the word and I'll stop."

She shivered, her pulse visible at the hollow of her throat. "What if I don't want you to stop?"

I chuckled, warmth rising in my chest. "Then you'll make me an extremely happy wolf."

She reached for my hand, pulled me close. "What else did Menace say?"

I sat beside her, our knees brushing. "He said you might get magical symptoms. Your bite mark could glow, you might feel cravings, or get overwhelmed if we're apart for long. But the bond—if we let it happen—will make us nearly impossible to separate. I'll know when you're sad. You'll know when I'm hurt. That kind of thing."

Her face lit up like she'd swallowed a star. "That's not scary. That's amazing. That's what I've wanted my whole life."

I stared at her, at this beautiful, stubborn, reckless woman who'd walked out of a nightmare and landed right in my arms. My wolf ached to claim her, and my human heart thumped so loud it made my ears ring.

"I want to do it right, Aspen. I want to make you mine in every way a man can."

She leaned in, her lips grazing my jaw. "Then stop talking about it and show me."

I let go finally, and the last wall between us came down.

I cupped her face, kissed her hard, her mouth sweet with the sugar she'd stolen from the grimoire pages. She opened to me, let my tongue sweep hers, and moaned low in her throat. My hands slid down, tracing the line of her neck to her shoulder, and I could already feel the heat building there, the spot where I'd leave my mark.

"Now what?" she whispered, voice sleepy.

I leaned down and whispered in her ear, "Go to the bathroom, Sunshine. Wash up. Come back naked and ready to do exactly as I say."

She shivered, hunger in her eyes. "Yes, sir."

She slid off the bed, legs wobbly, and padded to the bathroom, closing the door behind her.

I watched her go, every sense alive with anticipation.

We were about to seal the bond that assured we'd be together for the rest of our lives. The magic thrummed through the room in anticipation of what was about to happen. I heard the toilet flush and then water running in the sink. After a few minutes, she emerged. My mate, my Sunshine, the woman who had reminded me that the life I'd been living before I met her, hadn't been a life at all.

And now I would be hers, and she would be mine forever.

Chapter 16

Aspen

I shut the bathroom door behind me, hands braced on the porcelain counter, and for a moment just listened to the clattering rabbit-pulse of my heart. I'd been in here ten minutes, maybe less, but it felt like I'd crossed an ocean. The room was warm from the overhead heater; the mirror clean and clear showed me the version of myself I barely recognized.

Not just from the outside. Yeah, the leggings and bralette were gone, replaced by nothing but the promise of my own skin and the cotton of Papa's favorite shirt, still faintly warm from his body. But the real difference was in my eyes. They looked green as ever, but brighter now, sharp and wild in a way they'd never been before I met him. Maybe it was the light, or the fact that I was about to do something sacred and dangerous. Or maybe it was the magic that had started to burn in me since opening the grimoire. Either way, the woman staring back was not the one who'd run from her coven in the middle of the night, shaking and afraid and sure she was a cosmic mistake.

I touched my cheek, tracing the feel of the softness of the creamy skin. My hair was loose and dark and falling in waves around my shoulders. I daresay I looked beautiful; real. Like a woman about to do something life-changing.

I tried to picture what would happen next. Papa—no, Jonas, maybe I should call him that now, waiting for me in the bedroom, probably standing in that way he did with his arms crossed over his chest, thinking a hundred things and saying nothing. He'd ordered me to come out naked, and I was compelled to submit to him, not because he'd ordered me, but because I wanted to honor his wishes.

I squared my shoulders and let my hands drop to the edge of the counter. My nails were short and unpainted, fingers trembling only a little. I remembered Oscar's words from earlier in the night; *You are braver than you believe, Miss. And also possibly insane, but I suspect that will serve you well.*

I almost laughed, but I didn't. I took a deep, shaking breath and let it out, steady as I could. Then I reached for the doorknob. The handle was cold in my palm. I twisted it, gentle, and let the door swing open.

I stepped into the bedroom, the cool air brushing against my bare skin like a lover's caress. My heart pounded in my chest, each beat a drumroll announcing my entrance. Jonas—Papa—stood there, a mountain of muscle and scars, his body a testament to battles fought and survived. My eyes drank him in, every inch of him, from the broad chest that could shield me from the world to the narrow waist that tapered into thighs thick with power. His scars, those marks of honor and pain, told stories I could only imagine, and yet they only made him more beautiful to me.

"Come here, Aspen," he commanded, his voice low and rough, like gravel underfoot. His erection stood proud and thick, a monument to his desire for me. I walked to him, each step a surrender, a promise, a vow. The floor was cool beneath my feet, but the heat radiating from him was enough to make me forget everything else.

He tossed a pillow onto the floor and pointed at it. "On your knees."

I obeyed without hesitation, remembering the other morning when I woke him wanting to learn how to do this. I sank down onto the soft cushion, my knees pressing into the fabric. My breath hitched as I looked up at him, my eyes meeting his, and I saw the hunger in them, the need that matched my own.

"Take me into your mouth," he instructed, his voice trembling with restraint. "Just the head. Let it rest on your tongue. Get it wet for me. Let your spit run down the length."

I obeyed, lips parting, tongue out just a little. He ran his thumb over my lower lip, then dragged the head of his cock across it, smearing pre-cum in a slow line. The taste was sharp and salty, different but not unpleasant. I wanted more.

He pushed the head past my lips, and I closed around it, sucking gently as I could. His skin felt hot and alive. I let my tongue swirl around the tip, feeling the tiny pulse of his heartbeat through the thick skin. I looked up, wanting to see if I was doing it right.

His head was thrown back, eyes closed, mouth open in a soundless groan. He flexed his hips, just a little, pushing deeper, and I opened wider, letting him fill my mouth.

"Good," he grunted. "Take as much of me as you can. Use your hands for the rest."

I wrapped my fist around the base, stroking him the way I'd done the other morning, and let the drool slide down my chin. It was messy and a little obscene, but I loved the way it made him gasp, the way he shivered when I hollowed my cheeks and sucked harder.

He set his hands on either side of my head, not forcing, just guiding. "Look at me," he said, and I did, locking eyes with him as he rocked in and out of my mouth.

The sound of him—ragged breaths, low groans, the way he said my name like it was a prayer—made my pussy clench, wetness leaking down my thigh. I wanted to make him lose control. I wanted to be the reason he fell apart.

I bobbed my head, working him deeper, stroking the base with both hands. He was so big I couldn't fit more than a few inches, but he didn't seem to mind. He smiled down at me, sweat beading on his forehead.

"God, you're beautiful like this," he growled, voice thick.

I moaned around his cock; the vibration making him twitch in my mouth. I remembered what he'd taught me—how to cup his balls, how to squeeze just enough to make him gasp—and I reached under, cradling them as I sucked. He jerked, hips stuttering, and I tasted a fresh burst of pre-cum on my tongue.

"Careful," he said, voice strangled. "You keep that up, I'm going to come right now."

I slowed, licking up and down the shaft, then swirling around the head. I looked up, wanting to see how close he was.

He let go of my hair and cupped my jaw, tilting my head up. "Come here," he said, and before I knew it, he'd lifted me off the pillow and onto my feet, pulling me tight against his chest.

He kissed me hard, tasting himself on my lips. His hand snaked down between my legs, finding me soaked and swollen. He slid two fingers inside, curling them until I whimpered.

"See how wet you are?" he whispered, biting my earlobe. "You like sucking my cock, don't you?"

I nodded, desperate for him.

"You're mine now," his voice rough and possessive. He traced a finger down the curve of my hip, leaving a trail of fire in its wake. "Every inch of you."

I shivered, not from cold but from the intensity of his words. They weren't just words; they were a claim, a promise, a threat. And I wanted to believe them. I wanted to belong to him, body and soul.

He leaned down, his breath hot against my ear. "Do you understand what that means, Aspen?"

I nodded, unable to speak. My throat was dry, my heart pounding like a drum.

"It means," he continued, his lips brushing against my skin as he laid me on the bed, "that I own you. That you trust me to do whatever I want with you. And you'll let me. Because you want it. Because you need it."

I whimpered, the sound escaping my lips before I could stop it. His words were a knife, cutting through my defenses, leaving me bare and vulnerable. And I loved it. I loved the way he made me feel—like I was nothing but his, like I existed only for him.

"Touch yourself," he commanded, his voice low and gravelly. "Show me how much you want me."

I froze for a moment. I'd never done that much. And to do it in front of him. I know my cheeks were flaming.

"Aspen. Have you decided already that you'd rather not do what I want?" His voice was so stern, I felt more wetness spill from my pussy.

"No! No, sir. I will. I just have never...done that much." I was so afraid of disappointing him.

He leaned down and kissed my forehead. "Sunshine. Just like when you first sucked my cock, and I told you to just do what felt right. It's the same thing. I want to watch you give yourself pleasure. It will help me know what feels good to you. I can see you're even wetter than you were before, so it must appeal to you. Now, go on. Touch your beautiful dripping pussy for me."

My hand trembled as I reached between my legs, fingers brushing against my slick walls. He was right. I was dripping wet, already aching for him, and the slightest touch sent a jolt of pleasure through me. I moaned, arching my back, my fingers sliding inside me with ease.

Jonas watched me, his eyes dark with desire. "That's it," he growled. "I want you to fuck yourself for me. Let me see how much you need my cock."

I obeyed, my fingers moving faster, deeper, stopping only to rub my clit. I was gasping for air. My body was on fire, every nerve ending alive with pleasure. And still, it wasn't enough. I needed more. I needed him.

"Papa," I begged, my voice breaking. "Please, I can't. It's not enough."

He smiled, a teasing smile that sent a shiver down my spine. "Beg for it," he said. "Beg for my cock."

"Please," I whimpered, my fingers still working in and out of me. "Please, Papa, I need you. I need your cock. Please, fuck me."

He leaned down, his lips brushing against mine. "There's my good girl," he whispered, then kissed me hard, his tongue claiming my mouth as surely as his cock would claim my body.

He pulled my hand away, licked my fingers, leaving me panting, and positioned himself between my legs. I could feel the heat of him, the hardness of his cock pressing against my entrance. I spread my legs wider, inviting him in, wanting him to take me, to own me.

He thrust into me in one smooth motion, filling me completely. I cried out, my body arching off the bed, my fingers clutching at the sheets. He was so big, so thick, and it hurt so good.

"You are so perfect, Sunshine."

He started to move, slow at first, then faster, harder. Each thrust pushed me closer to the edge, my body tightening around him, my nails digging into his back. I could feel the sweat dripping off him, could hear the ragged sound of his breathing, and it only heightened my pleasure.

"You feel so fucking good," he growled, his hips slamming into mine. "So tight, so wet. You were made for me, Aspen."

I moaned, my body responding to his words, to his touch. I was lost in him, in the feel of him, in the sound of his voice. I was completely and utterly his, and I never wanted it to end.

He reached between us, his fingers finding my clit, and rubbed it in fast, tight circles. The combination of his cock inside me and his fingers on my clit was too much, too intense, and I came with a scream, my body shaking with the force of it.

He kept going, fucking me through my orgasm, his cock pounding into me with relentless force. I could feel him getting closer, his thrusts becoming more erratic, his breath coming in short, harsh gasps.

He groaned, his body tensing, and then he was coming, his cock pulsing inside me, filling me with his heat. I clung to him, my legs wrapped around his waist, my fingers tangled in his hair, as he emptied himself into me.

"You're mine now," he said. "Every inch of you."

After a minute or an hour—time was a joke, my body a riot of aftershocks—he kissed me again, this time hungry, devouring. He pulled back, face inches from mine, and brushed the hair from my eyes.

I lay there, my body still trembling from the aftershocks of my orgasm, Papa's cock still buried deep inside me. His breath was hot against my neck, his chest pressed against my back, and I could feel his heartbeat pounding in time with mine. His hands roamed over my body, possessive and hungry, and I shivered under his touch.

"I need you again," he said, not asking. His cock, impossibly, was already growing hard inside me.

"Again?" I whispered, my voice shaky, unsure if I could handle more. But the way he looked at me—the raw, primal need in his eyes—told me I didn't have a choice. I was his, and he was going to take what he wanted.

"Again," he growled, his voice rough and commanding. He kissed me again, this time harder, more demanding, and I moaned into his mouth, my body responding even as my mind screamed that I was too sensitive, too spent. But I wanted him. I needed him. I craved the way he made me feel—owned, claimed, loved.

He pulled out of me slowly, his cock slick with our combined fluids, and I whimpered at the loss. But before I could protest, he flipped me onto my stomach, his hands firm on my hips. He placed pillows beneath me, lifting my ass up, and I felt exposed, vulnerable, and utterly at his mercy.

"Fuck, Aspen," he breathed, his voice thick with desire. "Your ass...it's perfect. I could spend hours worshipping it."

I blushed, my face heating up, but before I could respond, he slapped my ass hard; the sound echoed through the room. I gasped, the sting of his hand turning into a deep, throbbing heat that spread through me. He did it again, and again, each slap sending a jolt of pleasure through me, until I was panting, my pussy dripping wet, aching for him.

"Wolves take their mates like this," he said, his voice low and gravelly. "From behind. It's primal, raw. And I'm going to claim you, Sunshine, now and forever."

I moaned, my body trembling with anticipation, and then he was pushing into me again, his cock stretching me wide, filling me completely. He gripped my hips tight enough to bruise, his fingers digging into my flesh, and I cried out, the pain and pleasure mingling into something overwhelming.

He reached around, his fingers finding my clit, and began stroking me in slow, deliberate circles. The combination of his cock pounding into me and his fingers on my clit was too much, too intense, and I felt myself spiraling towards another orgasm, my body tightening around him.

"That's it, Sunshine," he growled, his voice rough and possessive. "Come for me. Let me feel you."

He leaned over my back, his face positioned at my neck. I moaned, my body arching, and then he bit down on my neck at my shoulder junction, his teeth sinking into my flesh. The pain was sharp, intense, and it sent me over the edge, my orgasm crashing over me in waves. I screamed, my body shaking, my nails clawing at the sheets, and he groaned, his cock pulsing inside me as he came, filling me with his heat.

He held me there, his teeth still buried in my shoulder, until the last of my tremors subsided. Then he released the bite, licking the wound gently, and I felt a strange, deep connection forming between us—a bond that went beyond the physical, beyond the flesh.

I lost track of everything except the feeling of being completely, utterly possessed. His cock swelled inside me, the knot expanding until I was pinned in place, as my body responded to his tremendous size. The pressure was intense, almost too much, but Papa's hands on my hips anchored me—kept me from flying apart. The waves of orgasm didn't stop; they built on each other, smaller aftershocks that wracked my body until I was gasping into the sheets, drool and tears mixing on my cheek.

He didn't let go. He stroked my ass, my hips, and my sides as he spoke sweet words I can't remember. Even as the contractions slowed and my body went limp, he held my hips tight, his length pulsing inside me, still locked. I was so full of him I could feel the throb of his heartbeat in every inch.

"Can you handle more, Sunshine?" he growled, his voice gentle but so commanding it made me shiver.

"Yes," I whispered, barely able to talk. "Everything you have for me."

He pressed his chest to my back, so close I could feel his beard on my shoulder blade. His hand slid up my ribcage, fingers splayed wide, and his mouth found my ear.

He had leaned over my back again, mouth at my ear. "Will you mark me?" he asked, words rumbling through my bones.

I wanted to complete our bond more than anything.

"Please," I said, "let me."

He moved his hand to the nape of his neck, baring his shoulder to my mouth. "Bite," he whispered.

I didn't hesitate. I latched onto the thick muscle where his neck met his shoulder and bit down as hard as I could. The skin gave way, not with blood and pain but with something bright and hot and sweet. His taste filled my mouth—not copper, but the flavor of him. I tasted his memories, his wounds, his impossible goodness. I tasted love. My eyes were closed, but the tears flowed.

He shuddered, groaning deep, and ground his hips against me, forcing the knot even deeper. The sensation sparked another orgasm—smaller, more desperate, but still real. I cried out, not from pain, but from a joy so sharp it was almost unbearable.

I released the bite and licked the wound, wanting to seal it, wanting him to carry my mark forever. When I finally looked up, there were tears in his eyes. He blinked them away, then pressed his forehead to the back of my head, breathing in the scent of my hair.

He didn't say anything for a long minute. Neither did I. We just breathed together, bodies locked in place, heartbeats finally slowing.

When his knot finally softened, he eased out of me, careful and slow. I whimpered at the loss, but he scooped me into his arms, rolling us onto our sides. He spooned me, his big arm draped over my waist, hand splayed protectively over my belly.

"Are you alright?" he whispered, lips pressed to my ear.

I couldn't find words. Instead, I reached and tangled my fingers with his, holding his hand tight to my stomach.

He drew slow circles around my bellybutton, the gesture oddly soothing. I realized I was trembling—not from fear, but from the afterglow of something so intense I couldn't name it.

I felt him smile against my neck. "You did so good, Aspen. You're everything I ever wanted."

I turned in his arms so I could see his face, and he let me. Our noses bumped, and he wiped the tears from my cheeks with his thumb.

"I love you," I said, voice raw and shaky.

He kissed me, softer than before. "I love you more," he said.

We stayed like that, bound together, until the world faded away and sleep took us both.

I woke hours later, still in his arms, still held tight against his body. The house was quiet except for the faint hum of the heater and the wind against the window. I felt safe, warm, home.

I felt him everywhere. I knew I'd never be alone again.

CHAPTER 17

Big Papa

The sun wasn't up when I rolled Aspen out of bed, but that didn't matter. My mate always did her best work in the deep dark before dawn, and today, it was doubly important. It was the first day Buttercream & Blessings would open after we'd completed the mate bond—after we'd changed everything.

She sat shotgun, legs crossed at the ankles her hair soft and shiny in a pretty loose bun, dressed in a signature funky dress with tights and boots. There were no signs of last night's debauchery except for the bite mark on her neck that lightly glowed in the dark. She barely spoke, just sipped coffee from a battered travel mug and stared out the window, but the bond between us thrummed like a living wire. There wasn't a moment I didn't feel her in my chest now; a soft, electric warmth that took the place of the cold, anxious knot I'd carried since the day my convoy blew up outside Mosul.

I kept my left hand on the wheel, right hand on her thigh, thumb idly tracing circles. Every so often she'd lean over, bump my shoulder, and let out this little huff that meant she was excited and nervous at the same time. I loved that sound. I loved her. I still couldn't believe I was allowed to say it, to think it, to have her so completely.

When we hit Dairyville proper, the bakery stood out like a sunrise. She'd repainted the door last weekend, and even in the dead of night, the bright yellow screamed cheerfulness. I parked at the curb, cut the engine, and just watched her for a second.

She finished her coffee, wiped the sleep from her eyes, and smiled at me, soft as a secret. "Ready for round two?" she asked, voice rough from sleep.

"Always," I said. "I'm gonna stick around for a while. At least 'til you and Oscar get your wards in place."

She nodded her head, then hesitated. "I'd like that."

That made me happier than it should've.

Inside, the place was still and clean. Oscar sat atop the glass counter, tiny paws folded, looking like he'd been carved from cinnamon toast. He was wearing a navy corduroy jacket and an orange and navy plaid vest, because of course he was. When he saw us, he gave a regal nod.

"Good morning, sir. Miss," he said. "The perimeter appears undisturbed."

Aspen grinned and tousled his head, then busied herself turning on the kitchen lights and prepping the ovens. I wandered over to a table near the door, set up my laptop, and started in on the day's job: mapping the security and logistics for Bronc and Juliet's upcoming mating ceremony. I pulled up a shared doc, dropped a pin for the event site, and then typed out the supply list in the clean, military block letters Menace had drilled into me years ago.

But I wasn't really focused on the logistics. I kept glancing up at Aspen as she and Oscar started the protection rituals. It was a two-part system: Oscar took the right wall, Aspen took the left, and together they made a slow circuit of the interior. Oscar walked with precise, dignified steps, every so often pausing to tap a glowing sigil onto the baseboard. The light would linger, then fade, leaving a faint scent of fresh air and sage. Aspen followed, whispering lines from her mother's grimoire, shaking a tin of salt over the windowsills and doors.

I found it mesmerizing. She wasn't the bumbling, unsure girl who'd shown up in town weeks ago. She was in charge now. Her voice was clear, her hands steady, her magic alive and visible. She belonged here, and the bakery was her temple.

Every few minutes, she'd peek over her shoulder at me, green eyes sparkling, and I'd lift my coffee in salute. We didn't have to say anything—our bond did the talking.

After the first round of wards, she disappeared into the kitchen to start mixing dough. I watched the light come up over the street, painting everything a delicate pink. There was nothing threatening on the horizon, just the usual mix of half-asleep commuters and ranch hands grabbing coffee before work.

I went back to my list. Supplies: checked. Site perimeter: checked. Backup generator: requested. I was halfway through the communications plan when Oscar hopped onto my table, landing so lightly he didn't even ruffle the papers.

He eyed the screen, then me, then the screen again. "You are most efficient, sir. Have you considered a career in logistics?"

I snorted. "Had one. Wasn't as fun as it looks."

Oscar leaned in, as if about to whisper a national secret. "She's much changed, you know. Since last night."

I looked over at the kitchen. I could see Aspen's silhouette through the frosted glass, arms moving in a steady rhythm as she worked the dough.

"I know," I said, soft as a whisper. "She's... incredible."

Oscar twitched his nose, the picture of sage wisdom. "You are as well. A bit more...unrestrained this morning, if I may say so."

I laughed. "Yeah, well, some things are worth letting go for."

Oscar nodded, then fixed me with a stare so intense it might have punctured armor. "I shall inform you if anything strange is detected, sir.

Until then, please enjoy your...logistics." He said the word like it was a rare delicacy.

I shook my head and got back to work, but it was impossible to focus now. My mind kept wandering to the bedroom, to the way Aspen had trembled under me, the way she'd clawed my back and screamed my name like it was the only word in the world. I felt myself start to harden, just thinking about it.

I shifted in my seat, tried to distract myself with an email, but the bond lit up again—this time with a sharp jolt of amusement. Aspen must have felt it, because a second later she called out from the kitchen.

"Excuse me, sir," she said, voice sing-song. "You're making me wet in here, and I have to wear these panties all day."

I about died. Oscar made a strangled, scandalized sound, then covered his face with both paws.

I could hear her giggling, muffled by the swinging kitchen door. "You're not even in the room and you're already getting me in trouble," she said, still laughing. "I have a new rule. No making me horny when there's raw dough around."

"I'll try," I said, but didn't mean it. The warmth in my chest grew to a slow, steady burn. I'd spent years believing I was broken, unlikely to find this kind of happiness. Now it felt like the universe was making up for lost time.

Oscar composed himself, then pointedly straightened his cravat. "I shall be monitoring the yeast, Miss, should you require my assistance."

"Thank you, Oscar," she replied. "You're a true professional."

He puffed up, pleased.

The morning rolled on. I finished my work, double-checked the comms, then leaned back and just watched the bakery come to life. Aspen was in her element, humming along to an old Fleetwood Mac song, hands dusted with flour, hair coming loose from her bun a bit. Oscar busied himself with inventory, reading off ingredient lists in his perfect British diction.

I got up, stretched, and wandered to the front counter. I poured another mug of coffee, then perched on a stool, watching the street. It was quiet—nothing suspicious, nothing wrong. For the first time since I'd woken up in a hospital bed almost ten years ago, I felt completely, irrevocably right.

My phone buzzed. Maddie.

Hey, stud. Pearl's kitchen is doing lunch drop-off today. Me and maybe Parker will bring the goods. Is 11:30 cool?

I typed back: *Perfect. Aspen will want potato salad.*

Maddie's reply came instantly: *Your girl has excellent taste. See you soon, Big Papa.*

I smiled, pocketed the phone, and listened to the hum of the bakery. I could have stood there all day, just breathing in the scent of fresh bread and sugar, listening to Aspen and Oscar bicker about the proper pronunciation of "croissant."

At 6:00, we unlocked the front door. The first customer was a rancher in a battered Carhartt, who left with two dozen kolaches and a smile. By 7:00, the place was half full. Oscar stayed hidden in the back as Aspen worked the counter and the oven, and I played bouncer—discreet, but ready.

A woman in a gray jacket lingered outside for a minute, but she moved on, and nothing felt off. I let myself relax.

The moment I stepped inside the clubhouse, I was slammed by the familiar mix of coffee, leather, and motor oil. It was the smell of my second home.

Gunner and Arsenal were in the kitchen, arguing over whether brisket or ribs should be on the menu for Saturday's ceremony. Gunner had a heavy mug of black coffee in his grip and wore his cut over a plaid shirt that matched his boots, while Arsenal, true to form, dressed like he'd just stepped out of an urban sniper's fantasy. He saw me, narrowed his eyes, and nodded. That was about as much affection as Arsenal ever gave anyone.

"Hey, lover boy," Gunner called. "Heard you finally bit the bullet."

"Bullet's not the only thing I bit," I shot back, dropping my bag on the nearest chair. "And if you keep running your mouth, I'll let my mate put a spell on your pecker."

Gunner laughed, shaking his head. "I'm immune. My balls are sanctified by barbecue and bourbon."

Arsenal snorted. "I'm just waiting for the day one of you falls for a real monster. Then we'll see who's laughing."

"One of these days you're gonna fall in love with the exact wrong person," I told him, grinning. "Karma's a bitch, buddy."

He didn't answer, but the look in his eyes said he'd taken the hit.

Church started right on time, as it always did. Bronc presided from the head of the battered oak table, flipping through a dog-eared binder of schedules and supply lists. Maddie was there too, hunched over her laptop, eyes darting between her screen and the room like a bird of prey.

Bronc cleared his throat. "Let's get moving. First up: Saturday's ceremony. Papa, you got the site locked down?"

"Yeah," I said. "Oscar's helping Aspen with the protection wards, and I'll have extra bodies running perimeter checks. All the food's covered, Gunner's got the meat, and the cake's on Aspen."

Maddie typed something, then looked up. "We'll need extra chairs. Pearl says the entire pack plus a few other packs' members, vamps, etc. RSVP'd yes."

Bronc nodded, then turned to Arsenal. "Security update?"

Arsenal leaned forward, elbows on the table. "Morgantown's got two men in town this week, both low-level, but it's a red flag. No excuse for them to be here except to snoop. I've got eyes on them, but they're not making trouble."

Doc chimed in from the end of the table, his sleeves rolled up and arms crossed. "There was a stomach virus running through the pack last week. Hit five families, including two kids. Everyone's stable now, but if symptoms show up, they come to me—no exceptions."

That got a general nod. We'd never forgotten the water poisoning incident from a month back, and none of us wanted a repeat.

Bronc steered the meeting with a calm, steady hand. We hammered out the details, decided who'd run security shifts, and covered contingency plans for every likely disaster. By the time we finished, the sun was up, painting the windows with a hard, bright light.

He finally asked Wrecker to report on tech for the event.

"I know we'd thought drones were out because they made too much noise, but I've worked on a new prototype that is quiet as a mouse that will be perfect. So we'll have eyes in the sky that night."

Bronc just shook his head. "As if there were any doubt that you'd solve that dilemma."

It was then that Juliet came in, her belly a perfect six-months-round under a flowing blue dress. She looked like a goddess and walked like she owned the place, which, in a way, she did. Every head turned.

He stood and hugged her, then guided her to a seat beside him. The room got a little warmer.

Juliet glanced around, her eyes landing on the single men. "So, who's next to find their fated mate?"

Gunner shot his hand up, straight-faced. "Talk to the Goddess about it," he said, voice as slow and sure as Texas dust.

Juliet laughed so hard she nearly cried, and even Arsenal cracked a smile.

I caught myself watching her, the swell of new life, and I wondered if Aspen and I would ever have a kid. The thought hit like a truck, raw and sweet. I made a note to research how hybrid babies worked.

"Papa," Juliet said, catching me in my daydream. "Love looks good on you. You need to bring Aspen around more.."

I nodded, a little embarrassed. "She's a keeper."

Bronc met my eyes, all business again. "Anything else before we wrap?"

"Yeah," Arsenal said, looking at me. "Keep your witch from getting up to trouble. If the Morgantown bastards try anything, they'll target her first."

I bristled, but Bronc cut in. "She's one of us now. And when that Morgantown incident happened, she was with an Iron Valor wolf in Iron Valor territory, remember that. Check your attitude, Arsenal."

Head lowered and properly chastised, Arsenal agreed. "Yes, Alpha."

The meeting broke up, people peeling off to start their days. I lingered, pretending to nurse my coffee, but mostly just watching the way Bronc and Juliet glowed together.

Someday, I thought. That could be us.

I just had to keep her safe long enough to get there.

As the last echoes of the pack officers faded into the morning, Bronc lingered at the head of the table, thumbs drumming on the battered wood. The place felt bigger now, hollowed out by the absence of laughter and boots, the only sound the faint rumble of bikes on the county road and the tick of the kitchen clock.

He watched me for a minute, then jerked his chin at the empty chair beside him. "Sit, Papa."

I did, feeling the sudden weight of responsibility settle on my shoulders. Bronc didn't waste time with pleasantries.

"How's it feel?" he asked. "The bond."

I tried to put words to it, failed, tried again. "Like someone cut a stone out of my chest and replaced it with a live wire. She's always there, even if I don't look at her. It's... good. But it makes me want to break things if she gets threatened."

Bronc's mouth quirked. "That's how you know it's real."

We sat in the hush, sunlight slanting across the scarred table. I could see him weighing something, so I let the silence stretch.

Finally, he said, "Menace sent me his notes on witch-wolf matings. Didn't share much, but I know you had a talk."

I nodded. "Yeah. It's rare, but not impossible. The mate bond kicks in, and the magic... works itself out. She's getting stronger every day, and the bite went through just fine. So did the knot."

Bronc let out a laugh, low and real. "Good man."

"It's all good. Except for the part where every son of a bitch from here beyond the Mississippi wants a piece of her."

He grew serious, eyes sharpening. "What's your read on it?"

I shrugged. "Best guess? Verdant Hollow's pissed because she's not a dud, and now they're worried she'll use the grimoire against them. Morgantown's sniffing around, I figure because they've been put up to it."

Bronc nodded slowly. "They're coming for something. Either her, the book, or both. Maybe they think the book is a weapon."

"Could be," I said. "But it's Aspen they really want. Either to use, or to break."

Bronc leaned back, the old chair creaking. "You ready to fight for her?"

I didn't hesitate. "I'd burn the world down for her."

That got a real smile. "That's what I wanted to hear."

We sat for a minute, the hum of the bond settling me. Even from here, I could feel her—my Sunshine—working in the bakery, laughing with Oscar, alive and well.

Bronc spoke first. "Look, Papa. You've always had my trust. But now, you've got my pack's future in your hands. We need you sharp. We need you dangerous."

I looked at him and saw the worry behind the Alpha. "You think I'm not?"

He shook his head. "I think you're better than ever. I just want you to know what's at stake."

"I do," I said. "And I won't let anyone touch her. Or the pack."

He reached across the table; squeezed my arm. The gesture said more than any words. "Go home," he said. "Rest up. Tell Aspen she's got a family here, for life."

I stood, grabbed my jacket. "You too. Take care of your Luna."

He laughed. "She takes care of me."

I left the clubhouse with the sun high and the wind at my back. When I got in the truck, the bond lit up—Aspen, humming with pride, calling to me from across town.

I smiled, turned the key, and headed back to her.

By the time Maddie arrived with Parker in tow, the bakery was a living, breathing machine. Aspen's face was pink from the oven heat, her arms dusted in flour, but she looked happier than I'd ever seen her.

Parker caught my eye and grinned. "Domestic bliss suits you, JT."

I shrugged. "Could get used to it."

Maddie slid a cardboard box across the counter. "Pearl says congrats on the mate bond. Also, there's extra brisket."

Aspen ducked her head, shy but pleased. "Thanks, y'all."

We sat around a table eating brisket and potato salad, laughing about old pack stories. Oscar listened, occasionally interjecting with a dry quip. Even Parker seemed at ease, her eyes softer than usual.

After lunch, as the crowd thinned, Aspen slipped into my lap and kissed me, right there in front of everyone. I didn't care. I kissed her back, holding her close.

I looked around the bakery, at my friends, my mate, the prairie sun blazing outside. For the first time, I saw my future, and it didn't scare me at all.

I'd spent a lifetime preparing for war. But this—this quiet joy—was the fight I'd been born to win.

And I was never letting it go. We were ready for whatever came next.

Even if it burned us to the ground.

CHAPTER 18

Aspen

I'd always heard that the day after you bonded with a mate, the whole world changed. Parker described it like being plugged into a high-voltage line: colors seemed brighter, food tasted richer, and every glance from your partner carried the electric promise of sin and safety both. I'd assumed she was exaggerating. After all, I'd lived my life outside the fairy tale—hated by my coven, and lately hiding from ghosts and green-jacketed men.

But she hadn't lied. By noon, I was so tuned into Papa that when he stubbed his toe in the next room over, my own foot ached in sympathy. When he sneezed, I felt a tickle in my own nose. When he looked at me from across the bakery, something in my chest just...warmed.

The day was bright and dry as a breadstick. By 11:30, a line of regulars snaked out the door, all wanting their usual: kolaches, cinnamon rolls, maybe a danish if the world hadn't gone off its axis. But today, something strange was afoot. Every other customer asked if we had sandwich bread.

"Not today, but maybe soon," I found myself saying over and over. "Should I set some aside for you next week?"

By the third hour, I'd written "Sourdough Friday Coming Soon!" on the chalkboard in my best curly handwriting. Oscar, hidden in the prep area decked out in a tiny navy vest, watched the crowd with a patience I'd never seen in another living being.

"Is this common?" he whispered as a man in muddy overalls asked about rye. "The sudden demand for loaves?"

"Sandwich bread isn't glamorous, but people want fresh baked, no preservatives these days," I whispered back, "and if it pays the bills, I'll bake my body weight in it."

He snorted, but his little black eyes gleamed. "You underestimate the power of bread, Miss. Empires have risen and fallen on less."

The bakery hummed. I lost myself in the ritual: scoop, knead, proof, shape, bake. Each doughball was a little prayer for a day when the world might let me feed it. By two, the rush had died down. Only the real die-hards remained—the kind who nursed a single sticky bun for three hours, "just for the atmosphere," while using our Wi-Fi to get a little work done.

Papa showed up at 11:30 on the dot. He knew Maddie had brought lunch. I was happy he decided to stay and get a little work done himself.

The bakery was mine, but his presence filled the room. He wore a black t-shirt, blue jeans, and his Iron Valor jacket, the leather faded to near-gray at the elbows. He looked tired but happy, his eyes softer than I'd ever seen them. I wanted to drag him behind the counter and devour him in the walk-in, but I had some standards.

He took in the mess, the crumbs, the empty racks, and let out a low whistle. "Lemon bar riots, huh?"

"Don't mock my struggles," I said, leaning over the counter to kiss his cheek.

He grinned, rubbing the spot I'd kissed like he meant to keep it there all day. "Never."

Oscar hopped over to the espresso machine and set about making two shots, muttering, "At last, a man who appreciates strong brew."

Papa put the "CLOSED" sign on the door then squeezed behind the counter, grabbed a rag, and started wiping down tables like he'd worked here all his life. I stared at him for a moment, then shook my head and started on the next batch of dough for tomorrow. I hoped this would become our routine. We worked in tandem, no words needed, every motion smooth and easy.

Halfway through mopping the floor, he looked up and said, "So, was your mom a professional baker too? Is that how you learned to do all of this?"

"Not exactly." I snorted. "She owned an herb shop for about ten years. Mostly soaps, shampoos, and herbal remedies. The bakery was her side hustle. I worked with her after school and on the weekends. She claimed it kept me out of trouble, but mostly it kept the bullies in the coven from eating me whole."

He leaned against the mop handle, arms crossed. "That's your mother in those pictures, right? The ones by the register?"

I looked at the little frame with the faded photo of Mama and me, arms around each other, flour on our faces and smiles so big you could park a truck in them. "Yeah. She was the real deal. Not some Instagram witch. She could do things I still can't believe."

Oscar interjected, "Miss Waters's mother once brewed a tea that cured a high priestess's gallstones. She did not even use a cauldron."

Papa barked a laugh. "I believe it. Your magic's getting stronger every day."

I hesitated, kneading dough with more force than necessary. "I think she started that shop because she knew I'd never fit in with the others. Not really. She was getting me ready for another path."

He came over, took my floury hands in his, and brushed a stray hair from my cheek. "She did a damn good job."

Oscar cleared his throat. "Speaking as your familiar, Miss, I must say you are more powerful than you give yourself credit for."

I felt my face heat. "Having you here helps, Oscar. I never dreamed the fates would send me a familiar. Now, sometimes, I feel like I can actually do something."

Oscar bowed his head. "It is an honor to serve."

Papa squeezed my hands again. "I'd have killed for a family like that."

"Don't you have one?" I asked, brow furrowing. "You never talk about your parents."

He shrugged, his face closing off a little. "They're around. Oil business, lots of money, very little time for the actual work of raising wolves. My brother runs most of it now. I'm the family disappointment."

Oscar sniffed. "From what I hear, sir, you are considered a model citizen in at least six counties."

He grinned at that, but I saw the shadow in his eyes. "It's different for wolves, I guess. There's always a pack, a system. But it's not always a family, not really. Not the way you and your mom had it."

I wanted to ask more, to press my hand against his chest and see what memories I could dredge up, but the look on his face said it was enough for now. Instead, I put the dough in the fridge and shut the door.

"I'm glad you're here," I said. "For the first time in a long time, I feel...safe."

He looked at me, his gaze so intense I had to look away. "You are. Always."

The light outside faded to gold, then to gray. The bakery's lamps glowed against the deepening dark, casting long shadows across the counter. I wiped down the last tray, tossed the rag in the hamper, and switched off the ovens.

Oscar hopped onto my shoulder, whispering, "The sandwich revolution will not wait, Miss."

I smiled and ruffled his fur. "We'll get the recipe right tomorrow."

Papa stepped behind the counter, wrapped me in a bear hug, and pressed his lips to the crown of my head. We stood like that for a while, the world outside fading to nothing, the scent of vanilla and cinnamon clinging to our skin.

Finally, he let go. "You ready for dinner?"

"Always," I said. "But you're driving. My hands are shot."

He lifted my hands to his lips, kissed each knuckle, and said, "Deal."

We locked up, Oscar double-checking every window. The last glow of the day lingered on the glass, but inside, everything was warm and good and just for us.

As I stepped out into the cold with Papa at my side and Oscar on my shoulder, I knew that this was what home felt like. Not a place, but a promise. A little magic, a little mess, and someone to hold you at the end of the day.

And maybe, just maybe, a loaf of sandwich bread waiting for you in the morning.

Pearl's Bar & Grill was always busiest right after dark, when the last rays of sun fell through the high windows and turned the row of whiskey bottles into a stained-glass altar. The place pulsed with noise—old country on the jukebox, shifter kids running laps around the pool table, the thud and sizzle of someone in the kitchen tenderizing meat with a small mallet. The air was warm and crowded and tasted of fried onions, spilled beer, and something sweet and smoky I could never quite name.

Oscar had insisted on coming with us, though he'd have to pop out and pop in on his own. He'd popped in, sitting next to me the moment we sat at a corner booth, paws perched on the rim like a prairie dog at the edge of a foxhole. He made himself invisible to everyone but Papa, Pearl, and me.

"Evening, ma'am," he said to Pearl as she floated by, white hair piled high and lipstick brighter than the neon sign outside.

Pearl didn't even blink. "Good to see you again, Mr. Wild," she said, setting down two waters and a thick menu. "You want the usual, Papa?"

He nodded. "Chicken fried steak, double mashed potatoes, extra gravy."

Pearl grinned. "I figured. And for the lady?"

I tried to remember what was on the menu, but Oscar piped up, "Might I suggest the meatloaf? The tomato sauce is particularly delightful."

Pearl cocked an eyebrow at me, waiting.

"I'll go with the meatloaf and mashed potatoes." I said, blushing.

She winked. "Your mate bite sparkles, Aspen. Congrats. You two are perfect together."

I nearly choked. Papa grinned wide, reaching across the table to squeeze my hand. "Thanks, Pearl. We're happy."

The first ten minutes were a parade of shifters who stopped by the booth to say hi, slap Papa on the back, or, if they were female, give me the up-and-down and then a thumbs-up. Most just said, "Congrats" or "I'm so happy Big Papa finally found a wonderful girl," but a few asked real questions. Was it true I baked everything from scratch? Did I ever take custom cake orders? Was I really about to offer sandwich bread, or was that just a rumor?

Oscar wanted to field the questions, but I had to remind him that many of the people here were human and would freak out at a talking prairie dog.

The only one who didn't come over was Arsenal, who sat at the bar with his back to the room and a single whiskey in front of him.

Halfway through dinner, Gunner appeared, cowboy hat and all. He scooted in next to Papa and stuck his hand out for a shake. "Well, well, Big Papa, looks like you hit the jackpot."

Papa took the handshake, then flicked his eyes toward me. "I think I did."

Gunner turned his full attention to me, brown eyes sharp and kind. "You got some magic in you, don't you?"

I smiled, shy. "Just enough to cause trouble."

He laughed, loud and genuine. "That's all any of us ever need. If you ever want to trade secrets, I make a mean campfire chili, and I hear you got a scone that can stop a wolf dead in his tracks."

"I'd love that," I said, and meant it.

He tipped his hat, polished off Papa's water in a single gulp, and vanished back into the throng.

"Does he do that to everyone?" I asked.

Papa grinned. "Only the ones he likes."

Our food came hot and heavy and everything I needed after a day of baking. The gravy on the chicken fried steak was so rich I could've eaten it with a spoon. The meatloaf was tender, the sauce tangy and a little sweet. I took a bite and moaned, then immediately slapped my hand over my mouth in embarrassment.

He leaned in, voice low. "You keep making those sounds, Sunshine, and I'll have to carry you home before dessert."

Oscar covered his face with his paws. "Have you no shame, Miss?"

I grinned at them both, and for a moment, everything felt so normal I forgot I was being hunted by at least two different supernatural species.

Then Arsenal showed up at our booth.

He stood there for a second, eyes flicking from me to Papa and back. He looked tired, older than the last time I'd seen him, and his voice was even rougher than usual.

"Big Papa," he said. "Alpha wants you to call in tonight. Some security updates."

JT nodded, all business. "Will do. You sticking around for the music?"

Arsenal shook his head. "Got patrol. But I wanted to see for myself if the rumors were true."

He looked at me, then at the hint of the bite mark on Papa's neck.

I met his gaze, trying to look brave. "It's real," I said, my voice small.

He didn't smile. "Hope you're ready."

I swallowed hard. "As I'll ever be."

Arsenal gave a curt nod, then turned and walked away, boots silent on the old tile floor.

When he was gone, I let out a deep sigh.

Papa squeezed my knee. "Don't mind him. Arsenal trusts no one. Not even himself."

Oscar bristled, his voice prim. "The man is an oaf. He would not recognize a true mate bond if it bit him in the arse."

Papa snorted. "Don't judge a man too harshly unless you've walked in his shoes. I still think love is going to hit that one right upside his head someday."

We finished our meal, talking about nothing important—the best donut in town, whether or not Oscar could learn to play chess, what time I should show up at the MC for the ceremony. As we were walking out, Pearl caught Papa at the bar and wanted to discuss a few things about the ceremony. I was just about dancing with the urge to potty, so I excused myself to the lady's room.

"I'll just be a sec," I told him. "Nature calls." He leaned back and looked down the hall towards the restrooms like he was checking for predators.

"There and back," he ordered.

I handed him my bag, Oscar safely in tow, gave him a mock salute and headed that way.

The women's restroom was down a narrow hall lined with black-and-white photos of Dairyville's early days. Inside, it was the usual:

two stalls, a two-sink vanity, and a mirror that made everyone look haunt-ed.

I did my business, washed my hands, and stared at my reflection. The bite mark on my shoulder was half-hidden by my dress, but I could feel it pulsing with every heartbeat. I traced it gently with my finger, the memory of last night's passion still burning under my skin.

"Nice mark," said a voice behind me.

I spun around. A woman I'd never seen stood at the door, face pale and angular, her hair in a perfect twist. She wore a conservative navy dress that looked twenty years out of date, but her lipstick was red as blood.

"Thanks," I said, trying to keep my voice steady.

She smiled, but it didn't reach her eyes. "You know, some wounds never really heal."

I turned off the faucet, dried my hands, and edged toward the door.

She stepped in front of me, blocking my way. When she looked at me, her eyes went completely white—no iris, no pupil, just a film of milky frost.

"You can run," she said, her voice suddenly deeper, older, "but there's no hiding. I've found you, and I'm coming for you. No wolf in the world can stop me."

The air went cold. The lights flickered, shadows twisting on the tile. The smell of roses and rot filled the tiny room.

I staggered backward, clutching the edge of the sink.

The woman's lips curled. "That's right, Aspen. The Wyrdmother always gets what she's after."

I bumped the woman's shoulder as I tried to get to the door. She blinked, and her eyes turned normal again, but she looked confused, like she had no idea where she was.

I finally ducked past her and ran out of the women's restroom and straight into a wall of muscle and leather. My first thought was that the Wyrdmother's assassin had followed me out of the restroom, but when I looked up, I saw Arsenal's stony face staring back at me, eyes sharp as razors.

He grabbed my arms hard enough to hurt. "What happened?"

I tried to push past him. "Let go—"

He didn't. "You're shaking. What happened?"

I couldn't catch my breath. The hallway was too small, the lights too bright, the air tasted like bleach and old secrets. I was going to scream if he didn't let go.

"Hey!" Papa's voice boomed from the bar. He was on us in three steps, shoving Arsenal's hands off my shoulders with a growl.

"Let her go. Now." His tone was pure wolf, and for a second, I thought Arsenal would fight him right there in the hallway.

I twisted free, stumbling into Papa's arms. He held me tight, so tight I could barely breathe, but I didn't care. I needed something real to hold on to.

Arsenal stood there, arms crossed, jaw clenched. "What's going on?" he demanded.

Papa ran a hand through my hair. "Sunshine, tell me."

I tried. "There was a woman. In the bathroom. I—she—" My teeth were chattering, my whole body shaking.

Papa knelt to look me in the eye, gentle but relentless. "Start from the beginning."

I gulped air, fighting the urge to throw up. "She had white eyes. Pure white. She said the Wyrdmother's coming for me. She said—she said—'no wolf in the world can stop me.'"

The words hung in the air, heavy as anvils.

Arsenal's eyes narrowed. "Did she touch you?"

I shook my head. "She blocked my way. But I have protection spells. She couldn't touch me. She just wanted to scare me." My voice sounded hollow, even to myself.

Arsenal stalked into the bathroom, slammed the door, and returned thirty seconds later. "Empty," he reported. "No trace."

Papa pulled me closer, his hand splayed protectively over my spine. He turned to Arsenal. "See anything out of place?"

Arsenal shook his head. "Not unless you count a haunted mirror and an air freshener from 2005."

Papa didn't smile. "If you see anyone out of place, you bring the whole pack. We don't take chances."

Arsenal nodded, then left without another word, boots pounding down the hall.

I was still shaking. I took my bag from Papa so I could free Oscar from inside. His tiny head poked out.

"She's not here now, Miss," he whispered, his voice trembling. "It's safe to leave."

Oscar climbed instantly onto my shoulder, visible only to us. "Come on," Papa said, voice low and urgent. "We're going home."

He didn't wait for argument. We cut through the bar, past the pool table and the empty stage and the thicket of voices that suddenly seemed a world away. Outside, the wind had picked up, scattering gravel across the parking lot. Papa's truck loomed under the lone street-light, dust swirling around the tires.

He opened the passenger door, helped me inside, and then slid behind the wheel. He started the engine, but before he put it in gear, he turned to me.

"You're safe," he said again. "I'll never let her touch you."

I wanted to believe him. I really did. But all I could feel was the cold in my bones and the ghostly echo of that voice.

He called Bronc on the drive home, hands-free on the truck's Bluetooth. The conversation was short and sharp, like the crack of a whip. Papa relayed everything—the confrontation in the bathroom, the threat, Arsenal's check—and then listened as Bronc spat a string of curses I'd never heard before.

"We up security," Bronc said, voice like a stone wall. "We double down on everything. You said she's got her magic working now so she and Oscar can start getting wards up around the entire territory. I trust them to keep those fuckers out. Tell her to go about her business but keep her head on a swivel. We'll deal with the rest."

Papa grunted agreement, then hung up.

My heart swelled with the feeling of family.

"Bronc has no idea what those words mean to me. Besides my mother, I've never had a family before. This moment is the first time in my life I've felt like that's not the case." I know I sounded pathetic, but it needed to be said.

He reached for my hand across the console, his palm rough but steady. I let him take it, clinging like a lifeline.

The prairie was pitch black outside the cab. The only light came from the dashboard and the occasional sweep of headlights across fenceposts and barbed wire. The engine was a low, soothing rumble, and the smell of leather and sugar clung to my clothes.

"Sunshine," he said, voice soft now, "you okay?"

I tried to nod. "I'm sorry," I whispered.

He squeezed my hand so hard it almost hurt. "None of this is your fault. Don't ever say that."

"But—" My throat closed up. "If I weren't here, the pack wouldn't be—"

He cut me off. "Don't. You belong here. You heard what Bronc said. And I want you here. We'll protect you."

I wiped my eyes with the back of my hand. "I need to bake for the ceremony," I said. "I won't let them stop me."

He smiled, just a little. "That's my girl."

Oscar patted my ear. "You are braver than you believe, Miss."

I swallowed hard. "I can do it. I'll finish the cakes. I'll help with the wards. And if I have to—" I looked up at Papa, heart pounding, "—I'll leave. I won't let them hurt anyone else."

Papa shook his head. "No, you won't. Not unless I'm with you."

I smiled a thin, fragile thing. "Deal."

We turned onto the dirt road that led to his place—our place—and the headlights caught a pair of eyes reflecting in the brush. Deer, probably. Maybe a raccoon. But my witch senses tingled all the same.

"I've already warded the house. We're safe in here."

He parked in front of the house, then walked me to the door, never letting go of my hand. Oscar scampered ahead, checking every shadow before we entered.

Inside, everything was just as we'd left it: the scent of clean linen, the warmth of the wood stove, the silent promise of safety. Papa made me tea, real chamomile with honey, and sat with me on the sofa until I stopped shaking.

I stared at the fireplace, flames crackling and spitting, and made three silent vows: I would bake every cake on time. I would ward this territory, even if it cost me sleep and blood. And I would never let the past win, not even for a second.

Papa pressed a kiss to my temple. "We're gonna make it," he said.

I believed him. I had to.

Because when the monsters came, I wanted them to find me ready. Not hiding. Not afraid.

I fell asleep on the couch, Oscar curled on my chest, the fire dying down to embers. Papa stayed beside me, one hand over my heart, as if daring the world to try to take me again.

CHAPTER 19

Big Papa

Every wolf knew we didn't fuck around when we picked a fight. We rolled in with numbers, muscle, and enough reckless pride to take a beating just for the chance to give one back. Just like when we'd tangled with Greenbriar weeks ago, it was all blood and bone, and death. It was clear who the enemy was, where they were, and what they wanted to do to you. Straightforward work—a test of nerve, not a battle of ghosts.

Witches, though? That was a different hell. You trained for the wolves, ran drills and sparred until every move was muscle memory. But how the fuck did you fight a rumor, or a spell? How did you kill what you couldn't see?

I'd never say it out loud, but there was a part of me—the broken, still-mending piece under all that leather and bravado—that was afraid I couldn't protect Aspen from what was coming. Couldn't shield her from curses, or ghosts, or the kind of rage that only burned hotter when you thought you'd snuffed it out. I could put my body between her and a bullet. I could take a bite, a punch, a broken bone. But this? This was like chasing smoke.

I woke before dawn, restless, and padded barefoot through the dark house to the kitchen. Oscar sat on the windowsill, preening his whiskers and muttering to himself in the dim light. He saw me and nodded, grave as a judge.

"Good morning, sir," he said. "You look like you've been up since last Tuesday."

"Can't sleep," I said, not bothering with lies. "Want coffee?"

"If it's not a bother," he replied. "Heavy on the cream, if you please."

He watched, silent, as I ground the beans and measured the water, the quiet of the house settling over us like a thick wool blanket. When the brew was done, I poured a cup for each of us and set his tiny one by the window. He dipped his nose into the mug and let out a tiny sigh of satisfaction.

"She's safe for now," he said softly, staring out into the black prairie. "But they'll try again."

"I know."

"She's braver than you think. More than she thinks, at least."

"I know that too." I sipped the coffee and let the bitterness remind me I was alive. "Doesn't make it easier."

He watched me for a moment, then went back to his survey of the yard. "They'll come for her at the bakery. It won't do them any good. We've got the wards buttoned up tightly there."

"They won't give up I'm sure," I said. "But we'll be ready."

Oscar's mouth twitched, almost a smile. "We'll do our best to be."

By six, the bakery was humming. Aspen wore her new favorite dress—a little navy thing with a white collar and short sleeves, paired with black tights and tall boots. Her hair was up in a high ponytail, flour already dusting the tips black and white. She worked the dough with a confidence I'd never seen in her before, rolling and shaping like she was built for it.

"Papa," she called, "Kolache batch one's ready for the oven."

"On it," I replied, grabbing the trays with a kitchen towel and loading them into the big steel beast of an oven she'd inherited from the previous owner. The heat blasted my face, sharp and clean, and for a minute I could almost believe everything outside the bakery walls was just a bad dream.

Oscar perched on the counter, invisible to anyone but us, reviewing the orders on a clipboard nearly as big as his body. "Miss, you have a custom cake order for the Winthrop first birthday at ten. Kitty cat theme, I believe."

Aspen snorted. "Almost done with that one. Just gotta get that little kitty done."

I set out the scones and wiped the counter, then flipped the sign in the window to OPEN. The first customer of the day was a cowboy in starched Wranglers and a worn work shirt with pearl snaps. He looked me up and down—six-five, scarred, beard maybe a day over neat, and standing in a bakery like I owned the place.

He blinked. "Morning. Where's the, uh—"

"Right here," Aspen called, waving from behind the counter. "I'm training him. He's not as fast as me, but he's got a sweet tooth."

The cowboy grinned, and the tension snapped. "Got any of those jalapeno cheddar scones?"

Oscar slipped off the counter and scurried to the fridge, grabbing the special box before I could even answer. I handed it over and rang him up with a smile, and the man tipped his hat to Aspen as he left.

"He likes you," I said, winking at her.

"He likes the scones," she replied, face pink. But I could see the pride in her eyes. She was good at this. Maybe better than she knew.

For the next hour, we worked the morning rush: teachers grabbing coffee and cinnamon rolls, a group of women in athletic gear who gossiped loud enough to shake the windows, a tired mom with three kids in tow. I handled the register, Aspen ran the ovens, and Oscar handled quality control by stealing crumbs and giving them a tiny, judgy taste-test.

Every so often, someone would look at me and ask, "Aren't you Big Papa from Iron Valor?" or "Didn't I see you at the parade last month?" I'd shrug, say, "I get that a lot," and try not to laugh when they did a double-take seeing me in a bakery apron. It was a hell of a lot better than being recognized for the scars.

During a lull, Oscar hopped onto my shoulder, careful to avoid the flour dust.

"She's doing well today," he murmured. "No nightmares last night?"

"Not that I could tell," I said. "She slept like a log."

Oscar nodded, satisfied. "Keep her busy, keep her safe."

"Working on it," I replied, and meant it.

By eleven, the traffic had thinned. Aspen sat at one of the front tables, sipping a mug of coffee and reading her mother's grimoire, lips moving as she practiced a protection spell under her breath. Her hand traced the outline of the sigil on the cover, and I could see a faint shimmer where her skin met the leather. Magic, I guessed. It still gave me chills.

I cleared the last table and was about to pour myself a cup when the bell above the door chimed.

Bronc and Juliet walked in, arm in arm. He wore his usual jeans and a black tee under the club cut, silver glinting at the temples of his short-cropped hair. Juliet—pregnant now and glowing like she'd swallowed the sun—wore a green dress and a denim jacket, her hair down in waves. She moved slower these days, and Bronc hovered close, his hand never straying far from her back.

"Morning, y'all," I said, grinning. "To what do I owe the pleasure?"

Juliet beamed at Aspen. "Craving lemon tarts. Heard you were the only one in town who makes them right."

Aspen stood, smoothing her skirt. "Yes, ma'am. I'll box up half a dozen."

Bronc scanned the shop, eyes missing nothing. He nodded to me, then to Oscar—who gave a tiny, dignified bow from behind the espresso machine. "Everything quiet this morning?" he asked.

"So far," I said, keeping my voice low. "No sign of weirdness. No new faces, no trouble."

He relaxed just a little. "Good. We want to keep it that way."

I poured two cups of coffee—black for the men, chamomile tea for Juliet—and brought them to the table where Aspen was boxing the tarts. She glanced up at me, eyes green and bright, and I felt the mate bond pulse through my chest. It was like someone had run a live wire straight to my heart. Every time she smiled, the world made sense again.

Juliet caught me staring and grinned. "You're totally gone for her."

I shrugged, unashamed. "Who woulda thunk it?"

We all sat together, talking about the bakery, the upcoming ceremony, and the million little details that needed sorting before Saturday. Aspen gave a full report on the cake: "I'll have the layers baked and cooled, then wrapped and into the chiller. The delivery is at three on Saturday, so I'll do final assembly and decorating on site. I'm bringing Oscar for quality control."

Oscar piped up, "I have studied many wedding cakes, Miss. I shall ensure the buttercream is not too sweet."

Bronc snorted. "Don't let him near the chocolate. I hear he's got a problem."

Oscar looked offended, but only for a second. "Sir, I am a professional."

Juliet sipped her tea and sighed, content. "You two are going to make the prettiest cake on the continent. I can feel it in my bones."

I turned to Bronc. "How's everything on the security end?"

He rolled his eyes. "Church is running drills every night. Arsenal's got two teams watching the perimeter. If a witch so much as sneezes in Dairyville, we'll know."

I nodded. "Good."

Juliet leaned in, conspiratorial. "So what's the plan for the ceremony, Papa? I know you're in charge of the, uh, symbolism."

I grinned. "You'll see. I wanted something that matched the two of you. Wild, a little crazy, but still sweet."

Juliet looked at Bronc, eyes shining. "He's making us a ritual."

"I heard," Bronc said, pride and affection plain on his face. "Wouldn't trust anyone else with it."

We finished the tarts and let Aspen get back to work. When Bronc and Juliet left, Juliet hugged Aspen tight and whispered something in her ear that made Aspen blush bright red. Bronc clapped me on the back, then looked me dead in the eye.

"You're doing a good job," he said quietly. "She's stronger than ever."

"I just want her happy," I said, and meant it with everything I had.

"She is," he replied. "Keep it up."

They left, the door jingling behind them.

The rest of the day was slow, and Aspen used the time to prep doughs for tomorrow's marathon bake. Oscar took up a post on the windowsill, eyes half-lidded in the late-afternoon sun. I swept the floor, cleaned the counters, and tried not to think about the hundred ways the next few days could go wrong.

I slipped upstairs while Aspen was cleaning the bathrooms and dialed Wrecker. He answered on the first ring, like he knew I'd be calling before I even pressed send.

"What's up, Papa?" His voice was scratchy with fatigue, probably from an all-nighter patching up the club's security system.

"Hey, I got a weird request," I said, glancing at the stairs to make sure Aspen was still downstairs, humming to herself while she worked. "I was wondering if you could pull together some things for me from your playroom? Just the basics. Maybe a nice soft blindfold, some restraints, you know, beginner stuff."

He laughed long and low. "You planning on making your mate howl tonight?"

"Something like that," I said, running a hand through my hair. "I don't own any of that shit. Never thought I'd have anyone special enough that I'd need it. I just want to give her a night to really unwind. Like, the whole nine yards."

"Yeah, man, I got you." There was shuffling on his end, maybe him digging through the closet or a locked trunk. "You want the leather cuffs or the padded? I'll even toss in a soft flogger like the one you used at Kozlov's club."

I snorted. "Class act. Pack me a sampler, would you? I'll swing by after close. Aspen can wait in the truck."

He grunted, but there was affection underneath it. "She's good for you, Papa. Never seen you so alive."

"She's everything," I said, surprised at the catch in my own voice. "Thanks, brother."

"Anytime," he said, then hung up.

As we locked up, Aspen looked at me and smiled, tired but content. "Thank you for everything today," she said.

I cupped her face and kissed her softly. "Anytime, Sunshine."

She touched the spot where I'd kissed her, then nodded at Oscar, who was already snoring on his back, paws twitching like he was chasing something in his dreams.

"Let's take him home," I said.

She laughed. "He deserves a treat. And so do you."

We left the bakery behind, the prairie sun low and gold over the horizon, and I promised myself I'd make tonight special for her. After everything she'd survived, she deserved more than protection—she deserved to know what it felt like to be truly cherished.

I'd figure out how to do that, even if it killed me.

I locked up, double-checked every latch, then ushered Aspen out into the chilly dusk. She shivered, so I wrapped my jacket around her and held her close as we walked to the truck.

"What's the plan tonight?" She asked, eyes hopeful and a little shy.

I wanted to say, "Ruin you, in the best possible way," but I bit it back. "Something you won't forget," I said, and kissed her hair.

Wrecker's driveway was empty except for Parker's fancy sports car and his fancy Ford. I told Aspen to wait in the cab. "I'll be two seconds, I promise." Then I jogged up to the front door.

Wrecker answered in jeans and a t-shirt, bare arms covered in ink, his hair still damp from the shower.

"Got your care package," he said, handing me a heavy black duffel with reinforced handles. It clinked, like there were more than just restraints inside.

"Extras?" I asked, one brow up.

He shrugged, a wicked grin on his face. "I added the stuff you liked at Kozlov's club. And a couple new things, just in case you're feeling creative." His gaze softened, voice lowering. "She's gonna love it, man. Just be gentle. That one's got a heart like a biscuit."

"She's tougher than she looks," I said, but I smiled at the truth of it. "You and Parker doing okay?"

He nodded. "She's a handful. But she's worth the trouble." He patted my shoulder, firm and final. "Go knock her socks off, Big Papa."

I waved the bag and headed out; the gravel crunching under my boots.

Aspen watched me load the duffel behind the seat. "What's in there?" She asked, voice barely a whisper.

"Surprise for later," I said. "You trust me?"

Her green eyes were steady and clear. "Yes. Always."

Back home, I hung the duffel in the closet and told Aspen to meet me in the bedroom after she washed up.

She went, with a little nervous energy in her steps, and I could hear her run the faucet, brush her teeth, and whisper something to Oscar as he snoozed in his travel basket. I changed into a pair of black athletic shorts, then set up the room: dimmed the lights, drew the curtains.

She came in a minute later, wrapped in nothing but a towel, cheeks flushed pink. She stopped just inside the doorway, uncertain.

"Come here, Sunshine," I said, voice soft.

She obeyed, and I tugged her gently into my arms, feeling the warmth of her bare skin through the thin cotton. I kissed her temple, then slid the towel off her shoulders. She gasped, suddenly shy, but I kept my hands on her arms, grounding her.

"I want to try something tonight," I said, keeping my tone even. "If you hate it, say so. I'll stop. But I think you'll like it."

She nodded, breath trembling.

"First, I want you to relax. Can you do that for me?"

She nodded again, and I led her back to the bathroom, where I ran a bath for her. I added lavender and a handful of sage from the garden and made sure it was steaming hot. The air was thick with scent, and the water shimmered in the low light.

"Get in," I said, and she did, sliding under the surface with a sigh. The water came up to her chest, and I knelt beside the tub and traced a finger down her collarbone.

She shivered, but not from the cold. "You're so gentle," she whispered.

"Not always," I promised, and she smiled, anticipating what was coming.

I reached for some bath wash and a washcloth, then lathered her skin—slow circles on her arms, her shoulders, down the slope of her back and over her hips. She let her head fall back against the rim, eyes closed, trusting me completely. I lifted her leg and ran the cloth down one side and up the other. When I reached the top, I lightly grazed her pussy as I turned my hand and felt wetness that was more than the bathwater. Then I ran the cloth down her other leg.

"Mmm you're a tease," she murmured.

"Only a little bit," I said as I grazed her clit this time and she shuddered a little.

I leaned down and gave her a small kiss, my tongue reaching out and giving her lips a small lick as she tried to lean up for more.

"Uh uh. Tonight, you take only what I give you, Sunshine. But not to worry. I'm going to give you so much."

Her surprised face was so adorable.

When I rinsed her, the water turned milky with suds and herbs. I lifted her hand, kissed her palm, then trailed kisses up the inside of her arm to the hollow of her elbow.

She made a soft sound, half moan, half plea.

"Are you ready for what I have in store?" I asked, and she nodded, her eyes glassy with want.

I helped her out, wrapped her in a thick towel, and dried the ends of her hair with another. She stood there, flushed and perfect, while I finished toweling off her legs and feet. Then I scooped her up, carried her to the bed, and set her down on the fresh cotton sheets.

I went to the closet and returned with the duffel, unzipping it slow so she could see every step. She watched, curiosity and hunger fighting for space on her face.

I stood her at the foot of our canopy bed.

I pulled out the padded cuffs first—soft black leather, lined with lambswool. I showed them to her, let her touch the material, then wrapped one around her wrist and buckled it, snug but not tight. She shivered again, but this time with anticipation.

"Do you trust me?" I asked one more time.

"Yes," she said, voice strong now.

I cuffed the other wrist, then pulled her to me to the foot of the bed. I used the connecting strap to secure her hands above her head when I looped it over the wrought-iron bar of the canopy. She stood facing me, arms extended, breasts rising and falling with each breath.

Next came the blindfold—silk, soft and cool. I tied it behind her head, careful to keep her hair from snagging.

"You look beautiful. But I need you to stand with your legs spread for me please," I said, and she blushed, even though she couldn't see me. She did as she was told. Such a good girl.

"Now what?" she asked, voice a little shaky.

"Now you just feel," I said.

I let my hands roam—down her arms, over her ribs, circling her nipples with my thumbs until they stood hard and pink. She moaned, twisting her hips. I pinched one nipple, then soothed it with a kiss, switching to the other and repeating until she was squirming.

I reached for the next item in the bag—a small, soft leather flogger, the tails fine and supple as suede. I brushed it over her belly, her thighs, the curve of her hip. She jerked, surprised, but then melted into it as I flicked it lightly over her inner thighs.

"You like that?" I asked.

"Yes, sir," she gasped.

I worked up a rhythm, letting the strands tease her breasts, her belly, then back to her thighs. Each stroke left a faint red trail, and soon her skin glowed with heat.

I stopped and knelt between her legs, running my hands up the inside of her thighs. She was soaked, the scent of her need mixing with lavender and sage. I licked a stripe up her pussy, tasting her, and she arched up, straining against the cuffs.

"Please," she whimpered.

"Patience," I said, and reached for the next surprise.

But I paused just a moment to look at her—flushed, trembling, helpless and completely safe in my hands. She trusted me. She wanted this. And I wanted to give her the whole fucking world.

"Papa?" she whispered, and I knew she was ready for whatever came next.

I smiled, even though she couldn't see it, and bent down to kiss her, gentle, slow, promising her everything.

The real fun was just beginning.

I let her squirm for a moment before I moved on.

I reached into the duffel, grabbed the little purple vibe Wrecker had slipped in, and thumbed it on low. The sound was almost nothing, but Aspen flinched, her breath hitching in the sweetest way. I trailed the tip over her nipple—she jolted, almost yelped, then bit her lip. I circled it, flicked the speed up a notch, and watched her whole body tense.

"You good?" I asked, pausing just long enough to let the question register.

She nodded, hair falling over the blindfold. "It's so much," she said, voice thin with desperation.

"That's the idea," I said. "You tell me if it gets to be too much."

She whimpered but didn't ask me to stop. I alternated the vibe between her nipples, then down her ribs, then lower, brushing the insides of her thighs. She was panting now, hips rolling, knees getting wider like she was begging.

I held it over her clit, let the hum vibrate through her, and she made a noise that was part mewl, part sob. Her arms strained at the cuffs, fingers flexing and unflexing. She tried to close her legs, but I pressed them apart, holding her open.

"Papa, please—"

I clicked the vibe to high, pressed it hard to her clit, and she lost it. Her back arched and her body folded as much as she could while suspended, and she howled my name as she came, shuddering so hard I had to hold her down to keep her from pulling too hard.

I didn't stop. I kept the pressure on, working the vibe in slow, cruel circles until she was begging me to let up. I dialed it down, then slid it inside her, just an inch, and she gasped again—so sensitive, so close to breaking. I leaned in, licking her slick, and she moaned so loud I was glad the house was a quarter mile from the road.

She was a mess, sweat and tears and spit, but she was beautiful.

I set the vibe aside, wiped her down with a warm towel, then uncuffed her wrists. She sagged, boneless, in my arms. I laid her across the bed and peeled off the blindfold, and her eyes were wild, pupils blown black.

"You still okay?" I asked, voice hoarse.

She didn't answer with words. She lunged at me, legs around my waist, arms locked behind my neck, pressing her wet heat against my stomach. She climbed me, feral and hungry, and crashed her mouth to mine.

I caught her, pressed her onto her back, and lined up at her entrance. She was still quivering, but she needed this—I could feel it in the bond. I pushed in, slow at first, letting her adjust, but she rocked her hips up, desperate for me to fill her.

I obliged. I slammed into her, hard, and she screamed again, this time in pure, raw joy.

I fucked her like I'd never get the chance again; deep, fast, relentless. She clung to me, nails digging into my shoulders, legs wrapped around my ass. I felt the orgasm build in her, tight and hot, and when it hit she shook so hard it took everything I had to keep going.

She begged me to come, begged for it with words and moans and clawing need. I flipped her over onto her stomach.

"Present yourself to your mate, Sunshine."

She went up on her knees and looked at me over her shoulder. She looked feral.

"Take what your mate is offering, Alpha," she said deep and raw.

Something snapped inside me when she called me her Alpha. I knew what she meant. We both understood perfectly well that Bronc was the Alpha of this pack, but she just declared that I was the Alpha of this home.

I slammed into her again as she presented her perfect ass to me.

"You are the perfect mate for me. Magnificent in every way." I told her as I slammed into her over and over. I pulled out and stuck my finger in her pussy, getting it saturated with her wetness. Then I swirled it around her tight pucker, and her breath hitched.

"Do you trust your Alpha?"

She took a breath. "I do."

I pressed my finger into that tight ring of muscle, and it gave way. She moaned when I also slammed my cock back into her entrance. Her moans of ecstasy told me how much she loved the feeling of being totally filled by me.

"How can it feel so good?" She cried through her moans.

I could feel my knot start to swell as I continued to pound both holes.

"I live for your pleasure, mate."

I turned her body so she was on her back. I wanted to see her face. I looked down at where we were joined, amazed at how her body opened to make room for my knot. It was a miracle to me.

I knew she was close again, so I reached down and circled her clit with my thumb. Her release crashed over her, causing me to come in a torrent of release in a river of cum as she juddered her hips against me and I rocked as much as I could, emptying every ounce of myself into her.

We stayed like that, panting and sweating, for a long, long time.

Eventually, the knot softened, and I slipped out, rolling onto my back. Aspen curled up on my chest, hair tangled, skin flushed.

"That wasn't too much was it? I didn't hurt you?" I asked, stroking her hair.

She laughed, breathless. "It could never be too much."

I held her close, kissed her forehead, and let her breathe.

She was spectacular in every way. I told her so.

When I caught my breath, I grabbed a damp warm towel and cleaned her and then tucked her under the covers.

I left for the kitchen and came back with a tray of meat, cheese, fruit, and bread. She ate, starved, giggling at the way I fussed over her.

We finished the tray, then fell asleep in each other's arms, safe and whole.

The next day, we'd fight the world.

But tonight, she was mine, and I was hers, and nothing could touch us. If we could only keep the enemies from coming.

CHAPTER 20

Aspen

Bakery hours worm their way into your bones. Even if you go to bed at midnight, you're up at four, eyelids peeled open, heart drumming with the certainty that somewhere, a batch of cinnamon rolls is about to burn. I surfaced from the depths at 4:14, every cell crackling with energy, and spent a full minute cradled in the dark tangle of our bedsheets, listening to Papa snore soft and deep beside me.

That would have been enough for the old Aspen—just lying there, counting the seconds, watching the rectangle of moonlight crawl along the wall. But the new Aspen, the one who had completed her mate bond and survived it, was restless. My body tingled, every nerve ending humming like a live wire, skin still sensitive where his teeth had marked me.

I slid out from under Papa's arm, careful not to wake him, and padded barefoot to the bathroom. The shower stall was still damp from last night, and the whole room smelled like lavender and sage. I let the water run hot and stood under it, trying to reassemble my sense of self after being absolutely, undeniably ravaged by my mate. In the best way.

The memory of last night ran on a loop in my head—how he'd stripped me down, lifted me up, worked me open with tongue and hands and words so filthy I'd blushed in places I didn't know could flush. Our mate bond made every time we're together feel like a rush of sensation that made me see stars. It should have scared me. Instead, I felt… powerful. Like I could walk into any coven in Texas and hex the paint off the walls.

I toweled off and checked my reflection. The mate mark was beautiful: a bite-shaped crescent that had healed fast, surrounded by skin that glowed warm pink. My mother's green eyes looked back at me, brighter than ever, the whites clear and fierce. There were shadows under them, but they made me look powerful, not tired.

I threw on a pretty red dress with little white Swiss polka dots and a bow at the white collar. White tights and black boots completed my look. I dressed a bit unconventionally for Dairyville, but even if the people around here didn't know it, I *was* a witch after all. I pulled my hair up into a high ponytail and made my way to the kitchen.

The sight stopped me cold: Papa, fully dressed in a black Henley and jeans, was flipping bacon at the stove, coffee already percolating. Oscar sat at the table, whiskers immaculate, dressed in a tailored green jacket with a gold brocade vest and a crisp white cravat. The two of them looked like the opening to a very strange sitcom.

Papa turned at the sound of my feet. "Morning, Sunshine," he rumbled. "You're looking beautiful as always. Pretty as a picture."

"You're too sweet," I said, eyeing the plate of fluffy scrambled eggs and triangles of toast that waited on the counter. "You're spoiling me."

He shrugged, setting down the spatula and crossing the kitchen in three strides. He pressed a kiss to my forehead, hands gentle on my waist. "It's not spoiling if you deserve it."

Oscar cleared his throat. "Miss, I recommend the eggs before they lose their steam. There's nothing sadder than congealed yolk."

I grinned and slid into my usual seat, Oscar to my left, Papa on my right. The food was hot and perfect, the bacon crisp, the toast buttered to the very edges. I enjoyed every bite. I couldn't tell if it was the bond or just happiness, but I was starving.

Papa poured me a glass of orange juice, then sat back with his own coffee. "I'll be heading out after the store opens," he said. "Church at the clubhouse starts early. Bronc wants us on high alert until the ceremony's over."

My heart skipped. "You think they'll try something? The witches, or—"

He shook his head. "Don't know. But Bronc isn't taking any chances." He set his mug down, voice dropping. "We'll have teams running perimeter checks day and night. Arsenal and Gunner are handling inside security. I want you and Oscar to stick together. Don't go anywhere alone, not even to the back trash bin."

Oscar puffed up, tiny chest swelling with pride. "I shall attend to the Miss as though she were the crown jewels, sir."

I wanted to make a joke, but the worry in Papa's eyes killed it on my tongue. "We'll be careful," I promised. "I want to see Bronc and Juliet's ceremony go off without a hitch. They deserve it. And I don't wanna see anybody get hurt on my account."

"I know you don't sweetheart. And we want to give Bronc and Juliet a night they'll want to remember forever." Papa said.

We ate in peaceful silence for a bit. I could feel the energy between us—hot and sweet and hard to describe. I wanted to crawl into his lap and never leave, but Oscar would probably combust from embarrassment, and besides, I had work to do.

Oscar seemed to read my mind. "Miss, your bakery schedule is quite full today. Shall we review?"

"Go for it," I said, glad for the change in topic.

He pulled a tiny notebook from somewhere in his jacket, flicked it open with deft claws, and recited: "Kolaches, six dozen, to be delivered by ten. Sourdough proofing as we speak. You've a custom cake for the Hendricks party to be crumb coated today and finished tomorrow. The wedding cake layers are all baked and chilling. Tomorrow, assembly and piping at the venue."

I exhaled, tension bleeding from my shoulders. "We're ahead of schedule. That's a miracle."

Papa eyed me over the rim of his coffee. "*You're* a miracle, Sunshine."

I ducked my head, fighting a smile. "Don't make me blush before sunrise."

Oscar clicked his tongue. "There is nothing wrong with a healthy glow, Miss. I daresay it suits you."

We finished breakfast, and I stood. Papa lingered, clearing the table, then wrapped his arms around me from behind. His hands splayed across my hips, holding me steady.

"You good?" he asked, voice close to my ear.

"Better than I've ever been," I said, truth warming my chest. "Just a little overwhelmed."

He squeezed me gently. "We've got you. All of us."

I nodded, letting myself melt into his arms for one perfect second. Then I straightened, squared my shoulders, and said, "Alright, gents. Time to make the donuts."

Oscar hopped off the chair, bowing at the waist. "Lead on, Miss."

Papa watched us for a second, pride and love all over his face, before heading out to the truck. "Let's get this show on the road," he said as the screen door slammed behind him, and I let the quiet settle.

We all headed to the truck. He got me settled into my seat and fastened my seatbelt securely in place before heading to the driver's seat. Those little things he did spoke of more than his love for me; they said he cherished me. That meant almost as much. He didn't do it to make me feel weak. It was how he expressed to me how important it was to him that I was safe. I never wanted to rob him of that by fussing about the fact that I was capable of doing it myself. I liked the fact that I mattered to him, even in the small things.

The drive to the bakery took the usual fifteen minutes and gave me a moment to get my thoughts mapped out for how I wanted the morning prep to run. There was a method to how I ordered my mornings. Some doughs needed to be started so they could be in the proofing drawer before others if I expected to have rolls or breads in the case by the time we opened. Others could wait. It was all a balancing act. Some days I got it right, others, not so much. But each week the routine revealed itself, and I was becoming more comfortable with the curveballs of special orders.

When we got to the store, Papa unlocked the door and started turning on the lights. Oscar and I headed straight to the kitchen to get started. I grabbed a fresh apron and turned on the oven to preheat.

Oscar scampered onto the prep counter, paws folded. "Miss, if I may speak frankly—"

"You always do," I said, grinning.

He looked up, eyes sharp. "You are strong, but you needn't be alone in this. If anything troubles you—about the grimoire, the bond, or tomorrow's event—I am here."

"Thanks, Oscar," I said, softer than I meant. "I'll remember."

He beamed. "Now, shall we get to work?"

Papa popped his head into the kitchen and asked what he could do to help. I had him pull an enormous bag of flour from the storage closet. He was great for muscling things around. He set it out by my industrial mixer and got it opened and ready for me. I had him get the dining room ready, moving the chairs down from the tables and setting up the napkin holders and setting out the sugar caddies. We made a great team.

I set to work for a few hours, and the world shrank to flour and eggs and the rhythm of mixing, folding, rolling. Oscar read the orders aloud and double-checked every measurement. He even taste-tested the kolache filling, though I caught him sneaking some strawberry jam just for pleasure.

Papa headed out just after the open sign went on and the bell over the door started ringing.

The morning sped by, one perfect pastry at a time. And as had come my routine, I felt...prepared. Not just for the bakery, or the ceremony, but for whatever hell the world wanted to throw at me next.

Bring it on, I thought. I was ready.

The bakery always grew quiet after the first rush, the air thick with the ghosts of cinnamon and butter, the sun rising slow and lazy across the checkered tiles. I wiped the counters and let my mind drift, watching the dust motes spin in the pale beam slicing through the front window. Oscar, who had decided the best place for a familiar was directly in the patch of morning sunlight, perched on the prep table and looked every bit the dignified familiar, if you ignored the crumb of cheese danish clinging to his whiskers.

"Miss," he said, after clearing his throat twice for effect. "If I may, now might be an ideal moment to take another look at the grimoire. There's so much we haven't gotten to. It's usually quiet until eleven, and the protection wards are fully engaged."

I dried my hands and eyed the battered, iron-clasped book sitting on the shelf behind the prep table. "You make it sound like we're about to perform a heart transplant, Oscar."

He cocked his head, whiskers quivering. "In a way, we are. The book is at the heart of your legacy. We must treat it as such."

I couldn't argue with that. I walked over, running my fingers over the tooled leather. It looked ancient, older than any book I'd seen, and the sigil on the cover still glowed faintly when I brushed it. "Alright. Let's maybe figure out why the Wyrdmother wants it so bad."

Oscar hopped closer, his beady eyes sharp and bright. "Perhaps it is not the book itself, but the knowledge locked within."

I pulled up a stool and grabbed a safety pin from the counter. I gave my thumb a little poke and let the small bead of blood smear on the clasp and flipped it open, as carefully as I could. I wiped my thumb clean and started turning pages. There were notes in the margins, diagrams, stains of old herbs and maybe a scorch mark or two. My mother's handwriting danced across half the pages, but what caught my attention were the blank sheets.

Except, they weren't blank. Not really.

I ran my palm over one, and it felt warmer than paper should. Not hot, but faintly alive, like it was waiting for something. I frowned and turned to Oscar. "Why would there be blank pages between written pages in a spellbook? Wouldn't you want to fill every bit of space with something useful?"

He considered. "Some witches leave room for future generations, Miss. But more often, it's a sign of spells too dangerous to be written openly. Hidden in plain sight, as it were."

The notion made my skin crawl, but I couldn't help myself. I flipped another page, then another, each blank but not empty. My fingers tingled. I leaned in closer, nose almost to the page, and caught the faintest whiff—iron and roses and something sharp, like ozone before a thunderstorm.

"You ever see this before?" I asked.

Oscar shuffled to the edge of the book and sniffed. "There is something locked within," he whispered, his voice more reverent than I'd ever heard. "It's waiting for the correct key."

The bell above the door chimed, making me jump. A customer—just a regular, here for kolaches and coffee—poked his head in, exchanged the usual pleasantries, and left with a box of pastries so quickly I hardly remembered the exchange.

When I returned to the grimoire, it was as if it had inched closer, eager for attention. The light in the bakery flickered as clouds passed, and the faint glow from the page seemed to pulse with every breath I took.

I flipped another leaf and felt a sting on my thumb—a paper cut, quick and clean. I cursed under my breath, bringing the finger to my lips, but a bead of blood had already welled up and fallen onto the page.

At that instant, the room shifted.

The blood drop sizzled, spreading thin as ink across the paper. Black words began to crawl up from the point of contact, letters twisting and unfurling, coalescing into a script that was at once familiar and deeply wrong. Wisps of dark smoke rose from the book, curling into the shape of words and sigils I'd never seen. The air smelled of burnt sugar and grave dirt, and my heart jackhammered in my chest.

"Bloody hell," Oscar muttered, eyes wide.

The script that appeared was jagged, the lines trembling as if fighting to stay anchored in this world. I tried to read it, but my eyes slid off the letters, my brain refusing to latch on. It was like looking at a word in a dream—you could see it, but couldn't hold it.

Beneath the crawling text, in a frantic scrawl that could only be my mother's hand, a message appeared, written over and over in the margins:

DO NOT READ

DO NOT FEED IT

WIPE IT AWAY NOW

My breath caught. I sprinted to the bathroom, thumb throbbing, and grabbed the little bottle of alcohol and a handful of cotton swabs from the medicine cabinet. I returned to the table and poured the clear liquid onto a cotton swab, pressing it to my bleeding thumb and then, hand shaking, dabbed at the drops of blood on the page.

Each swipe erased a line of the nightmare text, the smoke vanishing with a hiss. By the time I erased the last drop of my blood, the page was blank again, though it still felt alive, hungry.

Oscar had gone utterly still, like a hunting hawk. "Are you alright, Miss?"

I nodded, even though my hands wouldn't stop trembling. "What the hell was that?"

He licked his lips, or tried to. "Some spells are too powerful and not meant to be used. They're meant for witches who wish to do harm to other witches. There is a spell that can drain power from other witches. I suspect your mother was trying to keep you—and anyone else—safe from the knowledge."

I stared at the page. "So if the Wyrdmother got her hands on this—if she knew it was my blood that could make that spell appear—she could..." I trailed off, stomach turning.

Oscar finished for me. "She could drain you of every last drop. Or worse."

I looked at my thumb, blood drying, and wondered how much it would take to open all the secrets in that book. Every drop of my magic? Of my blood?

I slammed the grimoire shut, the clasp locking with a hard, final click.

"Promise me something, Oscar," I said, voice low.

"Anything, Miss."

"If anything happens to me, if I get taken, or if I...if I'm lost, you burn this book. Burn it and scatter the ashes in the canyon."

He nodded, solemn as a priest. "It will be done."

I exhaled, a little shaky, but clear-headed. I couldn't figure out why my mother would have such a spell in her possession. Until I learned what else was in the book, I would continue to protect it.

The rest of the day passed in a blur of orders and frosting and customers, but every time my eyes glanced toward the grimoire, I felt its energy hum, hungry and patient and biding its time.

At closing, Papa called to let me know he'd be a little late. They were running extra security shifts; Arsenal needed backup. I told him it was fine, and not to worry, but the moment I locked the bakery door and drew the shades, the night closed in like a fist.

Oscar climbed into the window, visible only to me, gave me a curt nod, and said, "I shall keep watch from here."

I smiled. "Good. I need to finish the crumb coat on the cake."

He nodded, curling up on a folded napkin like a general preparing for battle.

In the kitchen, I piped frosting with hands that had finally stopped shaking, and let the comfort of sugar and memory do its work. My mother had known what she was doing when she hid the dangerous spells, and now it was my turn to keep the world safe from what lurked in those pages.

I finished the cakes, cleaned the kitchen, and climbed the stairs to my little apartment above the bakery. The window looked out over the street, and for a long time I sat on the sill, watching the empty darkness, wondering if the Wyrdmother was out there, searching for a way in.

If she came, I wouldn't cower.

I was the last Waters witch, and I had work to do.

CHAPTER 21

Big Papa

I told her I'd be a little late, but would try to be there at 6:00. I usually made a habit of being early, but tonight I forced myself to arrive exactly on time. Aspen had that effect on me—made me want to get it right, even if it meant white-knuckling the steering wheel for a full sixty seconds outside her bakery so I didn't come across as someone who expected her to rush for me. The clock on the dash rolled over, and I killed the ignition, took a breath, and stepped out into the dry evening.

The sun was setting behind Dairyville's one functional stoplight, laying long shadows across the sidewalks. The bakery glowed like a lantern in the middle of the block, every pane of glass scrubbed clean, the interior so spotless it looked staged for a magazine. Aspen was already waiting, posted up behind the counter with Oscar perched on her shoulder like a familiar out of a storybook. She wore the red polka dot dress I loved, white collar crisp and hair up in a high ponytail that made her look a little younger than she was and twice as fierce.

I took an extra moment to look at her through the glass. She'd set all the chairs upside-down on the tables, swept the black-and-white tile floors to a shine, and even left a single candle burning by the register—a homey little touch for a girl who'd lived in a small cottage with her mother. But she wasn't calm. Her posture was tight, hands clasped on the counter, her eyes darting not to me, but to the battered leather bag at her feet. Even Oscar seemed on edge, his tail twitching with the kind of nervous energy I associated with incoming mortars.

I knocked twice; a habit from nights on patrol, and let myself in.

"Evening, Sunshine," I said, voice gentle.

She gave me a smile, but it was thinner than usual. "Hey, Papa. You're right on time."

Oscar nodded gravely. "Punctuality is the mark of a gentleman, sir."

I shot him a wink. "Just trying to keep up with the bakery standard."

Aspen moved around the counter and came to me, but didn't reach for a hug. She stood a little to the side, the air between us full of things unsaid. I wanted to pull her in, cradle her against my chest, but I waited. She'd had a day.

"Shop looks incredible," I said. "You running a tight ship or just trying to impress the inspectors?"

She glanced at the ceiling, like she might find words up there. "Had a lot on my mind. Cleaning helps."

I nodded. "You hungry?"

She nodded, but it was more of a reflex. "Yeah. Oscar and I skipped lunch to catch up on orders. It's been a day."

Oscar straightened his vest. "I am famished, sir. I hope the menu tonight includes your renowned triple-stack burger."

I ruffled his fur, which made him chitter. "You got it, pal."

We fell into step toward the door. I went to grab her bag—the one with the grimoire—and she snatched it up first, hugging it tight to her chest.

I raised an eyebrow. "You expecting trouble tonight?"

She looked away. "Maybe."

The walk to the truck was quiet, just our boots on the sidewalk and the prairie wind. I got her settled in, then waited until we were on the road before I said anything. The sky was the color of bruised peaches, the kind of Western sunset that made you believe in God even if you didn't much care for churches.

About two miles out of Dairyville, she spoke up, voice so small I almost missed it. "Something happened with the grimoire today. I hate to say anything. But... it scared me."

I didn't look at her, just kept my eyes on the blacktop. "Tell me."

She fidgeted, one hand on the hem of her dress, twisting it around her finger. "Oscar wanted to study some, we've hardly had any time to go through it. Which I totally agreed. I was just flipping through it. Then—" She paused, biting her lip. "I got a paper cut. A drop of blood landed on the page, and everything changed."

I kept my voice steady. "What do you mean?"

She took a breath. "The blood made words appear. Dark words. I couldn't read them, but I knew... I knew it was bad. The air went cold. All these words started appearing on the page; scrolling across. Oscar said he thought it was a spell that could drain a witch's power. Maybe even kill them."

I felt my stomach ice over. "And then?"

She hugged the bag tighter. "My mom's handwriting appeared in the margin. It said, 'DO NOT READ. DO NOT FEED IT. WIPE IT AWAY NOW.' Over and over. So I cleaned it up—scrubbed off the blood. The more I removed my blood, the more the words disappeared. Then I shut the book and locked it. I think it's okay, but..." She looked at me then, green eyes wide and scared. "I think that's what the Wyrdmother wants. That spell."

I didn't say anything for a mile. I just drove, hands gripping the wheel until my knuckles hurt. My mind spun back to every story I'd ever heard about the Verdant Hollow coven, about the lengths power-hungry witches went to just to keep an edge over their sisters. If the Wyrdmother got her hands on Aspen, on her blood, it wouldn't just be an execution—it'd be a goddamn feeding frenzy.

"Can we destroy it?" I asked. "The grimoire?"

Aspen shook her head. "It's my mother's. It's the only thing I have left of her. I can't just—" She stopped, voice shaking. "I don't want to lose her twice."

I reached across the console and took her hand, squeezing it hard. "We'll keep it safe. Arsenal's got a perimeter plan, and Oscar's no slouch. Nobody's getting through the bakery doors without going through me first."

She tried to smile, but it wobbled. "You're not scared?"

I forced a laugh, but the mate bond made it impossible to hide the truth. She felt the fear in me, the protective rage, the way my body wanted to break something just so I could keep her safe. But I kept my words light. "Not as long as you're with me, Sunshine. I faced worse than witches in the service. You're stronger than all of them put together."

Oscar poked his head out of the bag, voice crisp. "He is correct, Miss. And I shall alert you if I sense any enchantments. The wards around the bakery are robust."

I nodded. "See? You've got the best team in Texas."

She clung to that, and I could feel the bond between us settle. Not calm, but at least steady.

We drove the last mile in silence; the radio played a country ballad about lost loves and hard-won peace. I pulled up in front of Pearl's Bar & Grill and killed the engine. The neon sign buzzed overhead, promising cold beer and hot pie, but tonight it felt like walking into a courtroom, not a diner.

I looked at Aspen, took in the way she smoothed her dress and checked her reflection in the visor mirror. She looked flawless, but her hands shook.

"There's, uh, something I forgot to mention," I said, voice low. "My parents are in town for the ceremony. They wanted to meet you. Just a quick dinner, nothing serious."

Her eyes went wide. "Your parents? Tonight?"

"Yeah. They're... well, they're a lot. My mom's a wannabe Texas debutante who never quite left the sorority house, and my dad's a numbers guy. Oilman. But they'll love you. I promise."

She made a sound halfway between a laugh and a groan. "You could've warned me."

"I didn't want to stress you more."

She breathed out slow, then took my hand in hers, grounding both of us. "Let's do this. Together."

I kissed her knuckles, then her cheek. "Always."

We got out and walked up the steps. I paused at the door, took a last look at her—my mate, my miracle, the strongest damn woman in Dairyville—and I knew we could take whatever the world threw at us.

Even if it meant walking straight into the lion's den.

Pearl's Bar & Grill was packed, typical Friday, and you could smell the fried onions and whiskey from the parking lot. The dining room pulsed with old country music and the whoop of some ranch hand at the dartboard, but my attention zeroed in on the back corner table—my parents' throne whenever they blew through town.

They were already seated, the whole damn tableau as perfectly staged as a bank commercial. My mother sat ramrod straight, shoulders squared, chin lifted half an inch above everyone else. Her hair was spun gold, slicked into a chignon so tight you'd think she was afraid of spontaneous movement. She wore a tan pencil skirt and cream cardigan, a string of pearls at her throat—real, not costume. Arms crossed, nails painted nude. She could have frozen a bottle of tequila with that gaze.

My father was the opposite: broad, hearty, dressed in an expensive navy suit that didn't quite hide the bulk he'd built up in a lifetime of deals and handshakes. He stood the second he spotted me, smile wide enough to show every capped tooth. His watch cost more than my first motorcycle.

Jacob, my older brother, sat to their right, already half a glass deep in something that was probably three parts bourbon, one part ice. He gave a lazy two-finger salute and didn't bother to stand.

I squeezed Aspen's hand once and led her to the booth, Oscar tucked discreetly in her bag with the grimoire. She looked like a goddamn vision—fresh, alive, something no Rice had ever brought to dinner. I'd warned her, but nothing could prep you for the slow-motion car crash of a Rice family reunion.

"Mom, Dad, Jacob," I said. "This is Aspen. My mate."

My mother's eyes flicked to Aspen's neck, zeroing in on the claiming bite like a heat-seeking missile. Her smile didn't move.

My father broke the tension first, thrusting out a hand. "Jonas! Son, you look like a million bucks." He turned to Aspen and took her hand, holding it just a touch too long. "So, you're Aspen. Jonas told us you're the pride of Dairyville. I can see he wasn't exaggerating."

Aspen blushed, but didn't wilt. "Thank you, sir."

Jacob finally looked up, eyes a perfect match to mine, if a little more bloodshot. "So you're the witch. Hope you like steak. They don't do vegan here." As though this were her first time here.

Aspen laughed. "If it doesn't moo, I don't want it."

That got a snort from Jacob. "I like her, JT."

Mom still hadn't spoken. She let her gaze roam Aspen up and down, taking in every inch: the dress, the boots, the wild shine of her eyes. "Polka dots and a bow are bold choices," she said finally. "But I suppose it suits you." Then, to me, "She's prettier than I expected. I was worried you might have gone for someone—well, less. She's certainly prettier than your last girlfriend. What was her name, Paul?" she looked at my father.

Jacob mumbled, "Rebecca is married now, Mom."

"Ah, that's right, Rebecca," she said while taking her seat.

I wanted to punch a hole in the table. Instead, I smiled as I pulled out the chair for Aspen. "She's perfect for me."

Before the next shot could be fired, Pearl herself materialized at the table, balancing a tray of biscuits and a crock of honey butter. Her hair was snow white tonight, teased into a soft halo. She gave my mother a hard look, then turned to Aspen with a warmth that could have melted a steel drum.

"Well, if it ain't our newest couple. Welcome, honey. We need to talk about getting another one of your chocolate cakes for the restaurant. The last one you made was gone in an hour. Can I get y'all started with drinks?"

Aspen ordered iced tea, and I asked for a Shiner. Pearl poured for both of us, then leaned in to Aspen, hand on her shoulder, and whispered something I couldn't catch. Aspen relaxed just a shade, and I made a mental note to thank Pearl later.

As soon as Pearl was gone, my mother launched into her version of small talk, which meant getting right to the point.

"So," she said, steepling her fingers. "Jonas tells us you're from Georgia. How does a girl from so far away end up in a place like this?"

Aspen met her gaze, not blinking. "It's a long story, ma'am. But I like it here. It feels like home."

"Does it?" Mom's mouth curled at the corners. "How sweet. I hope you'll find it welcoming. Small towns can be... insular, you know."

I felt Aspen bristle. "I haven't had any trouble," she said. "People here are good. Loyal."

Jacob gave a slow clap. "She even talks like one of us. Impressive."

My father, who'd been watching the show with a lawyer's interest, jumped in. "So how did you two meet? You know, your mother and I met at a fundraiser. Her folks said it was love at first sight, but I had to wear her down. Jonas never was one for the slow approach."

I looked at Aspen, letting her answer if she wanted to.

She said, "He came into my bakery to ask about a cake for Bronc and Juliet's mating ceremony. We just hit it off I guess."

Mom made a sound that might have been a laugh, or a cough. "That's our Jonas. Always on the lookout for a good woman. Even as a child, he brought home strays."

This time, I did squeeze Aspen's hand under the table. She squeezed back, harder.

Pearl delivered our food—steak for Jacob and Dad, a chicken fried for me, meatloaf for Aspen. Oscar poked his head out to sniff at the mashed potatoes, but I nudged him back in before anyone else noticed.

For a minute, the conversation drifted to pack business and the upcoming ceremony for Bronc and Juliet. My father wanted to know how many guests to expect, whether the local wolves could handle security, and if the humans would be a problem. Jacob asked about the music and whether the open bar was still a thing.

It was almost normal until Mom shifted gears, eyes back on Aspen.

"So Aspen. How is it you, a witch, happened to become mated to my son, a wolf? Isn't that terribly unusual? It just really doesn't happen? I mean and seriously, dear. Look at my son. I could understand it if it were Arsenal, or Doc, but clearly, the only thing my son truly had to offer was a very hefty trust fund and bank account. You don't expect me to believe that didn't play a huge part in your wanting to tie yourself to Jonas for the rest of your life. I mean, you never have to worry about anything now."

She said it with the smile of a woman who'd spent a lifetime getting away with murder. The air in the room crystallized.

I waited for Aspen to answer.

She took a breath and set her fork on the edge of the plate, each movement so deliberate it felt like time had slowed just for her. Her cheeks were fire-red, but her voice didn't shake. She sat up straight, squared her shoulders, and leveled a stare at my mother that would've cracked granite.

"Let me tell you something, lady," Aspen said. "I will not sit here while you insult, demean, and otherwise tell such despicable lies about my mate. To insinuate that I could only be interested in him because he has some kind of trust fund, which right this moment is the first I've heard of it, by the way, is to take away every amazing and wonderful thing about this man there is to know."

She pushed her plate gently away, hands folded, and leaned forward so every word hit my mother head-on. "You discounted his kindness, his gentleness, his heart, his amazing beauty that yes, he wears on the outside as well as the inside. Beauty that you clearly do not see, because you have no idea who he is. He is my shelter from the storms, my peace when I am troubled, he is laughter when I'm feeling down, and comfort when I'm alone. He is my anchor when I feel like I'm drifting out on unknown seas, and the only person I have ever known who has made me feel like I am enough. So you are the one, Mrs. Rice, who does not know who your son is, and it is you who owes him and me an apology."

She finished, voice ringing out through the sudden hush. Every head in the dining room had turned; even the dartboard shut up for a second. My mother sat frozen, lips parted, like she'd never in her life been spoken to that way.

And me? I thought I might explode with pride. My chest swelled until I thought it'd split the buttons on my shirt, and the mate bond between us roared so fiercely I nearly started howling in the middle of Pearl's Bar & Grill.

Oscar poked his head out of the purse and gave a tiny, dignified "Hear, hear!" before ducking back in.

My father gaped for a heartbeat, then started to laugh—really laugh, belly-deep and wheezing. "She's got you dead to rights, honey," he said, clapping my mother on the back so hard her pearls rattled. "Maybe now you'll let the boy live his life for once."

Jacob just whistled, low and impressed. "Damn, JT you sure know how to pick 'em."

Pearl appeared at my elbow, the tray of biscuits suddenly replenished. She leaned in, grinning, and whispered, "Never thought I'd see anyone give Juliet a run for her money."

For the first time in my life, I watched my mother blush. She looked at Aspen, really looked, and for a second I thought she might snap back with something cold or cruel. But all the ice had melted. She sat back, hands limp in her lap, and shook her head.

"I... suppose I was out of line," she said. "That was—well, it was quite a speech."

Aspen nodded once, firm. "It wasn't a speech, ma'am. It was, every word, the truth. I just don't think you've seen past your son's scars for some time. I wanted you to realize that there are many of us who do."

I squeezed Aspen's hand under the table, and this time, she squeezed back. Hard.

Nobody spoke for a long minute, but it wasn't the old, angry silence. It was something else—acceptance, maybe, or at least mutual respect. The food tasted better after that. The whole table seemed lighter. My mother even asked Aspen about the wedding cake for Bronc and Juliet, and didn't even flinch when Aspen told her she used real vanilla instead of extract.

The conversation drifted to safer waters. Jacob swapped stories about the wildest things he'd seen at the MC, and my dad relayed some half-true tales from the oil fields. Pearl brought pie, and my mother—of all people—offered to split a slice with Aspen, which was as close to a peace treaty as you could get in my family.

As we stood to leave, I caught a glimpse of us in the window—Aspen, radiant even after the battle, her hand tucked in my elbow; me, towering beside her, feeling finally, truly seen.

We walked out into the Texas night, the sky cold and clear and infinite.

And I knew right then, I would burn the world to the ground to protect her.

CHAPTER 22

Aspen

The drive home was all adrenaline and hot-wired nerves. I gripped Papa's hand the entire way, my body still vibrating from the dinner at Pearl's and the way I'd gone nuclear on his mother. Part of me was mortified; part of me wanted to strut down Main Street with a flag that read Suck It, Mrs. Rice. The mate bond buzzed like a live wire, equal parts pride and the simmering aftershock of rage, and it made my skin so sensitive I could hardly sit still in my seat.

I kept glancing over at Papa, searching his face for cracks. He played it stoic, all squared jaw and straight-ahead stare, but I could see the lines around his mouth, the way his knuckles whitened on the wheel. Every time we hit a dip in the road, the headlights would slice across his scars—the ridged one that creased his brow, the fainter silver slash along his cheek—and I'd catch his mother's words echoing in my head. *The only things my son truly had to offer were a very hefty trust fund and bank account.* It was an incredibly cruel thing to say, and now I burned to undo whatever damage she'd done.

When we pulled up the drive, Oscar wriggled in my bag, still in his smart daywear, and whispered, "I'd call that a successful mission, Miss. But perhaps the sir could use a... tonic?" He eyed Papa with concern, and I wanted to scoop both of them up and force-feed them honey and warm bread until everything felt better. I didn't get the sense that he was upset with me for what I'd said. His love and appreciation poured down our bond. But the evening had taken its toll; opened old wounds, and that was something I could not abide.

Inside, the house was dark but warm. Papa flicked on the lamp in the entry, threw his keys on the table, and let out a long, careful breath. I peeled off my coat and boots and waited for him to say something, but he didn't, just went to the kitchen and poured himself a glass of water. The silence was new; not the easy, shared silence we'd built, but a heavy, lopsided one. He turned his back as he drank, shoulders hunched.

I padded in after him, crossing the kitchen tiles on quiet feet covered in tights, and wrapped my arms around his waist from behind. I pressed my cheek between his shoulder blades and held on.

He set down the glass as he turned towards me, blanketing me in his arms.

I leaned my head back and looked at his face. "Hey, you know that everything she said tonight was the expression of a woman who is so out of touch with her own son, she resorted to being cruel, right? Maybe she's held resentment toward you because you rejected the family business. Or, it's possible she's a haint who simply puts too much stock in a person's physical beauty. Which, by the way, she's missed yours by a mile." I told him as I stood on tiptoes and gave him a small kiss.

I continued. "Nothing she said tonight matters diddly squat to me, my love. I don't care about her or what she thinks. She seemed bitter and unhappy. I actually pity people like her. Look at you. *You've* been directly to hell and back, and all I've ever heard people say about you is what a calming spirit you have. You bring peace to people's chaos. And there *she* sat, a woman who has everything, and she couldn't even be happy for her son who has found a mate who adores him? No, she'd rather try to do a gotcha and mention your trust fund, like I'm a gold digger."

He let out a low laugh, the kind that made my ribcage vibrate. "I know, Sunshine. I just… It's been years since I've seen her like that. I thought maybe if I brought you, it'd be different."

"I'm glad you brought me," I said, tightening my grip. "I wouldn't change a thing. You know, I'm just glad my magic didn't kick in. She might have walked out of Pearl's with donkey ears, cuz she certainly acted like a jackass."

He let out a big laugh and squeezed me tight. "Oh, Sunshine. You have a way of reminding me how good my life is. I'm so thankful to the Creator that he sent you to me."

"I love you, scars and all. Especially the scars."

He looked down at me. The light caught the furrow between his brows, and I wanted to smooth it with my thumb. "You really mean that, don't you?"

I smiled. "I'd show you, but Oscar is watching."

Oscar made a very dignified sound of retreat and poofed out of sight, leaving us alone.

"And for what it's worth, I don't think she really meant the mean things she said. I can't believe a mother would want to hurt her child like that." I was still trying to figure out how that was possible.

He huffed out another small laugh. "My father has needed to spank her ass and get her in line for years. That way, she wouldn't feel so out of control. I think that would solve most of her issues, and she wouldn't crush her son's spirit the way she does."

"This is something that works for wolves?" I asked, surprised and somehow tingly all over, remembering him giving me a taste of the flogger on my skin.

His smile was sly. "It works for more than just wolves, Sunshine. But yes, alpha wolves especially. Bronc isn't the only alpha in our pack, but he is the Alpha of our pack. All the officers of the pack and MC are alphas in our own right. We choose to yield to Bronc. He has the right to discipline us if we step out of line. It keeps our pack strong. We choose to submit to him because we honor the dynamic. It's the way our homes run as well. Wolves know this, and I haven't talked to you about this, but it's how I'd like our home to run as well. When you called me Alpha last night, it filled my heart with pride."

I'd never considered myself particularly feminist in my beliefs. I didn't like labels such as that. I always just wanted to be respected and treated equally as a man would be in business. But when I'd called him Alpha last night, I'd meant it.

"I'd never thought about it, but I like the idea of a mate who respects, cherishes, and only wants what's best for me. Everything else flows from there, I think. And I trust you to provide what I need. I can feel your love through our bond, so I have no reason to fear. But now I want to erase any bad feelings that may linger from what happened at dinner."

I took his hand and led him, slow and deliberate, down the hallway through our bedroom to the en suite bath. The tile was chilly on my feet, but I didn't care. I flicked on the vanity lights—soft, gold, forgiving—and turned the shower and let the water warm. The steam started to fog up the mirror almost instantly. He leaned against the counter, arms crossed, but there was no menace in it. He just looked tired, not physically, but soul-deep.

I stepped up to him and, with gentle hands, started to undo the buttons on his shirt. Each one came loose with a soft pop, my fingers brushing the skin beneath. The scars ran in thick and thin lines across his chest, his shoulders, his stomach. They looked brutal up close, old wounds, faded to white, but I found them beautiful, each one a story written in flesh and covered in tattoos.

He flinched when my fingertips traced a particularly gnarly one under his collarbone.

"I hate that one," he admitted, voice soft.

I reached up and kissed it, slow and unhurried. "I love it. It means you survived."

He shuddered, but let me keep going.

I worked the shirt off his arms and tossed it to the hamper. Then I moved to his belt, unbuckled it, and eased his jeans down, careful of the zipper over the uneven scar on his hip. He watched me the whole time, eyes never leaving my face, like he was waiting for me to show revulsion or even pity. I gave him neither.

When I reached his boxers, I hesitated—not because I was shy, but because I wanted him to see that every part of him was precious to me. I peeled them down, knelt on the cold tile, and wrapped my arms around his thighs, cheek pressed against the gentle swell of muscle. His hands went to my hair, fingers stroking my scalp.

I looked up at him. "You are the most beautiful man I have ever seen."

He made a noise in his throat, but didn't argue.

I stood, cupped his face in both hands, and kissed him, long and slow. He tasted like salt and heat and the faint tang of beer. When I pulled away, his eyes were damp, just a little.

"Now," I said, "get in the shower, and let me take care of you."

He stepped into the steam, his giant frame nearly filling the space, and held the glass door open for me. I stripped out of my dress and stepped in; the heat prickling my skin. The water ran in rivulets over his scars, highlighting every contour. I took a washcloth, lathered it with soap, and started at his shoulders, scrubbing gently. I worked my way down, pausing at every scar to press a kiss or run my tongue along its length. He didn't say a word, just let his head tip back, eyes closed.

When I reached his lower stomach, I knelt again, letting the water cascade over my head and down my back. His cock was already hard, thick and beautiful, resting against his stomach. I looked up at him, seeking permission.

He nodded, so I took him in my mouth, slow at first, savoring the feel of him. The water made everything slick and warm. He groaned, hands bracing on the tile above my head, hips rocking forward. I sucked him deeper, letting my tongue trace the vein that ran along the underside, one hand cupping his balls, the other gripping the back of his thigh. He tasted like skin and salt, and I wanted to memorize every inch.

His voice was rough. "Sunshine, you don't have to—"

I pulled off just long enough to say, "I want to. I want to love every part of you, inside and out."

He let me. His hands tangled in my wet hair, guiding me, but never forcing. I took as much of him as I could, gagged a little, but kept going. The noises he made were feral, desperate. He started to move, shallow thrusts at first, then deeper as he lost control. The washcloth fell from my hand; I gripped his thighs instead, holding on as he fucked my mouth, slow and careful.

"Fuck, Aspen," he groaned. "I'm close."

He tried to pull away, but I held him there, wanting him to let go, to trust me. He came with a shout, hot and bitter, filling my mouth. I swallowed, loving the way his whole body shook, how he looked down at me with awe and wonder.

I stood, wiped my mouth with the back of my hand, and pressed up against him, water and sweat and tears all mixing together. He hugged me tight, lifting me off the ground, and buried his face in my neck.

"Thank you," he whispered. "I needed that. I needed you."

"I know," I said, and meant it.

We stood like that, water pounding down, until the room was full of steam and the mirror had fogged over completely. He finally set me down, grabbed the shampoo, and washed my hair with such care it made me want to cry. Conditioner came next. Then he carefully rinsed until my hair was silky smooth.

"Lift your arms," he said, and I did, and he started washing me with a soft blue washcloth from before, lathered with lemon verbena soap. He started at my breasts, letting the cloth drag across my nipples just enough to make me whimper. He grinned, pleased with my reaction.

"Perfect," he murmured, eyes fixed on the way the water beaded and ran down my skin.

He knelt lower, trailing the soapy cloth over my belly, my hips, down the outsides of my thighs. His fingers were reverent, tracing every dip and curve as if memorizing me from the inside out. He paused at a faint scar on my left knee—a remnant from childhood—and pressed his mouth to it, soft and slow.

He set the cloth aside, running his hands over my calves and feet, then rose, towering above me. His cock was half-hard again, heavy and beautiful, bobbing against his thigh. Knowing that I caused that reaction in him was a heady feeling.

When he finished, he pressed my back against the cool tile wall, his hands lightly running down my body. His hand slid between my thighs, two fingers finding my slick heat and circling it, slow and purposeful. My head lolled back against the tile.

"Open for me," he said, and I did, widening my stance as far as I could.

He sank to his knees; the steam swirling around us, and buried his face in my pussy. The first stroke of his tongue was lightning, and I nearly slid down the wall. He held my hips, keeping me steady as he licked, sucked, and teased. The man was relentless, alternating between gentle flicks and deep, obscene thrusts that made my whole body clench. The water ran over his head, soaking his hair and streaming down his back.

I tangled my fingers in his hair, holding on for dear life as he devoured me. He lifted my right leg, placing my foot on his shoulder, opening me further. Every time I gasped or moaned, he doubled down, licking me harder, faster. The leg I was balancing on shook, and I thought I might fall, but he never let me slip.

The orgasm built fast, sharp and mean, and when it hit, I cried out, fingers twisting in his scalp as my hips bucked uncontrollably. I dropped my foot to the floor. He held my hips through it, licking me until I was shaking so hard I had to beg him to stop.

I tried to protest, but he lifted me bodily off the ground, setting me on the built-in bench in the shower. His hands were rough, trembling a little, but so careful with me. He slid two fingers into my pussy, pumping them as his thumb found my clit again. I melted, thighs falling open, ready for whatever he wanted to give.

"You're going to come for me again," he growled.

"I can't—" I started to say, but he shut me up with his mouth, kissing me hard as he fucked me with his fingers. The pressure built fast, spiraling out of control, and when I came again, it was explosive—my body shuddering, eyes rolling back, a sob wrenching out of my chest.

He stroked my hair, whispering sweet, filthy things as I shook in his arms.

When I finally caught my breath, he turned me and sat, pulling me onto his lap, his cock sliding against my pussy, hard and hot. He didn't try to enter me, just rocked against my clit, the head rubbing with perfect friction.

"Is this okay?" he asked, voice rough.

I nodded. "God, yes. I want you inside me. Please."

He hesitated, then slid in, slow and careful, stretching me until I thought I might break. He was so thick I had to breathe through the first few strokes, but once he was all the way in, it felt right. Because we were made for each other.

He moved my body up and down slowly, his hips rolling, every thrust sending sparks up my spine. The water was still running, steaming us both. I clawed at his shoulders, nails digging in, wanting him deeper, harder as I rocked my hips.

"Faster," I begged.

He obeyed, slamming into me from below with so much force I saw stars. I came again, tighter and longer this time, my pussy clenching around him as he groaned into my mouth. He lasted only a few more strokes before he shuddered, hips jerking, and emptied himself inside me. He didn't give me his knot in this position; we simply made love, connected to each other.

We sat there together; the water washing everything away.

He kissed my forehead, my cheeks, my lips. "I love you," he whispered, over and over.

I believed him with my very soul.

He washed me again, slow and sweet, then dried me in a fluffy towel. He gently sat me on the vanity stool and carefully combed every tangle from my hair. He surprised me when he grabbed the blow dryer and dried it so it wouldn't be a crazy mess in the morning.

If his mother could have seen us then, she'd have had to eat her pearls.

He didn't let me go—not even for a second. As soon as we made it to the bedroom, he set me down on the mattress and crawled in after, his weight a comforting pull. The sheets were cool and crisp against my back, a shock after the steamy cocoon of the bathroom. I shivered, but it wasn't the cold. It was the feeling of him—his eyes on my body, the way he surveyed me like I was a miracle instead of a mess.

"I love you," he said, voice barely a whisper.

I sighed, content. "I love you more."

We drifted off together, wrapped in each other, our worries melted away for the night.

Tomorrow, the world would come knocking. But for now, we had peace. We had each other.

And I wouldn't trade it for anything. Not even all the trust funds in Texas.

CHAPTER 23

Big Papa

On the morning of Bronc and Juliet's ceremony, I woke three minutes before the alarm. My brain was already in battle mode—scanning, prepping, sorting out every variable like the entire pack depended on me not screwing this up. Some things never changed, even when you finally found the one thing in this world worth living for.

The house was quiet. Aspen's head rested against my shoulder, her hair a black river tangled around my bicep. Oscar had found his way into the crook of her knees, the little bastard snoring soft and proper, like a clock wound for royalty. The bond hummed between us, low and steady, the undercurrent of her warmth telling me she was safe and dreaming.

I slid out from under them and started the coffee, moving quiet as a fox so I wouldn't wake her. The world outside was still dark, all star-pricked sky and wind. I stood at the kitchen window, mug in hand, and watched the first pale smear of dawn edge up behind the barn. You could feel it in your bones: today was the kind of day that split your life into before and after.

I ran down the mental checklist. Security at the club: tight, no fewer than a dozen trusted wolves running shifts. Wedding cake: Aspen and Oscar had it covered, a four-tier plus the two sheet cakes to cover all the guests. Food: Pearl's had that on lockdown. There will be enough to feed two fifty, easy. The only wild card was the guest list.

Today, Dairyville would see more supernatural royalty than a Vegas casino in October. Menace and Savannah—now officially King and Queen of the Midwest packs—were due in by 10:00 sharp. I was looking forward to seeing my brother and his beautiful queen. After the fight they endured to be together, they deserved every happiness. Next came the vampire king, Kazimir Kozlov, bringing his daughter Lucia. He was also the head of the Russian Bratva and ran a successful nightclub in Philadelphia. But Lucia was our Luna's best friend, so they were always welcome. If they kept their numbers small, I'd consider it a win.

On the maybe-list: King Archon Seraphael, angel of the high throne and unholy terror to anyone dumb enough to cross him. And if rumors were right, Rafe Mayfield, King of the Southwest wolves, would drop by "just to shake the Alpha's hand." That many apex predators in one place would make even the moon nervous.

I drained the first mug, poured a second, and padded back to the bedroom. Aspen had turned over, hugging my pillow, face hidden except for her nose and that beautiful mouth. She looked so peaceful I almost felt bad about waking her. Almost.

I leaned down and brushed her cheek. "Sunshine. Time to rise and shine."

She mumbled, "Five more minutes," then surfaced with a long, catlike stretch that somehow made her even cuter. She squinted up at me, hair wild, eyes bright and sly. "What time is it?"

"Quarter past four," I said. "Busy day ahead."

She sat up and rubbed her eyes. Oscar blinked awake and stood, wearing a Victorian nightgown, paws perched on her thigh.

"Miss," he said, "I believe today is the day you make history."

Aspen snorted. "I'm just the cake lady. Nobody remembers the baker."

"On the contrary," Oscar replied, "the baker controls the outcome of all major celebrations. I have read six books on the subject."

"Trust the rodent," I said. "He's the best-read mammal in the house."

I kissed Aspen good morning, and she pulled me down for a second one—sloppy, sleepy, and perfect. "Don't get into any trouble today," she said into my chest.

"I'll do my best. You stay close to Oscar. If you leave the bakery for any reason, you take a wolf with you. Non-negotiable."

She made a mock salute. "Aye, aye, sir."

Oscar nodded, solemn. "We shall be inseparable, sir."

We dressed quick, Aspen pulling her hair into a messy ponytail and slipping into a lemon-yellow sundress that made her look like the first day of spring, even though it was the third week of February. I stuck to jeans, boots, and a black T-shirt; we'd come back to dress later. The ceremony would run the gamut of attire.

Aspen's bakery was already lit with the overnight lights when we got there. She unlocked the door; Oscar darted ahead to do a security sweep, and I walked her in to help her with the tables and chairs.

"I'll come pick you up at 2:00," I said, giving her a kiss at the door. Lock up now. "You need anything, you call."

She smiled, soft and sure. "Go do your thing, Big Papa. I'll be ready when you get back. Might even save you a lemon scone."

I winked. "That's what keeps me going."

I left her to it, with Oscar standing guard at the back door, and headed for the compound. The sun hadn't yet tried to break the horizon. The roads were empty, and I let my mind drift as I drove. Public speaking never got easier, even after years of giving sermons to hard-bitten bikers and soldiers. I'd written my speech six different ways, none of them good enough for Bronc and Juliet. So I ran the words again in my head, chasing the perfect balance between "sacred" and "don't make the vampires puke."

At the compound, the place was a controlled frenzy. Pearl's crew was already cooking; you could smell bacon and cinnamon from the parking lot. The pack officers were gathered outside the big house, smoking and sipping from thermoses. Bronc stood at the center, tall and calm, arms folded across his chest like he was born for this. Juliet was beside him, glowing brighter than the sun. You could tell she'd gone all-in on "Luna" mode: elegant green dress, blonde hair perfectly styled, dark brown eyes shining, smile ready for everyone who came within ten feet.

I parked and went to join the crew. Arsenal was first to spot me, giving a tight nod before returning to his scan of the perimeter.

"Hey Papa," he said. "Things are looking good. All clear on the perimeter."

"Good. What about the guests?"

"Wrecker and Parker are on comms. They'll call out when anyone approaches the gate."

I looked to Bronc, who broke off his huddle with Gunner and came over.

"Papa," he said, voice low and steady. "You ready?"

"Getting there," I replied. "Guess we're gonna run with the big dogs tonight?"

He grinned, a rare flash of mischief. "Why not? Let 'em see how a real pack does it."

Juliet joined us, her hand sliding into Bronc's. "You look nervous," she said, tilting her head at me.

"I always look nervous when I'm about to officiate a mating ceremony for the Alpha," I said. "Plus, there's the whole 'potential for supernatural war' thing."

She laughed. "You'll do great."

Pearl stormed up, wooden spoon in hand. "If y'all don't come in for breakfast right now, I will tan every last one of you. Especially you, Bronc. You can't get married on an empty stomach."

Juliet laughed and tugged her mate inside. I followed, drawn by the promise of food and the scent of fresh coffee. The kitchen was a madhouse: stacks of pancakes, piles of bacon, eggs done every way you could imagine. Pearl moved through the chaos like a general, her staff falling in line behind her.

"Eat," she ordered, planting a plate in front of Bronc. "You too, Big Papa. You're skin and bones."

I looked down at myself. Two hundred fifty pounds, six-five, and "skin and bones" was the least accurate thing ever said about me.

"Yes, ma'am," I said.

We sat, the officers crowding around the big oak table. Wrecker and Parker arrived last, hair windblown from the ride in.

"Perimeter is green," Wrecker reported, walking in with Parker. "Got the drones up, and Parker's mapped the entire zone."

Parker grinned, her cheeks pink. "I even wrote a script to track the guest list as they show up. You should see the spreadsheet."

Gunner grabbed three biscuits and tried to stuff them into his mouth at once. "I heard that vampire's bringing his daughter. The tall one with the accent."

Wrecker snorted. "Focus, cowboy. We've got security on the agenda."

Pearl tapped her spoon on the counter. "You will not start a bar fight before noon, or so help me—"

Arsenal raised his hand. "Permission to address the Alpha?"

Bronc rolled his eyes. "Permission granted, asshole."

"Recommend a double check on fire protocols," Arsenal said. "Vampires don't always appreciate the open flame."

"Duly noted," Bronc replied.

Parker chimed in. "The lights are all LED, anyway. No heat. Just ambiance. And the flames are contained in butane patio heaters."

Doc sat down with a mountain of food piled on a plate. "Fire schmire. Kazimir ain't scared of shit. Fucker's a thousand years old. Think a little flame is gonna bother him?"

Arsenal gave Doc the stink eye. "Yeah, ya dick, but Kazimir's people ain't a thousand years old. Just tryin' to be respectful of our guests."

I butted in to keep a brawl from breaking out and Pearl from bringing in the wooden spoon to paddle their asses. "Alright, you two. Knock it off. Arsenal, point well taken. As Parker nicely pointed out, there's nothing to worry about since all flames are contained. Although a fire pit for s'mores might be nice at some point during the night." I used my best soothing tone, and everyone simmered back down.

I watched the room, the way everyone played their role. It felt like family, chaos and all. Even the nerves in my stomach settled. Juliet caught my eye, and for a split second, I saw the woman she'd been months before this. She'd shown up to be Bronc's bookkeeper without a clue that she had an ounce of shifter blood, much less Omega blood. Now she was Luna, and the world was about to bear witness.

After breakfast, we all moved to the meeting room for the pre-ceremony "church." Bronc stood at the head, Juliet at his side. The officers took their spots, with Pearl and Maddie sitting in as honorary members. The room buzzed with anticipation.

Bronc called the meeting to order with a simple, "Let's get this show on the road."

Wrecker gave the security rundown; then handed off to Parker, who shared the guest list, and the updated seating chart.

"Menace and Savannah will arrive with two guards at 10:00," Parker read from her tablet. "Kazimir Kozlov, plus daughter Lucia and two advisors, we think, 10:30. Archon Seraphael still hasn't RSVP'd, but his proxies say he's strongly considering attending. Time of arrival: unknown. Rafe Mayfield is a wildcard. Time of arrival also unknown."

Gunner snorted. "Figures the wolves would show up when the mood strikes."

Wrecker ignored the joke. "Every arrival point is covered. Arsenal and I will run double checks every fifteen minutes. Everyone will be directed to their guest houses. No one gets in or out without a full check."

Bronc nodded. "Anything else?"

I raised my hand. "Aspen and Oscar have finished the magical wards around the territory. Nothing gets through that isn't supposed to, and the cake is secure."

Juliet's smile could have powered the whole compound. "Tell Aspen I can't wait to see what she's made."

"I will. We'll deliver the cakes, and she'll finish the decorating after they're placed on the table."

The meeting wound down, the final prep details handled with the kind of efficiency you only got from years of military and pack discipline. Everyone filed out, peeling off to their assignments. Bronc lingered at the table, Juliet at his side.

He looked at me. "You got your words ready?"

I exhaled, long and slow. "Yeah. Just hope I don't choke."

Juliet squeezed my arm. "You won't."

Pearl ducked her head in from the hall. "Boys, I need you to help set up the chairs out back."

Bronc rolled his eyes. "Coming, Ma."

They left, leaving me alone in the big room. I pulled out my notepad and scanned the speech again, looking for holes. There was nothing fancy—just a promise, a blessing, and a warning to anyone dumb enough to cross the Iron Valor Pack. But I wanted it to be perfect.

I sat there for a minute, thinking about my life before Aspen, before this pack, before the wars and the scars. I thought about my father, always chasing something bigger, never stopping to see what he already had. I thought about my mother, cold and proud, but with a spine of steel. I wondered what they'd think if they really saw me now.

I stood, stretched, and went outside to help set up the chairs.

The rest of the morning flew by in a blur of motion. Every time I glanced at my phone, another half hour had vanished. By 10:00, the compound had taken on the feel of a festival: tables lined up ready for food, banners strung between the trees, and a sound system set up on the old wooden stage. The crew had even set up a "VIP" section for the out-of-towners, complete with shade tents and an espresso bar, courtesy of Parker's caffeine addiction.

Menace and Savannah's private jet landed on our airstrip just after 10:00. He looked every inch a king—tall, blonde hair slicked back, suit so sharp it could cut glass. Savannah clung to his arm, laughing at something he'd said, her own red hair catching the wind. They greeted Bronc with bear hugs and handshakes, then moved through the crowd like they owned it. Which, in a way, they did.

The vampires arrived next. Kazimir was a walking statue, tall and pale, black hair slicked back to show off his cheekbones. Lucia trailed him, wrapped in a blood-red dress that made every head turn. She spotted me and gave a sly little wave. I nodded back, trying not to blush like a kid at prom.

The angels still hadn't arrived. I wondered if Archon would grace us with his presence. He tended to avoid gatherings and showed up only when absolutely necessary. Since he'd touched me, I felt connected to him somehow and hoped he'd make it.

I made the rounds, shaking hands, doing small talk, but my mind kept drifting to Aspen and the bakery. Every time I checked the bond, I felt her moving—kneading dough, boxing cakes, making Oscar sample every new batch. She'd texted me at 9:30: "All good here. Oscar says the blueberry muffins are overcooked. Tell Pearl I blame the altitude."

I texted back, "You got this, Sunshine. I'm proud of you."

At 10:45, my phone buzzed with a photo: Aspen, flour-smudged and grinning, holding up a perfect pink wedding cake with four tiers. My heart damn near stopped.

She was perfect.

At 2:00 sharp, I pulled the club van up to the curb in front of Aspen's bakery. The van was technically a "delivery vehicle," but today, it was an armored transport for the most precious cargo in the Texas panhandle: Aspen's wedding cakes, boxed and stacked with military precision on rolling carts.

Through the plate-glass window I saw her, a streak of motion in that lemon-yellow sundress, hair swinging as she boxed up the last of the sheet cakes. Oscar was on the counter, issuing orders like a field marshal, and the pair of them looked so serious that I felt a laugh bubble up even as my hands sweated on the wheel.

Aspen met me at the door, pink in the face and out of breath. "We're ready," she announced. "I need you and your alpha muscles."

"Always at your service," I replied, sweeping the boxes onto the cart and double-checking each one for structural soundness. She'd written "DO NOT TIP" on every side in bubble letters, and Oscar had added a few warning stickers for good measure.

"Are you sure you don't want a seatbelt for these?" I asked only half-joking.

Oscar sniffed. "The cakes are sufficiently stabilized, sir. The real hazard is human error."

"Noted," I said, and maneuvered the cart down the ramp and into the van's back section. I locked each box in place with bungee cords, then ran a towel between them and the wall just in case.

Aspen climbed into the passenger seat, Oscar in her lap, and I started the engine.

The drive out to the clearing was twenty minutes on a straight shot of county road, the van's shocks tested by every pothole. I took them slow, hands at ten and two, hyper-aware of every shift in gravity. Aspen watched me, her lips twitching in a barely suppressed grin.

"I like seeing you this nervous," she said. "Makes me feel like my cakes matter."

"They matter," I said, not even hiding it. "And so do you."

Oscar looked up at her. "Miss, the mate bond is pulsing off the charts."

She blushed, then stuck out her tongue at him. "Oscar, hush."

We turned onto the dirt lane that led to the ceremony site, the evergreens closing in overhead, and even from the gate you could see the effect Maddie and Pearl had on the place. Edison bulbs hung in long zigzags from tree to tree, their filaments winking gold in the late light. Twinkle lights threaded the evergreens, and rows of folding chairs arced in a perfect half-moon around the makeshift altar—a table draped in linen, topped with candles and a huge wildflower arrangement. There were even "reserved" signs on the front row, each name written in Parker's handwriting.

Aspen went silent as we rolled to a stop. I saw the moment it hit her—what all her work, all her mornings and sweat and sugar had led to. She reached for my hand and squeezed.

"It's beautiful," she whispered.

Aspen let out a shaky laugh. "I'm a little terrified."

I leaned across and kissed her, gentle but sure. "You're never alone, Sunshine. Not now."

She nodded, and I could feel her steady herself through the bond.

We unloaded the cakes; I carried the big ones, Aspen did the detail work, and Oscar rode shotgun on the cart. I watched her slide straight into work mode, hands sure and quick as she unlatched each box, inspected every tier, and set up her arsenal of spatulas and piping bags.

Aspen's focus was absolute. Her hands didn't shake, not even a little, as she stacked layer upon layer, spun the turntable with her palm, piped intricate pearls of buttercream along each seam. Her lips moved as she worked, whispering measurements and prayers, and I could see the magic in every motion.

Oscar stood sentry beside her on the table, paws folded, his tail flicking every time someone wandered too close to the perimeter.

"Careful," he told a passing child. "Cake is at the heart of the event. It must not be disturbed."

The child blinked, then scurried off to find safer entertainment.

I checked the bond and found Aspen lost in her work. She was on the final touches now, dusting edible pearls onto the buttercream and arranging candied flowers in a spiral down the side. The sunlight hit her hair and made it glow, and for a second I just stood and stared.

She looked up and caught me watching.

"You're making me nervous," she mouthed, but she smiled.

Oscar snorted. "His face, miss. He's quite besotted."

She laughed, then smoothed her dress and went back to work.

Just then, Maddie came by the table. "Look at this," she said, eyes wide at the cake. "Aspen, you're a genius. Pearl is going to cry."

"Don't let her near the kitchen knives if she does," I said, and Maddie cackled.

Pearl herself came running up, flowered apron tied over a black dress. "You did it, honey," she exclaimed, pulling Aspen into a hug that left flour on both of them.

"It's perfect," Pearl whispered in her ear, and I could see Aspen's eyes go glassy.

We left them to finish the setup and headed home to change.

*

Aspen beat me to the closet, already unzipping the garment bag that hung on the back of the door. She held the dress up in front of her—a soft, almost-blush pink, the sleeves sheer to the elbow, the neckline square and modest, the bodice fitted and the skirt flaring out just enough to make her look like a 1950s movie star. It was the most beautiful thing I'd ever seen, and that was before she even put it on.

I showered quickly, then went to my side of the closet. The suit had arrived the week before, tailored by Menace's favorite shop in Amarillo: navy, with a black-and-blue brocade vest, white shirt, and a black silk tie. I tied it twice before I got it right, hands shaking the whole time.

I could hear Aspen on the other side of the bathroom door, humming as she did her hair. I finished dressing and turned to the mirror. For the first time in a long time, I didn't see the scars or the lines or the broken pieces. I saw a man who belonged here, who'd earned every inch of this moment.

The door opened, and Aspen stepped out, dress swirling beyond her feet, hair loose and shiny as a raven's wing. She stopped short when she saw me.

"Wow," she breathed, then again, "Wow."

I tried to say something, but the words died. She looked like a dream, and I think I loved her more in that instant than I ever had before.

She crossed to me and straightened my tie, her hands gentle. "You're so handsome," she whispered.

I shook my head. "You're perfect."

She blushed, then leaned in and kissed me, careful not to smudge her lipstick.

Oscar popped in, tail curled smartly. He wore a little black jacket and a high-collar white shirt with a black vest and gray silk cravat. "Shall we depart, sir, Miss?"

We laughed, and for a moment, there were no witches trying to harm my mate, no danger, no tomorrow. Just the three of us, standing in a sunlit room, ready for the rest of our lives.

I offered my arm. "Shall we, m'lady?"

She took it, and together we walked out the door, the late-day sun painting everything in gold.

The walk from the truck to the altar was only thirty yards, but the way Aspen clutched my arm made it feel like a parade down Main Street. Everyone was already in motion—pack kids running underfoot, Pearl and Maddie adjusting tablecloths and lanterns, the drone of the sound system testing in the background. The golden light of the day had deepened, and as we passed under the string of lights, the entire world glowed pink and orange.

I did a sweep of the clearing, noting the new arrivals. Parker had set up a command post by the espresso bar, logging every guest in real time. Gunner circled the perimeter, giving two-fingered salutes to anyone he knew. Arsenal manned the entrance, nodding to the VIPs as they arrived.

The first big arrival at the ceremony area was Menace and Savannah. They came in like the royalty they were, moving with a casual confidence that reminded everyone exactly who they were. Savannah wore a fitted green dress and cowboy boots, her hair tamed into glossy curls. Menace was all ice and steel, but the way he smiled at Savannah melted a little of the hard edge. I shook his hand, then guided them toward the altar where Bronc and Juliet were waiting for the official start.

Next up was the vampire King Kazimir. Lucia was close behind, plus a couple of enormous "advisors" who looked like they could rip the transmission out of a diesel truck with their bare hands. Kazimir greeted me with a predator's smile, sharp and gleaming, then turned his attention to the dessert table.

He moved with impossible speed and grace, and within seconds he was standing behind Aspen, watching her as she double-checked her cake.

"Miss Waters," he said, his voice silk over broken glass. "Your reputation precedes you."

Aspen nearly bumped into the cake. She spun around, eyes wide.

"Thank you, sir," she said, ducking her head. Her southern accent got thicker when she was nervous.

Kazimir nodded, then motioned to Lucia. "My daughter is an admirer of your work."

Lucia, tall and lithe, wore a black sheath dress and lipstick the color of cherry cordial. She leaned in and studied the cake.

"It's beautiful," she said to Aspen, her voice low and smoky. "You're an artist."

Aspen's cheeks went pink. "You're very kind."

Kazimir lingered another beat, then turned to me. "Congratulations on the occasion, Mr. Rice."

I gave him my best "business handshake" and made a mental note to keep the vampires away from the cocktail table.

The guests kept coming. My parents came down the aisle, and I stiffened. They walked up to the table, the look on their faces best described as sheepish.

"Son, Aspen. It's lovely to see you again." My mother's voice was strained but civil.

My father shook my hand.

I decided just to be myself. "Hi Mom, Dad. Y'all look nice."

Aspen spoke up also. "Mr. and Mrs. Rice, it's nice to see you."

My mother looked surprised that Aspen was civil to her.

"This is a beautiful cake, Aspen. You are very talented." Her voice was sincere.

"Oh, thank you so much." She replied with a heart-melting smile. There is no way you couldn't love this woman.

"Well, we need to take our seats, I guess." My dad was clearly ready to move on.

I gave Aspen a wink.

King Rafe arrived fashionably late, sauntering in with his own small entourage. He was decked out in what looked like a designer suit, probably Armani, looking more like a retired linebacker than a king. His presence quieted the crowd; you could feel the power rolling off him. I walked over to meet him. He clapped me on the back and said, "Damn good turnout, son. Who's the artist over there?" He asked, pointing at Aspen.

I told him Aspen was my mate, and his eyebrows shot up.

"Nice catch," he said, with genuine warmth.

I wanted to be certain he understood she belonged to me. Rafe was an unmated wolf. Didn't want him getting ideas.

By 5:45, the clearing was full. The crowd amazingly co-mingled together; vampires sat with wolves, and different packs sat together. This was a time for celebrating love, and everyone seemed to share the spirit of the occasion.

The last arrival was the most anticipated. Archon Seraphael entered with no fanfare, just a ripple through the crowd as every head turned at once. He was seven feet if he was an inch, dressed in white linen, his hair shining like spun glass. He moved with the ease of a man who had never in his entire existence, feared anything. He nodded at Bronc, then at me, then fixed his golden gaze on Aspen. She froze. For a moment, she was so still I thought she'd turned to stone. Then, he turned back to me.

"It's good to see you again, Jonas. Much better circumstances this time, I'd say," he said, his voice a song and a commandment.

I had no idea what to say, so I just nodded. "Thank you for coming, sir."

He left me standing there as he found his seat.

I took my place next to Bronc, squared my shoulders; it was almost time.

Chapter 24

Aspen

The clearing looked like a fairy tale had blown through it and gotten drunk on moonshine. Strings of Edison bulbs arched over the makeshift aisles, their warm gold tangled through the branches of pine and mesquite. Folding chairs fanned out in a lazy half-moon facing the altar, which was really just a raised platform swaddled in white linen and covered with wildflowers. Someone—probably Maddie—had set up a hand-lettered sign at the entrance: "Welcome to the Mating Ceremony of Bronc & Juliet."

The wedding cake sat on a separate square silver pedestal, its four tiers bristling with buttercream rosettes and piped inlays of lemon curd. Oscar had insisted on a band of candied violets for the bottom layer ("for contrast, miss!") and a tiny fondant motorcycle perched at the very top. A pair of matching sheet cakes—one chocolate, just in case someone was opposed to the lemon—waited behind the main event, ready for deployment.

I ran my hand around the cake stand, feeling the cold sweep of nerves. Papa had dropped me off an hour ago, the van packed tight with cakes, pastries, and Oscar's emergency "warding kit" of salt and chalk. After setup, I'd floated to the edge of the clearing, watching guests trickle in to take their seats. They looked different from when I'd met them earlier.

Now they were all dressed to the nines. No casual looks were to be found here. The first to arrive were the pack officers and their families, then out-of-towners, and finally, the parade of a few supernaturals who made my pulse skitter.

Menace was first. Savannah, his queen was impossible to miss: long auburn curls, eyes like rain-washed moss, a forest-green dress hugging every curve. They shook hands with Bronc and Juliet, then worked the crowd, Menace's laughter cutting through the cold air like a power tool.

Next was the vampire king. He glided up the path with his daughter on one arm, and for a second I thought they might float off the ground. He was beautiful, carved from marble, sharp in a black suit with a long purple overcoat that caught the light just so. He startled me when he approached the dessert table. I hadn't expected him to speak to me. His eyes, bright blue and slightly mocking, and I remembered I'd heard about the time he'd snapped a wolf's wrist at a business lunch and then complimented the local wine. But he was kind and surprisingly complimentary.

Rafe Mayfield—the king of the southwest—rolled in with an entourage of giants. He wore his power like a favorite shirt: comfortable, a little frayed, impossible to ignore. Papa spoke briefly to him and nodded to me. The king then pointed at my cake as he passed and gave me a thumbs up, the gesture so corny I laughed out loud.

But then, at the last possible moment, the clearing changed. The air shimmered, and every sound—from the drone of the crowd to the wind in the trees—shrank into a hush. And there he was, the angel king. He walked out of the darkness like he'd built the stars himself, bigger than life, white linen suit, with hair long and gleaming like silk, eyes molten gold. Even the wolves stepped aside as he moved. I'd never seen anything like him. No one had.

Oscar scrambled up my skirt and perched on my shoulder, his voice trembling. "He's real, Miss. The stories were true. He's not even trying to hide his power."

Archon stopped, scanned the whole crowd, and then locked eyes with me. He smiled, slow and kind, and nodded once in my direction. I clutched the edge of the cake table, knees weak.

"They say angels can see your soul," Oscar whispered, fluffing his fur.

"What did he see?" I managed.

"Everything," Oscar replied, and that was that.

People began to sit, the noise creeping back in like someone had turned up the volume by degrees. I scanned the seating, hunting for my spot, and found Maddie waving at me from the second row. She'd left an empty chair between herself and Queen Savannah, who was busy fixing the curl of her hair with a tiny gold compact.

I walked up, wiping my hands on my dress, and Savannah scooted over, beaming. "Aspen! Come sit with us. We need a buffer in case the vampires get feisty." Her accent was pure Midwest, honeyed and sharp at the same time.

I slid into the chair, my skirt hem rising to my knees. "Is it always like this?" I asked, watching the supernaturals jostle for seats.

Savannah snorted. "Lord, no. This is twice as many kings as you'd ever see in one place. Bronc just demands this kind of respect without even trying."

Maddie reached for my hand and gave it a squeeze. "Don't let them scare you, sugar. You belong here as much as any of 'em."

I tried to believe it. I wasn't the daughter of a line of shifter royalty, or a vampire princess, and even though my mother was a powerful witch, I sure wasn't. I was just Aspen Waters, a witch from the woods of Georgia, who'd only recently found her magic, who spent more time scraping burned sugar off baking pans than practicing spells. But for the first time, the idea didn't make me want to hide. I belonged here, even if I was a little weird around the edges.

The chatter faded as Bronc and Juliet took their places in front of the altar. Juliet looked like she'd walked out of a magazine, her gold dress shining, hair swept to one side in a cascade of soft curls. Bronc wore a dark tailored suit and looked so proud I thought he might burst.

Papa, my Papa, stood at the front, in his gorgeous black suit, vest and white shirt; silk tie shimmering slightly. He held a battered black folder in his hands. When he raised his eyes, the whole crowd fell silent.

"Family, friends, honored guests," he began, and his beautiful voice carried all the way to the back row, calm as water over stone. "We gather tonight to celebrate the union of Liam Bronc Baucaum and Juliet Marie Bettencourt—a love forged in battle, tested by fate, and sealed by the moon itself."

His eyes found Juliet, then Bronc. "Some of you came from afar. Some of you walked down the road. But everyone of you is here because you believe in something worth fighting for. In this pack, we don't choose the easy road. We choose each other. Even when it's hard. Especially when it's hard. We don't believe in backing down or backing away."

Juliet blinked hard, wiping her eyes with the back of her hand. Bronc just squeezed her hand tighter.

Papa went on. "The Great Creator formed us, and the Goddess of the moon made us what we are, and she created a specific person fated to be our other half, our mate. It's the one thing that's truly sacred, even when the rest of the world forgets what sacred means. A few of us are fortunate enough to find that person. Bronc is one of those lucky ones, for if ever there was a wolf who was fated to belong to someone, Juliet was made for this man."

He looked around the crowd, making eye contact with every king, every outcast, every wolf in the audience.

"We all come from somewhere. We all carry scars. But the only thing that matters is what we build together. Bronc and Juliet, you've already proven your love; already claimed each other. Tonight, you just make it official before the world."

He motioned for them to face each other, keeping their hands joined. The moon was just cresting the trees, silver light catching the edge of the altar, and for a second it seemed like all time had stopped.

"Juliet, will you take Bronc to be your mate? To share your strength, your laughter, your hope, and your sorrow? Will you be a support to him and this pack as his love, his helper, his Luna, for all the days you walk this earth?"

Juliet's voice was clear, strong. "I will, with all my heart."

"Bronc, will you take Juliet as your mate? To be her shield, her safe place, her protector, her partner, for every sunrise and every storm? Will you support her as she stands by you as you lead this pack into the future?"

Bronc didn't hesitate. "I will, as long as I have breath."

"Then by the bond of pack, by the witness of the Goddess of the moon and stars, and by the blood we have shed for each other, I pronounce you true mates for now and all eternity." Papa closed the folder, a smile crinkling his eyes. "You may now kiss your mate."

The clearing exploded with howls, applause, even a few tears from the tough old wolves in the back. Bronc dipped Juliet in a kiss so dramatic it made even the vampires cheer. Oscar tugged at my sleeve, dabbing at his tiny eyes with a napkin.

"I'm so happy for them," I whispered, feeling a stupid rush of joy.

Savannah leaned over, voice soft. "He did a beautiful job."

I smiled, a feeling of pride filling my heart. "He did, didn't he?"

She looked at me, her green eyes softer than I'd ever seen. "Feels good, doesn't it? The first time Menace looked at me like I was more than just a pawn. The first time I realized the world could be bigger than the life I'd been handed. It seemed almost too big."

I swallowed, nodding. "It's just... overwhelming."

She smiled. "Let yourself be overwhelmed, darling. It's how you know you're alive."

The crowd started to stand, chairs scraping dirt and voices rising. Maddie grabbed my hand. "Don't forget to grab some brisket before these wolves devour it."

I was pulled to the food table, with Oscar riding on my shoulder. For once, I wasn't just surviving. I was in the middle of the story. I was someone's mate, someone's miracle. Even if I just came into my magic. I felt it in my bones; I knew it was there, rising up. I felt more powerful every day, and I knew I was ready to make some magic of my own.

As I watched the guests line up for food—kings, vampires, wolves, every one of them smiling—I thought about the journey from Georgia to Texas, from outcast to pack, from loneliness to this blinding, ridiculous happiness. I'd never understood the power of a family, or of a mate, until now. And I was never letting it go.

Papa caught my eye from across the clearing. He smiled, and every doubt in me went quiet.

A feeling of family washed over me.

Pearl's crew outdid themselves. They'd parked two giant smokers behind the reception tent and spent the last twelve hours working them like a pair of atomic clocks. The result was enough brisket, sausage, and chicken to feed a small army, plus tubs of potato salad, coleslaw, beans, and every kind of roll and bun imaginable. Even the vampires ate: rare roast beef, slices of blood orange arranged like tiny suns. Lucia hovered near the table, eyeing the buffet with the polite hunger of a woman who could eat any man in the room but didn't want to mess up her lipstick.

I was so busy watching I didn't even get a plate for myself. I just hung out at the cake table, taking in the scene. I loved hearing the chatter. "The lemon's from scratch," "The buttercream's not too sweet," "That icing will make you see God." Parker took two pieces and then circled back for a third, blushing as she told me, "I have zero self-control. I'd eat the entire cake if I could." Her little dog Rocket trailed at her feet, eating every scrap that fell to the ground. His little tongue hung at an odd angle out of his mouth. He was so ugly he was cute. Oscar gave her a tiny bow and told her he'd make her a cake just for herself someday. There were servers cutting and plating, so I was free to mingle.

At one point, King Menace strode up to my table, took a bite of the chocolate, and said, "Goddamn, Waters. If you ever need a job in Missouri, let me know." He clapped me on the back so hard I almost face-planted into the buttercream, but it was worth it for the look of pure, wolfish joy on his face. Savannah followed, plate in hand, and leaned in conspiratorial: "He's not allowed very many sweets at home. You're going to make me the villain." Her smile said she didn't mind one bit.

Kazimir picked delicately at the candied violets, then motioned to his daughter. "Try the citrus," he murmured, and Lucia did, eyes lighting up with every bite. "You have gift, miss," she said. "I never expected cake to taste like sunlight." Her Russian accent wasn't as heavy as her father's but definitely colored her smoky voice.

But the person whose opinion mattered most stood back, hands tucked behind his back, just watching. Papa. He wore the smile of a man who'd never in his life doubted me, but who was still proud every time I proved him right. Every time someone praised the cake, his chest lifted a little more, like he was collecting the compliments to keep them safe for me later.

The moon rose higher, and the field filled with laughter and noise. Kids ran between tables, daring each other to get close to the angel king, only to chicken out at the last moment. Pearl moved through the crowd like a benevolent tornado, checking every table, refilling drinks, and sharing childhood stories.

Papa brought me a plate with a brisket sandwich. "Thought this would be easiest to eat." He had a spot of barbecue sauce on his tie.

I took a bite and savored the delicious flavor on my tongue.

Mouth full, I told him how much I loved it and appreciated it.

"Your service was beautiful," I told him with a swallow of water he offered me. "You captured the essence of what mates are and the importance of community as well. I loved it." I followed up with a kiss.

I loved how happy he looked. It was like everything had finally come together for him. Nobody deserved it more.

When the meal was over and the plates were mostly clean, Pearl stood up on a chair and called out, "Y'all clear out some space now. It's time for the first dance!" Her voice carried all the way to the back row, where a few of the more bashful shifters had tried to hide out.

The chairs vanished, replaced by a rectangle of open grass under the lights. Menace and Savannah led the way, gliding onto the makeshift floor like they'd been born to it. Juliet and Bronc followed, and despite his size, Bronc moved with the ease of a ballroom champion, spinning Juliet until her hair fanned out in a gold halo. Other couples joined: Gunner grabbed an unsuspecting young lady, Arsenal with Maddie, even Parker and Wrecker, who had a "let's see how many toes I can step on before she kills me" dynamic that made everyone around them grin.

I lingered at the edge, nervous energy crackling through me. I hadn't danced since the disastrous night at the County Line, and that had ended with a drunken FaceTime call to Papa, an unwanted grope by a stranger, and a promise never to make a fool of myself in public again. But then Papa appeared beside me, offering his hand, his eyes soft.

"Would you do me the honor?" he asked.

I nearly choked on my own heartbeat. "I'll step all over you."

He smiled, the lines around his mouth deepening. "It's worth the risk, Sunshine."

I let him lead me out to the floor, the smell of grass and sugar and grill smoke thick in the air. He set his hand on my waist, gentle but steady, and I followed his steps, focusing on the rhythm of his body instead of the blur of people around us. The music was old country, the kind you hear in a honky-tonk: a slow waltz.

My fingers dug into Papa's shoulder when the music shifted. Archon stood suddenly beside us like carved moonlight, trailing frost-kissed air where no breath should fog. "Might I steal your mate for a turn, Jonas?" His voice resonated through my bones.

Papa's arm stiffened around my waist. The clearing's murmurs died mid-sentence. For three heartbeats, though I know of Papa's great respect for the man, he wouldn't just give me to him. His hand fell from my back, warm imprint lingering through the dress. "Her choice," he rumbled, but the wolf in his eyes glowed amber.

Archon's palm hovered above my hip, never touching. "Thank you, son. She'll be fine," he murmured as violins swelled from somewhere unseen. My feet left the ground. Not flying—floating, grass brushing satin slippers I'd never owned.

"You have starlight in your eyes little one. And your cake's flavor was inspired." His gaze mapped constellations across my face. "Did you weave magic into your buttercream?"

Cold spread through my ribs. "Sir, you could put all of my magical ability into a thimble, I'm afraid."

"Hmmm. You doubt your magic?" His wings—when had they appeared? They shimmered at the edge of my vision. "Are you not a daughter of Georgia?"

I looked into his golden eyes.

The truth tumbled out like recipe ingredients measured twice.

"I am, but my mother died, and I've only just discovered my magic."

Archon's thumb brushed my jawline. "I'm sorry to hear about your mother. But know this, children often inherit unexpected gifts." Around us, dancers moved through syrup-thick air. "Listen, little cherub; there is light at your fingertips. You'll know when to use it."

My mind was racing. What was he saying? He knew I was from Georgia? Inheritance? I felt his arms hug me a little closer, and I was suddenly filled with an all-encompassing feeling of love. Not romantic love, but familial love. Why?

The music faded. Archon's wings dissolved into frost. "Your Alpha comes."

"Wait!" I grabbed empty air. His citrus-snow scent lingered, but the angel king had become starlight refracted through tears.

Papa's warmth hit my back. "You okay, Sunshine?" His nose brushed my hair, scenting for distress.

"I…" The confession about Archon and family died on my tongue. I thought perhaps he could have been my father. But if he had been, he'd have chosen abandonment. If that were the case, I'd rather not know. I pressed closer. "Can we dance again? Properly grounded this time?"

His low laugh vibrated through me. "Anything for you."

We twirled through ordinary time, to an ordinary song. But when I licked dry lips, they tasted of celestial honey and unanswered questions.

It should have been the perfect night.

Chapter 25

Archon Seraphael, Angel King

They say the breath of God is like ozone, that it leaves a stinging charge on the skin and a ringing in the ears that you never quite recover from. But the summoning that tore through my wings and set my bones to humming was nothing so gentle. It was the wrench of gravity at the event horizon, the memory of stars collapsing, the silent scream that cleaved the void when the Word first spoke and spun the dark into something more.

I stood at the threshold of the Creator's audience, a corridor whose walls and floor and ceiling were nothing but the curdled, living light of Heaven's innermost sanctum. The hall ran in both directions into infinity, but ahead, at the impossible vanishing point, pulsed a heartbeat that called my name. My wings, vast and white and impossible for any human to perceive, bristled with a thousand eyes. Each eye, in its own way, begged me to turn back. I did not. Disobedience in my line of work, was rarely an option.

I walked.

With each step, I felt the weight of the assignment I had just left behind. I had come from the earth, from a mating ceremony that echoed ancient rites, but the taste of celestial honey had barely faded from my tongue before I was ripped out of the world and deposited here, alone, to account for myself. I knew what this was. I knew I was being summoned to judgment.

At the hall's center, suspended in the air, was the very presence of the Creator—a column of golden radiance that spanned worlds, at once blinding and so intimate that it hollowed you out from the inside. The light didn't burn; it obliterated. It erased everything about you that wasn't essential, that wasn't precisely, painfully true.

I dropped to one knee, my seven-foot frame suddenly small as a wishbone. My head bent; my hair, platinum and heavy, spilled over my brow and fell in a pale curtain that glimmered in the radiance. My wings flared behind me, then drooped, ashamed.

The voice of the Creator was not a voice at all. It was a pressure, a Truth that vibrated my atoms and left me gasping. It pressed from within and without.

ARCHON, the voice thundered. YOU HAVE COME.

"I answer, as I always have," I said, though my words were less sound than arrangement of intention. "I am yours, as you will."

YOU BROKE THE GREAT LAW.

I tried to look up, but failed. "I did not intend—"

INTENTION IS IRRELEVANT. YOU TOUCHED THE MORTAL. YOU LOVED HER.

A soundless shudder passed through me. "I... Yes. I loved her."

FOR THIS, YOU HAVE BEEN SUMMONED.

My wings curled forward, a shield and a penance. I had known this was coming since the moment I first saw Laurel Waters through the haze of an Indian summer, her hair damp from the river, her laughter more holy than any chorus. I had known it would come to this.

I waited.

A beat passed, the silence dense as a neutron star. Then: THE CHILD.

My golden eyes flickered. "Aspen Waters." I tasted the name; it tasted of sunlight and wildflowers. "She is… She is good, my lord. I did not know she was of me. I swear this."

THE CHILD CARRIES THE SEED OF DIVINITY. THIS IS AN ABOMINATION.

The light flared, each photon a blade of judgment. For a moment I feared I would be sundered, made into ash, but then the intensity receded, like a storm's eye passing overhead.

"You made me your enforcer," I said, voice shaking. "You tasked me with the work that Gabriel and Michael would not do. I hunted the wicked, the abominations, the half-made things. I was your sword. I was loyal. I am fallen, but not forsaken."

YOU WERE MADE TO OBEY.

"And I have obeyed. Even in this—" my hands trembled, my hair clinging to my cheek "—I did not know, my lord. I did not know that the witch Laurel carried a child. I left her as I knew I must. She died before I could—" The words turned to dust. "I obeyed."

The Creator's presence built upon itself, pressure magnifying with the mercy of a red giant collapsing to diamond. His sorrowful caress, that question—Did you think I would not know?—hung in the vesper-bright air as the throne room began to pulse with a new frequency of light. I could not stand upright. My wings, those great ivory banners, curled inward as if to shield my soul from what was to come.

I felt every atom in my borrowed vessel turn to music—each note a chord of regret, longing, and the kind of love that can destroy creation. The marble floor liquefied into a marble sea, rippling with the reverberations of the Voice. My face pressed against it, and it did not yield. Nothing of me, not angel nor memory nor desire, was permitted to rise above the tide of that Presence.

When the Voice returned, it came as wind and rumor, as the taste of salt and myrrh. "You grieve for her, Seraphael." The words held neither blame nor comfort, only the impossible gravity of truth.

My tongue, made for supplication, rasped a reply: "Yes, Lord. I have grieved for her all the days of my existence, and all the days to come, if it please You."

The light in the chamber reddened; I heard the other Thrones shift their wings, the Song trembling in the high registers.

"She was mortal," the Creator said, "and yet she loved as only the divine are meant to love. She gave herself up for her child. Tell Me, Seraphael—what have you done with the days that I gave you?"

Every cell, every shadow of me, tried to shrink from the inquiry, but there was no refuge. I saw the life I'd lived: kept her safe from what darkness I could, and even then—forsaken her in her most desperate hour. I saw the times I had hovered at the edge of Earth's sky, aching to descend, to wrap her in feather and fire and sing her to rest. But Heaven has its laws, even for the architects of war.

I did what Laurel asked of me. I stayed away.

For an instant, the light dimmed, and the marble sea stilled beneath my cheek.

"Her soul is with Me now," the Creator said. The mercy in that simple phrase nearly undid the last of me.

Trembling, I dared to lift my head. The chamber was alive with starlight, every angelic courtier a silhouette of radiance, but none could match the sun at the center. I tried to speak, but my voice caught on a jagged edge: "Thank You, Lord. Thank You."

A gentle murmur, the laughter of nebulae, rippled through the room. "You are not done, Archon," the Creator said, and for the first time since I'd been called to judgment, I allowed myself to hope.

"Rise," said the Voice. I obeyed, though my legs would have buckled if the will of Heaven hadn't stitched me upright. My wings flared reflexively, arching over the marble like cathedral vaults. The chamber grew brighter, then focused—a spear of light aimed straight through my heart.

The Creator spoke, now as thunder: "Your daughter walks the Earth. Her soul is pure. Despite her inheritance—despite the blood that binds her to the old magic—she is of Me. She will wield great power, and there are those who will covet it. There are those who will kill for it."

At this, I nearly staggered. Not for fear—no, I'd stood against the armies of Hell and never once faltered—but for the knowledge that I had made her, and now the universe would turn itself inside out to test her.

"She is like the sunshine," I whispered, hoping her light might anchor her to safety. "She has found the wolf, and they are mated. But her kind will not let her live."

A long pause, measured in the heartbeats of dead suns. Then: "That is not your punishment," said the Creator, the Voice gentling until it was only the warmth of a mother's hand on a fevered brow. "That is your charge. You will guide her. You will protect her. She will live for centuries, and you will not let her become the monster the Wyrdmother dreams of."

Every lesson I'd learned in eons of warfare dissolved in the purity of that command. I, who had annihilated cities, now found my purpose reduced and distilled to the protection of a single spark—a daughter.

The shame of it, the joy of it, the terror—my wings trembled, and I threw myself to my knees, wings splayed to expose my throat, my heart, everything. "I beg Your forgiveness," I said, my voice ripped raw. "I beg for the mercy I could not give to Laurel. I beg for the wisdom to serve Your will through Aspen."

The Creator's light, for the first time, grew so gentle it almost hurt. Grace spilled through the throne room, slick and golden, and I felt it settle on my feathers, my hair, my tongue. "You are forgiven," said the Voice. "You are Mine."

I wanted to dwell there, in that golden moment, until the last heat-death of the cosmos. But the Voice was urgent, pushing me forward:

"Go now. Return to the world. Your daughter and her mate have need of you. The night gathers."

I looked up, and the stars above the throne burned with the cold blue of high winter. Every angel in attendance bent their heads, not to the Creator, but to me. I felt their love, their envy, their warning: The world would not thank me for what I was about to do. But that no longer mattered.

"Thank You, Lord," I whispered, and with that, I rose on wings of light and cracked the marble world apart.

Falling from Heaven is nothing like the old poets claim. There is no tumbling, no burning, no loss of station or beauty. To fall is to descend with purpose, every feather a blade of destiny. The rush of stars against your skin, the hiss of air in your lungs, the sudden pressure of time wrapping around your bones—this is how the Watchers once entered Eden, how the Morningstar himself once swept across the dawn.

I let myself become matter, sensation, desire. I shaped myself into a form that could walk the Earth, could touch her hand, could bleed if need be.

I landed, not in a crater or in fire, but in the narrow shadow between two heartbeats. The world around me came into focus: the scent of pine and damp moss, the prickle of winter air against my face, the distant pulse of Aspen's soul like a bell calling me home. I was not surprised to find that I ached for her, not as a lover, but as a father. Every memory I'd denied myself surged in—her infant wail, her first word, the tentative touch of her tiny hand against my own, all the joy and fear that makes a life worth having.

I knew at once where she was. And I knew, even before the wind changed, that something dark was moving toward her. Wolves were easy;

witches, I had learned to respect. But there were other things in the dark, things that whispered the old names, things that remembered what angels once were, and hated us for it.

I flared my wings, invisible to mortal eyes, but enough to clear the space around me of every shadow. I raised my hands and blessed the ground, the air, the night itself, calling forth every vestige of Heaven I was permitted to wield.

The Watchers had long ago learned that the only way to fight the darkness was with a darkness of your own. But I was not a Watcher, not anymore. I would fight for her as myself, Seraphael, the last of the Thrones, and I would damn the cost.

I stepped forward. The world bent before me, ready to be remade.

It was time to save my daughter.

CHAPTER 26

Aspen

By the time I'd boxed up my last spatula and wiped down the bakery's folding table, my brain was already pinging alarms. The relief and joy I'd felt just hours ago were thinning, replaced by a growing sense of wrongness. Papa should have been there to help break down the tables—he'd promised to haul all the bakery gear back to the truck, and if nothing else, the man never let me carry anything heavier than a cake box.

Except... he wasn't there.

Not at the cake tables, where Gunner and his nephews were fighting over the last wedge of lemon chiffon. Not by the fire pit, where the MC officers laughed and tried to one-up each other on who could roast a marshmallow without burning the stick. Not at the tables, where Juliet and her friends had begun the world's slowest game of Uno, the rules already devolving into local legend.

"Have you seen Papa?" I whispered, not wanting to start a scene. "He's been gone for... I don't know, over half an hour?"

Oscar flicked his tongue over a chunk of gouda from a cheese board and tilted his head. "Not for a while, Miss. I assumed he was conferring with the Alpha about something."

That tracked. But the pack was, for once, enjoying themselves, every officer accounted for and within eyesight. Even Bronc was letting his hair down, standing with his arm slung around Juliet and both their faces wreathed in uncharacteristic joy.

A few minutes later, I was in full search mode.

"Miss, I believe we have a situation," he said, voice barely more than a breath.

"What's wrong?"

My heart jackhammered in my chest. "You feel that too?"

Oscar nodded, whiskers trembling. "Something is… dampened. Like a blanket over a candle. Not snuffed out, but hidden."

For the first time, icy dread crept into my veins. "Come on," I said, scooping him up and hustling toward the main house. "We'll check the compound."

The walk felt like a hundred miles. The compound was still hopping—Pearl's kitchen crew cleaning up, the security wolves running post-event sweeps, children chasing each other down the hallways. I darted through the front door and found the entry empty, but music and laughter poured from the rec room. I followed the sound, only to find the entire pack leadership accounted for: Bronc and Juliet, Arsenal, Gunner, even Wrecker, who looked up as I barged in.

He clocked my face and came over immediately. "Something wrong?"

I tried to keep the panic out of my voice. "Have you seen Papa? He's not at the clearing, and I can't find him anywhere."

Wrecker's face changed—instantly, chilling seriousness. "He said he was going to check the perimeter, but he should have been back. Let me get Parker. Maybe she can pull the drone feeds."

He hustled out of the room, leaving me standing awkwardly with the rest of the crew. Arsenal caught my eye and jerked his chin toward the hallway, signaling for me to follow. He pulled me aside, his big hand gently on my arm.

"Hey," he said, "when's the last time you saw him?"

I did the mental math. "After the dancing, during cleanup. He kissed me at the cake table, then went to help. But that was, like, an hour ago."

Arsenal's mouth flattened into a line. "He'd never just bail on you. Not on a night like this."

I nodded, eyes burning. "I know. Something's wrong. The bond is murky."

Arsenal turned to the door. "I'll do a sweep. You stay here and wait for word from Parker."

I was ready to run out and keep looking, but the rec room door opened and Wrecker reappeared, Parker on his heels. She was already holding her laptop, typing one-handed as she walked.

"I'm running the feeds," she said, dropping into a kitchen chair. "Give me a minute."

The room seemed to shrink. Everyone—Pearl, Wrecker, even some of the clean-up wolves—crowded around. Oscar perched on my shoulder, silent, but I could feel him vibrating with anxiety.

Parker tapped away, lines of code flying. "I've got four drones on the east perimeter, two more on the west, and the cam at the entry drive. Wait... back it up, there—"

She froze the frame. On the laptop screen, Papa's figure strode along the tree line, his head down, hands in pockets. The timestamp said 9:13. She ran it forward—he paced the perimeter, checked a couple of outbuildings, then stopped by a small grove of juniper trees. He stood there for a full minute, looking at something out of frame. And then—just like that—he was gone.

Parker rewound, zoomed in. "He's walking, walking... and then nothing. No one else in the shot. No sign of a struggle. He just... vanishes."

I stared at the screen, willing it to show something else. A flash of color, a shadow, a clue. But there was only the darkness at the edge of the trees and the way Papa seemed to dissolve into it, like a drop of ink in water.

Wrecker grunted. "Play it again. Slower."

She did. This time, I caught a blur in the left corner of the frame—a flicker of movement, just as Papa turned his head. The motion was wrong: too fast, too smooth. Not a wolf. Not human.

Oscar leaned forward, his nose nearly pressed to the laptop screen. "Miss," he said, "that is witchcraft. He has been taken."

The world narrowed to a single, painful point.

I stepped back from the table, my knees weak. I tried to reach for the mate bond, but it was muffled, like trying to hear someone shout through a concrete wall. I knew he was alive, because I could feel a faint echo of him—fear, not for himself, but for me. That made it worse.

Bronc came through the door, his face dark with concern. "Report?"

Wrecker briefed him in two sentences. Bronc listened, then turned to me. "We'll find him, Aspen. I swear to you."

I nodded, but my heart was gone. I'd spent months thinking I was the target, that the witches of Verdant Hollow would come for me first. But Papa was my anchor, my whole world. I'd never considered that, in their twisted logic, they might strike at him instead.

Bronc barked orders, sending search teams into the woods and along the highway. Parker fired off a string of texts to the other packs. Within minutes, the entire compound shifted from party to war room, everyone moving with grim purpose. But I felt frozen in place, my entire self a hollow, echoing shell.

Juliet found me, her arm wrapped around my shoulders. "It's not your fault," she whispered, holding me tight.

But it was. It was my blood the Wyrdmother wanted, my magic. If I hadn't come here, none of this would have happened. I'd do whatever it took to get him back.

I'd changed out of the party dress into black leggings, tall flat boots, and a borrowed MC sweater that hung down past my butt and left my arms free to move. I'd cinched my hair into a high ponytail to keep it out of my face more than anything. I needed every neuron focused, every sense sharp, nothing falling into my eyes to distract me.

Wrecker's place was barely contained chaos. I stood just inside the door, pulse high and hot, as Parker flitted from one screen to another, her fingers blurring over the keyboard. They'd transferred their tech room to the living room. It had been gutted for this: coffee table banished, all furniture shoved against the walls to make room for a folding table packed with laptops, monitors, and charging cords. At the center, a flatscreen TV displayed a live grid of security feeds, each window labeled in all-caps: BARN, ENTRY RD, SOUTH TREE LINE, BUNKHOUSE, and more.

Juliet and Maddie hovered near me like an ad hoc honor guard, but I barely felt them. Every cell in my body was screaming for JT—for Papa—and the mate bond was no longer a lifeline but a noose cinched tight. If I could have reached through space and yanked him home, I would have.

The air in the house vibrated with the kind of tension you get in the last seconds before a tornado touches down. Arsenal and Gunner had been pacing the entryway, but they'd stopped now, arms folded tight across their chests, eyes pinned to the screens. Even the enforcers looked spooked; this was not a drill.

Kazimir stood near the window, backlit by the outside security lights, a presence so cold he seemed to pull the heat from the room. Every now and then he let out a low, almost-growl rumble, but mostly he watched the activity in silence, his jaw clenched like a bear trap. King Rafe, who had to duck to clear the ceiling fan, was camped out near the kitchen, arms crossed, feet planted like he was bracing for impact.

Oscar, in his best "crisis" waistcoat, had a front-row seat atop Parker's monitor, standing at attention. His fur was so puffed it looked like he'd stuck a paw in a live wire. He barely glanced at me when I entered, but I felt the faint nudge of his familiar magic at the edge of my senses, an extra buffer against the panic in my veins.

I tried to count the people in the room, tried to anchor myself in their presence, but my attention kept boomeranging back to the screens. Every time the outside cam flickered, my heart would jerk—hoping for a flash of blond hair, a telltale stride. I looked again and again, as if sheer force of will could conjure him back.

Parker muttered a string of curses at her monitor, then stabbed the enter key like it owed her money. "I've got the last hour of footage parsed, but he's just gone. One frame he's there, next frame he's smoke. This doesn't make any fucking sense. And there's not another person or presence anywhere to be seen. Not outside the fences, not on the highway."

Wrecker hovered behind her, eyes red, jaw set. "Rewind and scrub again. Look for any energy signatures—heat, electromagnetic, whatever."

Parker glared at him but did as told. "I've run six spectral filters already. There's nothing. No visual disturbance, no energy spike, no nothing. It's like he walked into a goddamn black hole."

Kazimir paced the window, steps silent even on the tile. "Witch-craft," he said, biting the word in half. "It's always power plays with these witches. Always want more."

King Rafe nodded, arms still crossed. "That bitch wants something that will position her above the rest of us. You can bank on that."

"My mother's grimoire. She wants my mother's grimoire." My words stilled the room as all eyes turned to me.

I licked my lips and took a deep breath. "She's obsessed with magic. Old magic. She wants to be the most powerful witch in North America—maybe even the world. But she's already top-tier. There's only one thing she doesn't have." My fingers fidgeted, nails scraping my thigh through the leggings. "She wants the grimoire. Or my blood. Or both."

Parker spun around in her chair, chair legs shrieking on tile. "Do you know why?"

"I'm pretty sure," I answered. "Oscar says there's a spell in the grimoire—one my mom hid—where a witch can drain magic from anyone, and make it their own. If the Wyrdmother had it, she could become a goddess." I paused, realizing the room was holding its breath. "Or burn the world down."

Juliet's hand found mine. Her palm was soft, but her grip was iron. "Aspen. Tell me you have the grimoire."

"I... It's in the safe at the house," I said, voice gone small.

Rafe grinned, all wolf, all menace. "She'll make contact with you, little witch. When she does, you bring the book. We'll take care of her then."

"Can we?" I asked. "She's way more powerful than me. Than any of us."

Kazimir's fangs glimmered when he spoke. "All the better. I like challenge."

Menace looked at me with a solemn nod. "We'll get him back, Aspen. But you need to be ready to run point. She'll want you, not the rest of us."

I was watching Parker tweak a new security script when the thought hit me. "She's probably waiting with a message for me at the bakery," I said. "Last time she tried to reach me, that's where I was."

Bronc, who'd appeared in the entry at some point, gave a hard nod. "Let's check it out. All of us."

I stood, legs shaky, and Oscar scrambled to perch on my shoulder. "I'll get the grimoire."

Juliet pressed a thermos into my hands. "Coffee. You're running on fumes."

I took a sip and let the heat settle my nerves. "Thanks."

Maddie hugged me so tight my ribs popped. "Bring him home, sweet girl. He's counting on you."

I nodded, throat too tight for words.

We rolled out, the whole rescue team moving with military precision. The cold outside bit my cheeks, and the moon was still hanging heavy and low, as if it wanted a front-row seat. Arsenal drove, Wrecker rode shotgun, Bronc and Menace flanked me in the back with Parker and Oscar in the third row. Juliet and Maddie stayed behind to coordinate any backup we might need, and I felt the loss of their comfort instantly.

The ride to the bakery took less than ten minutes, but every second felt like an hour. The closer we got, the more I felt the thrum of magic—dark and oily, seeping through the cracks of the world. The grimoire was in a satchel under the seat.

We rolled up to the bakery, the yellow glow of the streetlights giving the building an eerie, washed-out look. My heart hammered so hard I thought it might vibrate the bones right out of my chest, but I kept my hands steady as I unlocked the truck and led the way up the dark sidewalk. Behind me, Bronc, Menace, Arsenal, and Wrecker fanned out in a practiced wedge—men built for violence and for moments just like this.

The bakery's front window was dark, the neon "OPEN" sign off, but taped smack-dab in the middle of the glass was a sheet of paper—no, not paper, but thick, textured cardstock, the kind you'd use for invitations or funerals. There was something written on it in dark red ink that looked like it might have come from a vein instead of a pen.

I glanced back at Bronc, who nodded for me to go ahead. I peeled the tape, trying not to rip the edges, and the note came away with a sickening tack. I didn't realize my hands were shaking until I tried to unfold it.

On the front was a hand-drawn map—scrawled, but accurate, every turn and street labeled in a spiky, precise hand. There was a red X about fifty miles south of Dairyville, where the highway branched toward Morgantown. Beneath the map, in jagged script, were the words:

BRING THE GRIMOIRE TO THE STAR OR YOU'LL GET TO SEE YOUR MUTT IN PIECES.

Wrecker whistled, low and soft. "Subtle, ain't she?"

Menace took the note from my hand, eyes narrowing as he traced the lines. "This is deep in Morgantown territory. Not their usual spot for business. If she picked it, she wants the wolves watching."

Bronc studied the map with the calm of someone who'd run a thousand ops like this and survived all of them. "That explains why the Morgantown pack has been snooping around," he said, mostly to himself. "She's got muscle to back her play."

Arsenal stepped back from the bakery's entry, sharp eyes scanning the street. "There's activity up by the main road. Could be a tail."

"We knew she wouldn't make it easy," Bronc said, folding the note and tucking it in his vest. "Let's get moving."

Before we could even step off the curb, two sets of headlights swung into the lot: a matte-black Mercedes, and a new-looking Cadillac Escalade with the plates blacked out. Kazimir emerged from the Benz in a tailored suit, not a hair out of place, and Rafe rolled out of the Caddy, wearing his "Sunday best"—which, for him, meant a pearl-button shirt and jeans that looked poured on.

Menace strode over and handed Kazimir the note. He read it with a sneer, then offered it to Rafe, who just shook his head and muttered, "She's a real piece of work."

I caught Rafe's gaze—he was one of the few who could look me straight in the eye without flinching. "You ready for this?" he asked, voice pitched so only I could hear.

"Born ready," I lied. I was shaking inside, but I didn't have time to let that show.

Kazimir's gaze flicked to the bakery. "You have book?" he asked, blunt as a hammer.

I nodded.

Bronc clapped his hands, commanding attention. "Oscar, you have any idea what to expect at the drop?"

Oscar's face popped up over the third row seat. "There will be wards. Strong ones. I suggest Miss keeps the book close at all times—do not let them separate you."

Rafe gave me a quick, fierce smile. "We'll be right at your back, little witchling."

Menace had already started back toward the Expedition, barking assignments. Wrecker took the shotgun seat and glanced back and winked at Parker. Arsenal sat behind the wheel. I climbed in next to Bronc and pulled the satchel from under the seat to hold in my lap. I felt a reassuring squeeze of my shoulder from the third row. I was glad to have Parker along.

Oscar sat up straight, eyes clear and anxious when my phone rang. "Miss, I recommend you do not answer the phone number. It is a ruse. You will want to see her in person before making any deal."

Bronc smirked. "That's fine. We'll see her up close and personal."

I kept my hands in my lap, nails digging into the leather of the satchel, the only thing that kept them from clawing my own skin. Every mile we drove, the world got colder; the moon climbed higher, and the sky settled into a solid, bottomless black.

We rode in silence for most of it, the truck's engine the only thing steady. Every now and then, Bronc would glance over at me, checking for cracks. I made myself meet his gaze, even when my throat wanted to close up.

At the halfway mark, Arsenal clicked off the headlights and took the next ten miles by moonlight and the barest hint of dash back light. "No sense in giving them a clear shot at us," he said, which I assumed was code for "buckle up, this gets dangerous from here."

We crossed into Morgantown territory, marked only by a battered county line sign and the sudden, sharp stench of burned sage in the air. Witches used it to mask the scent of their workings, but to a wolf—or a witch bred for this—it was a dead giveaway.

We pulled off the highway onto a dirt road, winding deeper into the brush. I saw the map's red X in my mind, felt the bond to Papa stretch and twist like an over-wound wire. Somewhere out there, he was waiting. Somewhere out there, the Wyrdmother had set her trap.

Oscar shifted in my lap, voice barely above a whisper. "She will not harm him until she has what she wants. You must not let her have it."

"I won't," I whispered back.

The truck's cab was a tomb. No one spoke. Arsenal drove like he wanted to squeeze the last bit of life out of the steering wheel, both hands locked at ten and two, every muscle in his neck straining against the collar of his shirt. Wrecker's eyes were pinned to the dark horizon, lips moving silently as if he was counting seconds or bodies or both. I sat smashed between Bronc and Menace, the satchel now clutched to my chest, Oscar a barely contained tremor between Bronc and me. Parker's fingers clicked across her laptop keys as she still looked for hidden clues in the third seat.

Behind us, Rafe and Kazimir followed in their own cars, neither wanting to risk being boxed in. Gunner rolled up with several enforcers in the boxy MC van, which probably had more firepower hidden in it than a National Guard armory. I took a sort of mean comfort in that—if the Wyrdmother wanted a war; she was about to get one.

But mostly, I hurt.

The mate bond was still new and hadn't ever been tried. Now it felt like the bone had been yanked out entirely, replaced with a steel rod that pulsed cold with every mile we got closer to him. I wanted to scream, to claw the air, but I just hugged the grimoire and tried to breathe through the pain.

Arsenal grunted. "We park a mile out, go in quiet. Anything else is a fucking suicide run."

Bronc mapped out a strategy. "Menace and Aspen are with me. If it gets ugly, we'll need to clear a path. Wrecker, Parker, and Arsenal that's on y'all."

Oscar hopped up on my lap, voice the sort of calm that you get right before a volcano blows. "She will be expecting violence. And will be ready for every tactical approach. But the grimoire may distract her. If she is like other witches of her type, she will want to verify its authenticity before harming Sir."

Oscar's shiny black eyes fixed on me, the rest of his body covered by a leather jacket except for the tip of his white-furred tail. "Miss, do not allow her to touch your skin. If you can, do not allow her to speak your full name. She may try to leverage a blood name ritual to gain power over you."

"Can she really do that?" I asked, my tongue thick.

"Yes," Oscar said, and left it at that.

Bronc looked over at me. "She's not going to win, Aspen. We don't let our own get taken. Not ever."

I nodded, teeth set. "I know."

Arsenal slammed on the brakes a mile from the X on the map, rolling the truck behind a screen of juniper and brush. The air reeked of sage and bitter smoke. "It's time," he said.

The rest of the team fanned out. Rafe and Kazimir took the north approach, cutting through the dark with inhuman speed and grace. Gunner and his team ghosted west, barely visible as they melted into the trees. Menace led Bronc and me east, where bonfires crackled in the distance. God, I hoped they weren't naked.

The ritual site was laid out in a clearing ringed with rough wooden posts. At the center, three bonfires burned so hot I could feel the singe on my face from thirty yards away. Between the fires, I saw the Wyrdmother had Papa strapped to a large rune-covered wooden slab. It was set at an angle so he could see our approach.

Papa was bound to the slab by his wrists and ankles. Through his tattoos, I could see he was bleeding. He'd clearly put up a fight. He was stripped to his boxers, and blood ran down his arms, legs and sides onto the slab. His face was swollen where he'd been beaten. His chest rose and fell in quick, shallow breaths, but he was alive.

My knees almost buckled. I took a step forward, but Bronc's hand clamped around my shoulder, holding me steady. "Not yet," he whispered. "Let her come to us."

The Wyrdmother stood between two bonfires; coven sisters fanned out behind her like a murder of crows. She wore the same black robe, hood thrown back so her hair blazed silver in the firelight. Her hands glowed faintly green, crackling with power. Her eyes, when they landed on me, felt like stepping in front of a high beam—so bright they left spots dancing across my vision.

Kazimir and Rafe stepped into the clearing, and a look of fear passed across her face for a fleeting moment. She recovered before she spoke, gathering her power.

She called out in a voice that didn't belong in this world. "Well. If it isn't the little Waters bitch. Haven't you accrued quite an impressive team of support?"

Bronc bristled beside me, but I stepped forward, Oscar's weight steady on my shoulder.

"I'm here," I called. "Let him go."

She laughed, a sound like a crow choking on glass. "Do you think you can bargain with me, child?"

My voice came out steadier than I felt. "That's the deal, isn't it? The book for the man. Or are you a liar as well as a thief?"

She snarled. "Do you have the book or don't you?"

I pulled it from the satchel, holding it up so she could see the battered leather, the iron clasps, the faded sigil on the front. "Proof of life first," I demanded.

She considered, then flicked her fingers. One of the coven women slapped Papa's face. It jerked violently to the side.

He looked up, blood and sweat in his eyes. "Sunshine," he rasped.

I nearly broke, but Bronc's hand kept me grounded.

The Wyrdmother stepped forward, her feet barely disturbing the grass. "Give me the book, Dud. Or I'll start carving pieces off your mate, one finger at a time."

The air thickened with ozone. I felt the spell before I saw it—a crackling wave of green light that rolled out from the Wyrdmother's outstretched hands. My knees locked mid-step. Bronc's grip on my shoulder became stone.

Panic flooded my throat as I realized I was the only thing still moving.

"Clever trick, yes?" The Wyrdmother stalked toward Papa's bound form, her dagger catching firelight. "Your mongrels make excellent statues." She pressed the blade beneath Papa's jaw, drawing a bead of blood that slid crimson down his throat. "Now. The grimoire. Or I unmake your pretty wolf."

"Last chance, little moth," the Wyrdmother purred, her shadow elongating into talons. "The grimoire... or watch his blood water these boards."

My fingers twitched on the grimoire, the ancient leather warm as a heartbeat in my hands. The spell to rend power, I thought. To unmake every witch. Across the ground, Papa's eyes fluttered open—bright, achingly alive. His gaze found mine, and for a fractured moment, the world thawed.

"Don't," he rasped, blood flecking his lips as he strained against the chains. "You know what she'll become." His voice softened, a cracked plea. "I know what you are, Sunshine. Who you are."

My name in his mouth undid me. Days ago, it had been a beautiful song at my neck; now it was a dirge. I stumbled forward, the grimoire's weight suddenly unbearable. "I can't just—!"

"You can." Papa's smile was a blade. "You think I'd want eternity if it's built on your ashes? On everyone's?" His throat bobbed, the chains clinking as he lifted his head. "I loved you before I knew your face. Before time. Before reason. I'll love you after the stars burn out. But not like this. Never like this. Please don't trade our love for evil."

The Wyrdmother's snarl ripped through the moment. "Enough!" Her palm slammed down on the altar, veins bulging black beneath her parchment skin. "Choose, child—or I'll peel his beating heart from his ribs and let you wear it as a pendant!"

My hand closed around the grimoire's spine. I could feel its pulse now, ancient and hungry, pages whispering promises of desolation. Papa mouthed a silent no, tears cutting paths through the grime on his face.

Two futures split my soul:

A world drowned in the Wyrdmother's shadow, every heartbeat mine to crush.

A pyre of my own making, grief carving me hollow.

Happiness, I thought wildly. The word tasted foreign. Weeks stolen between doubt—Papa's laugh tangled with dawn light, his hands steadying me in the bakery when I picked up big cakes. His sweeping floors and refilling napkin holders. Simple things that were truly big things. Just the way he loved me. A lifetime's worth of peace crammed into stolen hours.

"I love you," Papa whispered, the words a sacrament. "Now end this."

My fingers tightened. The Wyrdmother lunged.

And I understood with devastating clarity that some choices aren't made—they're endured, teeth gritted against the fracture.

Chapter 27

Aspen

For a single heartbeat, I was paralyzed—watching my mate bleed out on a slab, the Wyrdmother looming over him with her knife like some high priestess at the altar of my nightmares. Bonfire light danced over her blade. The flames flickered over the wood, the blood, the tangle of runes carved across Papa's chest and arms. He didn't even scream anymore, just watched me with eyes that said, *"Don't do it, Sunshine."* He knew what the Wyrdmother wanted, and he'd rather die than see me hand it over.

I couldn't breathe. I couldn't move. The world shrank down to the shine of steel at his throat and the vein pulsing in the Wyrdmother's neck. It was like I'd been pressed flat by gravity—a hundred atmospheres crushing my ribs until something deep in me snapped. Then, all at once, the terror shifted.

It started in my chest, a coil of panic collapsing into rage. Not just anger, but something older, purer. Something that burned away fear and made room for a different animal. The world slowed. I saw the light as if I were inside it. The Wyrdmother's hand, the edge of the blade, the lines of runes in the bonfire's shadow—every detail went razor-sharp and bright.

My hands rose of their own will, and for the first time in my life, I felt magic the way a wildfire must feel its own heat. Every nerve ending sparked, my fingers searing with white-hot light. It hurt, but not in a way that wanted to be stopped. It wanted out.

The Wyrdmother saw the change a moment too late. She turned, mouth open to scream a spell, but my voice beat hers to the punch.

"GET AWAY FROM MY MATE!" I screamed, and the world split.

Lightning—pure, holy, blinding—shot from my hands. It hit her in the chest, not just moving her but unmaking her. There was no time for words or last curses. Her black robe, her crown of silver hair, her talons—all of it dissolved into a shower of green and gold sparks, then nothing at all. The force of it knocked the nearest coven sisters off their feet. The bonfires roared higher, caught up in the burst of raw power.

The energy didn't stop at the Wyrdmother. It spun out in fractal branches, arcing between the sisters, the trees, the standing stones around the altar. I swung toward them, hands still white with fury.

"And y'all!" I hollered, my voice bouncing off the clearing. "Not so funny now, is it? Not a dud anymore, huh?"

They cowered. Not a single one so much as reached for their own magic. They'd seen something they didn't understand and never wanted to see again.

Before I could let loose another blast, I felt a presence behind me. Warm, ancient, peaceful and terrifying all at once.

A hand—cool and gentle—closed over my shoulder. I flinched, ready to turn my power on whatever it was. But his voice froze me faster than a spell ever could.

"You did well, daughter. But that's enough for now."

I turned. Archon stood behind me, taller than the pines, white hair glowing even brighter than my hands. His wings stretched out behind him, so vast they cast their own shadow, eating the firelight whole.

It was like waking up from a trance. The power snapped back, stinging my palms. I staggered a step; the world lurching back to normal speed and color. I nearly toppled, but he caught me, guiding me to the ground as if I weighed nothing.

Then the bond snapped back—hard and fast—and all I could think of was Papa.

I spun, still reeling, and saw him slumped on the altar. Blood pulsed in a dark sheet from the cut at his neck. His lips moved, forming my name, but no sound made it out. Archon was there before I could scream, his hand pressed against the wound. Light spilled from between his fingers, blue and gold, so beautiful it hurt my eyes.

"Stay with him," Archon commanded, and I did, falling to my knees at the altar, grabbing Papa's hand in both of mine as the chains had fallen away. The runes carved on his skin smoked, burning away under Archon's touch. I wept openly, snot and tears running down my face, but I didn't care.

"Don't you dare leave me," I whispered. "You promised. You're my anchor."

He smiled, even as he bled. "Sunshine," he mouthed.

The clearing shook with a different kind of thunder—the sound of wolves tearing through brush. Gunner and his team burst out of the trees, armed and wild-eyed, ready to rip the world apart.

Bronc, breaking from his spell bellowed, "MOVE!" and Menace dove in, weapon drawn. But they both slammed to a stop when they saw Archon. Menace's mouth actually dropped open.

"What the fuck was that?" Menace said, looking from the scorched patch where the Wyrdmother had been, to the coven sisters huddled on the ground, to me with my hands still flickering with light.

Archon didn't even look up. "We can discuss later. Your friend needs to be stabilized."

Menace nodded, all the bravado gone. "Got it."

Bronc moved to my side, one big hand on my shoulder. I realized then that the coven sisters hadn't moved, hadn't even tried to run. They were frozen with terror. Maybe that was for the best.

Archon worked fast. The wound on Papa's neck shrank under his palm, the blood stopping as if reversed by the touch of God Himself. Archon's eyes went flat and bright, as though he was pouring everything into his touch. I watched the color return to Papa's face, the wild hitch in his breathing evening out.

"He's going to be fine," Archon said, finally letting go. "But he'll need rest. You all will."

Bronc's voice was low and grateful. "Thank you."

Archon turned to him, all warmth. "The wolves of Iron Valor always seem to keep me on my toes. Gather your people. We'll need to talk. In private."

Bronc nodded, then looked at Menace. "Secure the clearing, including the grimoire. Make sure no one follows us."

"On it," Menace said, and disappeared into the dark, his boots silent on the scorched earth.

Bronc turned to me, and for once in his life, he was at a loss for words. "Aspen..." He shook his head, pride and awe and something like fatherly terror all at once. "You did good, kid. Real good."

I wanted to say thank you, but my throat had closed up. I just squeezed Papa's hand until my knuckles ached.

"Time to get you home," Bronc said, and between him and Archon, they lifted Papa off the altar, cradling him like a child. I followed, dizzy and empty and still charged with whatever power I'd unleashed. My hands shook. I'd never felt more alive, or more scared of what I was.

We left the clearing behind. The coven sisters didn't follow. As we crossed back through the trees, I heard their wailing start—a song of grief and fear that carried all the way to the highway.

We got Papa into the van, Menace at the wheel and Bronc crammed in the back with Archon. I curled up next to Papa, my head on his shoulder, not caring that I was covered in sweat and blood and probably half-crazy.

He didn't say a word, just stroked my hair, over and over, as if to reassure himself I was still there.

Oscar materialized at my feet, his fur bristling with static. "Miss," he said, in a voice I'd never heard from him before, "you have just rewritten the rules of witchcraft. I suggest you do not do that again without warning me."

I almost laughed, but it came out as a choked sob. "I don't even know what I did, Oscar."

"Neither do they," he replied, glancing at Archon. "But I suspect he does."

Archon met my eyes across the van. There was pride there, but also something else—a warning.

"We'll talk soon," he said, and I shivered, not sure if I was more excited or terrified.

I closed my eyes, breathing in Papa's scent, letting the bond hum between us. His heart beat strong and sure under my palm. We were alive. We'd survived.

But nothing would ever be the same.

We got to the house just before dawn. Doc was waiting, medical bag open, sleeves rolled up. He didn't even blink when Archon handed Papa over and said, "He needs to be cleaned up, but the wound is sealed."

Doc took one look, nodded, and got to work. "I've seen weirder," he muttered, but I doubted it.

Oscar and I stood in the hall, watching through the cracked door as Doc cleaned Papa's wounds and wiped away the worst of the blood. Archon hovered at my shoulder, a presence I couldn't ignore.

When Doc finished, he beckoned me in. Papa. lay propped against the pillows, looking more alive than I'd thought possible.

"Hey, Sunshine," he whispered, his voice gravelly but his smile perfect. "You saved my life."

I pressed my forehead to his and cried for the first time in hours. "I almost killed half the forest to do it."

He just laughed. "That's my girl."

Archon cleared his throat. "You both need rest. But when you're ready, Aspen, we have much to discuss. About your powers. About your family and the likelihood that the Council is going to call an inquiry."

I looked up at him, feeling the old fear slide back into place. But this time, I wasn't alone.

I had Papa. I had my pack. And apparently, I had the literal Angel King for a father figure. I nodded, wiping my eyes. "I'll be ready."

He smiled—a real, dazzling smile—and in that moment, I thought things were going to be okay.

But first, I crawled into bed next to Papa, wrapped my arms around him, and let myself drift into the sweetest, deepest sleep I'd ever known.

Tomorrow, the world could wait.

The next morning, I woke to the sound of a blood pressure cuff inflating on Papa's arm and the low, steady voice of Doc muttering numbers under his breath. Sunlight blazed through the bedroom windows, painting stripes over the mess of blankets and pillows across the bed. Oscar sat sentry at the headboard, his fur slicked and neat as if he'd spent the entire night prepping for a royal visit. The grimoire—my mother's, and now mine—rested on the nightstand, its battered clasp glinting in the sunlight.

Papa looked almost normal. His neck was wrapped in a loose bandage, and his hand found mine the second he spotted me awake. The mate bond purred and hummed between us, not as electric as it had been after the blast, but settled, warm, alive.

Doc finished with the cuff and made a note on his phone. "You'll live," he said, one eyebrow raised at the two of us. "But you need to rest for a couple days. No heavy lifting, no moonlight strolls, no…" he made a vague gesture that I knew meant sex "…vigorous exercise."

Papa managed a wry grin. "Can we define 'vigorous' for science?"

Doc shook his head, grinning. "For your age? You can probably walk to the mailbox by tomorrow. Just listen to your body, and if anything feels weird; like, supernatural weird, call me."

I glanced at his hand. The knuckles were raw, stained with pink from scrubbing off Papa's blood. His nails were chewed down to the quick, and his collarbone was tight as a bowstring. Doc was not made for house calls, or for being around archangels. Speaking of—

Archon stood in the bedroom doorway, arms folded behind his back, watching the sunrise as if he'd personally set the lightbulb to "stun" this morning. Even in faded jeans and a t-shirt, he looked regal; like an emperor slumming it in suburbia. He radiated presence, and I could feel Oscar's hackles spike every time he so much as moved.

Doc packed up his bag, then made for the door with the hurried energy of a man who'd rather lance boils than make small talk with an angel king. Archon turned and nodded to him, a gesture that held so much dignity it almost made Doc bow. Instead, he froze halfway, then did an awkward two-fingered salute and vanished into the Texas morning.

Papa let out a snort. "He'll need therapy for a year."

I squeezed his hand. "You're the one who almost bled out, Papa."

He smiled, but it didn't reach his eyes. "But you're the one who saved the world. And me."

That brought the memories back, flooding my skin with goosebumps: the heat in my chest, the fire in my hands, the sight of the Wyrdmother shattering like a mirror dropped off the roof. I wanted to shrink away from it, but the memory didn't let me. I wasn't afraid, not really. Just—changed.

Archon's voice cut through the hush, softer than velvet but sharp enough to slice. "Aspen, if you're up to it, we should talk."

I expected him to sound formal, all thunder and commandments. But he didn't. He sounded like a dad who'd never figured out how to be a dad, which made my heart twist even more.

I licked my lips. "Can Papa join? I don't want to have to repeat everything to him later. He'll just make me tell it, anyway."

Archon's smile flickered. "Of course. In fact, I'd prefer it."

Papa and I made our way to the living room and got comfortable on the couch, and I placed the grimoire on the end table.

Archon strode to the kitchen and poured himself a mug of coffee, just, you know, like archangels do, and came back to the couch, perching on the edge of the ottoman like it was a throne. He fixed his golden gaze on me, then on the grimoire, then back to me. The air in the room prickled with something that felt holy and dangerous and more than a little like home.

I waited for him to start, but he let the silence stretch, watching the dust motes swirl in the sunlight.

Finally, he said, "Your mother was the most wonderful woman I ever knew."

My breath caught. He'd never said her name. Not once, even at the wedding.

Archon saw it. He nodded, like he understood exactly what I was thinking. "I met Laurel at a council in Geneva twenty-seven years ago.

She was already the strongest elemental witch in her coven, and she argued like she was born to it. But she was kind, too. Gentle, in ways that surprised everyone. Including me." He looked down into his coffee, the faintest frown at the surface. "We weren't supposed to fall in love. That's... forbidden, for angels. But we did. And then, you happened."

Papa squeezed my hand. Oscar let out a long, low whistle.

Archon's eyes were far away. "She didn't tell me she was pregnant. She cut all contact. I thought it was just too much having to be secretive with everything. So, I stayed away." He shrugged, a celestial gesture that somehow still looked sad. "Your mother was very good at hiding. I never knew you existed until last night."

I stared at the floor. "She never told me, either. Not even at the end. She just said my father was 'other'."

"She was protecting you," Archon said. "If the angelic host had known, you'd have been a target. From all sides. So she hid you. Hid your power, too, as best she could." His gaze flicked to the grimoire. "But she left a way for you to find it. For you to find yourself."

I felt tears burning behind my eyes, but I forced them down. "So I'm a... what? Witch-angel hybrid?"

He gave a single, small nod. "That's as close as any language can get. You are unique. The first and only of your kind, as far as I know."

Papa gave a low whistle. "Damn, Sunshine. No pressure."

I punched his thigh, laughing through the sting of tears. "No kidding. I just wanted to bake cakes and pay my bills."

Archon actually smiled at that. "You're allowed to want simple things. Even the most powerful beings crave peace. But you must also know that word of this will eventually spread, likely has already. And in the event that the Council calls for an accounting, I will be there by your side."

Papa spoke up. "If the Council should call for an accounting, you should know that Maltraz was involved in this."

I looked at Papa surprised.

"I'm sorry I didn't tell you Sunshine. But the symbol that green-jacketed man left was a demonic tracking sigil. Wrecker figured it out. By the time he did, you'd already been confronted by the crazy lady. I didn't see a point in adding to your stress."

Archon didn't look surprised. "This is not a shocking revelation. Those who seek power are predictable. Maltraz can usually be counted among the top on that list. I'm sure the Wyrdmother promised him something. She was certain she'd get the book and would have the power to destroy all who stood against her. It could have been how she got the demon king to do her bidding."

I looked at Papa. "I'm not happy that you kept this from me. But I understand. Let's just not make it a habit, please."

He kissed my forehead. "I promise."

I thought about the blast, the feel of raw magic in my bones, and looked at my father. "I've honestly just discovered my magic. I'd always been a dud magically and have certainly never done anything like *that* before. Should I be worried? That seemed pretty dangerous."

His gaze sharpened. "It was. Immeasurably so. Your power is not only magic, but the force of creation itself. You must be careful when you use it. Control will come, but for now, do not call it unless there is no other choice. The backlash could be... catastrophic. For you, for those around you. But," he reached out, taking my hand with a gentleness that shocked me, "you are not alone. You have Papa. You have Oscar. You have your pack. And if you wish, you have me."

Oscar coughed, looking at the ceiling. "I will do my utmost, Miss. But I must admit, I am entirely out of my depth."

Archon grinned. "That's true for most of us, Oscar."

I tried to absorb it all. The room felt too small, the coffee too bitter, my skin too thin. I looked at Papa, who smiled like he'd always known I was something special.

"I'll be honest, the prospect of having a living parent in my life is really appealing. I always thought my father wasn't in my life because he had chosen to be absent. That does a number on a person. I always thought there must be something wrong with me if one of the people who helped make me didn't want to have anything to do with me." I hated how pathetic I sounded. I also hated that I was freaking crying again. I was almost 26 years old, for Pete's sake.

Archon took both of my hands in his.

"Aspen. I promise you, had I known of your existence, I don't care what the consequences might have been, I'd have been in your life. I'd have been the best father I could have been, and you'd have known that I loved and wanted you."

"That means so much to hear you say that." I told him through my tears. "So, what happens now?"

Archon sipped his coffee. "Now you live. You heal. You learn to wield your power, but you do it on your terms. I will help you if you let me. The Creator knows all about you. He has forgiven me and has blessed me with being your protector. I will stand behind you always. But your path is yours, and no one else's." He stood towering above us even in the little living room. I stood with him. He reached out, brushed a thumb along my cheek. It felt like starlight and forgiveness. "I am proud of you, daughter. You are more than I could have dreamed."

"Dad? Can I call you that?" I asked him awkwardly.

"Of course, child. I love the sound of that."

"How do I get in touch with you if I need you?"

He picked up my phone and handed it to me.

"Just search under *Dad* and shoot me a message. That's the quickest way. But I'm also connected to both of you. I can sense when you're in trouble as well. I'm never far. Now, I think you and Jonas likely need some time alone to process the events of the past several hours, so I'll take my leave. But remember, you can contact me anytime."

With that, he turned, left his coffee half-finished, and walked out the door. A moment later, I heard the whir of wings, and he was gone.

It took a long time for my brain to reboot. I curled up next to Papa, Oscar perched at my feet, the grimoire heavy and alive on the table.

"You okay, Sunshine?" Papa asked, voice softer than a summer night.

"Not even a little," I answered. "But I think I might be someday."

He pulled me onto his chest, careful of the bandage at his throat. "You're going to be amazing. Hell, you already are."

I wanted to believe it. I really did.

I let my fingers trace his scars, then his lips, then the line of his jaw. Every inch of him felt like home.

"Thank you for not dying," I said.

He laughed, the sound vibrating through both of us. "Thank you for saving my life. Again."

Oscar cleared his throat. "If I may, Miss—I believe you are owed several cake orders, and perhaps a nap."

I snorted. "You always know just what to say, Oscar."

Papa rolled us both off the couch, and we ended up tangled on the rug, laughing like fools. It felt good. It felt like a beginning.

I looked at the grimoire, then at my mate, then at the prairie dog who'd stood by me through hell and high water.

"I think we're going to be okay," I said. And for the first time in my life, I meant it.

Because if I'd learned anything from angels, witches, and wolves, it's that you don't have to be just one thing to belong. You just have to love with all your weird, wild heart.

And I did.

Epilogue

Arsenal

Council headquarters, Chicago, looked exactly like I'd always imagined the Vatican might, if it was run by people who considered the Inquisition a blueprint for office design. The building soared thirty stories of black stone and gold trim, hunched at the end of Michigan Avenue like a mausoleum for dead empires. Getting through security took an hour—retina scan, handprint, magic sniff test, then a wolf shifter in an Armani suit "escorting" us up in a private elevator, flanked by two more just in case we decided to assassinate another world leader before lunch.

Inside, every surface gleamed. Marble floors so polished you could check your hair in them, columns as thick as a redwood forest, ceilings stenciled with spells and what looked a lot like machine gun ports hidden behind angels and gargoyles. I'd been in war rooms before. This was the first one that felt like it might double as a sacrificial altar if the wind changed.

Big Papa walked with his usual slow authority, not a damn bit thrown off by the silent threat in every corner. The bandage at his throat showed above his collar—an unmissable souvenir from last week's bloodletting—and the look on his face told the world that he would not be giving up a single inch of territory ever again. Aspen stayed at his left, hand resting sometimes on his arm, sometimes at her own wrist, her eyes scanning every face, every shadow. There was something new in her step, a kind of assurance that came from knowing you could burn down the planet with a single mistake. I was the designated security for this little reunion, but I doubted anything mortal could touch us now.

The Chamber was bigger than a basketball court, U-shaped with three tiers of seating. Each seat was filled: wolves, witches, vampires, and one king-sized demon holding a stylus and a notebook the size of a car battery. At the head of the U was the Council itself, every member in a black suit and red tie, the sort of people who treated the Geneva conventions as starting points. They all turned to watch us as we took our seats at the defense table. Three microphones, three glasses of water, three coasters with the old Council sigil.

I slouched back and sized up the opposition. Not bad, as far as kangaroo courts went. The new Wyrdmother of Verdant Hollow was a heavyset woman with purple hair and a dress that looked like it had eaten six other dresses for breakfast. The vampire delegation was headed by Lucia Kozlov, her smile more genuine than most in the room, but her eyes all knives. King Rafe Mayfield represented the Southwest, which meant he wore a bolo tie and a sneer. Menace was there, the King of the Midwest, and Iron Valor, truth be told. There were other faces, other eyes, none of them friendly.

Papa cleared his throat. "Let's just be honest, gentlemen and ladies—none of you really wants to be here, do you?" His voice was like a church bell: loud, old, impossible to ignore.

A few smirked from the back rows. The demon's eyes didn't move. The new Council chair, an elder called Pietro, rapped a silver pen against the table. "We are here because three Council leaders have perished in the past year, and each time, the Iron Valor Pack was present." He let it hang. "Perhaps you would like to explain that?"

"We don't kill for sport," Papa replied, "and we don't kill unless we have to. You've read the reports. We didn't instigate a single incident."

Pietro nodded. "We have. The problem, Mr. Rice, is that each time the culprit is dead. Or, as with the most recent event, is incinerated beyond identification."

I watched Aspen's shoulders tense. She hadn't meant to turn the Wyrdmother into cosmic fertilizer, but I wasn't about to let her take the fall alone. I raised my hand, not for permission, but as a warning. "You want testimony, I'll give you testimony."

"Jess Regan. Please," Pietro said, and a dozen Council pens moved to take notes.

I spoke in the clipped monotone of a man who'd spent half his life in a debriefing room. "At 2321 hours local, the Wyrdmother and a coven of five forcibly abducted Jonas Rice from his pack territory in Dairyville, Texas. They then chained him to a rune-inscribed altar and, after beating him bloody, the Wyrdmother was in the process of murdering him by slitting his throat during a bloodletting ritual. He survived barely. I witnessed this with my own eyes." I nodded at Papa's bandage. "The wound is documented. The tools used were recovered and are in custody. The scene was secured by Iron Valor and the Midwest King's detail. Aspen Waters confronted the Wyrdmother in a clearing. Moments before, the Wyrdmother threatened to kill Rice unless Waters surrendered a magical artifact."

Pietro's gaze flicked to Aspen. "Did you comply?"

She shook her head, voice clear as a glass bell. "The artifact belonged to me. Jonas and I knew it was too dangerous for that madwoman to get her hands on. So no. I did not give it to her. That in no way justifies her attempting to murder my mate. So I stopped her."

Shasta Tierney, the High Flame Caller from the Emberthorn Witches, leaned in. "And how, Ms. Waters, did you accomplish that?"

I felt the tension spike next to me, but Aspen just said, "With magic." Her accent was as thick as the syrup at Pearl's Bar & Grill. "It was instinct. I'd never done anything like it before."

The demon lawyer at the far end finally raised his head. His eyes glowed like brake lights. "You are not a fully trained practitioner, Miss Waters. How is it that you were able to destroy one of the most powerful witches in the world?"

Aspen didn't blink. "Turns out, my father's the angel king. Guess I inherited something."

A chill ran through the room. Even Pietro looked shaken. The demon showed his teeth in what could have been a smile. "Archon Seraphael?"

"That's the one," I said, not hiding the pride in my voice.

The doors at the far end boomed open, and the world tilted. I've been in gunfights, bombed-out cities, places where you could taste death in the air. None of that prepared me for what it was like when Archon walked into the room. He was seven feet of blinding light, hair like a comet's tail, a suit so white it made the marble look dirty. He didn't walk—he drifted, every eye in the place locked on him. He ignored them all and strode right up to the defense table, standing behind Aspen.

He nodded to the Council, but it was all formality. "I apologize for my tardiness," he said, voice calm and beautiful, but edged with the kind of threat you only heard in thunderstorms. "I see the matter is already underway."

Pietro actually stammered, which would have been funny if not for the fact that I could see his hands shaking. "We—uh—were just reviewing the circumstances of the Wyrdmother's demise."

"Then allow me to clarify," Archon said, and with a snap of his fingers, the chamber darkened. A three-dimensional image hung in the air above the table—Aspen's bakery, the bloodied sigils on the paper bag, the face of the green-jacketed man, captured by security cam. Maltraz glared at the crowd. The display shifted—next, to the clearing where Aspen destroyed the Wyrdmother, the entire event replaying in supernatural slow motion.

"There was a demon tracking sigil in the bakery," Archon continued. "The demon Maltraz must have collaborated with the Wyrdmother to orchestrate the abduction and forced transfer of magical power from my daughter to herself. This was not just an attempted murder. It was a breach of Council law, the inter-species treaty, and the Magical Convention."

He paused, letting the information settle over the room like fallout. Even the demon lawyer paled, then he spoke. "This evidence is circumstantial. Any demon could have influenced that man. There is no proof it was Maltraz."

Pietro cleared his throat. "We agree. This evidence is damning, but we cannot ascertain who left this sigil. And Archon, we... appreciate your clarification. But there is still the matter of the, ah, excessive force used."

Archon folded his hands, all patience. "Would you have preferred my daughter's mate and my daughter die?"

"No, of course not—"

"Then the matter is settled," Archon said. He looked at Aspen, pride shining out of him like heat. "She is not a threat. She is not a weapon. She is a young woman who defended her mate and her family. Anyone in this room would have done the same."

Silence. It stretched for an entire minute, the longest sixty seconds of my life. Then the Council chair scribbled a note, whispered to the others, and rapped the table with his pen. "This session is adjourned. Iron Valor is cleared of all charges. Ms. Waters, you will submit to regular magical evaluations, to be overseen by the angel king himself. Is that acceptable?"

Aspen nodded, too stunned to speak. Papa's eyes closed with what I could only call a prayer.

We were ushered out by the wolf shifter in the suit, back through the marble and gold and the endless security. In the elevator, it was just us, Archon shining like a thousand-watt bulb, Aspen and Papa holding hands, me staring at my boots and realizing, for the first time, that maybe Iron Valor could survive the next hundred years after all.

As the elevator dropped, I looked at Aspen, at the small pink scar on Papa's neck, at the face of Archon. "You okay, kid?" I asked her.

She smiled, a little bit shaky. "Yeah. I think I might be."

Archon clapped me on the shoulder, nearly knocking me through the back of the elevator. "You did well, son. You all did."

The doors opened on the city below. Outside, the wind howled, and the old world waited for us to come back. I took a breath and braced for whatever came next.

I could still feel the weight of all those eyes, the endless scrutiny, the suspicion. But for once, it didn't feel like a death sentence.

It felt like hope.

The next morning before "church," Pearl insisted on feeding us all breakfast. The scent of fried bacon hit you at the threshold, a wall of comfort and cholesterol, followed by the even heavier thump of biscuits drowning in sausage gravy.

I found my usual seat at the corner of the big table, back to the wall, direct sight line to the kitchen and both exits. Habit. Gunner was already there, two plates in, mop of auburn hair wild from his morning run. He looked up and grinned, brown eyes bright. "You're late, city boy," he said, and slid a pile of bacon onto my plate.

"Don't start," I shot back, but took the bacon anyway. He was right. I preferred this—real food, real faces, real problems—to the politics and artifice of Chicago. The memory of the Council chamber still sat like a stone in my gut.

Pearl herself ran the kitchen, apron smeared with flour, voice carrying over the crowd. "Sit down, eat, then you can solve all the world's problems," she shouted, and every shifter in the building obeyed without question. Even Bronc got in line for the buffet. He wore a black T-shirt stretched tight over his chest, arms folded, eyes always scanning.

Aspen and Papa walked in just as Pearl started pouring the coffee. Aspen was a changed creature. No trace of the scared, hungry ghost she'd been at the edge of the clearing just days ago. She laughed easily, bumping hips with Papa and making a beeline for the cinnamon rolls. Even Oscar, her furry sidekick, had a fresh swagger. She spotted me and gave a little salute with her fork.

We piled our plates and then settled in for the morning ritual. Bronc called us to order by clearing his throat and rapping his knuckles on the tabletop, sending half the drinks sloshing.

"Alright, shut up and listen," he said, tone half-serious, half-fatherly. "We're here because we have unfinished business. The Council cleared us, but the job isn't done. Wrecker, you got an update?"

Wrecker set down his fork, wiped his mouth with the back of his hand, and leaned forward. "Morgantown Pack is dirty. I've been digging in their books—there's weird wire transfers, shell corporations, and a whole lot of cash that ain't going through legitimate channels. They're not just running a chop shop. They're moving product. Maybe people."

A growl ran down the table—real, low, animal. Even Gunner's voice dropped half an octave. "Trafficking?"

"That's the best guess," Wrecker said. "And every time we get close, something blows up. Last week, their Beta got shot in a parking lot in Fort Worth. No one's talking."

Bronc nodded, chewing it over. "So what's the play?"

"We need eyes on Steiner," Wrecker said. "He's the only one with a clean record. Never seen him in the same room with any of the heavy hitters. He's more like a mafia kingpin than an Alpha."

Bronc's gaze moved to me. "Arsenal, you and Gunner are on recon. Nothing fancy. Watch, learn, report. We don't want a fight. Yet."

I gave a nod, and Gunner thumped the table, eager. "About damn time."

Pearl swooped by, dropping off another platter of eggs, and leaned down to whisper, "Y'all be careful out there. Steiner's got friends in high places, and a lot of money buys a lot of bullets." She winked at Gunner, then kissed the top of Bronc's head before heading back to the kitchen.

Across the table, I watched Aspen lean close to Papa, her hand on his forearm. She whispered something, and he covered her hand with his, squeezing gently. For a second, I felt a pang—a memory of something lost. But it was gone as quick as it came.

Bronc tapped the table again. "Alright. Gunner, Arsenal, roll out tonight. Wrecker will feed you everything he's got by sunset. The rest of you—run the routes, keep the businesses up, and keep your ears open. We're not letting anyone in this pack get blindsided again."

He paused, blue eyes sweeping the table. "And if you see anything strange—witches, vamps, or anything that doesn't smell right—you call it in. No more solo heroics."

Everyone nodded. The meeting adjourned itself, and the noise picked right back up, louder than before.

I finished my coffee, then stood to go. Gunner followed. Outside, the Texas sun was already burning off the night, the world turning gold and bright.

He clapped me on the back. "Bet you wish you'd stayed in Chicago, huh?"

I snorted. "You kidding? This is home. At least here I know who wants to kill me."

He laughed. "Fair. Race you to the truck?"

I grinned. "You're on."

We ran, both of us a little lighter for it, the weight of the past few weeks fading with every step. There was work to do, wolves to hunt, secrets to uncover. But for the first time in a long while, I looked forward to it.

Let the world try to keep up.

Recon was my element. Nothing calmed my nerves like long hours of surveillance, the taste of burnt coffee and the slow piecing together of a target's life from patterns and probabilities. Gunner wasn't built for patience, but he played the part—he could sit for hours, as long as you gave him a snack every forty minutes and let him snark about the parade of idiots we watched from the battered pickup parked outside the Morgantown Pack's "compound."

The place was a joke. Three metal buildings: a machine shop, an auto body garage, and a dive bar that looked like it survived on meth and karaoke. Supposedly thirty wolves belonged to the pack, but most of the traffic was in-and-out muscle types—never the same faces twice, no females, no pups, and not a single sign of a real home. It was a front, and not a good one.

Steiner, their Alpha, wasn't even here. Wrecker finally found his true headquarters outside Fort Worth. We hit the road and headed east with a list of several businesses he apparently owned. A fancy restaurant, a dive bar, and a high-toned strip club were included in the mix.

"Interesting that there's no sign of an MC patch in sight." Gunner said, voice low. "I think that's just bullshit back in Morgantown just for show."

"He's compensating," I said, keeping the camera on Steiner. "Everything about this operation is surface. No real discipline. No family."

"Maybe he ate them," Gunner said, deadpan. "Wouldn't be the first psycho Alpha who culled his own pack."

I nodded, not disagreeing. The itch in my scalp told me there was a bigger game in play—maybe trafficking, maybe worse.

Just past 2200, a black Escalade rolled up. Steiner got in, followed by his muscle, and they headed west. I nudged Gunner awake. "Showtime."

We tailed them for 25 miles, right to the outskirts of downtown. They parked at a fancy-looking strip club disguised as some kind of oasis. He went through a side entrance marked PRIVATE. There were valets in bow ties and fancy cars in the parking lot.

"What the fuck is this place?" Gunner muttered. "Think we're overdressed?"

"Stay sharp," I told him, palming my knife. "If Steiner's meeting, he's meeting someone with teeth."

The club inside was a fever dream—mirrored walls, leather booths with blackout curtains, bartenders in designer dresses pouring top shelf for a crowd of men who looked like they were handling million-dollar business deals. Others could have been members of the Russian mob. The bouncers were the biggest tells: they wore tailored jackets, but the bulges under their arms said they preferred Glocks to persuasion.

We took a table at the back, ordered two beers, and watched. Steiner moved like a man who owned the world, never looking twice at the talent, heading straight for a private booth by the stage. He sat, back to the wall, his muscle flanking him, eyes everywhere.

Then the first dancer came out, and I nearly dropped my glass.

She was five feet, six inches of perfection. Legs like blades, blonde hair in a waterfall down her back. Her skin glowed under the lights, but it was the eyes that got me. Blue, sharp, and all business, like she saw everything and cared about none of it.

Gunner whistled, low. "Holy hell. That's not your average party favor."

My heart hammered so hard I thought I'd bust a seam. She stalked the stage, fluid and perfect, never once glancing at the crowd. On the second turn, her eyes locked with mine. For a half-beat, the whole club faded out. Her expression shifted—recognition, then shock, then something like shame. She looked away so fast it felt like I'd been shot.

I couldn't breathe. I couldn't think. The rest of the set was a blur. When she finished, Steiner's man flicked a folded bill onto the stage, and she scooped it up, vanished behind the curtain.

Gunner looked at me, worried for the first time all night. "You okay, man? You look like you just saw a ghost."

"Let's go," I said, voice rough. "Now."

We hit the parking lot, air like a slap to the face, and I doubled over by the truck, trying to keep my lunch down.

Gunner hovered. "Who was she?"

I pressed my fist to my chest, forcing the words out. "Harper fucking Larsen. She was... She used to be... nobody."

Gunner let the silence stretch. "You want to go back in?"

I shook my head. "No. I need to think."

We climbed in and headed for the highway, headlights slicing through the black. Every mile, the memory of her face—those eyes—burned hotter, brighter, until I wanted to claw my own skin off just to get free of it.

For years, I'd buried Harper. Buried everything about her. I'd thought it was dead and gone. But it was back now, and I didn't know what to do with it.

Gunner drove, silent, hands steady at the wheel. He didn't push, didn't joke. He just let me work through it, like a true brother.

When the lights of Dairyville finally glowed on the horizon, I found my voice again. "Thanks, Finn."

He nodded, eyes never leaving the road. "Anytime, Jess."

Everyone thought I was a hardass, that I never gave the women they brought to the pack a break, even though fate had brought them together. That's because fate had given me a mate too. But fate can't keep your mate from rejecting you. Looks like things didn't work out so well for mine after she left me. You'd think that would bring me some kind of satisfaction.

But deep down, I knew better. It only made me want her all over again.

THANK YOU

From the depths of my heart, thank you. Thank you for joining Big Papa on this raw, emotional journey as he finally found the happiness and the love he so deeply deserved. Writing his story, and watching Aspen see past his scars to the beautiful, resilient soul beneath, has been one of the most rewarding experiences of my creative life. And yes, I fell head over heels for Aspen too—how could I not? Oh, and with a sidekick like Oscar, life will never get boring.

This series has always been about more than individual characters; it's about the pack. The fierce, unbreakable bonds that tie these wolves together. The way they fight for one another, love without limits, and keep showing up, book after book, like old friends you never want to let go. Your enthusiasm for the way they show up, their quirks, and their loyalty has meant the world to me. They're family—and now, so are you.

And that epilogue... oh, Arsenal. My heart aches for him. His story is one of heartbreak, healing, and a love that will shake the very foundations of the pack. I've been itching to get my hands on him, and his story is going to get you right in the feels.

Your support, your messages, and your love for these characters fuel me. Thank for your encouragement and support. It means the world to me. Y'all make me wanna howl at the moon!

With gratitude,

Dex

ALSO BY DEX

If you loved Big Papa, and you somehow missed books 1, 2, and 3 in the Wolves of Iron Valor MC series, you need to read them NOW! BRONC Book 1and MENACE Book 2and Wrecker Book 3

And if you're a fan of romantasy, my first series is a fun tale of an orphan from Texas who realizes she's actually not so much from Texas as she is from an entirely different realm. She's tasked with saving the realm from destruction by a power-hungry goddess. Along the way she meets her mate, a dreamy shadow-wielding vampire king, as well as a host of other fabulous creatures, including dragons, of course. Read the completed hot and steamy Kingdoms of Eldoria series **Claiming Starlight, Starlight & Luna Rising, and Starlight & Fire**, where you'll meet Olivia and Cade as well as the Dragonia and group of wonderful friends and family she comes to know and love. You'll find yourself on the edge of your seat with the heart-stopping action and needing a fan to cool yourself off as the steam heats up between several couples.

ACKNOWLEDGEMENTS

Having people I trust read what I write and give me honest feedback and catch mistakes before the book goes to the masses is so damn helpful. I'm lucky to have a few ladies willing to do this for me. And they do it just because they love my books and more than that; they are just good people. I want them to know how much I appreciate it. **Denise Pruitt**, **Patti Kapusta**, and **Kathy Connley** my heartfelt thanks to all of you.